Madeleine's King

King Brothers Investigation Services

Clarice Jayne

Cover design by: B. P. Designs

Contents

Foreword

I don't usually feel the need to write anything other than a dedication at the beginning or end of my books, but in the case of Madeleine's King, I thought there was a place for it. Maddie's story has been a hard one for me to write, taking me longer than planned, but it made me realise finally that I needed to get help. Madeleine's King does contain triggers on non consensual sex, and violence towards women. So please consider this before reading the book if you feel you may be affected by it.

Most of the stories I write are pure imagination, but in the case of Sienna's King and Madeleine's King, I have drawn on experiences from my past. Experiences that I have fought to forget for the past thirty years. In some respect getting the words down on paper has been quite cathartic, but also very distressing.

I myself was physically, mentally and sexually abused by a boyfriend in my late teens. To the point I thought I might die at his hands. If it wasn't for my knight in shining armour who I have now been happily married to for nearly twenty-five years, I probably would have done. I guess I chose to write bits of it in my stories to get it out of the box I had kept it locked up in for so long. I needed to finally accept what happened to me and how far I have come. I have sought help, and am working through everything together with them.

So please understand when you read, or if you have already read this book, there is light at the end of the tunnel. If you have or are experiencing abuse in any way, please don't lock it away. Don't try to forget what has happened to you, it will only eat away at you, as it has done me, for so many years.

Remember there are people out there to help. If you can't speak to a friend or loved one, then contact one of the numbers below if you are in the UK. I know people in the US, Australia and around the world will all have your own helplines and crisis centres.

Please don't suffer in silence. Ask for help. You don't have to be alone.

Clarice Jayne

Rape Crisis - England & Wales - www.rapecrisis.org.uk

Women's Aid - www.womensaid.org.uk

Dedication

To any woman or man who has ever been the victim
or is currently the victim of domestic violence or rape.
Remember you do not deserve what has happened, or is
happening to you. There are people out there who can help.
Please do not suffer in silence. This book is for you.

Clarice Jayne

xxx

*** *Please Note* ***

Madeleine's King

Has been written by an English author in UK English. You
may therefore assume there are some spelling errors within it,
however, it is just the way we spell things in good old Blighty.

Chapter One

Tyler

C hristmas and the New Year had been great. Spending time with all the guys and their families had been just what we all needed. Christmas Day had been amazing, and it was easy to see why all of Robert and Elizabeth's staff loved working for them. They had included them in all the day's activities, even giving them presents which they were expected to open with the rest of their friends and family. We had all received something from them, and it was obvious that Sienna and Jayden had been asked about us, as the presents fitted our personalities perfectly. I had received a transforming USB Flash drive which changed from a drive to a leopard in true Transformers style. It was fantastic, and something a geek like me could truly appreciate. Dinner was amazing and the fireworks display they put on for New Year's Eve rivalled any display I had been to. To add to that, the news that Jayden and Sienna were expecting a baby, along with Brandon and Ashleigh getting engaged had made the holiday period even better..

There was just one thing missing though, one person I had wanted to spend the holiday with. Maddie. She had declined Robert and Elizabeth's invitation to come and stay with them, choosing to open the café instead over the holiday period. Jess had tried to convince her, as had I, but she was determined to spend the holidays on her own.

It saddened me to think that she was back in Kings View alone, but nothing I could have said would have changed her mind. She was determined to keep Jess's business running with or without her being there. Something told me that she wanted to be alone. That there was a reason she didn't want to celebrate, and that reason was also why she wouldn't let me get close to her. I had spoken to her both on Christmas Day and New Year's Eve to let her know we were all thinking of her. She seemed happy enough, but there was a slight sadness in her voice when I spoke to her. It was as though she wanted to be here with us, but whatever was keeping her from getting close was holding her back.

I had spoken to Jess about it and explained my worries. She agreed that she was as worried about Maddie as I was, but we just had to give her time to open up to us. She was sure there was something in her past that was still haunting her, but until Maddie was ready to tell us, we just had to be there for her, helping her whenever we could. Part of me was angry that she wouldn't let me in, wouldn't allow me to be there for her, to help her through her issues. There was even a part of me that thought about walking away and leaving her to it. But every time I thought about it, I felt a pain in my heart, reminding me that she was the woman I wanted to spend the rest of my life with. I wanted what Mason, Jayden, and Brandon had. I wanted someone to be there for me every day when I came home. Someone to spend the rest of my life with, and as far as I was concerned, that someone was Maddie. I just needed her to realise it as well.

There was something different about Nathan as well. He was far more subdued over the holiday period than normal. Whilst he seemed happy to be spending it with us as friends, it was as if there was somewhere else he wanted to be. Or perhaps, with someone else? We were all positive now he was seeing someone. As everyone was finding their life partners, our weekly trips out were happening less and less. We were lucky to get out once a month now. Nathan, being the youngest of us all, was usually the first to try and get us out. But lately, he had seemed more reserved. Even Kye couldn't convince him to go out, and hell, he was a party animal. I wondered how things would be in the future, once we all found the woman we loved? Even if it was a woman. I had my suspicions about Richard, but would never mention them to either him or the guys. I was positive he was gay. Not that it bothered me, he's a great guy and I have enjoyed working with him over the past few months. He loves investigation work as much as I do, and the fact that he seemed to love computers as I did, meant he would be a great help to me.

Knowing I had to get going, I said goodbye to the guys that were still around, Robert and Elizabeth, and was just getting into my car to head over to my parents' house to spend a couple of days with them, before getting back to work. Mason had decided to close the office for a few extra days to allow us some time with our families. Business was good, and we were busy, but Mason had given all the work to contractors over the holiday period so we could have some well-deserved time off. The past couple of years had been hectic, to say the least. What with Jess, Sienna, and Ashleigh either being kidnapped or forced to leave with someone. We had been kept busy in both our personal lives and work. I was thankful that nothing had happened to Maddie. I just hoped it stayed that way.

Driving back to Surrey, I arrived at my parents' house in a little over two hours. The roads were quite clear for New Year's Day, and I was thankful for that. It had been a late one and although I hadn't had too many drinks, knowing I had to drive this morning, I was still tired from lack of sleep. The thought of being caught up in a traffic jam filled me with dread. I pulled up outside the house, noticing that my sister Kelsey's car was still there. When I spoke to her yesterday, she said she may not be here as she was meeting up with her friends for a couple of days. I had really wanted to chat with her before she left. I knew that she and Nathan spoke occasionally, she saw him as a big brother as well, seeing as we spent so much time together when we were kids. I wanted her to see what she could find out from him regarding what was up, and whether he had mentioned anything to her.

Getting out of the car, I grabbed my overnight bag from the boot and walked up to the door. Despite this being my family home, I still never let myself in, even with my key. I knocked on the door waiting for someone to come and let me in. Dad answered within a couple of minutes and greeted me as usual.

"Hi, Son. When are you going to use that key you have to let yourself in? You know this is your home too."

"Hi, Dad. You know I don't like to let myself in. I haven't lived here for nearly ten years now so don't see it as my house anymore. Anyway, it helps to keep you fit."

Raising his eyebrows at me, and letting out a small laugh, he pulled me into a hug.

"It's good to see you, Son."

"You too, Dad."

"Come and see your mother and sister, before she deserts us for the rest of the holidays."

I placed my bag at the bottom of the stairs ready to take to my room and followed Dad into the kitchen, where I found Mum busy getting everything ready for lunch and my sister sat at the table drinking coffee. Walking up to Mum I put my arms around her and gave her a big hug.

"Happy New Year, Mum."

I guessed she hadn't heard me arrive or walking up to her by the way she nearly jumped out of her skin as I spoke.

"Jesus, Tyler. Make more noise when you come in will you? You're lucky I didn't attack you with this knife in my hand."

Placing a peck on her cheek, I smiled.

"Old army habits obviously die hard, Mum. Never allow anyone to know when you are approaching. It keeps you alive."

"Well, in this case, old habits will get you killed, if you do that to me again!"

I looked over at Dad and Kelsey as they both laughed at my Mum's reaction. Walking over to Kelsey, I gave her a kiss on the top of her head as I spoke.

"Hey, Kiddo, are you keeping out of trouble?"

"Of course, Ty. When are you going to stop using that nickname for me? I'm twenty-five next birthday, which I believe makes me an adult."

"You'll always be my kiddo, Kelsey."

I could see the look of disgust on her face, but I knew deep down she loved it and she loved me. Although I know she would never admit it.

"When are you heading out, Kelsey?"

"In a little while. Why, do you miss me already, Ty?"

"Like a hole in the head. But that's beside the point. I wanted to have a quick chat with you before you went. Have you got a few minutes?"

"Yeah, sure."

Getting up from her chair, I followed her out of the kitchen and into the living room.

"What's up my big brother, need some help with your love life?"

"Nope, and even if I did, I wouldn't ask you. No, I'm worried about Nath. Has he said anything to you?"

"What about?" I was quite taken aback by how she sounded, almost defensive.

"I don't really know. He seemed a bit off over the weekend. Is he seeing anyone, do you know?"

"How would I know if he is seeing someone? Last time I spoke to him we just chatted about nothing in particular. We never talk about our personal lives, same as I would never talk to you about it."

I wasn't sure exactly what it was about this conversation, but she wasn't telling me the whole truth. Thinking I would try a different tact, I continued, "So he hasn't mentioned any problems or worries he's having then?"

"Nope. Why don't you try asking him instead of me? Now, I want to finish my coffee if you don't mind. I'm meeting my friends in half an hour, so I need to think about getting ready to leave."

With that, she turned and walked out of the front room and into the kitchen. I stood there for a minute, dumbfounded at the conversation we had just had. Kelsey and I had never been really close, but we always spoke. The way she just spoke to me was as though I was an enemy that she wouldn't tell a single thing to. I would just have to chat with Jayden to try and find out what was happening because I couldn't let this go. Walking back into the kitchen I found just my Mum and Dad busy getting ready for lunch.

"What did you say to Kelsey? She seemed really annoyed when she walked back in here."

"I just asked her if Nathan had said anything to her to explain why he was in a strange mood over Christmas. I know they always chat, so I thought he might have said something. She almost snapped my head off when she answered."

"Let her be, Tyler. You know she has always had a soft spot for Nathan," Mum replied. She always came to Kelsey's defence over me. I knew they were close, and that is what worried me sometimes, especially when I knew how much Kelsey liked Nathan. I'm sure Mum just wanted them to be together. However, having seen what Nathan could be like, there was no way I was letting him anywhere near my little sister, twenty-five years old or not.

I looked at my Mum and Dad and shook my head. I knew this wasn't a fight I was going to win. I just had to hope that my little chats with Nathan had sunk in, and he knew how I felt about the two of them being together. I loved him like a brother, but his attitude towards women wasn't one I wanted for my sister, and I would do anything to protect her from him. Although, I had to admit, his interactions with women recently had been few and far between. In fact, I'm not sure I had seen him out with a woman in the past year.

Grabbing my coffee, I sat down at the table just as Kelsey walked back into the room, together with her overnight bag.

"Where are you planning on going, dear?"

"Only round my friend's place, Mum. We're just spending a couple of girly nights in. Nothing special. There's no need to worry about me," she said as she walked over to Mum and gave her a hug. She gave our Dad a quick hug and kiss and then turned to me, her scowl still clear to see on her face.

"Come on, Kiddo, you know I only care about you. Just as I'm worried about Nath."

"You have a fine way to show it sometimes. Ty, I am twenty-five years old, I don't need you protecting me any longer."

Getting up from my chair I pulled her into a hug.

"I will always try and protect you, Kelsey, even when you are married with kids. Now go and enjoy yourself. I'll try and catch up with you in a couple of weeks, okay?"

She squeezed me back. I knew she wouldn't be able to stay mad at me for too long. As her big brother, I had to annoy her like this occasionally, but that didn't mean I didn't love her. I knew deep down she loved me too, but again, being the little sister gave her the right to be mad at me.

"Love you, Bro."

"Love you too, Kiddo."

"Right, I better get off. I'll see you in a couple of days."

With that, she rushed out of the house and off to her friends. Although I had a strange feeling her friend was of the male variety rather than female, and something told me it would come to bite us all soon.

Chapter Two

Madeleine

··············· ❦ ···············

Another year where I'd spent Christmas and New Year alone. Another year where I refused to let anyone in. It was the way I wanted it. Life was easier alone. I didn't have to let anyone know my feelings or try to be happy around them. The truth was though, I hated it. Hated that I felt I had to distance myself from my friends over the holidays. I desperately wanted to spend time with everyone from Kings over the Christmas period, but doing that meant opening my feelings. It was hard enough seeing Jess with Callum every day, but being with them twenty-four hours a day over the break? I just couldn't do it. I knew I would crack. I would tell them everything about my past and risk losing them as friends forever. No, I had to stay strong and protect myself and them from knowing my past.

Then there was Tyler. The man I desperately wanted to spend

the rest of my life with, but knew I could never have. If he knew the truth about me, knew what I had done...I'm sure it would make him run a mile. He would just look at me with pity and disgust every time he walked into the shop. Not that I would still be working there, as Jess would probably fire me on the spot. I sat in my room looking at the Christmas tree I had put in the corner, I could feel the pain and hurt building in my chest. It was the same every year. Christmas Day, Dad would try to contact me and leave me a message on my answerphone. Then the same again on New Year's Day. As yet, I hadn't listened to either of them. I hadn't got the courage to and didn't want to hear the disappointment in his voice. That's what I was to him and the rest of the family, a big disappointment.

I picked up my mobile. Why I hadn't changed my number I'll never know. I guess it was just in case they decided to message me to let me know something was wrong. Then again, why would they? As far as my stepmum was concerned I was a liar and a whore. She was the one that threw me onto the streets all those years ago. I guess she kept that bit of information from my Dad as he tried to contact me regularly. Calling my voicemail, I sat there and listened to my messages,

You have two un-played messages. Message One BEEP.

Hey, baby girl. Happy Christmas. Just wanted to talk to you. We all miss you so much. Please call me. I just want to understand what I did to make you leave. Rosie misses you. Please Mads, please call me. I love you.

I pressed the button to delete the message, tears pouring down my face.

Message Two BEEP

Hey, Mads. Happy New Year, baby girl. Let's make this the best year ever. Please contact me, so we can meet up. It can just be the two of us if you want. You not being around has put a strain on my relationship with Michelle. I'm not sure how much longer we

will stay together. I'm not trying to make you feel bad, just wanted to let you know, you don't have to worry about her being around. I think it's over between us. I don't love her like I used to, she's changed. Please just let me know you're safe and okay. I'm back home soon, perhaps we can meet up and chat. I love you, baby girl and miss you more than you will ever know.

I closed the phone without deleting the message. Tears poured down my face. It was the longest message my Dad had ever sent me. Part of me was pleased that it seemed his relationship with my stepmum was over. Not that they were married, but she still liked to call herself that. Then there was Thomas, her son. He was a few years older than me and he liked to remind me of it. He hated me and told me so on many occasions. I threw my phone across the room, narrowly missing the pictures on the table. I hated what had happened to me. My entire family and the life I loved had been taken from me after one drunken night. More than that had been taken though, my innocence was taken as well. I was still haunted by that night, the night that changed my life forever. Thanks to that nightmare evening, I could never bring myself to have a proper relationship with anyone. I remembered the day I finally left my family home, the day when I'd finally had enough.

I'd been arguing with Michelle for the past two months. She wanted to know the truth. Dad had been on deployment for nearly a year then. The longest time he had ever been away, and I was stuck here with his bitch of a girlfriend and her devil spawn. Of course, whenever my Dad was around, they were both as nice as pie to me, acting like the doting family. However, as soon as he walked out of the house, their true colours came through. He didn't know anything about the situation I had gotten myself into, didn't know about the surprise that was waiting for him when he came home. It had been a normal morning for me. I got up and saw to myself and Rosie. I had planned a day out for us both, anything to get out of the house after the blazing row I had the night before with

Michelle.

I drifted off into my thoughts of that day replaying them repeatedly in my head.

"Come on, Poppet, let's get out of here before the rest of the house gets up."

I gathered Rosie up in my arms and grabbed all her stuff and headed downstairs, hoping not to run into Michelle and Thomas. Luck wasn't on my side this morning as they were both sitting in the kitchen drinking coffee. I tried to walk past without being noticed, but unfortunately, Michelle looked up just as I was walking past the door.

"Where do you think you are going?"

"Rosie and I are going out for the day, not that it's any of your business."

"As long as you live under my roof, it is my business."

I looked at her in disgust. How the hell she could say this was her house when it had been my family home for the past twenty years was beyond me. I had more of a right than either of them to be living here.

"I do believe this is my house and has been for the past twenty years. You aren't my mother and never will be, Michelle. You're just my Dad's current flavour of the month. As soon as he gets bored with you, you will be thrown out like the garbage you are. You and your devil son."

I knew I was pushing my luck, that I shouldn't be saying any of this, but the memory of the things she had said to me last night was still running through my head. How she was going to tell my Dad everything that had happened whilst he had been away. Not that anything she would have told him would have been true. No, she just wanted to spin a web of lies to make him hate me. The problem was, I couldn't understand why? As soon as I saw Thomas get up from his seat, I knew I had gone too far. Stalking over to me, hand raised, I pulled Rosie into me to protect her from what was about to happen.

"Don't you dare talk to your stepmum like that, you fucking bitch."

"She isn't my stepmum. In case it had escaped your notice, she isn't married to my Dad. Therefore, she is just my Dad's girlfriend and has no relationship to me."

He lunged towards me but stopped in his tracks as soon as Michelle spoke.

"Thomas, that's enough. Not with Rosie in the room."

Much as I hated her, I had to admit, she never allowed Rosie to ever be in harm's way. At least she was treated well by them both. Then again, she should be, she was just an innocent child after all. I saw the look of anger that came over Thomas' face as he mouthed to me that I would pay for this later. It wouldn't have been the first time he laid his hands on me. He turned to his mother and walked back over to the chair and sat down.

"Now, Madeleine. We still have unfinished business from last night before you go anywhere."

"I told you last night, I don't want to talk about it, ever. You wouldn't believe me even if I told you the truth, so what's the point?"

"Sit down now. Thomas, take Rosie and put her in her playpen."

I didn't want to give Rosie up, especially not to him. I knew he wouldn't hurt her, but I hated the way he was with her. Walking over to me, he went to take Rosie from my arms. I held her close but knew it wasn't worth arguing with either of them. If I did, it would only end up with someone getting hurt, and I didn't want that to be Rosie. I handed her over to Thomas and he walked out of

13

the kitchen to place her in the front room. I knew she would be fine there, and we could still see her through the doorway.

"So, Madeleine," Michelle continued in her sickly sweet, sarcastic tone that she seemed to save for only me. "I have been patient with you, but looking after Rosie costs money. With you not working, having an extra mouth to feed is putting a strain on my finances. We need to know who the father is so he can pay his way for her."

I couldn't help but let the laugh escape from my lips. If only she knew, would she be so high and mighty then?

"What makes you think he will be in a position to pay, and would he even want to. I told you I would never tell you what happened. So, leave it there. If I'm causing you so many issues, then I will just take Rosie and leave. Would that make you happy?"

Michelle went to speak but we both looked around in shock when Thomas' booming voice sounded through the kitchen.

"You aren't taking Rosie fucking anywhere. She is staying here with us."

I couldn't believe what I was hearing. The devil son himself was now telling me what I could do with my own daughter.

"Since when did you get a say in this, Thomas? If I choose to leave and take Rosie with me, that is my decision. NOT YOURS," I was screaming at him. I hated him, hated everything that he had done and said to me.

"We have spent all this time looking after her, keeping the pair of you in this house. That gives me every right to have a say in what happens to Rosie. She is basically my niece, after all."

I saw a look pass over Thomas' face, almost a smirk as if he had a plan and it included Rosie.

"I will ask you again, Madeleine. Who is the father of your child?"

I was hurt, angry that they wouldn't leave me alone. Wouldn't let *me forget what happened that night. That they had to try and keep dragging up the past and make me remember what happened. I could feel myself starting to shake as the tears of anger fell down my face. Before I knew it, I said the words I vowed would never leave my lips.*

"If you really have to know, I was raped, okay. Happy now? Someone I know got drunk and decided that it would be fun to torment me and then rape me!" There it was, out in the open. The secret I had been holding onto all of Rosie's life. The reaction I wasn't expecting was the slap around the face as Michelle hit me.

"You're just a liar and a whore, who couldn't keep her knickers up and ended up with that bastard child in there. Raped indeed, is that the best you could come up with? Next thing you will be telling me that it was Thomas. I suggest you leave this house today. Unless you want me to tell your father exactly what a lying, promiscuous child you are."

I was dumbfounded. Completely speechless. I couldn't believe what she was saying to me. Not only was she accusing me of lying about being raped, but she was throwing me out of my own house. A house I had grown up in. I had given up everything to have Rosie. There was never a doubt in my mind. No matter how she had come into this world, I still loved her and there was never a moment I thought about getting rid of her. I had given up any chance I had of finishing my university degree in Psychology. Any chance I had of finding a man that loved me. And now she was just turfing me and my daughter out on the streets. Finally coming to my senses, I spoke, far calmer than I was feeling inside.

"Fine, I will leave and take my bastard child out of your hair, as you so finely put it. I will get our things together and leave. You won't have to worry about us ever again."

I walked out of the kitchen and upstairs to grab a bag and put some stuff into it. We didn't have much between us, but we had enough to get by. I packed a case for myself and a bag for Rosie and walked back downstairs. I found Thomas standing in the hallway, waiting for me, with a smirk on his face.

"All packed?"

"Yes. You should be pleased that I'm leaving."

"Oh, I am pleased you're leaving, but you aren't taking Rosie. She stays here with us. She is far too valuable to let you have her."

I rushed into the front room to grab Rosie, but she was gone. I turned, the tears falling down my face to see Thomas standing in the doorway.

"Mum took her out. You aren't taking her away from us, Mads. As I said, she is far too valuable. So, I suggest you just walk out of that front door and forget about us, and Rosie. Because we never want to see you again."

I woke suddenly, sobs consuming my whole being. It took me a moment to realise that it had all been a dream. Getting up from my chair I walked across the room and picked up my phone. Opening it, I brought up the last picture that Dad had sent me of Rosie. Sitting back down, the tears were pouring down my face. This pain was my punishment for what I had done. Walking away from my life and the child that I loved. I didn't deserve to be happy. I didn't deserve to be loved ever again. I was destined to live the rest of my life alone.

Chapter Three

Tyler

It had been two weeks since I had been in Kings View. I'd had a lovely time with Sienna's family along with my own, but I was glad to finally be back near Maddie. I had called her yesterday before I left my parents, just to check how she was. Something told me that she was upset, that she had been crying. She said she was fine, but there was sadness in her voice. I just wish she would let me in and tell me what was wrong. There wasn't anything she could tell me that would change my mind about her. I loved her. I was just scared of what my love would mean.

Would me telling her three simple words push her away completely? *I love you*, such simple words that meant exactly how I felt about her. The problem was, I had a feeling those words would be the end of us. That I would scare her away by saying them. The problem was, what if I didn't say them?

Would that lead to the same result? Me alone, without the woman I couldn't live without. She was the reason I got up every morning to face the day.

I was sitting at my desk completely lost in my thoughts when I suddenly jumped at the hand placed on my shoulder. Turning around I saw Brandon standing there.

"For fuck's sake, Brandon. Give me a little warning next time, will you?"

"Tyler, when are you going to remember everything you learned in the army? Never let the enemy know you're coming. You shouldn't be so lost in your own thoughts there. Anyone we know?"

"As my mother said to me the other day when I did the same thing to her, one of these days it is going to get you killed. And of course, you know who I'm thinking about. The only person I ever think about."

Since Brandon and Ashleigh had moved down here into a rented house while they waited for theirs to be built, I had spent a lot of time talking to them. Brandon had always treated me like a younger brother and until recently we hadn't been close. More and more, I found myself confiding in him and Ashleigh about my feelings towards Maddie.

"You really do have it bad, don't you Tyler?"

"You don't have to ask me that. She is the first person I think about when I wake in the morning, and the last just before I fall asleep. I truly love her. I just wish she would tell me what is holding her back. I guess something must have happened with a past boyfriend. I just hoped she would have realised by now that I'm not that kind of guy."

I could see Brandon, standing there pondering what to reply. I really couldn't understand why, as we have had this conversation countless times before. He pulled up a chair and sat down next to me.

"You know I have told all of you never to have secrets from each other, as they only ever lead to pain. The problem is Maddie just isn't ready to let hers go. I guess it's something that to her, is just so big, that she is worried about what everyone will think when we find out. I'm not just talking about you, but all her friends. I know for a fact she hasn't mentioned anything to Jess.

Jess wouldn't tell me exactly what she said, if she did tell her, but she would at least let me and you know if she had said something. You just need to keep being there for her and slowly chip away at her defence."

I knew Brandon was right, but how much longer could I do that? We had been seeing each other as friends for nearly a year now, and I was still not getting any closer to her. I wasn't desperate to sleep with her, but I wanted to show her how much I truly loved her.

"Why is love so difficult?"

Brandon chuckled next to me.

"If I had the answer to that question, I would be a billionaire. Saying that, I don't think it is love that is difficult, but relationships. It's easy to tell someone you love them, whether you really mean it or not. And before you try to say anything, I know you love Maddie. No, the difficult part is holding onto the relationship, or even starting it in your case."

"State the fucking obvious, Brandon. Look, it doesn't matter anyway. As long as she is still here in Kings View, I can keep an eye on her. Just be around for me when it all goes wrong and I fall apart."

Chuckling, Brandon got up from the chair next to me and placed his hand back on my shoulder.

"Always, Tyler. Hopefully, it won't come to that, but you know me, and Ashleigh will always be there for you."

I gave him a chin lift as he walked out of the office and headed off for his day. Things had been a bit quiet for me over the past few weeks, so Richard was going to head down here to work with me, learning the basics of my job. He was going to be staying with Mason for a couple of days, so he didn't have to travel every day. I looked through my work for the week, deciding what I could give Richard to look at. I had already seen some of the work he had done with Jayden and had to admit I was quite impressed. His computer skills were second to none, and I wondered why he had never been picked up by one of the big computer firms in London. I knew he had some learning difficulties, but still, you wouldn't know it from what I had seen so far.

Hearing the front door open, I got up from my desk and headed out to the reception area. We didn't have a receptionist here like in London, but it didn't really bother us as normally we would be expecting someone, or if not, one of us would head out there. Walking round into the main foyer, I found Maddie standing there, complete with breakfast and coffee in her hands. Smiling, I walked over to her.

"Hey, Mads. Happy New Year, let me take that off you."

Smiling, I walked over to her and took the box she was carrying, and placed it on the desk in front of me.

"Hi, Tyler. Happy New Year to you too. I hope you had a good one."

We had already had this conversation on the phone yesterday. But I couldn't help feeling warmth about having it in person. Pulling her into a hug, I gave her a kiss on the cheek. I could see the blush come over her face as I pulled away. This was as close as we got, a hug and a kiss on the cheek. I wanted so much more, but knew no matter how hard I tried she would just push me away. I would just steal these odd moments whenever I could.

"It was good. Glad I could get home and spend some time with my family. I take it Jess is at the shop as you managed to get down here."

"Yes, and I better be getting back before the morning rush. You know how busy it gets."

"Okay, I will come round for lunch later. Can you have it ready for everyone? Guess it will be the usual plus Richard."

"Will do. See you later."

She paused for a second before turning and walking out the door. I heard her talking outside to someone just before Nathan and Richard walked through the front door.

"Thank God, breakfast is here waiting."

"Do you ever think of anything other than your stomach, Nathan?"

"Nope," Nathan replied to Richard as he was picking up a coffee and croissant and headed off to his office to work.

"Looks like Jess let Maddie know you were coming as there is an extra coffee here. Why don't you grab it and meet me in my office, and I'll get rid of these, then we can get to work."

***

Although I didn't have much work on now, it had picked up for me since we had completed the job for Mr. Jarvis at Jarvis Designs. My computer skills were starting to be well used. I had spent time there just before and after Jess had been kidnapped, trying to figure out who was taking his clients away from him and designing their websites for them. It turned out to be one of his employees, their best designer in fact, Peter Knowles. We established he had been doing it for years, probably costing Mr. Jarvis a few hundred thousand pounds in lost revenue.

The employee wasn't prosecuted as we knew it would be difficult for any court to convict him of anything other than stealing, and that would still be a grey area. Mr. Jarvis had fired him on the spot, stopping all payments to him under gross misconduct and had warned other web design companies that he knew of what Peter had done. To say Peter was pissed was an understatement and I was sure that was not the last Mr. Jarvis was going to hear from him.

For us as a company, though, the recommendations that we had received from Mr. Jarvis had brought the work rolling in. I was spending most of my days investigating money laundering and stealing through computer fraud or espionage and earning Kings a lot of money doing so. Currently, we had two jobs looking into the same thing. Money appeared to be syphoned off of the accounts, but as yet, the owners couldn't prove exactly who was behind it. They had their suspicions but just needed the proof.

Walking into my office, I found Richard setting up his laptop, ready to get on with his day. It was pleasing to have another computer geek on the payroll. For years I had been made fun of by the rest of the guys, not in a nasty way and it was only because I tended to use my brain more than my brawn. In some respects that had made me the lucky one. During my time in the forces, I had not seen what my brothers had seen, the wanton violence that war brought with it. I was also lucky enough not to have been there when we lost our friend Mark, only Nathan and Jayden had seen that. It still affected me though, and I was glad when Mason had suggested that we get out and come to work for him. Now I just got to do the job I loved but without the chance of being shot or killed.

Sitting down at my desk, I turned to Richard.

"So, what has Jayden been getting you to do up in London then?"

"Oh, this and that. Just investigating people's spending habits really, trying to link them to purchases they have given their bits on the side. Pretty easy and boring stuff really. I know I have to start at the bottom and have a long way to go before I get to your standard, but it's just too easy for me. I'm sure if Jayden actually put his mind to it, he could do that himself."

I knew that Jayden could do that, and he had on several occasions. I guess he just wanted to first prove to himself that Richard could do the job, and second make Richard realise that sometimes our role in the company was just that. Easy, dull, and boring.

"Well, you will be pleased to know, what I need you to start working on is nothing like the spending habits of a cheating husband you have been doing up to now."

I saw Richard's face light up in delight, almost like looking at a kid who was just told he was going to Disneyland. I went through the two jobs that we currently had, both with remarkably similar situations.

"Has either company thought about setting up a dummy account? They could speak to their bank and set up dummy transactions going into the account for orders, and the same going out. In reality, no money will ever be changing hands. However, if money is transferred to an account that hasn't been set up, we would then be able to trace it. I'm sure the fraud department of their bank would be able to set up the accounts and we could keep a trace of them. I could look into the transactions every day and see who has been working on them."

I had known that Richard was good, seeing what he had already done, but this even surpassed me. I had never even thought of doing something like that. I was probably too much of a geek. I tended to just think of what we could do within the computer system, or how we could interrogate it to find out what we needed. Richard thought out of the box and came up with solutions to get the perpetrator to slip up, to make themselves known to us.

"That's a mighty fine idea, Richard. I knew there was a reason why I asked you to come down here. I wouldn't have thought of that in a million years."

"It was just a suggestion. If you don't think it will work then you don't have to go ahead. I know you probably have different ways of doing things."

I could see that Richard was almost embarrassed that he had suggested something I hadn't thought of and was worried that I would think he was stepping on my toes.

"Richard, it's a great suggestion. You don't have to worry about coming up with an idea or solution that I hadn't thought of. I suspect it will happen a lot. I'm great when it comes to getting the information out of a computer, but not always how to find how it is getting in there. Don't be embarrassed or afraid to come up with suggestions, there is never a wrong answer, and no one will laugh at you. If it is a suggestion, we will discuss it. If we don't think it will work, we will say so. But it will always be after the whole group has investigated it, it will never be immediately thrown out. Unless of course, it is complete nonsense, but then I wouldn't expect that of you."

I could see him visibly relax at my words. It was as though he saw me as someone to look up to, despite the fact I was slightly younger than him.

"Come on, let's get some work done, then we can go and get lunch."

Chapter Four

Madeleine

········✦····· ⟣⟢ ·····✦········

It had been a normal morning. I woke as usual with a start, my recurring nightmare tearing me from my sleep. For once, I wanted to wake up without the remnants of that night going around my brain, the memories of the reason why I had to leave my entire life behind me. It had been the same for the past few years. Every morning I would wake screaming remembering what he had done to me. How he had violated my body without a care. Left my room laughing at what he had done. Then there was the year of verbal and physical abuse I had received afterward. I just thanked the lord that he had only touched me in that way once. It had been a one-time deal for him, but that is probably because I had always locked my bedroom door after that one night.

My morning had greatly improved today, however. It was great seeing Tyler again. I had missed him these past couple of weeks. Even though I wouldn't allow him to get too close to me, just knowing he was around calmed my nerves. I almost caved this morning, telling him exactly how I felt about him. When he walked over to me and placed his arms around me I felt loved, felt safe, and protected from the world around me. Then when he kissed me so gently on the cheek, I could feel another piece of the armour I had put around my heart falling away.

For me, the issue has never been whether he loved me, or even if I loved him. He has never said the words to me, but I know exactly how he feels about me. Even a blind man could see how he feels about me. I know he loves me, and I guess the reason why he won't tell me is that he is afraid of what those words will do to me, to us. I don't know how to make him see that I am no good for him. I don't deserve the love and kindness that he is showing me. The only way I know is to tell him the truth, but once that secret is out, it can never be taken back. It will mean the end of my life again, only this time I don't think I will be able to come back from it.

I'd walked back into the shop with a huge smile on my face. Jess immediately knew who I had seen. Neither of us would admit we were seeing each other, everyone around us knew.

"I see Tyler is back."

"What makes you say that?"

"Because this is the first time in the past week I have seen a smile like that on your face. Therefore, someone must have put it there. Knowing that the only person that has been missing up until today is Tyler, he must have put it there."

"I don't know what you are talking about. Now if you don't mind, I have lunches to get ready."

Walking out the back, I could hear Jess chuckling away. As things were very quiet here in Kings View, I was able to spend the next thirty minutes or so getting all the orders ready for lunch. Not that there were many, just Mr. and Mrs. Duncan from the newsagents and now Mr. Stewart from the Pharmacy who has taken to coming in every day. I also prepare for the guys every day that Jess insists we must do. Not that I mind, they are always appreciative of their breakfast and lunch. It also meant that I got to see Tyler nearly every day. Having got all the lunches ready, I headed back out to the shop, to find Jess sitting in her usual corner with Callum. I headed over and sat down to the waiting latte she had made.

"So, are you going to admit that your happy mood this morning is thanks to Tyler being back?"

"I will neither confirm nor deny that statement." The smile on my face said it all. There was no way I could hide the happiness I felt having seen him again. "Okay, yes, it's because Tyler is back that I'm happy. Will you be quiet about it now?"

"I will stop mentioning it," before she could finish her sentence, the shop bell went as Mr. Stewart walked in to get his lunch.

"Afternoon, Mr. Stewart. Let me just get your lunch from out the back."

Returning from the kitchen I handed him over the sandwich. "Anything else for you today?"

"No, that's all. Thank you, Maddie. Here you go, that should be the right money for you."

"Perfect as always. Enjoy your lunch."

With that, he left the shop and I started to get two lattes ready for the Duncans who I knew would be here in a short while. I didn't have long to wait as within minutes Mr. Duncan walked through the door.

"Ah, there they are, my two favourite ladies. Good afternoon,

Maddie and Jess. How are you both today? And how is the little man? He is growing up so quickly." Mr. Duncan walked over to Jess who was holding and feeding Callum. I loved how he was always so thoughtful and caring to us both, almost like a father to us, seeing as ours weren't around.

"We are both doing well. As you can see our little man is hungry as usual."

"It's good to see him doing so well. And how are you, Maddie? Did you actually have any time off over Christmas? You seemed to be open every day."

"Only the same time as you, Mr. Duncan."

I heard him laughing as I walked out the back to get their lunch together. He knew exactly how much time I had off over Christmas and New Year, because he was in my shop every morning, I was open. Walking back out I placed the bags on the counter and put the lattes with them.

"Thank you, Maddie, dear. I don't know what we would do without you."

"I am sure you and Mrs. Duncan would cope. Enjoy your lunch."

"We will," and with that, he walked out of the shop.

"I guess I best start the coffee for the guys. I'm sure one of them will be in soon."

"Yeah, it is about that time. Callum's asleep if you need a hand."

"Only if you want to. I can cope, you know."

"I know you can, I just like to feel useful in my own shop sometimes."

"I know."

It didn't take us long to get everything ready and before we knew it we heard the shop door open, and Tyler and Richard walked in.

"Hi, Jess. How's my favourite coffee shop owner and adopted nephew?"

"We are fine Tyler, and don't let Mason hear you saying Callum is your adopted nephew. He will kill you if you say that in front of him."

"Aww, he knows we all see him as our nephew. He will be fine."

Turning to me I saw his face light up like it had this morning when I walked in.

"Hey, Mads," he said as he walked over to me and gave me my second kiss of the day. I could feel myself start to blush as he pulled away looking into my eyes smiling. I stood there speechless, unable to talk or look away from his eyes. He gently placed his hand on my face, and I found myself leaning into it, remembering how he had held me this morning. Our private, or should I say public moment, was broken when Richard spoke.

"Hi, Maddie. Did you have a good Christmas and New Year?"

Taking a moment to register that I was being spoken to, I turned as Tyler removed his hand and smiled at Richard.

"I did, thank you. How about you? Did you go to Sienna's parents for Christmas?"

"Yes, Mum and I went. Sienna wouldn't take no for an answer when we said we would stay at home. It was great. It was a shame you couldn't make it. We all missed you."

I saw Richard glance over at Tyler and I saw an expression come over his face I couldn't make out. Pushing it aside I walked over to the counter to finish off the coffees.

"There you go, all ready for you."

"Thanks, Mads," Tyler said as he walked over towards me. He looked over and saw Richard chatting to Jess. "Can I come round and see you tonight? I missed you."

I could feel myself start to blush again as he placed his hand back on my face. Not trusting myself to speak, especially as we had gone back to him using my nickname, only he called me, I just smiled at him and nodded my head. Although, I still had doubts about him coming around. Especially after the affection he had shown me today.

"Thanks, I'll meet you here after work. I can help you lock up."

Picking up the box I had got ready in front of him, he gave me another kiss on the cheek and turned to walk out.

"Come on, Richard. We best get back before we get in trouble with the boss, and Nathan puts out a search party for his lunch. See you later, Jess."

"Okay, I'm on my way. Mason I can deal with, but Nathan without food? Hell, that is something I don't want to see. Jess, Maddie, thanks for lunch."

With that, they both walked out of the shop, and I was left standing there, with a blush on my cheeks and Jess looking at me with a huge smile on her face.

"I think you need to make us both a drink and then sit down here. We need to talk about Tyler and you."

I could feel my eyes roll in my head. I knew I wouldn't get away from this conversation, not after the display Tyler had just shown. We had always been close together whenever we were together, but this had been the first time he had shown that level of fondness. Quickly getting our drinks ready, I walked back over and sat down with Jess. Callum by now was fast asleep and Jess had put him back into his pram.

"So now you have admitted to me you are happy that Tyler is

back, are you finally going to tell me what is going on between you two? Before you say nothing, nothing doesn't include the way he held your face and kissed you on the cheek. I have been around enough lovesick men now to know that Tyler is madly in love with you. Are you going to deny you love him?"

I sat there digesting what she had just said. I knew that he loved me, but did he really have it that bad? Was he at the same point as Mason, Jayden, and Brandon had been, that he couldn't live without me?

"It's not as easy as that, Jess. I can't get close to Tyler, not to anyone. If he was to know the truth…"

I stopped immediately when the words left my mouth, slamming my hand over it. I had said too much to the wrong person. Jess wouldn't let this be now. She would try and get the full truth out of me. I could feel the panic start to rise, and my breathing became erratic as my anxiety built. I felt Jess's hand on mine, and I looked up and saw the concern on her face. I was dreading the next question that was going to come out of her mouth. But I was surprised when she finally spoke.

"Maddie, I know something happened to you in the past. Some of the conversations we've had over the years have made that plainly obvious. I have never pushed you to tell me, and I never will. When you feel you can let everything out, I will be here. You know you can talk to any of us. Sienna, Ashleigh, or me. We all see you like our little sister and will love you no matter what. Believe me when I say there is nothing you could tell us that would make us feel any different about you."

"I'm not so sure about that."

"Well, that is a decision only you can make, Maddie. Now apart from whatever is holding you back. How do you feel about Tyler? Because you need to tell him if you don't have any feelings for him. I couldn't stand for either of you to get hurt."

"I love him, Jess. He is the only guy I want to spend my life with. I'm just frightened if I tell him the truth that I will lose him, that I will lose the life I have built up here. I'm just not ready to let it out yet. I know all of you have said before that keeping secrets only causes pain, but all I can think is if I tell mine that it will be the end for me. That everyone I love and care about will see the real me and will hate me. I know I would. I hate myself."

"Maddie, I'm sure it isn't that bad that we would all hate you."

"As I said, I hate myself, so I'm pretty sure you would too. I will tell you sometime, but not yet. I'm really not ready to let my secret out."

"Well, when you are, I'm here for you. No matter what, we will get through it together. I know you, Maddie, and I know the wonderful caring woman that you are. Whatever is troubling you, I'm sure it won't cause any of us to hate you. Now you better get everything ready for tomorrow as you have a guest tonight."

"Yeah, I best had. And thank you, Jess. I know you are there for me, I just wish I was brave enough to tell you the truth now."

I walked out the back to get ready for the next day. I still wasn't sure that letting Tyler come round tonight was a good idea. Up until now, we had always met here in the shop or just went out for a walk. I had never allowed him in my flat. But how he had been today, I couldn't refuse. It was everything I wanted, yet everything that I was afraid of. I just had to take it slow and see where things went. Hopefully I wouldn't make a fool of myself in the process, or worse, break my heart forever.

Chapter Five

Tyler

I walked back to the office, happier than I had been in a long time. Maddie had finally agreed to let me go up to her flat with her this evening. It was a step closer to the outcome I wanted, Maddie being mine completely. I just need to take things slow and convince her that I was the man she needed in her life. I was completely lost in my happiness and didn't realise that Richard had been speaking to me until he called out my name for what I guessed was the umpteenth time.

"Tyler, are you actually with me, or still back in the coffee shop with Maddie?"

"Sorry, it's just the first time Mads has agreed for me to spend the evening with her outside of the coffee shop. I guess I just got lost in my happiness. What were you saying?"

"Let's get into the office and deliver these lunches, then we can talk. I'm guessing you have a lot on your mind, and I'm a good listener."

Smiling, I gave him a quick nod as we walked through the door of the office. Taking round the lunches, I walked into my office and closed the door. I could do with another perspective on my predicament. Not that it was really a predicament, just a worry. It was great having Brandon and Ashleigh there for me, but I felt I was putting all my worries onto them when they had just got together and had far better things to be doing with their time.

"So, come on then, tell me about you and Maddie. It's obvious you're in love with her, and from the looks of things she really cares about you too. What's stopping the pair of you?"

"If only I knew."

I went through the whole story, how I felt about her, my concerns, everything. Richard just sat there and listened. I knew he had spoken to Sienna a lot over the years, and they were almost like brother and sister. For a while, I think it annoyed Jayden like hell, but it wasn't long before he just came to terms with it, especially when he realised how much he had spoken to Jess in the past. We all had. She was like the big sister most of us never had. When I finished my explanation, Richard spoke.

"Well as I see it, you both love each other. That much is obvious, and I'm sure I'm not the first person to tell you that. Just take it slowly, let her feel comfortable around you, and just slightly push the boundaries each time you see her. I'm guessing today is the first time you kissed her in public, going by the blush on her face."

"You noticed that?"

"Yeah, she tried to hide it, but both Jess and I saw it."

"In fairness, today is the first time I have ever kissed her in that way. Of course, we have given each other a hello peck when we see each other at a gathering. Then again, most of the guys have, except you and Kye, and I suspect that is because you haven't known her that long. Today just felt different for me. I've missed her so much over the past couple of weeks and when she dropped off the breakfast this morning, I just needed to hold her, so I did and gave her a kiss. It just felt so right. Shit, I just don't know what to do about these feelings. Do I tell her how I feel?"

"You've already said you're worried telling her exactly how you feel will push her away. I guess the question is, are you ready to fight for her? Are you ready to be rejected but keep pushing? That's what you need to ask yourself before you do anything that might cause her to tell you to leave her alone."

"I guess you're right, I have a lot of soul searching to do. I think I will just take it slow for now and see how things go. The problem is, the more time I spend with her, the more I know I want to spend the rest of my life with her. Anyway, enough about me, what about you? We have known you now for at least a year and have never seen you with anyone. Is there anyone special in your life?"

I saw the colour almost drain out of his face. I knew then that this was a question he didn't want to answer.

"Sorry, I shouldn't have been so nosey. You don't have to answer that if you don't want to."

"It's not that I don't want to answer it, it's just …" he paused for a moment, contemplating exactly what he was going to say. "I guess I have to tell someone soon. It will become plainly obvious at some point. It's just I haven't told anyone who knows me about this, not even my mother."

I had a sneaking suspicion I knew what the next words were going to be out of his mouth. I had thought that there was something different about Richard, about the way he acted around us. Not that it bothered me, but I guess it bothered him. I looked over at him and could see the look of worry in his eyes.

"Richard, I think I know what you are going to say. If it is what I think it is, then it doesn't mean I will feel any differently towards you. You're a great guy and who you love is who you love. It shouldn't make any difference to who you are as a friend and colleague. If you do the job to the best of your abilities, I don't give a shit who you prefer to go out with."

"You knew I was gay?"

"I didn't know, but had an idea."

"Well, now you are the only person that knows, apart from anyone I go out with, and that hasn't been anyone in a long time. I'm just worried that people will treat me differently, especially the guys. They are all military guys, alpha men if you will. I've heard the stories of how gays are treated in the forces."

"I'll stop you right there. You may have heard how they used to be treated, but there is a big difference now. Perhaps I should tell you about Mark. He was one of our friends, our brother in the army. The four of us were always together when we were in camp. Jayden, Mark, Nathan, and I. Mark was gay, but he never made a thing of it though. Yeah, he used to wind us up every now and then, but it was never done maliciously, and he never made a play for any of us, because he knew we were all straight. But we still loved him like a brother, right up until the end."

I could feel the pain building in me. It had been a long time since I had spoken about Mark. It had hit Jayden worst as he had to watch him die in his arms after the sniper attack. But each of us had grieved in some way because of his death.

"I'm sorry. I didn't mean to bring up bad memories for you."

"It's fine. It's been a while since I talked about him. Thinking about it though, you are the only person I have told he was gay too. Not because I was embarrassed by it, but just because it didn't occur to me to tell anyone. He was just Mark, our brother in arms who we loved. I guess what I am trying to say is, I think you will be surprised at the reaction of the guys when you tell them. But that is down to you. When you're ready, you will be the one to tell everyone. Believe me, though, it won't make a difference."

"Are you really sure about that?"

"If I'm honest, they will probably be relieved that you have told them. I think they have all been walking on eggshells not wanting to say anything to you. I'm sure Jayden and Brandon have seen the signs, Jayden more so because of Mark."

"Thanks for being so understanding, Tyler. It's been worrying the hell out of me all this time, thinking of how people will react when they find out. Knowing you don't see me any differently than before I told you makes me feel a little easier. I don't think I'm ready to tell everyone yet though, so can we just keep it between us. I don't like asking others to keep secrets, but I just need some time. I guess my Mum should really be the first to know."

"As I said, Richard, you will be the one to tell them and not me. But if you need me there for moral support when you do tell them, I will be there for you."

He gave me a smile and a nod of acknowledgment. I felt I had come a long way to know more about Richard today. He was finally coming out of the shell he had placed himself in. He just had to realise that it didn't matter to any of us that he was gay.

"Let's get on with some work, then I can get back to Maddie and spend the evening with her."

"Okay, lover boy," Richard said, almost bursting into hysterics as he said it.

"You can really go off people, you know."

Richard and I had been working together all afternoon and got a great deal further than I expected us to. We had already spoken to the companies we were working for, and they were putting everything into place with the dummy bank accounts, and we had started work setting up the interrogation programs to trace any rogue transactions that occurred. All we had to do now was wait and see what happened.

Looking down at the time on my laptop, I saw it was getting on towards 5:00. I was just about to turn to Richard and tell him to knock it off for the day when Mason walked into the office.

"So, Richard, how was your first full day working with this taskmaster? I see he hasn't let you get away from the desk all day."

I could see the smirk on his face, just daring me to say anything. Shrugging my shoulders, I just turned to Richard.

"We've had a good day, haven't we? Got to know each other a bit better and got a lot of work done. All in all, I would say it's been a good day, wouldn't you?" I gave Richard a smile and a quick wink. We got to know each other well today. Not only had Richard confessed to me his one secret, but I had found out just how good he was at the job. I would make sure both Mason and Jayden knew that mainly to stop giving him such menial tasks. He was far better than that.

"Yeah, it's been a good day. I have really enjoyed it," he replied with a genuine smile on his face.

"Ready to head off for the day then?"

"Is that okay with you, Tyler? If we still have things to look at then we can carry on for a while and I will head down to your place when we are finished, Mason."

"You're okay, Richard. If the boss says it's time to go then it's time to go. Plus, I have plans of my own, remember," I said with another wink.

"Yeah, good luck with that."

I could see Mason look at both of us with his eyebrows raised.

"Do I detect a bit of a geeky bromance going on here?"

I looked over at Richard as he looked over at me and we just burst out laughing. After everything we had spoken about today, the idea of us having a bromance, a geeky one at that, was hilarious. Trying to calm down my laughter, I just turned to Mason.

"Something like that, yeah. Go on Richard, you two head off home. I'll lock up here."

Mason just shook his head and walked out of the office. Richard was just about to leave when he turned to me and spoke.

"Tyler, thanks for today. I really mean it. You have made me feel far better about myself and working for you, knowing that I am accepted by you for who I am is a great weight off my mind."

"Anytime. Now get yourself out of here before the big boss starts getting arsey."

He pulled me into a hug, which knowing what I knew, should have made me feel uncomfortable. But I was surprised when it didn't. I didn't have an issue with gay men. As I said before, one of our best friends was gay, but since we lost Mark, I had never been around any other gay guys that I was aware of. This just felt like a good friend thanking me for helping him out, which is how it should be. Pulling out of the hug, Richard just gave me a nod of acknowledgment and headed out of the office.

I continued to pack everything away for the evening, smiling to myself that I had managed to bring some peace to one person's life. Now I just had to do it for one more person. Well, two. Maddie and myself. Closing the office door, I headed out and met Nathan standing in the reception.

"Fancy coming for a drink tonight?"

"Thanks, but I kind of have plans tonight. Maybe the weekend?"

"No problem. I'll let you lock up," and with that, he was out of the office and heading off.

I locked up and headed down to the coffee shop. My mind, still reeling over the conversation I just had with Nathan. He was never that quick to dismiss me when I turned him down for a drink. He would always try and argue with you, to convince you to go out with him. The guys were right, something was happening in his life. Something had changed his outlook and I was sure we would find out what it was, and soon. I couldn't think too much about that though, because tonight, I was going to get to spend time with the woman I loved.

Chapter Six

Madeleine

········

I t was getting close to 5:00 and I was starting to finish up for the day. Everything was ready for tomorrow morning and the shop was now empty. I loved running the café now that I had completed my Psychology degree. I just had to wait for my results and then see where I went from there. After having Rosie, I never thought I would be able to go back to university, having left part way through the second year to have her. Here I was, all these years later about to graduate with my degree. I had been lucky they had allowed me to go straight to the second year when I applied again.

I was still apprehensive about tonight and Tyler coming round. It was the first time I had allowed him to come round to the flat. Usually, we would just meet in the shop, and he would spend some time with me here. But being a quiet January night, it didn't seem right just to sit down here with no chance of customers coming in. We had gone for a few walks together up to the park in the summer, which had been really nice, but again being the middle of winter it was far too cold for that.

I just couldn't stop thinking about my past. What would Tyler think if he knew the truth? I just had to try and keep it from him for as long as I could. Perhaps if he grew to love me enough, he could forgive everything I had done in my past. After all, all the guys had forgiven Kye for his part in Sienna's kidnapping. I just hoped they could be as forgiving as me. But I wasn't so sure they would. Then there was the issue of getting close and intimate with him. I had a few boyfriends after that night. But as soon as it came to them touching me, I panicked. I couldn't bear anyone touching me in any intimate way without memories flooding back to me of that night. Of course, they ran a mile as soon as I freaked out. Would Tyler do the same? So far he had never touched me, but I could tell he wanted to. I just wondered if he sensed my fear and decided that he would take things slow? I hoped that he did and that he would wait until I was ready. I just didn't know if I ever would be.

I was out the back lost in my thoughts and didn't hear the shop bell ring. So when Tyler spoke to me, I nearly jumped a mile.

"I'm sorry, Mads. I should have shouted that I was here before I said anything. I forget you can't always hear everything out back."

Holding my chest, I brought my breathing back down to normal, as he slowly approached me, placing his arms around me and bringing me into a hug.

"I'm sorry, Tyler. I was kinda lost in my own thoughts and didn't hear you come in. I didn't mean to jump like that."

"It's okay, sweetheart, I'm sorry I scared you."

I felt a warmth come over me as he held me in his arms and

called me *sweetheart*. I felt safe in his arms and wanted to be in them forever just so I could forget the past. He placed a soft kiss on the top of my head, and I could feel myself start to blush. This was the most intimate moment we'd had together. I was surprised I hadn't started to freak out. But instead, I just felt warm and safe, happy in the knowledge that Tyler was with me. It gave me hope that what this was between us could work. Pulling away from me, Tyler looked down into my eyes. I hadn't realised until this moment just how gorgeous he was. Okay, he wasn't as buff as some of the other guys, but that was what I loved about him. The other thing I loved was his eyes. They were almost grey in colour and whenever you looked into them, it was as if you were looking right into his soul. They were beautiful. I was lost in them at this moment as we stood there looking at each other. I could see his hesitation as he looked down at my lips. Taking a deep breath, he pulled away further and let go of me as if sensing I wasn't ready. Part of me loved him for it, but deep down inside I wanted him to kiss me, to feel his lips on mine. I was just worried about where that kiss would lead. I felt the warmth leave me as he stepped away, immediately wishing he was back. Smiling down at me he spoke.

"I'm sorry, Mads. I should have asked before I held you like that. I just wanted to feel you close to me."

"It's fine. I liked it. I just …" I wasn't sure where I was going with this. How did I tell him what I had gone through without saying all the sordid details of my story? As if sensing the trouble I was having, Tyler just smiled.

"It's okay, you don't have to explain to me until you are ready. Let's just take things one step at a time, okay?"

Stepping over towards me, he gave me another kiss on the top of my head. "So, are you nearly finished for the evening?"

"Yeah, I just need to lock everything up and then we can head upstairs. I hadn't really thought about dinner though. I can get us some soup if you want?"

"How about we just order something in? I don't mind getting it, as I invited myself round to your place. We can just grab a pizza and sit down and watch a movie. You've been on your feet all day, so I wouldn't want to make you cook for me as well. I just wanted to spend some time with you," he paused for a second, appearing that he wasn't sure if he should say what he was thinking. Within a moment though, he carried on. "I missed you."

It felt so good to hear him say that. I had missed all of them over Christmas and New Year, but to hear him say that he specifically missed me made me feel so good inside. Smiling back at him, I spoke.

"I missed you too, and that sounds like a perfect evening."

"Okay, what pizza do you fancy? I'll get it ordered now so it will be here when we get upstairs."

"Just a chicken feast for me, thanks."

"Okay, I will order while you lock up."

Walking out to the front of the shop, I locked the door and made sure everything was switched off before heading back out the back to pick up my bag and head upstairs.

"All ordered, should be here in about thirty minutes. You ready?"

"Mmmhmm, let's go."

Walking out the back, I locked everything up and headed up the stairs to my flat. I could feel Tyler's hand resting on my back the whole way upstairs and it felt amazing. The more time I spent with this man, the more I fell for him. Opening the door to my flat, I walked into the kitchen and placed my bag on the table.

"Did you want something to drink? I have tea, coffee. There might even be a bottle of wine in the fridge." I turned to find Tyler right in front of me, smiling. He gently placed his hand on my cheek, and I found myself immediately leaning into his touch, relishing the warmth of his hand.

"Anything is fine, I just want to spend the evening with you."

I grabbed a couple of glasses and pulled out a bottle of wine from the fridge. Walking into the front room, I placed down the glasses and switched on the TV to find something to watch. Hearing the knock at the door, Tyler walked over and grabbed the pizzas from the delivery guy and brought them in. We sat down and ate, just chatting about our day. It felt so comfortable having Tyler here and I wondered why I had never done this before. Finishing our food, I found myself sitting next to him, and immediately leaned into him as he placed his arm around me.

Resting my head against his chest, I felt at home. This was where I wanted to be. Deep down inside though, I knew it was only a dream, one that would never come true. There was no way that I could have this forever. No way I could have him holding me so tenderly every night. As soon as he found out the truth about my past he would never want to see me again. I was so lost in my thoughts that I didn't realise that Tyler had been stroking my hair and tenderly kissing me on the head until he spoke.

"What's going through your head, sweetheart?"

"Nothing really. Just wish I could stay like this forever. Just forget everything except this moment and being with you."

I felt him shift slightly and turned to meet his eyes gazing down at me.

"Mads, sweetheart. Whatever happened in your past, I don't care. It won't change how I feel about you. You do realise that?"

I could feel myself start to lose it again. The tears, just waiting to fall. Just as I was about to pull away and speak, he just pulled me to him again and gently placed a finger on my lips.

"Don't say anything, Mads. When you are ready to tell me, you can. For now, let's just enjoy this moment together. Okay?"

I looked up at him smiling. If there was a reason why I had fallen so hard for this guy it was in that one statement. He was willing to wait for me to tell him my story. The problem was, I didn't think I would ever be ready to tell him, along with the heartbreak that it would bring. But, as I sat there gazing into his eyes, I started to hope. Perhaps Jess was right? Perhaps it wouldn't make a difference. I don't think either of us was really paying attention to the film. We were just sitting there gazing into each other's eyes. I saw Tyler quickly look down at my lips. Was he thinking about kissing me? Did I want him to kiss me? It was something I had thought about since I had met him.

Slowly, Tyler lowered his face towards mine until our lips were just a hair's breadth away. Gently he placed his lips on mine as he held me. He didn't try to deepen the kiss, just lingered his lips on mine. It felt amazing, it was almost too much, yet it wasn't enough. He broke away and smiled at me.

"I have waited two long years to do that, sweetheart."

I wanted to pull him towards me, to kiss him again and show him how much he really meant to me, but I was so worried about where it would lead. As if sensing my uncertainty, he just smiled and placed his hand on my face.

"I will never take it any further than that, until you are ready, Mads. I'm not going to ask you what happened in the past, you will tell me that when you are ready. Just know that I am not like the person in your past. I would never hurt you or do anything you didn't want. If it takes another two years, I will be happy if I can spend time with you like this."

I could feel the tears forming in my eyes at his words. He was so sensitive and caring, I just couldn't hold back as the tears began to fall. Wiping them away, Tyler just pulled me into him and allowed me to cry, gently rubbing my back as he held me. I had never known what it was like to feel this way with a man. No one had ever been this caring towards me, but I liked it and wanted it so much more. Managing to get my emotions under control, I sat there in Tyler's arms, enjoying how safe I felt in them.

"Thank you, Tyler."

"For what?"

"For this. For being so patient with me. I wish I could tell you everything, but it will change how you feel about me. I know it will."

Gently he moved my face around with his hand, so he was now looking directly into my eyes with his. Those gorgeous eyes that I just couldn't get enough of.

"Sweetheart, if you told me that you had murdered someone, I would still feel the same way about you. As I said, I will not pressure you to tell me, but I will be there to pick the pieces up when you finally do. I'm not going anywhere, except by your side. Now let's just enjoy this moment together and watch the film."

I turned back to watch the tv, a sense of relief washing over me at his words. If he truly meant what he said, that it didn't matter what I told him, he would still love me, then there was no reason to worry. I started to wonder what life would be like with Tyler in my life constantly. Would it be like this? Could I dare to hope that we could have a relationship with him knowing everything, and if he did, would he accept Rosie into his life? As I allowed these thoughts to go around in my head, feeling the warmth of Tyler wrapped around me, I felt my eyes grow heavy as the weariness of the day took over my body and

I fell into a sound sleep.

Chapter Seven

Tyler

earing Maddie breathing slowly, I knew she had fallen asleep in my arms. I couldn't explain exactly what I was feeling right now. This was what I had wanted for years, to have her in my arms like this. To me, it seemed that was where she belonged and always would. I just needed to convince her of that. I could tell she was worried about me finding out about her past, and I had meant every word I said to her. I didn't care. She could have murdered someone, and I would still love her. She was the only woman I would ever love, and I never wanted to let her go.

When I kissed her earlier, I had wanted so much more. I wanted to pick her up in my arms and take her into the bedroom and make love to her all night long. I knew I couldn't, knew I had to take my time. But I still wanted to feel her body under me and touch every part of her skin. It was as though she was the air I needed to breathe. I sat there gazing down at the sleeping beauty in my arms. She was my everything. I loved everything about her, her quirkiness, how she was different from every other woman I had known.

She had the most gorgeous red hair. Yeah it was dyed, but I loved that. It suited her fiery personality. Then there were those magnificent brown eyes with golden flecks. I lost myself in those eyes every time I looked into them. With her body nestled against me, I knew she was mine, that we fitted together perfectly.

As I sat there, I thought back to my conversation with Richard earlier. Was I willing to fight for Maddie? Could I take being rejected and keep pushing to be with her? At this moment I immediately knew my answer was yes. There was no question, and I didn't have to think about it anymore, my answer would always be yes. I never wanted to let this woman go. I was never going to walk away from her and let her live a life without me. I would do everything I could to make her see we were meant to be together, even if that took the rest of my life. There was no doubt in my mind that this was meant to be, that we were meant to be.

I had seen Mason, Jayden, and now Brandon find the women they wanted to spend the rest of their lives with. I'd seen how Mason and Jayden had already started to raise a family of their own. And I wanted that. I wanted to have the whole family with kids, to finally settle down. I loved my parents and my sister, but I wanted to have a family of my own. To create a life with the woman I loved a life that was mine.

Leaning down, I gently placed a kiss on top of Maddie's head and rested my head on top of hers. I knew I should put her into bed and either leave the flat and head home or just get comfortable on the settee alone. But for one evening, I just wanted her here in my arms. If this was going to be the only night I got to spend with my sweetheart then I was going to make the most of it. I closed my eyes, breathing in her scent. The combination of perfume, bread, and coffee invaded my senses, warming me to my core. Closing my eyes, I just lay there for a moment. Just a few minutes, I thought, and then I would put her to bed. Before I knew it though, I had fallen asleep with my woman in my arms.

I was jolted awake as I felt Maddie thrashing in my arms. She was having a bad dream, and if I was to guess it was more of a nightmare. I tightened my hold around her, trying to calm her down. I knew I shouldn't wake her. I had seen Jayden go through so many nightmares after Mark was killed to know how she could react to that. I needed to try and calm her down and slowly pull her out from her terror. Holding her, to try and comfort her, I quietly spoke.

"Maddie, sweetheart, wake up for me baby."

I could feel her heartbeat was out of control as she started thrashing in my arms as though she was trying to get out of my grasp, or the grasp of the person in her nightmare. I knew I shouldn't, but if I didn't try and wake her soon, I was worried that she was going to hurt herself. I was just about to speak again when I froze, hearing the words that came out from her mouth. It was almost a whisper, but it still filled me with dread.

"Please, don't do this to me."

Whatever she was reliving in her head right now, had to be the reason why she wouldn't let me get close. Part of me was desperate to know what it was, but the other part of me knew I shouldn't be listening, that these were her personal thoughts, and she wouldn't want me hearing them.

"You're hurting me. Please stop, I don't want this. Please stop."

Hearing how scared she was, I could feel the anger burning inside of me. I was just starting to realise exactly what she had been through, or what I assumed she had been through. I could be wrong, but it would make so much sense as to why she wouldn't let me get close to her. I could feel myself starting to lose it as she fought against my hold. The thought that she had been hurt by another man, that he had … I couldn't even bring myself to say it, the pain in my chest was too much.

I tried to hold her as close to me as possible as she fought to try and escape me. I could hear her cries as her sobs wracked throughout her entire body.

"Sweetheart, it's Tyler. It's okay, I'm here. No one is going to hurt you."

She continued to try and fight me in her sleep. Her cries were now frantic as she thrashed about in my arms. My heart broke in two when I heard the scream that came from her mouth as she suddenly awoke in my arms. The look of fear and hatred in her eyes as she met mine would be a picture that would be forever ingrained in my mind.

Chapter Eight
Madeleine

The sound of the bedroom door opening aroused me from my sleep. I had never been a heavy sleeper and at this moment I was thankful I wasn't. I smelt him before he even got close to the bed. He'd been drinking again. Usually, this meant a night of verbal abuse towards me. He would tell me how much he hated me and wished he didn't have to live in the same house as me. Tonight though, I had a feeling tonight was going to be different. He never came into my room. Usually, when he was this late coming home he would just crash around the house and head to his bedroom.

Then again, usually, my Dad or step mum were in the house. Tonight though, it was just the two of us. I felt the bed dip as he climbed onto it. I could smell his breath as he closed the gap towards me. I lay there, with my eyes closed, trying to stay calm, pretending to still be asleep. I hoped that this would be enough to make him leave, that not paying any interest to him, he would just forget about me.

When I felt the cover being lifted off me, I knew I wasn't going to be that lucky. I could feel my heart starting to beat faster as fear started to grip my entire being. I could feel his body next to mine, feel his erection pressing up against me. I couldn't help but let the fear take over as tears started to fall across my face. Slowly he started to caress my body. If this had been anyone else it would have been sensual, arousing almost. Knowing, however, that it was Thomas, my so-called stepbrother, just made me feel dirty. He hated me, so why was he here?

"Mads, are you awake?"

The way he spoke was almost caring, as though he had genuine feelings for me, but I knew he didn't. He couldn't care less about me.

"What do you want, Thomas?" The disgust was clear to hear in my voice. Whatever he wanted, he wasn't going to get it. Not without a fight.

I could feel his hand moving around and grasping my breast. I hissed slightly in pain as he started to squeeze it hard. Turning slightly, I found myself pinned underneath him, his body pressing me down into the bed. I could feel my fear growing as I looked into his eyes. They were dark with lust and disgust. It was obvious he still hated me, but his need was greater than his hatred.

"What do you think I want, Mads? I want you. Well, not specifically you. I just want to fuck someone, as you just happen to be the only woman available, then you get the pleasure of me fucking you tonight."

"Thomas, you don't really want this. You're drunk and don't know what you're doing. You hate me, so you will only regret it in the morning. Just leave and we won't say any more about this."

I was almost begging him to leave my room. I knew he would hate himself in the morning when he realised what he'd done. Not because of the fact he had hurt me, but because he had sex with the one woman he hated more than his mother. What came out of his mouth next, filled me with horror. He laughed. He looked down into my eyes and he laughed at me.

"Oh, I know exactly what I am doing, my dearest Mads. I know how much I hate you, and that is why I am here now. I know you're still a virgin, so I am going to take that precious cherry from you now. I am going to ruin you for every other guy that follows me. I am going to make you feel so good, that no other bloke will ever live up to what you experience tonight."

Before I could even take in what he was saying, he suddenly forced his tongue into my mouth as he kissed me angrily, grabbing both of my hands and holding them above my head. I was struggling to breathe as he pressed down on my chest and continued to kiss me. Pulling away from my mouth, he looked down with a smirk on his face.

"Please, don't do this to me."

"Oh, Mads. I know you want this as much as I do. I've seen the way you look at me. I know you want my cock inside you, pounding you. I will make a slut out of you yet. Once I'm done, you will be begging me to do this to you every night."

I could feel the tears streaming down my face. I just needed him to let go of my wrists, and then I would be able to fight him off and get away. I was sure of it. As he lifted off me and straddled my body, I was ready. Waiting for him to let go. As if sensing what I was planning, he took only one hand off from my wrists but continued to hold them down with the other. I struggled to try and break free from his grip until I felt the pain in my face as his fist, landed on it.

"Don't try that again, Madeleine. It will only end with more pain for you."

Pulling off his belt he placed it around one of the slats in the headboard and then fastened it around my wrists so I couldn't move. I tried to pull away, but it just got tighter and tighter around them. I could feel the panic start to rise in me.

"There, that should keep you in place while I fuck you senseless."

He ripped my t-shirt over my head and pulled down my shorts. I wanted to kick him, but I couldn't move. The fear had totally taken over my body. I felt like I was a stranger looking down on myself and what was happening. I was still struggling to breathe as my fear and sobs were going through my body. Getting off the bed, I watched as Thomas removed his trousers and boxer shorts, freeing his cock for me to see. Not that he impressed me, it just disgusted me how he thought he could do this to me.

Climbing back onto the bed he yanked my legs apart as he settled in between them.

"Now to do what I have wanted for a very long time, ruin your life."

I felt Thomas place his cock at my entrance. As he placed his hand on my throat he squeezed slightly and thrust into me. I felt the pain go through my body as he took everything from me. He had taken my virginity without a care in the world. The pain was unbearable as he lay on top of me squeezing my throat.

"You're hurting me. Please stop, I don't want this. Please stop."

He just ignored my pleas as he kept ramming into me over and over again. I closed my eyes not wanting to see his face, smirking down at me as he crushed my soul. He said he was going to ruin my life, and in one night, he was doing exactly that. He had taken everything from me. The pain was too much as I heard Thomas groan as he obviously found his release and I felt the blackness take over my body as I started to pass out.

I screamed as I woke from my dream, two strong arms around me were holding me down. I could feel the panic rising in me again as I met his eyes. I tried to push him away, I didn't want him touching me anymore, he had already taken everything from me and now he wouldn't leave me alone. I pushed and pushed, but he wouldn't let me go.

"Let me go, you have already taken everything from me. Please just let me be."

"Mads, sweetheart, it's me, Tyler. I'm not going to hurt you. Please calm down baby."

I suddenly realised where I was and who it was holding me. It wasn't Thomas, it was worse. Now Tyler would realise exactly what had happened to me and wouldn't want anything to do with me. I had ruined everything. How could I have fallen asleep in his arms, allowed him to see me at my worst? The tears were still pouring down my face as I looked into his eyes. They were full of hurt and anger. He hated me, I could see it in his face. He knew I was broken, that I was dirty and tarnished, he was disgusted by me.

"Let me go, Tyler. Get out, just get out."

"Sweetheart, it's okay, we can get through this. Just talk to me please."

I saw hurt in his eyes. Did he really mean that? Did he really want to get through this? I couldn't risk it. Couldn't risk the pain it would cause when he found out the full story and left me alone again, with no one, nothing.

"JUST GET OUT!" I shouted at him. The shock was clear to see as he immediately let me go. He sat there for a moment just looking at me, watching the tears pouring down my face. Slowly he moved his hand up to touch my face and try to wipe away the tears. I swatted it away. I felt dirty. I didn't want anyone touching me again. The thoughts of Thomas's hands all over my body were still fresh in my head.

"Please, just leave Tyler. Don't argue, just leave."

I could see the hesitation in his eyes. He didn't want to leave me alone, despite it being exactly what I wanted. He got up from the settee and looked back at me.

"Mads, whatever happened, it doesn't matter. It really doesn't. I want to help you get through this. I will wait as long as it takes, but just remember I am here for you when you need me."

He picked up his coat and walked towards the door. Opening it, he turned back and then said three words I never expected or wanted to hear from any man.

"I love you, sweetheart."

With one final glance, he walked out the door and closed it behind him. I broke down in tears. As soon as he walked out, I wanted to run to the door, to beg him to come back, and say that I loved him too. But I couldn't do it. I couldn't let him get any closer to me. Everything I had done in my life, meant I had to be alone. I had brought it all on myself. Had allowed myself to be raped by my stepbrother. I had a child with him and then left that beautiful girl with him and his mother. What kind of a mother and woman was I? How could I have done that?

She would be nearly three years old now. Two years older than when I left her with them. She probably didn't even remember who I was. Not that I had a choice in leaving her. Thomas made it quite clear that I was leaving, and my precious Rosie was staying with him. All he was bothered about was the money she brought into the house. That was all they were both worried about. God only knows what they had told my Dad. He probably thinks I was a tart that got knocked up by some punter and then left them to pick up the pieces. Well, if Michelle and Thomas had anything to do with it, that's what he would think. I would be one big disappointment to him.

I fell to the ground, hugging my legs to my chest, allowing the pain and sadness to curse through my body as the tears fell. I was right to make him leave. Tyler was better off without me. Everyone was better off without me. As soon as I could, I would leave Kings View and make a life somewhere else. I had a bit of money saved up so I would be able to survive a little while. Once I had my degree confirmed, I would be able to get myself a good job.

Looking over at the clock, I could see that it was already 04:00 in the morning. There wasn't much point in trying to get any sleep now and I needed a hot shower to try and get rid of the dirt from my skin. I felt filthy, knowing what he had done to me all those years ago. Pulling myself together, as I always did, I got up from the floor and headed to the bathroom to shower and get ready for the day.

Chapter Nine

Tyler

L eaving Maddie sitting there with tears pouring down her face was the hardest thing I had ever done. But it was what she wanted. She had made that quite clear. I couldn't help but tell her I loved her as I walked out the door. I needed her to know that I would always be there for her. I stood outside her flat for a while, hoping she would come to the door and ask me to go back in. Part of me knew she wouldn't, but the other part wanted her so much.

Currently, I was walking back to the office. There wasn't really much point in me heading off home now, and there was a shower there, so I could get cleaned up for the day. I always kept a set of clean clothes there as you never could tell what was going to happen. Walking down the road, I let the events of the evening run through my head. Everything up until we had both fallen asleep had been wonderful. I couldn't have asked for a better evening. I thought I was finally getting somewhere with Maddie, that she was finally learning to trust me. But in one fell swoop, all of that hope and trust was taken away by that one nightmare.

It made me realise that I had to help her. Somehow, I had to get her away from those nightmares. She needed to let everything out, Jayden was proof of that. But how was I going to help her when she wouldn't let me? I didn't want to involve Jess in this, since she had too much on her hands with Callum. I know she would help, but I didn't want to burden her with this as well. I guess I would have to go to Ashleigh. She had become friends with Maddie, so I'm sure she would be able to talk to her. In the meantime, I needed to find out as much as I could about Maddie before she came to Kings View. I knew I shouldn't, but the more I could figure things out, the more I would be able to help her. I realised it was an intrusion into her life, but if she wouldn't open up to me it was the only way I could find out the truth.

Walking up to the office, I opened the door and turned off the alarm. Getting out my phone I waited for the text message or call I was bound to receive from Mason. He would have known someone had entered the building at a ridiculous time and seen the video footage, so I could expect some form of contact. As I walked down the corridor, my phone started to ring.

"Don't ask, Mason. It's been a long couple of hours. I am fine and the office is okay. I didn't fancy driving home at four in the morning. I'm grabbing a shower and maybe a couple of hours sleep."

I heard the silence at the end of the phone, so Mason was obviously surprised at my response to his call.

"Mace, you there?"

"Yeah, just a little shocked at your answering the phone. Okay, I will let you get on. But I think you have some explaining to do when I get in the office."

"Okay, boss. See you later."

With that, I headed to grab a shower and try to get my head down for a couple of hours.

It was just after 08:00, and I had managed to get three hours of sleep before I started my investigation work on Maddie. I was sitting in Mason's office waiting for the lecture I was about to get. He had dropped Jess off at the coffee shop this morning and when he saw Maddie standing there looking a complete mess, he almost lost it. Especially since he knew I had been round there last night and then came back here at four this morning. He walked in carrying our coffees and sat down behind his desk. I could see he was not a happy boss this morning.

"So, are you going to tell me what the fuck, happened last night at Maddie's? Why was she in a complete state this morning?"

I took a deep breath. This wasn't the conversation I had wanted, especially not with Mason.

"Before you start having a go at me, I didn't do anything. We had a pizza, sat down to watch a film and I kissed her. That was it. She fell asleep in my arms and the next thing I knew, I woke up to her having a nightmare."

I could still feel the anger in me, knowing what she had been going through in that dream.

"She was thrashing about so much, I tried to wake her up. She eventually did wake up screaming. Then she threw me out of the flat."

I saw the realisation on his face. He knew me well enough to know I wouldn't intentionally hurt Maddie. He may not have known how much I really cared for her, but he knew I would never intentionally hurt a woman.

"Do you know what the nightmare was about?"

I looked down at my coffee cup. I didn't want to bring myself to say the words. But I knew I had to.

"She still won't tell me what happened. Shit. This is difficult for me to say. I think she was raped, Mace, and by someone she knew."

I heard the sharp intake of breath that Mason had taken and knew he was probably as angry as me. I just couldn't look at him to see. The thought of what happened to my sweetheart was killing me inside. Especially since she wouldn't let me help her.

"What are you going to do about it?"

"I don't think you want to know. It isn't entirely ethical."

I looked up and saw his eyebrows raised, almost daring me to tell him.

"As long as it isn't illegal, I don't want to know. Just don't expect me to pick up the pieces when it all goes wrong. Remember she works for my fiancé, who loves her dearly. I will take Jess's side over you any day. Hell, I have to live with her, and me being in the doghouse with Monty is not something I want to even contemplate."

"It isn't illegal. Well, not yet anyway. Believe me, when I tell you, I don't want to hurt Maddie. I guess it's time to be honest with you, and myself. I love her, Mace. I can't see me ever wanting to be with another woman, even if she tells me to get lost."

"Well thank fuck, you finally admitted it. If you need any help, you know where I am. I know you've been chatting to Brandon and Ashleigh, and before you say anything, they haven't told me what about. I'm guessing it's Maddie. Just come to me before things get out of hand. We've had enough problems in the past year or so, and I don't want any more if we can help it."

I just nodded my head to Mason. I knew he would do everything to help any of his friends, and although I was strictly Jayden's friend, I knew he would have my back if I needed him. I got up from the chair and headed towards the door.

"Get Richard to give you a hand, but all our jobs still need to be done. So any time spent on Maddie needs to be made up and I won't be paying overtime for it."

"Sure thing, boss."

I looked at Mason, and although I knew he was being serious, his eyes told me he wasn't angry, that he knew I had to do this, and he was behind me. He loved Maddie because she was so important to Jess, and he wouldn't want to see her upset or hurt, even if it is from her past. Walking out of his office I headed down to my office to carry on my investigation.

I found Richard already sitting at the desk next to me, starting up his laptop as I walked through the door.

"Hey, Tyler, how did things go last night?"

"They were fine until Maddie had a nightmare."

"Shit, Tyler. Is she okay?"

"I don't know. She threw me out of the flat and I ended up here at four o'clock this morning. I do know one thing. Something terrible happened to her. I think she was raped by someone she knew. I need to find out as much as I can about her past. I know it's not right to invade her privacy, but I need to try and help her, and this is the only way I can do it without her actually telling me what happened."

I could see Richard looking worried. He knew as well as I

did that this was unethical. It wasn't a job. This was just personal, but we had to try. He sat there for a moment, just contemplating what I had said, then he turned to me and smiled.

"What do you need me to do?"

"I can't ask you to help me with this. You know as well as I do, we shouldn't be doing it."

"Tyler, it may be wrong, but you need to know. Hell, I need to know now. I may not know Maddie as well as you all do, but I know that she is a wonderful and kind young woman. If there is anything we can do to help her through this, then I want to be part of it. If you think what happened to her did indeed happen, then we need to help her get through this. No woman should have to deal with that. I'll do whatever you need to help, and take the consequences with you."

"Thanks, Richard. But we still need to work on the rest of our jobs, Mason made that quite clear."

"Sounds like I will be spending a bit more time down here than I originally planned then."

I smiled at the guy sitting next to me. We hadn't known each other that long, not really known each other at all. But in the space of a couple of days, he was already there beside me, helping me with Maddie. He had my back, and for that, I would always be thankful. I just hoped that he found someone to make him happy and that when he did, I could be there for him helping him along the way.

"I'll start looking through her social media sites. Can you see what you can find about her parents?"

"Sure thing. I just have a couple of bits to do on the jobs we started yesterday and then I will get straight on it. That should keep Mason happy as well."

With that, the pair of us got our heads down and started our investigation. All the while I was truly hoping that what I thought wasn't true.

Chapter Ten

Tyler

························· ❦ ·······················

Richard and I had been working all day trying to find out everything we could about Maddie before she came to Kings View. Unfortunately, it hadn't been much, but at least it was a starting point. Richard had found out that her parents Brian and Natasha had been happily married for nearly thirty years before Natasha had unfortunately died when she had an unexpected epileptic fit whilst driving home from work about 6 years ago. She died instantly when her car went out of control and hit a tree. Brian was a serving Lieutenant Commander in the Royal Navy and was often away on deployment. I wasn't even going to ask how Richard had found that piece of information out. I knew how difficult it was to get information on serving members of the armed forces, so how he had established that even impressed me.

I had determined that he was seeing a woman called Michelle

Smith, and she and her son Thomas appear to have moved into Brian's house a little over four years ago, two years before Maddie had moved here to Kings View. What wasn't clear was what their relationship had been like with Maddie. There were never any pictures of them together on any of their social media sites. In fact, the only one that seemed to be posting regularly was Thomas, and when he did, it seemed to be a different girl every time.

"Well, there's not much to go on I'm afraid, Tyler. We have to start somewhere and what we have is a starting point."

"I know, although there is something about Thomas that sends shivers down my spine. Check out the pictures on his Facebook account."

"Hell, there is a guy you wouldn't want to meet in real life. Something about him screams arsehole. How many different women has he been with in the past month?" Pausing for a second, he looked over at me and I could tell he was starting to think the same thing as me. "You don't think …?"

"I'm not sure, Richard. But he is someone I want to know more about if we can. It's not just the pictures. Maddie's nightmare, it was as if she knew exactly who was doing it to her, this wasn't a stranger. We may be jumping to conclusions here, but I don't have much more to go on."

Thoughts were going through my head. Was Thomas behind everything? As Richard had said, he looked very much like an arsehole and seemed to be with a different woman every weekend. But the fact of the matter was, he was effectively her stepbrother. Although we had already seen what a 'step' anything, had meant to Ashleigh's stepfather. He was quite happy to make Ashleigh his wife and have kids with her, whether Ashleigh wanted it or not. The more I thought about it, the more it was starting to make sense. Lost in my thoughts, I forgot that Richard was still sitting next to me until he placed a hand on my shoulder.

"Look, it's getting late. I'm going to pack up and get back to Mason's. I haven't got any plans for the evening, so I will do a bit more work there tonight."

"Richard, you don't need to spend your entire time helping me. You should be relaxing in the evening, not ..."

"You can stop right there, Tyler. I don't have anything better to do than help someone I would like to call a friend when he needs help. Maybe one day, I will be calling on you to help me. Now, you need to get some rest as well. Neither of us will get anything done properly if we stay here all night. So, come on, get packed up, and head home."

Smiling, I started packing everything away. I knew there was no point arguing with Richard. He may not be built like the rest of the guys, but I got the impression he could take care of himself if needed, and if the truth was known, I was still knackered from my restless night's sleep. Just as we were about to head out of the door, Brandon walked into the office.

"Hey guys, how's it going?"

"Not bad, Brandon. Just heading off for the evening. I'm sure Tyler will fill you in. I'll see you in the morning and will let you know if I find anything tonight."

"Thanks for today, Richard. I really appreciate everything."

"Anytime. See you both in the morning."

With that, Richard walked out of the office, leaving me standing there with Brandon.

"So, Mason said you had some news about Maddie. Do you fancy coming to our place and talking about it? I'm guessing you don't really feel like going home tonight."

"You guys have put up with me enough in the past few months.

I'm sure you have far better things to be doing than listening to me all night again. I'll just grab something to eat and put my head down for a few hours here."

"Ashleigh would never forgive me if I let you sleep in the office tonight. Come on, I've already spoken to her and told her to expect you. She is making dinner for us all. Then you can tell us exactly what has happened."

He walked over to me and placed his hand on my shoulder. I was close to breaking point now. What, with everything that had happened last night, and then the help and compassion that Richard, Mason, and now Brandon were showing me, it took all my strength to hold back the tears. I wasn't usually an emotional man, but when it came to my sweetheart, everything went out the window. Brandon could see the change in my mood and smiled.

"Come on, let's get you home. You can sleep in our spare room tonight. I don't think Ashleigh would want you being alone tonight, and in fairness neither do I. We can grab something to eat and then sit down and chat things through, okay?"

Smiling, I gave him a quick chin lift and grabbed my stuff. Heading out of the office we made our way over to Brandon's house.

***

We had just enjoyed a fantastic meal and were now in the sitting room. Brandon walked in and passed me a beer before sitting next to Ashleigh.

"So, are you going to tell us what happened last night between you and Maddie?"

"Shit, Brandon. I don't really know how to say this."

I took a deep breath and continued to explain everything that had happened last night at Maddie's. I hated telling anyone, especially seeing as I hadn't discussed anything with Maddie, but I needed help. I couldn't do this on my own. I'm sure in the end she would forgive me, I just had to hope that she wouldn't get too mad when she found out. I looked over at Brandon and Ashleigh when I finished explaining. It was obvious Brandon was as angry about the situation as I was. There wasn't a man working at King's that agreed with any woman being hurt.

"You have to try and help her, Tyler. If there is anything I can do that you think would help, I will."

"I appreciate that, Ashleigh, and nothing would please me more than to help her. The problem is, she still won't let me in. I know whatever happened to her is eating her up inside, and the look on her face when she woke up last night, how scared she was, it killed me inside."

I saw Ashleigh's face drop. The tears were starting to form in her eyes. We all wanted to help Maddie, but she had to want to be helped as well. We couldn't just force ourselves on her and expect her to gladly take our help. Deep down, we all knew she was going to fight against us, that unless she admitted to us she needed that help, she would never accept it because she didn't feel like she needed it.

"Whatever Maddie is hiding or holding back, she thinks it will change how I feel about her. She told me that much last night before she fell asleep. If she was raped, and I hope to God she wasn't, in her mind she thinks that will change the way I feel about her."

"You don't believe that, do you?"

"Of course, I don't believe that, Brandon. It would just mean I would take things slow with her until she can trust me. Basically, what I'm doing now."

All this while Ashleigh had been sitting there silently,

apparently going through everything in her mind. Suddenly she turned to me and spoke.

"There is another possible reason, other than being raped."

I looked over at Ashleigh, confused by her statement. I wracked my brain trying to work out what other reason there could be. Ashleigh looked at me realising that I couldn't think of any other reason for me changing my mind about her.

"If she was raped, and it is sounding like a high possibility, what if there was another outcome because of it? One that she is so ashamed of, she thinks it will change everyone's thoughts about her."

I was still confused. I couldn't think of any outcome from her being raped that would make me feel any different about her. A man brutally raping her would just leave her scared to be around other men, not wanting any physical contact or sex with them. I mean, she didn't have a baby with him … my eyes immediately flew up and met Ashleigh's, understanding exactly where she was going with this.

"You don't think …?"

"It's one reason why she would be ashamed."

I could see Brandon sitting there, totally confused at the conversation we were having without actually saying words.

"Will someone please enlighten me as to what is going on here? You have obviously come to the same conclusion as each other, but I am still way in the dark here."

I looked at Ashleigh, I couldn't bring myself to say it. Especially if it was true. Would that change my feelings about Maddie? I wanted to say it didn't, but my heart pounding in my chest was saying otherwise.

"What if there was a consequence of her being raped? What if she got pregnant? She could have had an abortion, or given the child away, and that is the reason why she thinks our feelings towards her would change if we found out."

Brandon immediately realised exactly where Ashleigh had gone with the conversation. He immediately took Ashleigh's hand in his. I knew there was a high chance that they wouldn't be able to have children together, and that hurt Ashleigh more than any of us would understand. If Maddie had an abortion, that would upset Ashleigh more than anyone else. What she said next both surprised and filled me with warmth.

"I know there is a chance that I can't have a child naturally, but even if Maddie decided to have an abortion because she got pregnant after being raped, it wouldn't change how I feel about her. I can't say that I would do the same, but the thought of bringing up a child brought into this world in that way may have been too much for her to take. I know people out there will argue with me, saying it is still murder, but it's a personal choice that every woman would have to take. And they should get that choice, it shouldn't be pushed upon them, either way. If that is what she needed to do, then if I had been her friend at the time, even knowing I possibly couldn't have what she had been given, I would have stood by her to help her through it."

I saw the tears starting to fall from her eyes again as she spoke, the thought of what Maddie must have gone through clearly affecting her. I saw Brandon squeeze her hand tightly. I couldn't bear it any longer. I got up from my seat and sat in front of her, taking her other hand in mine. I knew Brandon was sitting there glaring at me, but I just needed to be there for Ashleigh.

"I'm sorry if I have made you upset thinking about this. It was never my intention to do that. I should have thought about how this might affect you. Both of you have been there for me over the past few months and I cannot thank you enough. For a moment there I wondered if I could still feel the same way about Maddie if I knew she had a child, but I realised now the answer is yes. Everything you said is true. She should have that choice and I shouldn't make a judgement about what she should or shouldn't have done. After all, it is her choice, and she is the one that must live with it. I wouldn't feel any different about her. I would still love her no matter what. I just need to be there to help her and support her no matter what. Thank you for making me realise that."

Ashleigh squeezed my hand and smiled down at me.

"You are going to make Maddie a wonderful husband one day, Tyler. I can see how much she means to you. Now we just have to make Maddie realise that."

"Easier said than done," I said as I returned to my seat opposite them.

"So, what have you done so far? Mason said he gave you permission to have Richard help you."

"I'm not sure you should know, Brandon. Plausible deniability and all that. Safe to say, it is not illegal, just not exactly ethical."

"I'm sure what I was doing for two years, wasn't exactly ethical, but I still did it. Remember I followed Ashleigh across Europe trying to track her down. That isn't exactly how I should have acted as a private investigator when it wasn't a job."

Spending the next hour going through everything we had done and found out, I waited with bated breath to find out what Brandon and Ashleigh thought.

"I hate to admit it, but Thomas sounds like the most likely to have caused this, but unless Maddie is willing to tell us that, we won't know."

"And there is the issue, Brandon. She couldn't even bear to look at me last night. She literally threw me out of her flat as I tried to comfort her. I even told her I loved her as I walked out the door."

"Let me talk to her, Tyler. I can go there during the day and offer to listen to her. If it is her stepbrother that did this to her then I will understand better than most what she is going through."

"How are you going to approach her? She will know I have been talking if you say anything."

"I will just say you were worried about her, that's all, I won't mention anything else. I will leave it for a couple of days, so it doesn't look that obvious."

"Well, I appreciate any help I can get, so thank you, both of you. It's probably best if I steer clear of the shop for the moment, I don't want to make matters worse. Now, if you don't mind, I'm going to head off to grab a shower and then get some sleep. I didn't get much last night, and I could do with an early night."

"No problem. I'll have breakfast ready for you in the morning."

"Brandon, I think I love your fiancé as much as I do Maddie."

"Just remember to keep your hands to yourself and get your arse to bed."

Laughing I headed up to my room for the night to get some rest and get ready for another day.

Chapter Eleven

Madeleine

I hadn't seen Tyler for two days since I threw him out of my flat. I knew I shouldn't have done that. It wasn't his fault what happened, not really. I was just angry with myself for allowing him to chip yet another piece of my wall away. I had nearly told him everything after he kissed me so tenderly. At no moment did he try to take advantage of me, never tried to make it anything more than it was. Then when he said he wouldn't care if I had murdered someone I nearly caved, but I knew I couldn't. Then when I found him holding me after I woke from my nightmare, the only person I could see was Thomas smirking back at me, so I had to throw him out. I couldn't bear to look at him anymore. It wasn't until he was leaving, and he turned to me and said he loved me, that I wanted to take it all back. I knew deep down he loved me, but he had never said those three words to me.

What hurt the most is that he hadn't even come to pick up the breakfast or lunches for the past two days. Brandon and Nathan had come. I guess he was just giving me the space I had asked for, but still, it hurt. I missed him. I hated to say that, but it was true. I couldn't understand how he could so easily break down the wall I had built around myself for the past two years. That alone should worry me, but truth be known, I wanted him to. I was scared about telling him the truth. One voice inside me kept saying that he would understand, that he would be there for me. The issue was the much louder voice, my voice of reason said he would run a mile, especially when he found out about Rosie.

It had been a normal morning for me, everything except being here on my own for the day. Jess was out with Joan all day. She had wanted to spend some time with her today, picking out an outfit for their upcoming wedding. It was a day I was both looking forward to and dreading. Spending the entire weekend with everyone worried the hell out of me. The thing was that Jess was my friend, she had been there for me when I needed a job, and I couldn't thank her enough. But the idea of being around everyone for so long filled me with dread, especially as she had asked me to be one of her bridesmaids. I was desperately trying to find a way out of it, but every time I went to say something I just thought about how it would break her heart if I said no. So, I always chickened out.

Mr. Duncan had been in for his morning order and had just left with his lunch. I was just getting the coffee ready for the guys, hoping that Tyler would walk in when the door opened, and my heart fell when I saw Richard here on his own. I smiled as he walked over to the counter, but I think he immediately saw my disappointment as he walked over.

"Hey, Maddie. You, okay? You seem a little down."

"Hi, Richard. Yeah, I'm okay. Is Tyler not with you?"

I saw the look of understanding come over his face. I wasn't sure how much he knew about what had happened the other evening, whether Tyler would even mention it. I just needed to know that he was okay.

"No, he was busy working, so I thought I would come down instead."

He stood there for a second and sighed.

"Maddie, it's not my place to say anything. I know that Tyler is worried about you. I guess he just doesn't want to make things worse than they are."

"It's not his fault, it was mine. I didn't mean everything I said. Tell him … Just tell him I miss him. Please."

"I will. Just remember he would never do anything to hurt you. He really does care about you, a lot. Whatever he does, he only wants to help you."

Richard smiled at me, and I couldn't help but feel comfort in what he had said to me. Tyler was only worried about me. I knew he loved me before he had said the words, but hearing them had only made it more real. I passed the box containing their lunch over to him and decided that I couldn't leave things the way they were.

"Thanks, Maddie. I'll see you around."

"Richard, before you go. Could you let Tyler know I want to see him? I think I need to apologise to him about the other night."

"I'll let him know. And you look after yourself as well. You look tired."

"I will, and thanks."

Watching Richard walk out of the shop, I felt a sense of relief wash over me. There was no reason for me to blame Tyler for what happened the other evening. He really was just trying to help me and calm me down after my nightmare. I just wasn't used to having someone there for me. It was going to take some time, but perhaps I should let him in. Perhaps it was time to be honest with someone. I was living a lie at the moment on my own. If it went wrong, what difference would there be? I just had to hope that he meant everything he said that he wouldn't care what happened in my past. Well, tonight would be the start of that journey. I was sure of it.

The small lunchtime rush was over, and I was left alone in the shop. I had already nearly got everything ready for the next day. Hearing the front door of the shop I headed out to the front to see who the next customer of the day was. I was surprised to see Ashleigh walking through the door. I had got to know Ashleigh quite a bit over the last few months since she and Brandon had moved down here. In fairness, it made sense that they were down here. Brandon and Mason were best friends, and I couldn't ever see them living anywhere but here in Kings View. Their house was in the progress of being built next to Mason's and they were currently renting a house here in the town.

"Hi, Ashleigh. Jess is out with Joan today and isn't around if you are looking for her."

"I know, Brandon told me this morning. I was actually coming to see you. I haven't managed to get to spend any time with you in a while and thought it would be fun to catch up, seeing as we are going to be bridesmaids soon for Jess."

I wasn't sure how to take that. Yeah, we had chatted a bit when Jess had been here in the shop, but I wouldn't have considered Ashleigh to be my friend. I got on well with everyone, but the only person I guess I really thought of as a friend was Jess, because she had been there for me before she had got together with Mason. However, I wasn't going to turn Ashleigh away, and if it took away the boredom of the afternoon, it couldn't be that bad.

"Let me get us a drink, and we can sit and chat. What would you like?"

"I'll just have a latte, if that's okay."

"Sure, take a seat and I'll bring it over and join you."

Making us both a drink, I grabbed them both and went and sat in our usual corner. Even when the shop was full, all the regulars would leave one table in the corner by the window free for Jess or me. It was kind of an unwritten rule that it was our table, and no one ever sat there. It was only during the summer that a stranger would come in and sit there if Jess wasn't in. Placing the drinks on the table, I sat down across from Ashleigh.

"How are things going with the house? Jess said they have already started building. I must say I was surprised that they would start with the weather as it has been."

"I think that had something to do with Brandon. He has been bugging them to start for the past three months. He wants his own house so he can get his dog and start a family."

As I listened to Ashleigh, I heard a slight sadness in her voice when she mentioned a family. I wondered if that was something she really wanted, or if she was just keeping Brandon happy.

"You don't sound like you want a family, Ashleigh."

She looked up at me and smiled.

"It's not that, it's just I'm not sure if I will ever be able to have a child naturally. The doctors have always said I could have problems. If it happens, it happens. But, there are plenty of children out there like Amelia that need parents to look after them. We have both agreed that we will adopt if it doesn't happen for us."

I could see she genuinely meant everything she said, although there was sadness in her voice. She was happy that she had Brandon standing by her side.

"I'm sorry Ashleigh. I didn't mean to bring up sad memories. I know Brandon is absolutely devoted to you. He hardly ever stops talking about you when he is here. You are a very lucky woman to have him. Jess said he was going out of his mind all the time you were missing. I'm just glad to see him finally happy."

"It's fine, and I know I am extremely lucky. Although I'm not sure Jess has quite forgiven Mason after she heard how Brandon proposed. Anyway, enough about me. How are you? Brandon said you've seemed a bit down the last couple of weeks. You know we all missed you over Christmas and New Year."

That was when alarm bells should have started to ring, but me being the gullible woman I always was, I just took it as any normal question, especially from Ashleigh.

"I'm okay. I just have a lot on my plate with running this place for Jess, waiting for my degree results, and then seeing if I can find myself a permanent job. I love working for Jess, but it does seem a waste of my psychology degree to be running a coffee shop. I thought I could have a chat with Mason, thought I might be able to get some work with him. I'm sure I could put it to good use in his business. So, what about you, have you found a job you want to do yet?"

"I found a few, but for some reason Brandon wants me to stay at home. It's not like he believes the good wifey must stay home and look after hubby, I just think he wants me near him all the time. Like he is worried that I will be taken away from him again. At this rate, he will have me working in the office."

"You can always come and give me a hand here. I know it isn't always busy, but at least you will be close and be doing something, instead of just sitting at home."

"You know, that might not be such a bad idea. I'm not really worried about the money. I still have plenty from the sale of my parents' house. It would just give me something to do each day. Although me, you and Jess together? The guys might be a little worried we are plotting against them."

I had to laugh. The guys probably would think that. They were always worried when they walked in here and found us all sitting together, but if it gave Ashleigh some sense of purpose, something to break up the monotony of the day, then I wouldn't stop her. I was starting to wonder though, what the real reason was for her being here. We never really had these conversations before, and I was starting to think that she was just building herself up to start a conversation she didn't really want to have.

"Ashleigh, you didn't come here just to chat about this, did you? Why are you here?"

I saw her look down at her hands and then look at me with an embarrassed smile.

"You're right, I did come here to speak about something else. Before you get annoyed, please just hear me out. Tyler is really worried about you. He came to speak to me and Brandon the other night after what happened at your place. He didn't know where to go."

I could feel the anger starting to build. How dare he go to someone else and tell them what happened. He had no right. That was between the two of us, not that he really knew what happened. I was just starting to trust him, just starting to believe that he really was going to be there for me, and was going to help me. But I knew I shouldn't have believed him. He was like every other guy I had met. The first sign of trouble, they went running to others and told them everything.

"He had no right to do that. All I did was chuck him out of the flat. He had no right to discuss that with anyone."

I was shaking with anger. I couldn't believe he had got Ashleigh to come down here to speak to me.

"I guess he was too scared to discuss this with me himself, so he sent you instead, did he? What, will it be Jess next, then Brandon and Mason? How many people has he spoken to, Ashleigh? Does the whole team know? I thought he was different. I thought I could trust him. I should have known he was the same as all the other guys I had met."

Ashleigh went to place her hand over mine to try and calm me down, but I immediately pulled it away. I didn't want her pity. I didn't want Tyler's pity.

"Maddie, please. He was worried about you. I don't think he has spoken to anyone else. He was devastated when you threw him out of the flat and he couldn't do anything to help you. He just wants to be there for you, Maddie. He loves you."

"And he couldn't come here and tell me all this himself? He had to send you to do it?"

"It wasn't like that. He didn't ask me to come. I wanted to help. I just thought after everything I had been through, I would be more understanding. I don't think he really wanted me to interfere."

"Well, at least he has some things right. Look, I don't want to talk about it, and neither of you had the right to interfere. I think you should just leave now."

I got up from my seat and grabbed my cup to clean it up. I was done with people interfering in my life. They didn't need to know what I had been through. I didn't need anyone in my life and I was going to tell Tyler that as soon as I saw him next.

"I'm sorry, Maddie. We just wanted to help you, to be there for you."

"Well, I don't need anyone's help, thank you. Goodbye, Ashleigh."

I saw the look of hurt and defeat on her face, as she got up from her chair and placed her mug on the counter. Turning, she went to walk out the door, but turned back round just before she reached the door.

"Everything I said about Tyler is true. He really does love you. Don't push him away because he wants to help. I know what that feels like and nearly lost the only man I loved. Don't make my mistake, Maddie. Please."

I could see the silent tears falling from her face as she turned and left me alone again with my thoughts. It didn't make a difference though. I now know I cannot trust another man again. That included Tyler.

Chapter Twelve

Tyler

I had avoided Maddie and the coffee shop now for the past three days. I thought it was best to give her a chance to calm down. She had made it quite clear that she didn't want me around so that is what I did, gave her space. The problem was I missed her immensely. I wanted to be with her, helping her, holding her close to me. The time I'd had her in my arms was still ingrained into my memories. Those few moments when my lips touched hers so tenderly, were in my dreams every night. It had been the perfect evening until she re-lived those darkest memories in her mind. I just wished I could take them away from her.

I had spent the past two nights at Brandon's. I hadn't wanted to, but Ashleigh insisted. I think she was worried I would do something stupid if there wasn't someone there to keep an eye on me. She really didn't need to. I wasn't about to do anything stupid. I was never a big drinker, so I wasn't going to go down the same route as Mason and Brandon. I just needed some time to get myself together, to try and understand exactly what was going on.

Both Richard and myself had been intermittently looking for as much information as we could about Thomas. We had established he was currently not working, and neither was his mother. They were basically living off the money that Maddie's Dad was sending them home whilst he was on deployment. Part of me wanted to reach out to Brian, to try and find out what was going on. He must have known something was wrong for his daughter to have left three years ago. Or was he the issue? Was he the reason she had to leave? My mind was going in circles trying to work out exactly what to do. I really couldn't think straight and started to understand why Brandon and Mason would hit the bottle. It was easier than trying to deal with the pain and confusion. Just as I was starting to have these thoughts, Richard walked back into the office with lunch.

"Time for you to take a break and eat something before you get yourself in such a state you can't think straight. Although in fairness, it already looks as if you've gone past that point."

I grabbed lunch from him and turned to him.

"Thanks for this, and you're right, I'm already past that point. I can't find anything to help us. I only have one other route to take now, and I'm not sure I can take it."

"What's that? Apart from actually coming out and asking Maddie, that is."

"Ashleigh did come up with an idea last night, but up until now, I have been too frightened to look. What if she had a child because she was raped. She could have had it adopted or even …"

"It is a possibility, but I think both you and I know that would be a step too far. There is being unethical and then downright illegal. Searching through someone's medical records or adoption records is just a step too far."

"Don't you think I know that, Richard? I know it's illegal, but …"

I felt his hand come on my shoulder, obviously seeing the distress I was in. I didn't mean to lash out at him. It wasn't his fault.

"I'm sorry …"

"No need for apologies. I know you're hurting, that you just want to help Maddie, who by the way is missing you. I forgot to mention that when I came in. I think she was going to say something else, but stopped just before she let the words leave her mouth. She asked me to tell you she wants to see you, that she needs to apologise to you. So, it's not all bad. Giving her some space allowed her to sort herself out."

"Thanks, Richard. I needed to know that more than I realised. Come on, let's get on with some real work, and then I can get to see my woman, even if she doesn't realise she's mine yet."

We had spent the rest of the afternoon working through the cases we had. We had nearly everything buttoned up and were just waiting to see if any of our traps were going to catch anyone. We had been working in silence when there was a knock at the door.

"Yeah."

I was horrified when I saw Brandon walk in with his arm around a clearly upset Ashleigh.

"What the hell happened?"

"Maddie is what happened. I'm just about to go down there and give her a piece of my mind, Tyler. I don't care if you love her or not, I'm not having her upset Ashleigh like this."

I saw Ashleigh place her hand on Brandon's chest and turn to him.

"It's not her fault. She was right, I really shouldn't have got involved. I just couldn't handle the thought of her going through whatever she is alone without trying or offering to help. I'm sorry, Tyler, but she is pretty upset and angry. I don't think you will get a good reception if you go around there."

"Don't worry about it, Ashleigh. In all honesty, I thought this might happen. She is a very private and proud woman, I'm not sure she wants anyone's help. But we had to try. I guess I'm walking into the lion's den this evening then."

"You know you are still welcome to stay at our place, Tyler."

"Thanks for the offer, Ashleigh. But I think I have outstayed my welcome with Brandon. You two should be enjoying time together and not have a bachelor like me hanging around. Plus, I think from the look on his face, he wants to kill someone, and I think I might be at least second on that list if not top."

I could see Brandon's demeanour immediately change at my words, as he sighed.

"Tyler, of course you're welcome to stay with us. It's not a bother. I didn't mean to come across so cross at you, or Maddie. I think the whole situation is getting to all of us. We all want to help Maddie, but it's very difficult when she doesn't want you to help her. Stay tonight at least. If things go as bad as I think they are going to, I don't want you driving back home, or even to your parents. I know you won't do anything stupid, but your mind will be elsewhere, and you might be distracted. I don't think any of us could live with that, should something happen, especially when that is something we can avoid. I just hate seeing my Chérie upset."

"Thank you. To all of you. You have all been there for me, no matter what was going on in your own lives. I'm sure I will need you all over the next few days. Like you, I suspect this afternoon isn't going to go well. In fact, I think this could be the end for me and Maddie. No matter what, I will try and help her, even if that means I never get to make her mine. Anyway, I better get on with some work before the boss sacks me. I'll see you guys later, okay?"

Richard and I had spent the afternoon working through our cases. We had basically done all we could at finding out about Maddie without doing something illegal, so I had to drown myself in work. My heart wasn't in it though. All afternoon, I had been worrying about going to see Maddie. I was at the point of calling the whole thing off and just heading home to try and get a good night's sleep, something I hadn't had since the last night I spent with her. Every night was just a rehash of everything that happened. I would go to sleep thinking about holding her and kissing her so tenderly and would wake up dripping in sweat as I relived her nightmare and her throwing me out of the flat.

I knew our next meeting wasn't going to go well. It would probably end up with her never wanting to see me again. I knew that, but deep down in my heart, I knew I had to try. What now had become a regular occurrence, it wasn't until I felt a hand on my shoulder that I was pulled from my thoughts.

"It's past 5:00. I think it's time you went and faced the music, Tyler. I know you have been worrying about it all afternoon, but you have to do it at some point if you want to keep her."

"I know, Richard. It's just I think this will be the end of us. She hates that I got Ashleigh involved with this, and no matter what Ashleigh said to her, she's going to know it was me."

"Well, you aren't going to find out sitting here. Do you want me to come with you? Hold your hand for moral support? And I do mean that literally."

I saw the smirk fall across his lips. I know he didn't like me in that way. He'd said that although I was a great guy that he considered a friend, he wasn't interested in me in any other way. Still, I think part of him liked to joke with me, as I was the only person in the business that knew his secret. For a split second, I was starting to wonder if he really did mean it romantically. That was until he gave me a wink and then started to laugh.

"I thought for a minute then, you were being deadly serious about that."

"I know, your face gave you away. Just trying to lighten the mood. Sorry, that was uncalled for. But the offer still stands, without the hand-holding of course. That would just be weird."

He chuckled to himself again, and I couldn't help but join in. I loved the friendship we now had and wanted him to stay down here forever. But I knew he would have to go back to London at some point. He was so much like Jayden in that respect. He didn't really like the countryside, preferred the hustle and bustle of a city. Plus, it allowed him to feel comfortable about his sexuality, in a place where no one knew you and didn't care. Here in Kings View, almost everybody knew your business, and if they didn't, they soon would if Mrs. Duncan found out. I smiled, turning to him.

"Thanks for the offer, but I think this is something I need to do myself. I just need to be a big boy and face my fears. Come on, let's get out of here."

Walking out of the office, I said my goodbyes to everyone and started the walk up to the coffee shop. I just hoped it wasn't for the last time.

Walking into the shop I was happy to see that there weren't any customers in there. I didn't want them to see us fighting in the middle of the shop. Hearing Maddie calling out from the back that she would just be a minute, I braced myself for the reception I was about to get. It wasn't long before I found out exactly how the rest of the evening was going to go. Seeing her walking out to the counter, I smiled and said hello.

"Hi, Maddie. Can we talk?"

Her smiling face ready to greet her customer, immediately turned to anger and hatred as soon as she saw and heard me standing there.

"You've got a fucking nerve showing up here, Tyler. How dare you get Ashleigh to come here after you told her everything that happened the other night. You had no right to tell her anything."

"Maddie, if you will just let me explain for a second."

I could see Maddie starting to shake with anger, the tears falling from her face. This had not been the meeting I had wanted, but one that I knew was coming. I just had to hope that she would see reason and calm down enough to explain.

"Well come on, Tyler. I am dying to hear your excuses."

I started to move towards her, hoping that my proximity would calm her like it had the other evening. The problem was, it didn't, it only seemed to raise her anger more.

"Don't come another step closer. Just say what you have to say."

Stopping dead in my tracks, I looked at my sweetheart, standing there with tears flowing down her face. I just wanted to hold her. To make her realise just how much I loved her. I had to try and make her realise that I was there for her. It was now or never.

"Maddie, I was devastated when you told me to leave the other night. All I wanted was to be there for you, to help you get through whatever you were dealing with. I didn't tell Ashleigh everything to make you mad. I just needed help. Needed to try and work out exactly what you were going through. I meant every word I said to you the other evening, especially as I walked out of the door. I love you, Maddie. All I want is to be with you, for the rest of my life if I can. I want to help you."

She looked at me for a second, and for a moment I thought I had managed to get through to her. That I started to make some progress where she would at least speak to me. The next words she spoke, however, cut through me like a knife, and I knew things were never going to be the same again between us.

"All you wanted to do was help me, Tyler. Is that so? You say you love me. Well, you have a funny fucking way of going about it. You tell everyone what I am going through. Tell everyone what happened to me. Is that the act of someone who loves me?"

"How can I tell anyone what you have gone through when I don't even know myself?"

I was hurt. I did love her and all I wanted to do was help, but she was throwing it back in my face.

"You're no better than the fucking arsehole that caused all of this. I trusted you. But that's gone now. In fact, I never want to fucking see you again. I don't want you to be part of my life, and I don't want you anywhere near me."

I knew she was hurt and angry. I could see the tears pouring down her face. I knew if I could just hold her, get her to let everything out, she would come back to me. If I could just get her to take her anger out on me, she would see that she needed me. I started to walk over to her, ready to scoop her into my arms. She looked at me and her hand immediately came up to stop me.

"Don't come anywhere near me. I don't want your fucking pity. Just leave."

There it was. The twist of the knife in my heart. I had tried everything. It wasn't enough.

"I'm sorry." It was almost a whisper from my mouth as I slowly turned and walked back to the door. It was taking all my strength right now not to break down in front of her. I could feel the tears starting to form in my own eyes. I got to the door and opened it. I wasn't going to leave before I said it one more time. Turning back, I saw the look of pure hatred in her eyes.

"I really do love you, Maddie, no matter what you think or want to believe. I will always be there for you … Goodbye, Maddie."

I walked out the door and into the street. I managed to get back to my car and get in before I allowed myself to crumble. The tears falling. I had lost her. She would never be mine. But, whatever the future held, I was going to try and help her in any way I could.

Chapter Thirteen

Madeleine

I watched him walk out the door. I couldn't believe the audacity of Tyler. He only wanted to help me. What, by telling everyone what had happened the evening he stayed over? He was no better than Thomas. He was only interested in me for one thing, what he could get from me in the bedroom. He might not have raped me, but he was still playing with my emotions. Telling me he loved me than going behind my back and gossiping about me. I hated him. Hated what he had done to me. So why was I now standing in the middle of the room, tears pouring down my face, and a pain in my chest that was only growing stronger?

I knew exactly the reason why. Because I loved him and wanted to be with him. I needed him, but I couldn't allow him to get close. That much was obvious. If I had told him exactly what had happened to me, he probably would have already told

Ashleigh, who in turn would have told Brandon, then Mason and Jess and where would that leave me? No, that was it. No matter how much it hurt, I couldn't allow Tyler in. It was easier this way, easier just to deal with the pain in my heart from losing one person than losing my entire life here in Kings View.

I knew I wouldn't be able to face seeing another customer this evening, so I walked over and locked up the shop. Picking up my bag and phone, I noticed three messages already. Two were from Ashleigh and one from Tyler. I didn't have it in me to read them now, so I threw the phone in my bag and locked up, then headed upstairs to my flat.

Walking up the stairs, I half expected to see Tyler sitting outside my door, waiting for me to come home. I was almost grateful when I got there to find no one there. Then there was that pain again, the one that had hoped he would be there, resting by the door ready to pull me into his arms and tell me everything was going to be alright. The same way he had tried after my nightmare.

Opening the door to my flat, the tears started to pour again as I slumped down onto the floor. I had lost everything. My family. My daughter, and the only man I had truly loved. Was there any reason for me to carry on? What was the point of my life if I was going to forever be alone? I couldn't stop the sobs wracking through my body. I had never felt pain like this before. I didn't know how I would carry on with my life the way it was. I hated myself. I hated everything about me. The way I had left my own daughter with that monster. He might have been her biological father, but he was still a monster and didn't deserve her, didn't deserve to be in her life. I hated myself for ruining the one chance I had of being happy.

Picking myself up from the floor, I walked into the kitchen and grabbed the bottle of wine I had in the fridge. Pulling a glass out of the cupboard, I also pulled out the box of co-codamol, along with a box of paracetamol and ibuprofen I had in the cupboard. Walking into the front room I placed them all on the coffee table in front of me and poured myself a glass of wine. I couldn't find a good enough reason to carry on living the life I had. There really wasn't any point. Pulling out my phone I decided to read the messages from Ashleigh.

> *Maddie*
>
> *Please don't blame Tyler. He only wanted to help. We all want to help. Call or message me, please.*
>
> *Ashleigh*

I moved on to the next message, tears continuing to pour down my face.

> *Please message me, Maddie. I'm worried about you. Please let me know you're alright at least, and I will leave you alone.*

I knew I had to message Ashleigh. If I didn't, she would only send Brandon round to check on me. I sent her a quick text to say I was fine and just needed some time to myself. I couldn't really be mad at her, even if I wanted to. I know they all cared about me, but I just wanted my private life to be private. I had never been one to share my life with anyone, and that wasn't about to start now. I looked at my phone, staring at Tyler's name on the screen. I hovered my finger over the message, my anger and fear were stopping me from opening it. I hesitantly pressed on the message and started to read.

> *Sweetheart,*
>
> *I know you hate me right now and never want to see me again. Although that is heartbreaking to hear, I understand. I can't take back what I have done, and if I'm honest, I would do everything the same again, given the chance. I love you. Nothing will change how I feel about you. Even if you never change your mind, I will always love*

you. There will never be another woman in my life like you. All I want to do is help you through whatever has happened in your life. I will only ask one thing of you. Please do not leave or give up. Even if I can't be with you, I want to know you are safe.

I will always be there for you, Maddie.

Tyler

The tears were pouring down my face as I read the message. Any hate I felt for him before reading that message was slowly turning into the pain of losing someone I loved. I looked at the bottle of wine in front of me and the packets of pills. Looking back at the message and remembering the ones Ashleigh had sent, I knew then I couldn't do it. I had to stay strong. If there was ever a chance that I could get my Rosie back, I had to try and to do that I had to be alive. I picked up the packets and the wine and walked back into the kitchen to put them away. Deciding I needed to get some sleep instead of spending the night with a bottle of wine, I headed to get ready for bed.

I laid down on my bed after a quick shower and willed sleep to come quickly. I just hoped that when it did come, the nightmares didn't come with it.

"All packed?"

"Yes. You should be pleased that I'm leaving."

"Oh, I am pleased you're leaving, but you aren't taking Rosie. She stays here with us. She is far too valuable to let you have her."

I rushed into the front room to grab Rosie, but she was gone. I turned, the tears falling down my face to see Thomas standing in the doorway.

"Mum took her out. You aren't taking her away from us, Mads. As

I said, she is far too valuable. So, I suggest you just walk out of that front door and forget about us and Rosie. Because we never want to see you again."

I looked at Thomas in complete horror. He couldn't take my daughter away from me. Rosie was mine, not his. He might be her biological father, but there was no evidence to say she was. I had purposely not put his name on the birth certificate for that reason.

"Thomas, you can't do that. Rosie is my daughter. You don't want anything to do with her."

I could see the anger in his eyes as he rushed over to me. Grabbing me around the neck I was immediately taken back to the night he raped me. I could feel the fear running through my entire body, and Thomas could tell. A smirk appeared on his face.

"That's the Madds I remember the night I took your precious virginity. That scared little girl that turned me on so fucking much. I had forgotten how much I enjoyed that. Seeing you so scared below me. Perhaps I should do it one more time for good measure before I throw you out of the house."

I was gasping for air as his hand constricted my airway.

"Thomas, please. Don't do this to me. You've already got what you wanted once. You aren't interested in me."

"Oh, that's where you are wrong, my dear girl. I love seeing a woman scared when I have sex. That's why I loved taking you, seeing you struggle and panic below me as I rammed into you. Shit, I can feel myself getting horny and hard just thinking about it."

He let go of my throat and I took deep breaths, compensating for the air I was unable to breathe before. I could feel the hot tracks of my tears down my face, but still, Thomas just stood there laughing at me.

"I have already said I am leaving, and I will be taking Rosie with me."

I felt the air move before his fist connected with my face and I fell to the floor in a heap. My cheek and eye throbbed in pain.

"I already fucking told you once. Rosie is staying with me. She is worth too much money to let her go. At least she brings in some money each month, unlike her bitch of a mother."

He stood over me and pointed to my face.

"Take that as a warning. Get out of the house now and never come back."

"I've already told you, I am not leaving Rosie here with you."

I was screaming at him now, despite being so scared of what he was going to do to me. I didn't have to wait long until I found out when his boot contacted my stomach and ribs, three times. I was struggling to breathe as the sobs and pain went through my chest. He grabbed me by my shirt and pulled me up off the floor, then threw me across the room like a rag doll.

"This is your last warning, Madeleine. Get out while you still can, alive anyway. If you leave now, then I promise I won't hurt Rosie."

"You wouldn't," I replied in almost a whisper.

"Do you want to stay and find out? Now get your sorry arse up and get out of the house. NOW."

I was in agony. I knew the damage he had done was severe. But I was angry, and I wasn't going to give up easily. I struggled to my feet and started to walk over to Thomas, ready to argue again. When I was within reach of him, he immediately grabbed me by the throat again, this time completely cutting off my airway.

"This is your last warning, Madeleine. When I let you go, get your bag and walk out of here with your life. If you do that, you will also save the life of your child."

I gasped as he let go of me. It was heartbreaking, but I knew I had to leave. I loved Rosie more than life itself. No matter what happened to me, I couldn't risk her life. I struggled over to the bag that I had left in the hallway. Without saying another word, I picked up the bag and walked to the front door, opened it, and left my family home for the last time.

I woke suddenly with tears pouring down my face. I couldn't carry on like this, I knew that now. I needed help, but would anyone still be there to help me after what I had said and done? I know both Ashleigh and Tyler said they wanted to help, but after today would they still say that? There was only one way to find out. I needed to speak to someone, but I couldn't face Tyler after what I had said to him today. Picking up my phone I sent a message to Jess and Ashleigh asking them to meet me at the coffee shop after lunch. All I could do now was hope they would turn up.

Chapter Fourteen

Madeleine

After the night I had, I was glad that the morning had been uneventful, especially as I had overlaid and didn't get down here until nearly 6:00. I managed to get back to sleep after I woke suddenly from my nightmare, and I guess finally deciding to talk to someone and messaging Ashleigh and Jess, must have eased my conscious enough to sleep as long as I did. The problem was I didn't know if either of them would turn up. Especially Ashleigh. I had said some terrible things to her, that at the time I had meant. I was hurt that she involved herself in my business, but now, well I just wanted to accept her help.

Hearing the bell go above the front door I grabbed Mr. and Mrs. Duncan's lunch from the counter where I had just finished preparing it. I wasn't surprised to find Mr. Duncan standing at the counter waiting as I walked from out the back.

"Good afternoon, Mr. Duncan. I have your lunch here ready for you."

"Madeleine, you really are a lifesaver. I don't know what we would do without you."

I laughed. We had the same conversation every day.

"Mr. Duncan, you say that every day. I am sure you would survive without me here."

"I know we would, but I wouldn't spend as much time with my beloved Mabel if you didn't. Anyway, enough about us. How are you? You look tired, my love. I really don't like seeing you like this. You need to take some time off."

"I'm fine, Mr. Duncan, really I am. Just need to get some more sleep."

Well, I need some uninterrupted sleep if the truth is known, I thought to myself.

"You know Mabel will always help out if you need it. I can run the newsagents on my own. She would be more than willing to come over so you could grab a couple of hours' sleep."

"I know she would, and that is really sweet of you to offer. But as you said, you want to spend more time together, not less. I am fine, and I have Ashleigh who can pop in if I really need it, but thank you for thinking of me."

"Anytime my dear. Please look after yourself."

"I will, Mr. Duncan."

"Right, well, I better be getting back before Mabel sends out a search party. Thank you for lunch and I will see you in the morning as usual."

"You're welcome, see you tomorrow."

With that, he walked out of the shop and I was left alone again.

In some ways, I loved the winter. It was easy to keep the shop running as we tended to only have our regular customers. But it also got boring during the day, especially as now I didn't have my studies to keep me occupied in between customers. Now I only had my thoughts to keep me company, and that usually meant remembering everything I had left behind at home. Deciding I needed a coffee, I started up the machine to make myself a latte when I heard the shop door open again.

Looking around I saw Jess and Ashleigh walking through the door. I could have cried, in fact, the tears were already forming in my eyes. They had turned up. After everything I had said to Ashleigh yesterday, she still walked through the door. As usual, Jess was holding Callum, although I knew that wouldn't last. He had already started to walk a few steps on his own and it wouldn't be long before he was tearing around the shop causing both his mother and me no end of heart attacks. I smiled at them both as they took a seat in our usual corner.

"The usual for you both?"

"Yes please, Maddie, and could you get a juice for Callum and perhaps a cookie. That will hopefully keep him quiet for a little while."

"No problem. I will get one of his cups from out the back."

Getting everything together, I walked back out to the front of the shop and made Jess and Ashleigh a coffee. Walking over, I found Callum was already in his high chair. Passing him a cookie and drink, Jess turned to him.

"Say thank you to Maddie, Callum."

"Tar, tar."

I smiled down at Callum.

"You're welcome, soldier. Here you go, lattes for both of you."

I sat down in the chair and looked at Jess and Ashleigh sitting in front of me. I knew I had some explaining to do, especially after the early morning text message, but first I needed to apologise to Ashleigh.

"Ashleigh, I just wanted to say …"

"Maddie, you don't need to apologise to me. I know I overstepped the mark by involving myself in your relationship with Tyler. I shouldn't have done that. But he was so worried about you that I couldn't help myself. I know how much secrets can hurt a relationship. Hell, I was without Brandon for two years because I couldn't tell him the truth about me. I just didn't want to see you and Tyler make the same mistake."

"I know, Ashleigh. I shouldn't have said all those things to you. I'm just worried that if I tell you the truth, you aren't going to want to be my friend anymore, and I am not sure if Tyler will want to be with me when he finds out. I know you don't want me to say it, but I am sorry, Ashleigh. I was hurt and I lashed out."

"Maddie, you know we all love you like a little sister. We all want to help, and I am sure whatever happened in your past will not change how we feel about you."

I looked over at Jess and gave her a weak smile. I wasn't so sure about that, but there was only one way for me to find out.

"So, I guess you are both wondering why I asked you to come here today?"

"I think we both know the reason, but why don't we let you tell us," Ashleigh said as she took my hand and gave it a squeeze.

"Well, I think it is time for me to be honest with everyone and tell you the real reason I came here to Kings View."

***

I spent the next hour explaining my story to Jess and Ashleigh.

Try as I might, I couldn't help the tears pouring down my face. Every so often I looked up to see Ashleigh and Jess's shocked faces and the tears that were also appearing in their own eyes. I couldn't gauge how they felt about the situation, or what they were going to say at the end of it, but I was too far down now to worry. I felt emotionally drained as I finished my explanation and looked up at them both.

"So, there you go. That's my story. I understand if you want me to leave now. I know you must both hate me for leaving my daughter behind. Especially you, Ashleigh. I know how difficult this must be for you, given your situation."

I was met by stunned silence for a moment. I could see tears flowing down Ashleigh's face. I knew my answer then, she hated me. Hated me for leaving a child behind, when there was a good chance she would never have one. I looked down at the table for a second, and then went to move my chair and leave. Just as I was about to get up, a hand grasped mine and I was immediately engulfed in a hug from Ashleigh. I froze for a second before I completely lost it and allowed the sobs to leave my body. We sat there for a moment, just crying together. Pulling away, she smiled at me.

"I know that was hard, but thank you for finally opening up to us."

"You're not angry at me?"

"Why would we be angry?" Jess asked.

"Because I abandoned my daughter."

"And probably saved her, and yourself in the process. Of course, we aren't angry, not at you anyway. The man who raped you basically threatened to kill you and your daughter. You did what any scared mother would do, protect your child. I know you think that me possibly not being able to have children would mean I would hate you for what you have done, but I could never do that, Maddie. I probably would have done the same as you in your situation. But that doesn't mean we are going to end the story there."

"What do you mean?"

"It's time for you to allow us to help you. All of us, including the guys. We can help you be rid of Thomas for good, and get Rosie back. That is if that is what you want?"

"It's all I have ever wanted,…but what will Tyler think? Will he still want me when he knows the truth? I don't want to lose him," I looked up at them both with tears pouring down my eyes.

"Why is that, Maddie?" Jess asked as she took my hand in hers.

"Because," I looked down again, not able to look either of them in the eyes. Not wanting to open my soul to them. I sat in silence for a few seconds, not sure if I should say the words out loud. Finally, I said the three words I had been holding back for the past year at least. "I love him."

"Well, thank God you have finally admitted it. I thought I was going to have to fight that out of you."

I looked up at Ashleigh in shock. What did she mean finally admitted it? Had she known all along? Realising my confused look, she took my hand in hers.

"I think all of us, Tyler included, knew you loved him. You could just never say those words and having heard your story we can understand why. Why do you think we have been encouraging you all this time? Both of us knew you loved Tyler, you just needed to admit it to yourself. The next question is, what are you going to do about it?"

That was the question. What was I going to do about it?

"What can I do about it, Ashleigh? After everything I said to Tyler last night I'm not sure he will ever forgive me, or if I can come back from that. I could see how devastated he was. I know he said he still loved me and wanted to help me when he messaged me last night, but was that just his guilt talking? Or was it that he still meant every word and wanted to be with me? I'm scared I've lost him forever."

I had kept it together for a while now, but as soon as the reality kicked in that I could have lost Tyler forever, the tears started flowing again.

"Maddie, I won't lie to you, Tyler was devastated when he got back to our house last night. I had to practically drag his arse out of bed this morning, and before you say anything, he wasn't drinking last night. I managed to get him up by telling him you had asked to see me today. I'm not sure how much work he would have got done today, but at least he wasn't moping around the house."

I felt terrible. I had caused that pain. Everything I had said to him, telling him that I never wanted to see him again. All the hurt he was feeling was down to me.

"So, what do I do now?"

"Well, I think you start by being honest with Tyler and tell him everything. I know it is going to be hard for him to hear, but he deserves to know. If he decides he wants nothing to do with you, not only is he a complete fucking idiot, but he will have me to answer to. However, I'm sure it won't come to that. I'm sure he will still love you and be there for you. I also know he will do everything in his power to get Rosie back. All of the guys will...What do you say, Maddie?"

I looked at Ashleigh and Jess both sitting there. They were my best friends. My only friends. I knew they were both right. I couldn't carry on anymore. I needed help, I knew I did, and they would be there with me every step of the way, just the same as I was for Jess all those years ago.

"You're right, Ashleigh. I can't let this rule my life forever. I will message Tyler and ask him to come over this evening and tell him everything."

Ashleigh took my hand in hers and smiled. It wasn't out of pity, but a genuine caring smile. I knew I had made the right decision. They hadn't judged me for what I had done. They might not have agreed with it, although they didn't say as much, but they understood why I had done it. Now I just had to get the courage to tell Tyler everything.

"Have you got everything ready for tomorrow?"

"I still have a couple of things to do."

"Let me and Ashleigh sort those out. We can lock up here. You just get yourself together, have a nice long hot bath, and be ready for Tyler when he comes round tonight, okay?"

"Thanks, Jess. I think I will. And thank you, both of you. I think I have the best and most understanding friends as my besties. I love you both."

The tears were pouring from all of us now as we all pulled together in a hug.

"Go on, get out of here," Ashleigh said as she let me go.

"Yes, ma'am," I replied with a chuckle.

I went out the back and grabbed my bag to head upstairs to my flat, run a shower and work out exactly what I was going to cook Tyler for dinner tonight. Walking into my flat and looking through the cupboards and fridge, I realised that a takeaway was probably in order, but first I had to make sure he was going to come. My hand was shaking as I opened up my phone to send him a message and begin to type.

> *Tyler,*
>
> *Words can't say how sorry I am for the way I treated you*

last night and the things I said. I spoke to Jess and Ashleigh today and realised that it's time to be honest with everyone.

I hope you will forgive me enough to come to my flat this evening to hear me out. No more secrets, I think you deserve that much.

Then you can decide.

I love you.

Madds xx

I sent the message hoping it was enough. Hours seemed to pass, which in reality was probably less than a minute before I received a notification. My hand was shaking as I opened it with fear and trepidation.

What time do you want me there?

Chapter Fifteen

Tyler

I'd hardly slept a wink all night. The events of yesterday just kept going over and over in my head. Maddie didn't want me in her life. She never wanted to see me again. I'd sent her a message trying to tell her exactly what I wanted to say, but she never replied. So, that was it. Any chance I had of us getting together, or of me helping her was gone. I would just have to keep an eye on her from afar, but I would never get to feel her in my arms again. Laying here in bed was where I was going to stay all day. I had already messaged Mason to let him know I wouldn't be in today. I couldn't face seeing anyone, especially to let them see how much of a wreck I was and how I had been crying most of the night. I was grateful that my room was far away from Brandon and Ashleigh's, so at least they wouldn't have heard me.

A knock on the door pulled me from my thoughts.

"Come in."

The door opened and I saw Ashleigh standing there, a look of pure shock on her face.

"Tyler, please tell me you haven't been like this all night. If I'd have known I would have spoken to you sooner than now."

"Okay, I won't tell you then. I've phoned Mason. I'm not going in today if that was what you were coming in to remind me of. The time that is."

"Well, it was one thing. You can't stay here alone all day. It won't do you any good and you know that."

"Going to work isn't really going to help either, Ashleigh. I can't concentrate as it is worrying about Maddie. Now she wants nothing more to do with me. How do you think I am going to function then? I haven't slept at all and all I want to do is crawl into a corner and die."

"Tyler Edwards, you don't mean that!"

"Sorry. No, I probably don't, but it's how I feel right now."

"Well, you can stop feeling sorry for yourself, get your arse out of bed, and get ready for work. Breakfast will be on the table in thirty minutes and then I will tell you my news."

"I'm really not up to any happy news at the moment, but thanks for trying."

"You will get up, showered, dressed, and be downstairs in the next twenty-five minutes or I will get all the guys to come round and get you up. Now do as you're told, because believe me, you're going to want to hear what I have to tell you."

I smiled as best I could at Ashleigh before she walked out of the room. I knew she was right. I couldn't mope around here for the rest of the day. I was working well with Richard, and I didn't want to let him or the rest of the team down. That wasn't in my nature. I got myself out of bed and headed to grab a shower and get ready. I was downstairs within my given time limit and found Brandon and Ashleigh in the kitchen. Brandon was sitting at the table nursing a cup of coffee, while Ashleigh was just plating up breakfast.

"I'll grab you a coffee.

You look like you could do with one. Take a seat."

Both of them knew what had happened last night with Maddie. I had to tell someone, and these two were the closest thing I had to family now after my own.

"Thanks, Brandon. And thanks for everything. I will be out of your hair soon. There isn't much point in me staying around now. Richard goes back home after today and I may as well go back to my place, now Maddie doesn't want to see me."

"We can talk about that later. First, eat breakfast," Ashleigh said as she placed a plate down in front of me.

I hadn't realised quite how hungry I was until I started eating. Ashleigh was an amazing cook and I could see why Maddie liked her helping out around the shop. This was one thing I was going to miss like crazy. A good home-cooked breakfast and meal every evening, but I knew I couldn't impose on them much longer. They had their own lives to live, especially as they had only just got back together.

"Now, for my news," Ashleigh said as she sat down with a coffee. "I got a message last night from Maddie. She wants to see me and Jess at the coffee shop this afternoon. She apologised for everything she said to me and said she was ready to talk. I think she is going to finally tell us what happened. At least that is what I am hoping for. So, don't give up on life yet."

"Are you just telling me what I want to hear, Ashleigh? Please say it's the truth."

"Tyler…"

"No, Brandon. Remember what kind of state you were in. Don't start on Tyler. He clearly has had a rough night and wants confirmation. Yes, Tyler, I am telling you the truth. Maddie wants to talk, and I am going to do everything in my power to get you two back together. Jess is meeting me here this morning and we are going to have a chat first. Then go and speak to Maddie. I will get her to contact you, even if it almost kills me."

"Thank you, Ashleigh, and I'm sorry if you thought I didn't believe her, Brandon. My life has just been turned completely upside down these past twenty-four hours. I don't mean anything by it, I've just never been hurting as much as I have since last night. Thank you, both of you. I wouldn't have survived the past couple of days without you."

"You know we will always be there for you. Neither of us has a family, so we see all our friends and colleagues as our family. You know I would do anything for you. You were there with me when I lost Ashleigh and nearly died in the process."

"Is that a roundabout way of saying you love me, Brandon?"

"I guess it is, just don't go around telling everyone."

We finished breakfast, and my outlook on the day was a lot brighter than when I got up this morning. I just had to hope that Jess and Ashleigh were able to convince Maddie that she needed me in her life too. All I had to do now was wait, and this was going to be the hardest day of my life.

Today had dragged, especially as I still hadn't heard a word from Ashleigh or Maddie. Brandon was almost at the point of murdering me, with the number of times I had asked him if he'd heard from Ashleigh. How I had managed to get through the day, I never knew. But I had and was just starting to pack everything up and head back to Brandon's.

"I'm going to stay on until the end of the week, if that's okay, Tyler? We still have a few bits to go through so there doesn't seem much point in heading home yet."

"No problem, Richard. To be honest, I enjoy the company. Even if I haven't exactly been very good company myself today."

"No need to explain. I understand."

My phone notification went off to tell me I had a message and I stopped dead in my tracks when I saw who it was from.

"Anything interesting?"

I stood and read the message, not quite believing what I was reading.

"It's from Maddie. She wants to see me tonight. She wants to tell me everything."

"That's great news. At least then we will be able to help her."

"Let's hope so," I said as I messaged her back asking what time she wanted me there. Her reply was almost immediate.

Head over when you've finished work. So, I guess I'll see you soon.

"Well, good luck, and I'll see you in the morning."

"Yeah, see you, Richard."

I headed out of the office and started to walk up to Maddie's flat. I had to admit, this wasn't a journey I thought I would ever be having again. I just hoped I didn't fuck it up again. I couldn't believe that she had finally told me that she loved me. I know it was only in a text, but she would never have admitted that before. I think all of us knew how she felt, but it's different to think you know, and to be told. My whole mood had gone from devastation to elation in a matter of ten minutes, I just needed to stay calm and listen to everything she had to say. Walking up to her door I knocked. When Maddie opened the door, my heart sank. Seeing her red, puffy eyes almost killed me. I didn't think, I just pulled her into my chest and held her. No words were said as I allowed her to cry in my embrace. Slowly pulling away, she looked up into my eyes and smiled slightly. This wasn't the Maddie I knew. The woman in front of me was hurting and broken, and I was going to do everything in my power to help her.

"Tyler, I'm so, so sorry."

"There is no need to apologise, Maddie. Let's just sit down and talk."

"I've ordered pizza. Sorry, I realised when I got home that I didn't have anything in the house to eat. It shouldn't be too long."

Just as she finished speaking, the doorbell sounded, and I got up to answer it. I didn't want anyone thinking that Maddie had been hurt, and the way she looked now would probably raise too many questions. Grabbing the pizza and thanking the delivery guy, I closed the door and headed back into the front room.

"Let's eat first, and then we can talk. If that's okay with you."

"Sounds perfect. Let me just say one thing. Thank you for coming, Tyler. I don't deserve you being here after everything I said."

"No more of that," I leaned over and gave her a kiss on the cheek and was rewarded with a smile and a blush. I couldn't be happier, seeing that was almost like having my Maddie back. I just had to make sure I kept her this time. We sat and ate in relative silence, just chatting about the mundane parts of our day. Neither of us wanted to really admit how we had felt about last night, but we knew it was going to come up sooner or later. Having finished the pizza, Maddie picked up the empty box and placed it in the kitchen.

"Sorry, I should have asked earlier. Do you want something to drink?"

"Whatever you have that is cold will be good."

She walked back in with a beer and a glass of wine for herself. Passing the beer to me, she then sat down on the settee next to me.

"So, I guess I owe you an explanation for everything, don't I?"

"Only if you're ready to tell me, sweetheart. As long as I can spend time with you, I don't care if you tell me tonight, or never. But I would rather you did, so I can help you."

"I said no more secrets, and I meant that. Although, what I am going to tell you won't be easy for you to hear. It's hard enough for me to tell, especially as this will be the second time today. I realised last night that I couldn't hold it back anymore. I needed to tell someone. Jess and Ashleigh know, so I suspect Mason and Brandon will know by the end of the evening. It's only fair that I tell you as well, considering I have admitted my feelings towards you now. Can I just ask you to do two things for me?"

"Anything."

"Please don't say anything until you've heard the whole story, and can you just hold me? I'm not sure I will be able to tell you this if you are looking at me all the way through."

"Come here," I pulled her into my side, loving the way she felt next to me.

"Okay, here goes. It happened about three years ago, just over a year before I came to Kings View. I was living with my Dad's girlfriend and her son in my family home. My Dad was on tour in the Royal Navy. I never got on with Michelle and Thomas, especially Thomas. He would often argue with me and sometimes get physical with me. He hit me several times in the past, but never enough to hurt me very badly. For the most part, they both left me alone. Both had made themselves at home and thought they owned the place. It happened one evening. Michelle had gone out, probably to shag some unsuspecting bloke, and Thomas had been out with his friends. It wasn't unusual for Thomas to come home blind drunk. When he did, he would usually just crash around the house and then end up in his bedroom and pass out until the next day. There had been a couple of occasions when he had hit me, but I could deal with that."

"I was lying in bed and was woken by him crashing through the house. I lay in bed holding my breath, hoping he would just walk past my room. Unfortunately, this time I wasn't so lucky. I don't want to go into details with you, but the short story is, he raped me. I was still a virgin at the time, and he revelled in the knowledge that he was my first. He was going to ruin it for every guy that followed him."

I could feel my anger building inside. We were right. She was raped and it was Thomas. If I ever got hold of him, I would make sure he realised how not to treat a woman ever again. That was if he survived, because with the way I felt right then I would probably kill him. I wanted to speak to tell her everything would be okay, but I had a suspicion that there was more to this story, that perhaps Ashleigh had been correct. I gave her a squeeze and placed a soft kiss on top of her head, all the while running my fingers down her arm to give her some reassurance, I couldn't let her see how angry I was. That was probably why she had asked me to hold her.

"That's not everything though, is it, sweetheart?"

"No...About a month later I realised that I was late for my period, so I took a test, and I was pregnant. I decided no matter what I was going to keep the baby. It caused a lot of friction in the household, especially with Michelle, as she wanted to know who the father was. I couldn't tell her it was her son as she would have never believed me. So anyway, I had my daughter, Rosie. She was the most amazing thing that ever happened to me, no matter how she came into the world. I loved her. My Dad was on a long tour and knew nothing about this. It all came to a head a few months after Rosie was born. I'd had a blazing row with Michelle again the night before and was going out for the day with Rosie. The argument continued and I decided that I was going to leave and take Rosie with me. After I packed, I came back down to find Thomas still there, but Michelle and Rosie had gone. I had an argument with Thomas, and he beat me up badly. He told me if both Rosie and I wanted to live I should walk out there and then and never come back."

I could hear her voice starting to crack and knew the tears were now falling down her face. Immediately, I pulled her up into my lap and just held her, allowing the tears to fall. We had guessed some of what happened to her, but I was still shocked to hear it. Maddie had always seemed a strong and independent woman, I couldn't believe that someone could have that kind of hold over her. That someone could do that to such a sweet woman. We sat in silence for a moment, just holding each other. I tried to give her the strength she needed to get through this, and she would. No matter what happened in the future between us, I was going to make sure Thomas was out of her life forever and she was going to get Rosie back. After a few short minutes, I decided to speak.

"Sweetheart, I must admit I am shocked by this and can't understand what you must have been through. But it doesn't make any difference to how I feel about you. In fact, it makes me love you more, that you felt you could tell me what happened to you. I can't imagine how hard it was to leave your daughter behind with a man who not only hated you, but probably was only using his daughter as a tool to manipulate your life."

I gently pulled her face around, so she was looking into my eyes. I wanted her to see that what I was about to say to her was sincere.

"I love you, Madds. What you have just told me will never change that. Knowing what you have been through and how you have managed to still live a near-normal life...I can't imagine how you have managed it. Whatever it takes, I will help you to get rid of Thomas from your life and get Rosie back. I hope that we can be there for each other throughout this, but if you decide that you don't want a relationship with me, I will understand. But believe me when I say I will love Rosie as much as I love you and hope I can be part of her life in the future."

I saw the tears appearing on her face again. I didn't know if they were from relief or the hurt that she thought she needed to reject me. I meant every word of it. I wanted Maddie and Rosie in my life. I couldn't think of anything better than to have a family with Maddie. There was just one thing I wanted at that moment though, one thing I wanted to do. Looking back into her tear-filled eyes, I gently brushed away the tears that were falling down her cheeks.

"Sweetheart, can I ask you for one thing? Can I kiss you?"

I didn't want to make a move without permission first. After everything she had told me, I finally understood why she seemed so reluctant at any form of intimacy, and knowing that I knew I had to take things slowly. She didn't say a word, but a beautiful smile came over her lips as she nodded to me. Slowly I leaned down to her face and placed my lips on hers. I rested there for a while, not making any move to deepen the kiss. I felt one of her arms move from its position on my back and rest in my hair. Her lips parted slightly, and I felt her tongue slide along my bottom lip. She was finally letting me in. Finally allowing me to be with her. Slightly deepening the kiss, I allowed her to take the lead as she pulled my head closer to hers. I had my answer as she kissed me slowly with so much passion. She wanted me, wanted me to help her and I was damned sure that after this moment, I was never going to let her go.

Chapter Sixteen

Madeleine

I was surprised when Tyler asked me if he could kiss me. His whole reaction to my explanation surprised me in fact. To be fair, I couldn't understand why he was still sitting here with me in his arms. I had imagined him storming out of the flat once I'd told him. I thought he'd be angry that I kept the secret that I had a baby with another man from him, well, from everyone, for so long. I could feel by the way he was holding me that he was angry. At first, I thought it was towards me, but when he spoke to me, told me how much he loved me, and wanted both me and Rosie to be in his life, I couldn't be happier. I knew when he pressed his lips against mine that he wouldn't take it any further. If I wanted to get over my fear of being intimate with him, it was me that would have to make the first move. I was relieved when he opened his mouth as I ran my tongue along his bottom lip, but again he was allowing me to take the lead with the kiss. He never took things too far, but responded to me in a way that showed me how much he loved me but wanted to take it slow.

I didn't want the kiss to end. I had waited so long for this moment, and I didn't want to stop. Tyler was everything I ever wanted in a man, and I just hoped that this kiss showed him that. If only he'd have been Rosie's Dad. My life would have been so much different. Pulling away, I looked up into his eyes and saw nothing but love and happiness in them. After everything I had put him through the past year, and everything I said to him last night, he still loved me. Placing his hand on my cheek, he just smiled down at me.

"Thank you, sweetheart. You don't know how long I have been waiting for that kiss."

"Probably as long as I have. Tyler, I'm sorry…"

He put his finger to my lips to stop me from talking.

"We are not going to play the blame game anymore. I can understand everything now I know the truth, and you have absolutely nothing to apologise for."

"I do though, please let me finish. I just wanted to say that I was sorry that I didn't tell you this sooner. I guess I just expected everyone to hate me for leaving a child behind, especially Ashleigh. I didn't want you to hate me because of my actions. I realise now how stupid and selfish that was of me. I probably could have had my daughter back a long time ago if I had been honest from the start."

"Well, that's all in the past now. We can't keep living on ifs and maybes. Now we can do something about it. Let me and the guys help you to get Rosie back. I think we both know we love each other now, but I want to take that further. I want to spend the rest of my life with you and Rosie if you will let me?"

"I'm sure you will get bored with us soon enough."

A sudden realisation came over me, a wave of sadness which Tyler obviously picked up on.

"What's up, sweetheart?"

"Tyler, I haven't seen Rosie in nearly two years. I only have pictures of her that Dad has sent me. What if she doesn't remember me? What if she is calling another woman Mum?"

"We can deal with that when the time comes. I do have to ask though. What does your Dad think of all this?"

"He doesn't know. The only person at home who knows Thomas is Rosie's father, is Thomas. That is unless he has confessed, but I think that is highly unlikely. I was called a slut by Michelle when I finally admitted I had been raped, I just never told her who by."

Tyler just pulled me into him, holding me and drawing circles on my back. It felt reassuring, comfortable. He was here for me, and I knew at that moment, he always would be, he always had been, despite me never letting him in. No matter how many times I tried to push him away, he always came back to try again. He would make the perfect dad for Rosie, I knew it.

"Do you want to see a picture of her?"

"Of Rosie? I would love to. I bet she is as beautiful as her mother."

I could feel myself start to blush, as I reached down onto the table to grab my phone. Opening Messenger, I pulled up the last photo Dad had sent me. It was on her second birthday and was of him and her. I was pleased he never sent me any pictures of Michelle and Thomas, they were only of Rosie or of them together. Passing the phone over to Tyler, I saw his face completely light up as he looked down at her.

"She's beautiful, Madds. I can see so much of you in her. I take it that is your Dad with her."

"Yes, it was on her second birthday. He always tries to message me on important dates, birthdays, Christmas, New Year, etc. telling me how things are going and how much Rosie misses me..."

The tears started to fall again. I had always been able to hold back these emotions. Now that it was out in the open, I didn't have to do that anymore. I could openly grieve, for want of a better word, at the loss of my daughter. I knew she wasn't dead, but she wasn't with me either.

"I miss her, Tyler. I miss her so much."

"Well now I know, we can do something about that. If you want me to go down there with you and get her back then that is what we will do. But I think I should speak to Mason first. He knows far more about this kind of thing than me. I know she is your daughter, but she is Thomas's too. We wouldn't want to do anything that could prevent you from ever seeing her again. And we don't want to put Rosie in a situation where she might get hurt or be in danger."

"I understand. As I said, Mason and Brandon probably already know by now. So, it won't matter if you speak to them. I do want to do this the right way. I want to know that she can come home with me and there is nothing anyone can do to take her away again. Although, I might have to find another place to live. Having a three-year-old in this flat won't be easy."

"We can look at that when the time comes. That is if you will let me help?"

I snuggled into Tyler's embrace. This is all I had ever wanted. For Tyler to be mine, to be loved by him. But now that I thought that could actually happen, I wasn't sure how to say that was what I wanted. How do you tell someone that you have lied to your entire time together that you needed them to be part of your life? I guess Tyler understood the internal dilemma I was going through because he didn't say a word. He just continued to hold me and place kisses on my head to let me know he was there.

"I don't know how to accept help," I said after a while. "All my life I have only relied on myself, worried about what people would think of me. You have done so much for me, Tyler, probably without even knowing it. You have always been there for me, no matter how horrible I was to you. I'm not sure what I can ever do to repay you."

"Nothing, sweetheart. I love you, that's all you need to worry about. I would move Heaven and Earth for you and expect nothing in return. And I mean nothing. I'm not saying that I don't want you in that way, I'm just saying that I don't expect it just because I'm helping you. If, when, and only when, you are ready and want to sleep with me, it will be one of the happiest days in my life. But it can only be when you are ready. We can take our time, take as long as you need. I'm in this for the long haul. Me, you, and little Rosie. I want us to be a family."

I was an emotional wreck. I could feel the tears falling down my face again. This time, they weren't tears of anger or pain, they were tears of joy. Although, from the look on Tyler's face you wouldn't have thought so. He looked distraught that he had said something wrong.

"What did I say, sweetheart? I didn't mean to upset..." It was my turn to place a finger against his lips as I smiled and started to chuckle.

"They're tears of joy, Tyler. I love you too, and I want to be with you as a family. I think you would make a fantastic dad to Rosie. I want to feel loved again. I have never felt the way I do about you with any other man. I tried to have boyfriends, but Thomas and his actions always got in the way. You are the only man who has managed to break down the wall I put up to protect myself."

I didn't have time to think this time before Tyler kissed my lips again, just a brief touch before he pulled away and smiled down at me.

"What was that for?"

"Just for being you, Madds. Also, for saying you think I would make a fantastic dad."

"So, where do we go from here? I mean now that we have finally admitted our feelings for each other, and you know my entire story."

"Let's just take things one day at a time, shall we. There is no need for us to rush into things. We have waited a year to get this far. However, the situation with Rosie is the most important. I'll have a chat with Mason tomorrow, and we can start work on getting her back. Whatever happens between us, I want to know that I at least helped you two be together again. For tonight, let's just sit here for a while and watch a movie or something."

"That sounds perfect."

We found a movie to watch. I don't think either of us was too bothered about what it was. Just the fact that we were snuggled up together on the settee was all that bothered us. Tyler continued to draw small circles on my arm as he held me. Every so often I would feel him place a slight kiss on my head. These small gestures made me realise I did want more. I wanted to be able to be intimate with him. I knew he wouldn't let me go that far, not this evening anyway. How did I make him realise what I wanted? That I felt ready to at least try? I want to know what it feels like to have someone who truly loves you that close and intimate. I know Jess and Ashleigh used to joke about it with me, well they did before they knew the truth. I guess now they feel terrible for some of the things they said. I wanted what all those women in romance novels I read had. I wanted to feel my whole being was being consumed in passion, and I wanted Tyler to be the reason for it. I knew it would take him a long time to give me that. I guess Tyler must have sensed my internal thoughts as he placed a kiss on my head and spoke.

"What's got your thoughts being tied up in knots, sweetheart?"

"Nothing, really. Well actually…" God, how did I put this? "Will you stay here the night with me?" I just blurted it out as quickly as I could, hardly taking a breath between words.

"Of course. I've done it before. I'll just sleep on the couch as usual. That wasn't anything to be so worried about, now was it?"

He didn't get what I meant. This was going to be so much harder than I thought it was.

"Tyler, that's not what I meant. Will you sleep with me in my bed tonight? I mean … we don't have to do anything, just snuggle like this. But I …"

Tyler leaned down and gave me a quick kiss.

"Sweetheart, if that is what you want, then yes, I will stay with you tonight. But I don't want to rush things. I don't want either of us to ruin what we are starting to build here. If you find me lying on the settee in the morning, please don't be disappointed. I just don't want to do anything that might make you feel worse, okay?"

"I understand."

I had said I understood, but I still felt disappointed that he felt he had to sleep on the settee. I knew he wouldn't do anything to hurt me, so why did he feel the need not to sleep in the same bed?

Chapter Seventeen

Tyler

········•···•··➤ ❧ ➤··•···•········

I couldn't believe Maddie had just asked me to sleep with her tonight, and in her bed. I was suddenly filled with both elation and dread. This had been everything I wanted since I had first met Maddie, but I didn't want to ruin things between us. I suspected I would be sleeping on the settee by the end of the night, merely due to the fact I knew I wouldn't be able to stop myself from waking up with a hard-on, the longer I spent with her. Not that I would do anything with it, not with Maddie anyway, but I didn't want her feeling pressured into anything.

Looking at Maddie now, I could see she was disappointed with what I'd said, even if she said she understood. I needed her to realise exactly what I meant. Carefully I pulled her up into my lap and held her, guessing it wouldn't be long before she realised exactly what I was getting at.

"Sweetheart, please don't look so disappointed. I know you think it's not necessary, and yes, I can keep control of myself. The issue is my friend down there, who you can probably feel right now. I just don't want you to wake up and cause you any distress thinking I was trying something when I wasn't. I know I'm not explaining myself well."

Maddie leaned down and placed a kiss on my cheek. I couldn't get enough of her soft lips and that was another reason why I was starting to think this was a bad idea. That, and the fact that my cock was now extremely hard and twitching in my trousers. If Maddie couldn't feel it, then God knows what I had to do. She obviously had as she started to giggle as she leaned into me closely, placing her head on my shoulder. She was going to be the death of me.

"I think I understand well enough, Tyler. And yes, I can feel your not-so-little friend down there. I'm sure I will be fine and won't try to kill you during the night."

"Madds, I'm trying to be serious here. I want things to work between us and I don't want anything that could remind you of that night. The last time I fell asleep here and you woke up in my arms ..."

"I know, Tyler. Sorry I didn't mean to make fun of the situation. But I feel so much more relaxed now you know the truth, I'm sure it will be fine," I felt her breath against my neck, she was doing nothing to help my predicament. In fact, if I wasn't mistaken, she was doing it on purpose. When I felt her lips on my neck, I knew she was.

"Sweetheart..."

"Tyler, look I know you are trying to be a gentleman here, and I love you for it. But I just want to feel again. I know there is probably only so far we can go before I do start freaking out a little, and I know I must build myself up. But please, let's have some fun tonight. Even if it is only making out."

I took in a sharp breath as she slowly moved on top of my cock. God, I loved this woman. I just needed to remind myself of what she has gone through.

"Okay, but we are going to take things slowly. We can try something for a while until you are comfortable, then take it up a level. But, under no circumstances will I be having sex with you tonight. I don't want to take things that far yet."

I could almost see the pout on her lips. She thought she was ready for that big step, but I knew there was no way she was. Not after confessing everything to me.

"You can pout all you like, sweetheart, but it's still no," I kissed along her jaw until my lips were just next to her ear and whispered. "That doesn't mean, however, that I'm not going to make you come again and again. There are other things I can use, you know."

I heard the sharp intake of breath Maddie took as she sat there in my arms. I could talk as much as I wanted, but I was still going to take things as slowly as she would let me. I was starting to think that it wouldn't be as slow as I first thought. But for tonight, I was just going to make her feel alive again, even if it meant me having a really long cold shower in the morning. Maddie lifted her head and looked into my eyes again. The smile that was now on her face was beautiful, and knowing that I had put it there filled my heart.

"I think I'm going to grab a shower. I would ask you to join me, but I know you'll refuse. But I hope you won't refuse to meet me in bed?"

"I won't refuse that, no, but if you don't mind me grabbing a shower after you first?"

Smiling, she placed her lips on mine again, coaxing me into a smouldering kiss. Maddie was experienced when it came to kissing, which was both a blessing and a curse. I loved feeling her pour her love into the kiss, but what it did to my body was killing me. I wanted to say to hell with it and take her there and then. Breaking away I gave her a quick slap on her bottom.

"Get in that shower, before we both do something we'll regret."

"Okay, I get the message. I will leave a towel in the bathroom for you, and shout when I am finished."

Giving me a kiss on the cheek, she got up and headed into the bathroom to get ready. I shook my head as she walked off. Tonight was going to be a long night, but one I was most certainly looking forward to.

I was pleased I had chucked some clothes in my backpack before I left the office this evening. At least I had some sweatpants to put on after having my shower. There was no way I was just going to sleep in my boxers this evening, not with the beauty I was going to have to lay next to anyway. Maddie had tried everything for me to undress her when she came out of the shower, but there was no way I was going to do that, not yet anyway. What happened when we were in bed though, I had no idea, but it was already starting to worry me. I wasn't sure how far I could take things tonight. I wanted so much to make it special for Maddie, but I didn't want to take things too far that I frightened her or took her back to that evening with Thomas. I guess I just had to let her guide me as to how far she wanted to go.

Walking into her bedroom, I found her lying in the bed, thankfully covered by the sheets. Although I had a sneaky suspicion that under those sheets was a very bare body.

"Feel better for that?"

"Much, thank you."

I walked around to the other side of the bed and climbed on top, there was no way I was going inside, not yet. I needed to keep myself calm this evening, and a naked Maddie was not going to allow that.

"You can get in the bed, you know. You don't have to lie on top all night."

"For the moment, I think it is best. I can think clearly up here, and I suggest we have a chat about tonight."

"What is there to chat about? I do believe you promised me multiple orgasms."

"I know what I said, but we do need to talk about this. Now I know for definite what you have been through. I don't want to do anything to make you uncomfortable. I don't want you taken back to that night again. So, we are going to take things slowly and if at any point I think you are starting to feel uncomfortable or scared I will stop. I hope you understand, we have a long life together ahead of us and it will take as long as it takes, okay?"

Looking down into her eyes I could see she was still disappointed, but she nodded her head in agreement. I knew it was the right thing to do. I saw her eyes fall to my lips as her tongue slowly licked her bottom lip.

Lowering my head to meet hers I placed my lips on hers. I didn't have to wait long for her reactions. She immediately let me in as our tongues duelled for dominance. Her arms came up around me with one on my back and one of her hands tangling through my hair. This absolute beauty in my arms was mine. There was no way I was ever letting her go. All I had to do now was make her realise it. I knew she loved me, but we had a long way to go before she could truly trust herself with another guy. But that all started tonight. Pulling away from the kiss, I placed kisses along her jaw and up to her ear, gaining a slight moan from Maddie's lips.

"Have you done anything since that night? Either with someone else or by yourself?"

"Only kissed other guys. I have never let any of them touch me, but I do have some toys. I'm not completely celibate, I have made myself come many times."

I almost groaned at her words. This was going to be harder than I thought. Part of me wished she had been celibate since that night. I just needed to make this special for her, try to erase all bad memories of what was happening and replace them with memories of us.

"If you need me to stop, just say, and I will stop. Just remember it is me here with you. Me giving you this pleasure and not him, okay?"

Nodding her head, I started placing kisses down her jaw again, heading down her neck and towards her chest. I pulled down the cover and saw her beautiful breasts there waiting for me to pleasure, her nipples already puckering up through the temperature change. I knew Maddie was quite big-chested, she had never made a show of it at work, but I always wondered what they looked like. Now seeing them I couldn't wait to get my lips and hands on them.

"God, you are beautiful, sweetheart."

I kissed down her breasts and pulled her nipple into my mouth, causing a moan of satisfaction to fall from her mouth which unfortunately was going straight to my cock. I had to ignore that. Tonight was all about Maddie and making her feel good. I was allowing her to have happy memories of being with a man. I knew it was going to be painful and uncomfortable for me, but I could deal with that later. Running my tongue around her nipple, I could hear her breath hitch at every touch. The sound of small moans came from her mouth. This had been what I wanted for two years, but until tonight, I never thought I would ever get it. I moved over to her other breast and gave it the same attention. I loved how her nipples puckered as soon as I touched them. Soon, I was going to get lost in those breasts, but not tonight. I placed kisses down her stomach and towards her pelvis. All the time I could hear Maddie's soft moans urging me on. Placing a kiss right above her mound, I felt Maddie tense under me.

"Just remember, sweetheart, it's me here. I'm not going to hurt you and you can tell me to stop at any time."

I wanted to reiterate what I had said earlier to her. It would kill me to stop now, but I would do it in a heartbeat if she was that worried or scared.

"I'm sorry, it's just been so long since … you know?"

"It's fine, sweetheart. I have all night and believe me, I am going to make the most of it, for as long as you will let me."

I smiled against her smooth flesh beneath me. I hadn't been with a woman since I had met Maddie. She had been the only one I wanted all this time. I carefully moved between her legs, allowing her to move to accommodate me. There was no way I was going to put any pressure on her, she was the one who was going to let me in. Lowering my head, I looked up into her gorgeous eyes as she gazed down at me, a slight look of concern on her face. As I looked at her a slightly nervous smile graced her lips and she nodded at my unspoken question. She was okay for me to continue.

Gently I parted her lips and slowly took my first taste of her sweetness. God, she tasted divine. Maddie took in a sharp breath and bucked her hips immediately at the touch of my tongue. Usually, I would hold a woman down, but with Maddie, I knew I couldn't. I just waited for her breathing to slow slightly and when it had, I went in again. Slowly I circled her clit with my tongue spurred on again by the moans Maddie was making. She was starting to relax more and enjoyed both the feeling and moment we were sharing together. She was already so close to her first release, the wetness from her core seeping onto my chin. Continuing my slow but methodical circles, we were both taken by surprise when her orgasm hit. Maddie screamed my name as the pleasure took over her body. My pace didn't change as she trembled beneath me and I looked up to see the beauty below me in the throes of ecstasy. Slowing down, I eventually stopped and looked up at her, waiting for her eyes to finally open and meet mine. Maddie, my sweetheart was truly gorgeous in this state, and I knew there would be no other woman for me. When her eyes finally opened and she looked down at me, a smile formed on her face.

"Tyler, that was … amazing. I never thought I would feel like that."

I moved up the bed and pulled her into my chest, our naked flesh together was doing nothing for the pain I was feeling in my groin right now. But I would suffer this a million times just to see the look on the face of my woman next to me now. Placing a kiss on her forehead she moved and placed her head on my shoulder, resting her head in my neck.

"What about you? You must be uncomfortable there?"

"As I said, tonight isn't about me. It's all about you. I can take a few nights being uncomfortable until you are ready. And before you say anything, you are not ready yet. Let's take things one step at a time. Now get some sleep for the moment, because I'm not finished with making you feel good yet tonight."

With that, I pulled the covers up on top of us and lay there with my sweetheart in my arms, exactly where she was meant to be. I heard her breathing slowly as she fell asleep in my arms, her heart beating against my chest, slowly allowing sleep to take over me.

Chapter Eighteen

Madeleine

·····✦·❊✦❊✦❊✦❊✦ ❧ ✦❊✦❊✦❊✦❊·❊·····

Opening my eyes, my heart jumped as I felt the heat of his body next to me, our arms and legs intertwined. It took me a few moments to realise who was lying next to me, and when I did, a sense of relief washed over me. Tyler. He had stayed the whole night with me in bed. That had also meant I hadn't had a nightmare for the first time in weeks. He had held me all night, and I had never felt safer or more loved than I did right now. Looking over at the clock I saw that it was still only 4:30 and I didn't need to get up for at least another thirty minutes. I was amazed that I was so awake at this time of the morning after the night I had. Tyler had made me feel good many times during the night, taking things a lot further than I had ever gone before. I was desperate to take care of him, to let him take me. But he would always stop me telling me I wasn't ready yet, and he was probably right. But it wouldn't be long before I was ready, and I was going to make sure he felt the way I did right now.

Snuggling into his body, I felt his arms pull me towards him as he came round from his slumber and placed a soft kiss on the top of my head.

"How are you feeling, sweetheart? I'm guessing you had a good night's sleep as we are both lying here together."

"I have never felt better. It is the first time in a long while that I have woken up without it being from a nightmare of that night. Thank you. Thank you for last night and for not giving up on me, Tyler. I really don't know how to thank you. Well, I do, but you won't let me," I said as my hand glided down his hard chest. His hand immediately covered mine and stopped me in my tracks.

"I've already said that time will come. Last night was amazing, and I think you have overcome some of your insecurities, but not all of them. I don't want to rush this, sweetheart. I love you, and I want that kind of relationship with you. But you need to be ready and overcome everything you have been through. That's not going to happen overnight. We pushed a lot of boundaries last night, but each time we can go one step further. I want to be the one to overcome them with you. Be the one who makes you feel good. I want to replace your nightmares with dreams of me and what I can do to you."

"I want that too, Tyler. But ..."

I buried my head into his neck. I was too afraid to say the thoughts that were in my head. Too afraid that he would reject me as soon as I said it. My life wasn't just my own. I had a daughter to consider. No matter how much I loved Tyler, she had to come first in my life. I just wasn't sure how honest Tyler had been last night when he said he wanted to be part of her life, our life together.

"What's going through that head of yours, sweetheart?

Whatever it is, let's talk about it. We agreed no secrets, remember? And I intend to hold up my side of the bargain. But you have to too. If we are going to make this work, you need to tell me what is going through that beautiful head of yours."

"Tyler, I love you, I really do. But I must think of Rosie. She should be the most important person in my life, and at the moment I am just thinking of myself. I should be working out how to get her back."

"Sweetheart, I have already told you that we will get Rosie back. I love you, and if that means I have to welcome Rosie into my life as well, of course, I am going to do that. I meant every word I said, that I want both of you, not just you. I know you come as a package deal. I want a family, what Mason and Jayden both have, and I am determined that family will be with you."

He pulled me into his side again, just holding me. I couldn't help it as the tears started to fall from my eyes. If I could ever fall more in love with this man, it was from those words.

"I'm sorry, I shouldn't cry. I just can't believe how much you would do for me. That you would give up your life just to look after me and Rosie."

"I will give up everything for you, sweetheart. Now, much as I would love to spend the day in bed with you, I know you have to open up the shop soon. So, you better get yourself in the shower and get ready. I'll make you a coffee and grab a shower once you are ready. I can't risk taking one with you."

Placing a chaste kiss on my lips, he got out of the bed and headed out to the kitchen. Smiling to myself at how lucky I was to have Tyler in my life, I got out of bed and headed to the bathroom to shower and get ready for the day.

I walked into the shop today in one of the best moods I had been in for years. At last, things seemed to be going my way. I had got everything ready for the morning and already served Mr. Duncan from the newsagents and was now sitting with Tyler drinking my first coffee of the morning before he had to go off to work.

"So, how are you feeling this morning, sweetheart?"

"It's all a bit surreal at the moment. I have been wanting this for so long that I never thought it would actually happen. I'm just happy and sad at the same time, I guess."

Tyler took my hand in his as a look of concern came over his face.

"Why are you sad? I thought you would be ecstatic after what we did last night."

"Don't get me wrong, I am very happy about what happened last night. It's just, without Rosie here I can never be truly happy."

"We are going to do something about that, and if you don't mind I would like to talk to Mace and Brandon about it as soon as I can. I don't want you to be without Rosie for a minute longer than necessary," he immediately replied, giving my hand a squeeze.

"Thank you, Tyler, and of course, it's fine to speak to the guys. It's the only way I will get Rosie back."

I looked at the time and seeing it was nearly 8:00 I thought it best to start on the coffees for the guys. Getting up from my seat I went to the machine to start the drinks running.

"Who's in today?"

"Just the four of us today, Mace, Brandon, Richard, and myself."

"Okay, I'll have lunch ready at the normal time for you all. If anyone wants anything different or one of the other guys turns up, just give me a call."

Turning to place the drinks on the counter, I jumped when I found Tyler standing next to me.

"Tyler, don't do that. You nearly gave me heart failure."

Pulling me into his side, he placed a kiss on my cheek.

"I'm sorry, I just couldn't bear to be apart from you another minute longer. Richard's gonna hate me today. I'm going to be unbearable."

I laughed as I looked up at him, but seeing the look in his eyes, my heart rate increased. A look of pure love was there and I couldn't help but move my lips closer to his. As our lips met, we immediately pulled each other closer, our kiss going from PG to PG-15 at a rapid rate. Neither of us heard the shop door open until we both heard Mason's dulcet tones as he walked over to the counter.

"Well, about fucking time. Perhaps you won't be so much of an arsehole now."

"Mason, leave them alone. You know what Maddie's been through," Jess, who had obviously come in with Mason, replied as she slapped him on the shoulder, whilst holding Callum in her arm.

Pulling away from the kiss, Tyler rested his forehead on mine as he laughed at their little exchange. If anyone was in love with each other it was those two. So much so, even a little argument like that was light-hearted.

"Hi, Mace. I have just finished your drinks. Are you staying, Jess?"

"After what I just walked in on, I think that is a stupid question, don't you think?"

I could feel myself start to blush. I knew this day would come, especially after all the times I had teased Jess about Mason at the beginning of their relationship. I guess it was my turn now, and I was sure Tyler would get it ten times worse from the rest of the guys.

"Okay, sit down and I'll make you a drink. I just need to get these guys their pastries and then I can chuck them out for our girly chat."

I could almost hear Tyler pouting behind me as Mason chuckled away to himself. I had barely got the pastries in the bag before I was swept into Tyler's chest again as he gave me one final kiss, out of sight from the bosses of course.

"We don't have any more time for that, Tyler. We have work to do and from what I heard last night I think you are about to add to it," Mason said as if almost knowing what we were doing in here.

"I'll try and get back here at lunchtime, but if not, can I come round again tonight?"

"If we are going to continue where we left off early this morning, then you better believe I want you there."

"Okay. I love you, sweetheart."

"Love you too."

With that, he picked up the bag and walked out the front to a laughing Mason. Saying their goodbyes to Jess, I made her a drink and sat down in her usual corner with her.

"So, I take it last night went well then?"

"There were a few tears and a lot of making up to do on my part. But overall, yes it went well. Hell, what am I saying? Oh My God, Jess. It was amazing. I never knew things could be like that. After denying myself all this time. I just wish …"

She placed her hand over mine.

"You needed that time, Maddie. It needed to be right for you. Have you slept with him yet?"

"We slept in the same bed together, but he wouldn't sleep with me in that way. He wants to make sure I am truly ready for that, and he doesn't think I am yet. He won't even let me take care of him. But I will say, he did take good care of me last night," as soon as I said it, I could feel my face blush.

"I'm sure he did, and I'm glad he is thinking about you first. What did he say about Rosie? I'm guessing he was okay with it, as I'm sure you wouldn't have let it go that far if he wasn't?"

"He wants us to be a family, all three of us. He's going to speak to Mace and Brandon today to work out how we can get her back. It was the first thing he said, apart from saying she was adorable when he saw her photo."

"You have a photo and never showed us!"

I got up from the table and grabbed my phone from my bag out back. I walked back to the table and pulled up the last picture of Rosie that my Dad had sent to me. Handing it over to Jess I saw the smile that lit up her face, the exact same smile I had whenever I saw her.

"She is beautiful, Maddie. How old is she now?"

"She will be three next birthday. I have missed her first two birthdays ..." I could feel the tears start to form in my eyes at the thought of all the time I had missed my beautiful daughter.

"Maddie, please don't get upset. I know Mason will not let you live the rest of your life without her. He will do all that he can to help Tyler get her back for you. If he doesn't, he will have to answer to me."

I had to laugh at that. I had gotten to know Jess very well over the past two years, and I knew that once she had something in her head, she would never let go of it. There was no way that Mason wouldn't help me to get Rosie back, not if he wanted to sleep in the same bed as his fiancé. Or even in the same house come to think of it.

"I know, it just upsets me to think that for the past two years she has been living with that monster of a man. He may have provided the sperm to make that beautiful girl, but he is no father to her. He was happy to rape me and let me live with the consequences. The only reason he kept her was because of the money he could get having her at home. He doesn't love her and neither does Michelle. The only reason why Rosie is treated well is because of my Dad."

"Well, when she comes home, we are going to have one hell of a birthday party for her. She can meet Callum and Amelia. You know they are going to love her. You know you are like a little sister to me, so I get to be an honorary auntie to her. And believe me, she will have six uncles who are going to protect her with their lives, along with one man who is going to be a fantastic Dad. She is going to have so much love around her that she will be one of the happiest little girls in the world. You just have to be a little patient, but she will be back with you soon."

"Then I just have to work out where we will live and what we need to get, and ..."

"Let us all worry about that. Big sis here lives with a millionaire. We can help with anything you need, and before you say anything. Let's call it payment for all those months you worked for me and refused to accept any money. You don't even accept a share in the profits here when you are running the place."

I would never accept that kind of money from her. I accepted the wage she gave me, but a share of the profits just because I was running the place, that was too much. I ran the shop because I enjoyed it, it gave me something to do to keep my mind off Rosie and what happened to me. That brought another question. When I did get Rosie back, I might not be able to put the hours into this place. How was I going to juggle the life of a Mum and running a shop?

"Before you ask the next question, Ashleigh is more than happy to either help out here or help look after Rosie when you are working. Brandon really doesn't want her working, but is happy for her to hang out here. So, it will help both of you out. Ashleigh won't go stir crazy from sitting at home and you can continue to work here. You know she even offered to work the reception at the office, just for something to do."

"Is she really that bored?"

"You try spending days at home on your own, after travelling over Europe."

"I guess you have a point. Jess, I just wanted to say thank you. Not just for the job, and for being here and understanding. Thank you for being my friend. I have never really had many friends in my life but you have always been there for me."

"Hey, just returning the favour with everything that happened with Chris, and because that is what a big sister does."

I knew right then, no matter what, I was never leaving this town. Rosie would be coming here to live with me, Tyler, and the wonderful friends that I now called family here in Kings View.

144

Chapter Nineteen

Thomas

It had been nearly two years since I had forced Madeleine to leave the house and Rosie behind. At the time it had seemed the most sensible suggestion to get rid of her before she told the truth about me being Rosie's father. I was sure Mum had realised it was me, but so far, she hadn't said a word. I was just lucky that she looked more like Madeleine than me. Brian had been beside himself when he came home from deployment to find out not only was he a grandfather, but his daughter had left home and her daughter behind. Whenever he was home, he spent all of his time trying to find her. When he was on deployment, he employed private investigators to try and find out where she was.

It was obvious that this was putting a strain on his relationship with Mum. She had been spending more and more time out on the streets earning money as only she knew how.

With a bloke between her legs. She thought I didn't know what she did when she went out for all hours of the day and night. But I knew. Part of me felt bad as I was one of the reasons behind it, but if the truth be known, I couldn't stand her. The only reason I was still here was that it was rent-free, and I could come and go as I pleased. The reason I didn't have a job at the moment was that it was now left to me to look after Rosie.

I had grown to love the little girl, but there was no way I was going to give up the life I had to look after her for the rest of my life. I had planned on putting her up for adoption, but Brian had immediately put a stop to that. I knew that he was going to be gone for a while this time, so I reached out to a few of my friends to find another solution. A child, even one of Rosie's age, could make a lot of money if sold to a couple that couldn't get through the adoption process and really wanted a child. I had made enquiries and had been offered £50,000 for her. There was only one problem. I wasn't named as the father on the birth certificate. My own words to Madeleine had now come back to haunt me.

"I want nothing to do with that kid if you are going to keep it. If you ever tell anyone that it is mine, I will deny it."

Those words now meant that I had no legal right to the child. I could get a DNA test, but again, I would need Madeleine here to get that done. Then of course there would be the argument that followed from my Mum when she did find out the truth. No, I needed to take Rosie away and then get Madeleine to come to me. Then I could force her to name me as the father and then get rid of the brat. The money would be mine and then I could fuck off away from this place and my Mum. Let her wallow in her own pity when Brian throws her out after finding out exactly what she has been doing for the past two years. And I would make sure that he did.

Try as I might, both Brian and myself had been no closer to working out where Madeleine was. She couldn't have gotten that far as she didn't have that much money when she left here. I was certain she wouldn't have made a life with another guy wherever she was. The way I had treated her that night, I was sure she would never be able to sleep with another guy again. Perhaps she had turned and become a lesbian. Now there was a thought that made my cock hard. Much as I hated Madeleine, I had always wanted to have her. The problem was I was such an arsehole that she would never have fallen in love with me of her own accord. I had to force things, so I had that night after coming home blind drunk from my friend's house. I must admit I was surprised that I had even managed to get it up, let alone knock her up in the process.

Just remembering how she screamed for me to stop made my cock hard again. Perhaps when I got her to come and see me, I would have her one last time, for old time's sake. Just before I blew her world apart by taking her only daughter away from her for good. She would agree to everything I said, or she would watch as I tortured her daughter. I didn't care that she was mine as well. I only provided one night of passion for her, and I didn't want to live with the outcome for the rest of my life. No, I just wanted the money that she could bring. Perhaps I would keep Madeleine? I could lock her up and use her as a cash register. Get her popping out babies that I could sell to the highest bidder. I knew she wouldn't go for it, but she would agree in the end, if she wanted to live, that was.

My phone started to ring as I sat there pondering that thought. Looking down it was one of the contacts I was using to try and find Madeleine.

"I hope you finally have good news for me, with all the money I am paying you."

"Lovely to speak to you too, Tom."

"Fuck the pleasantries, and the name is Thomas, not Tom. Now tell me what you've got."

"We haven't found her, but do have a lead. Seems that dear Maddie went back to University, down at Southampton. So, she must be in that area somewhere. I have a few *friends* searching through the records to find her. There is a PI company in the Winchester area that also might be able to help us, but I will save that as a last resort, mainly due to the cost of hiring them."

"About fucking time, you had some leads. Check it out and as you said, keep the PI company in mind, but only use them if you really need to. The fewer people that know about this the better. If you found her, then that means that Brian may have found her too. We need to be careful and get to her first. I need this brat gone, and soon."

"Okay, no problem, Thomas. I'll keep you up to date."

"Just see that you do."

With that, I dropped the call and threw my phone down on the chair next to me. This was taking too long. How could someone just disappear without a trace for nearly two years and only be a couple of hundred miles away? The longer it took, the less chance I had of selling Rosie for a decent amount of money. I just needed to make sure that I found her before Brian did. At least then I could get exactly what I wanted. If he found her first, things would get complicated, and I really didn't need to go down the route that I was contemplating in my head. No, my contact would find her first, and then the money and Madeleine would be mine.

Chapter Twenty

Tyler

Walking out of the coffee shop with Mason, I was happier than I had been in years. Finally, Maddie and I were together. We had overcome all the secrets she had been holding back and were working through them. Now I just had to get little Rosie back for her and we could start to live a life together as a family. I knew there was a long road ahead of us before Maddie would be able to trust me one hundred percent, even if what had happened wasn't my fault. But I was willing to spend the time and work things through with her. If it didn't work out between us in the end, as long as I knew I had gotten Rosie back and done everything I could, I would be happy.

"So, you finally got it together then?"

"Well, we are officially seeing each other, if that's what you mean. I'm sure you know what happened to Maddie?"

"Jess told me some of it, but I am sure there is a lot she didn't tell me."

"Did she tell you about Rosie?"

"No, who is Rosie?"

"Shit, I thought that would have been the first thing she told you."

"I'm guessing that we need to sit down and have a chat?"

"I was going to ask if I could speak to you and Brandon, yes. I will probably need Richard's help as well, but I can fill him in with what he needs to know. I'm not sure if Maddie will want him to know everything, but she was happy for me to tell you. I guess, like me, Maddie thought Jess would tell you everything."

"Of course, we can have a chat. I assume it's bad, especially if Jess wouldn't tell me all there is to know. Let's get settled in for the day, have our normal morning meeting and then we can sit down and talk."

"Thanks, Mace. I really appreciate this, and I know Maddie will too."

"I'm just happy that you two finally got things worked out. I hated seeing the two of you unhappy."

"We have a long way to go, but we will get there."

The pair of us continued to walk up to the office. Richard and Brandon were already there, standing in the reception area as we walked through the door. A knowing smirk came across Brandon's face as I walked in. He would have known where I was last night, considering I was staying at their place and didn't come home.

"I was just going to send out a search party to find you, seeing as you didn't come home last night. No word, no message, me and Ashleigh were starting to worry."

I could see the look of mischief in his eyes. Brandon wasn't usually the one to make or play jokes on people. But since he had got back together with Ashleigh, his whole outlook on life seemed to have changed. He had become more of a joker than Jayden, and he was bad. I couldn't begrudge him though. He had been without Ashleigh for three years. At least Maddie had been close by, regardless that she wouldn't let me in.

"I'm sure you knew exactly where I was, Brandon. Maddie said she had told Ashleigh and Jess she was going to invite me round."

"She did. But what if Maddie had murdered you or chucked you out on the streets and you had a car crash. So many possibilities had us worried sick."

I could see the smile starting to form on his face, so I knew he was only joking with me.

"I'm guessing all is good with you two then?"

Before I could even reply, Mason answered for me.

"Oh, it is definitely good between them. You should have seen what me and Jess walked into at the coffee shop this morning. It was not a friendly kiss, I can tell you. Would have made even you blush, Brandon."

"And I missed it! Any chance of a repeat at lunchtime? I can be there at one."

"Will you two leave it off? I have work to be getting on with and we need to talk," I said looking at the pair of them. Brandon just gave me a chin lift, making me think that he probably knew more about the situation than Mason. That would make things easier later.

Walking towards my office with my coffee in my hand, I sat down at my desk and took a deep breath. My life had changed so quickly, and I wasn't sure where to go from here. I had so much that I needed to sort out, the first of which would be finding a new house here in Kings View. I had to make sure that we had room for when Rosie came back into Maddie's life. But I didn't want to jump the gun on things. I needed to sit down with Maddie and work out what we were going to do. I would gladly buy a house down here. I had enough money, but I didn't want Maddie thinking that I was just doing it for her to stay with me.

I'm not sure how long I had been sitting there with thoughts going around my head. Or exactly when Richard had walked in the office, but I nearly jumped when I looked over and saw him sitting there smiling at me.

"You could have said you were in the office."

"I did, several times. But you were so deep in thought I gave up. I knew you would look over at some point. Anyway, I take it your chat went well last night, especially after what Mace said this morning."

"It did go well. We talked about everything, and she told me the truth. I hate to say that Ashleigh was right. Thomas did rape her, and she has a daughter with him, Rosie. She is nearly three years old and absolutely adorable."

"Right, so I guess our plan of action is to get Rosie back."

"Yeah, that's the plan. I'm going to sit down with Mace and Brandon this morning and work out exactly what we need to do. We must make sure we do everything by the book. I don't want us to do anything that could lead to Rosie being taken away from Maddie permanently. I want to be a family with them both. I've already fallen in love with Rosie and have never met her. I'm sure we were meant to be together."

"I'm pleased for you, Tyler. So that's four down and three to go then."

"Well, I'm sure Nathan already has someone, I just don't know who. I don't think I can ever see Kye with a steady woman. He's more of a playboy than Jayden ever was. So, I guess that just leaves you, Richard, and I know you will find someone who loves you soon. You're a great guy, we just need to get you out there in more ways than one."

"Why does that fill me with worry and dread?"

"Trust me, have I ever led you astray? Nope, don't answer that. Let's get on with the last bits of our investigation so we can report back at the morning meeting."

With a hesitant and worried laugh, Richard just nodded his head and we got down to finishing everything we had to do.

"So, is there anything else we need to discuss?"

The meeting seemed to be dragging today. I guessed it was because I was eager to speak with Mason and Brandon about the situation with Maddie. My normal bored demeanour during our meetings had gone today. I had been chattier and happier to discuss everything, which hadn't gone without notice as I received a few glances from both Jayden and Nathan. Kye didn't know me that well, but even he seemed surprised at the way I was today.

"Yeah, I just have one question, bro."

"Go ahead, Jayden."

"Tyler, did you get laid last night? You are never this happy on our calls. Have you and Maddie finally got your arses in gear and admitted you love each other?"

I looked over as Brandon nearly choked on the coffee that he had been drinking before Jayden had started to speak.

"For fuck's sake, Jayden. Give a guy a warning before you ask a question like that."

"Well?"

"Maddie and I have started seeing each other, yes. But leave it there please, Jayden. There is a lot you don't know, and I'm not about to broadcast it to everyone. I'm sure you will find out at some point, but not today, okay?"

"Everything alright, Tyler?"

"As Tyler said, bro, there is a lot more you don't know. We will fill you in as and when we need to. Just leave it at that for the moment."

He just gave a chin lift and said no more.

"Well if that's everything, we will say our goodbyes and speak again tomorrow probably."

"Mace, wait on the line a second," Jayden said before Mason cut off the call. The guys all left the room at the London office. I was about to walk out before Jayden spoke again.

"Tyler, can you stay behind for a second."

I sat back down at the conference table with Mason and Brandon as Richard left the room and closed the door.

"Tyler, I didn't mean anything by my comment. I'm sorry, I was just having a laugh. Didn't mean to hurt your feelings, man."

"It's okay. I know you didn't mean anything by it. It's just there is a lot you don't know about Maddie. I'm not going to say anything here. Once it's all sorted and you come down, I will be able to explain. Everything will be okay, it might just take us a while to get there."

"Safe to say, bro. We have another mission related to one of our women. That's all I'm going to say for the moment. We may need Richard to stay down here for a while longer."

"Anything you need, just let me know. We can all be down there in an hour if you need us. Maddie is safe, isn't she? You know we all see her as our little sister."

"She is safe and thank you. I will let you know if I need anything."

"Sure thing. Okay, I will let you get on."

Jayden shut down the connection and I was left in the conference room with Mason and Brandon. I took a deep breath.

"So, I guess you want to know why I wanted this talk?"

"Well, I think I probably know why, but I'm not so sure that Mace here knows as much as me. So do you want to explain it to him?"

I looked between the two of them. This wasn't going to be easy, even with, I suspected, Brandon knowing most of the story.

"Okay, I guess I will start at the beginning. It's not going to be easy to hear, believe me. I had to hold back my anger last night when she finally told me. Maddie was living at home with her Dad's new girlfriend and her son Thomas. Thomas seemed to take a dislike to Maddie and often got very verbal and then started to get physical with her. While her Dad was on tour in the Navy, Thomas got drunk one night. When he came home it was just him and Maddie in the house. Long story short, he raped her."

I could feel my anger starting to build again. With the thought that he was Maddie's first and he fucking did that to her, the tears started to fall down my face. Not really because I was upset, but because I was fuming.

"You okay, man? You don't have to say anymore if you don't want to."

"No, you need to know everything, Mace. It gets worse, believe me."

I looked over at Brandon who just nodded for me to go on. He knew more than Mason, obviously.

"He was her fucking first time, Mace. He raped her when she hadn't been with anyone else before that and to top it off, she got pregnant."

I thought the table would split in two the way Mason hit it. I could see the anger in his eyes. It was almost the same look I'd had when Maddie had first told me.

"I take it she got rid of the baby?"

"No, and that is what we need to talk about. She decided that no matter what, she couldn't have an abortion. She had a daughter, Rosie. Mace, you should see her, she is fucking adorable. I love her already and that's before I've even met her. The problem is, she is still living at her Dad's place, with Thomas and Michelle, his Mum. He forced Maddie to leave. Beat her up pretty bad from what she explained. He said that she wasn't taking Rosie with her, that she was too valuable. I'm frightened that he is going to try and sell her."

I could see the anger in both of their faces as I suggested that. But to me, it seemed the most sensible reason for a guy to keep hold of a child that he didn't really want. Plus, to say that Rosie was too valuable to allow Maddie to take her away, would also suggest the same thing.

"What do you need us to do?" Mason immediately asked.

"I promised Maddie that I would get Rosie back to her and that we would be a family. So that's what I need help with. I need to do this right and make sure there is no way that Thomas can get her back. I don't think he is named on the birth certificate because he didn't want anything to do with her. The only people outside of us here who know who the father of Rosie is, are Maddie and Thomas. She didn't even tell her Dad. The first he knew about it was when he returned from his tour to find Maddie gone, and Rosie there."

"I hope you don't mind, Tyler, but I have already reached out to our solicitors, to find out the legal side of this. Ashleigh told me everything last night when she came back from the shop. I guess she thought I would take it better than Jess thought Mason would. Don't get me wrong, I was fuming last night and almost ended up outside Maddie's flat. But Ashleigh reminded me that she was going to be explaining everything to you, so I thought better of it. Christian said he is going to look into everything and get back to us a bit later. Then we can decide where to go from there."

"Thanks, Brandon. I appreciate that."

"Okay, so I guess we'll wait to hear from Christian and then get a plan together. I assume Rosie is still at Maddie's old house?"

I was just about to answer Mason when there was a knock at the door.

"Come in, Richard."

"Sorry to bother you guys, but there is someone here to see Tyler."

"Does it need to be now, Richard?"

"Tyler, it's Lieutenant Commander Brian Lewis."

My head immediately snapped around to Richard.

"Is that who I think it is, Tyler?"

"Yeah, it's Maddie's Dad"

Chapter Twenty-One

Tyler

"You better show him in here, Richard."

"Will do, Mason."

Richard walked out of the room, and we all sat there looking at each other. None of us knew exactly what to say, the shock clear on all our faces. I could feel the worry running through me. How did Brian find us here? Why would he come down if he didn't know that Maddie was here? There were more questions than answers. A knock at the door pulled us all from our thoughts, as Richard walked back through the door with Maddie's Dad. He was clearly a military man, which I hoped would work in our favour, as we had all served our time in the forces. Granted we were in the Army and Lt Cdr Lewis was in the Navy, but that didn't matter. We all had the same mindset.

Mason walked up to him and greeted him.

"Lieutenant Commander Lewis, it's a pleasure to meet you. My name is Mason King, and I am one of the owners of King Brothers. These are my colleagues Brandon James and Tyler Edwards."

"Mr. King, thank you for agreeing to see me without an appointment. Please call me Brian. I am not in uniform today. I know you have all served your Queen, so will understand."

"Of course, Brian, and please call me Mason. Why don't you take a seat? We must say we are surprised to see you here today of all days."

Brian's eyes immediately met mine. I wondered how much he knew, and whether he thought I was the one who had gotten Maddie pregnant. When I looked in his eyes, I only saw a father who was worried about his daughter. There was no anger or resentment towards me. That had to be a good sign.

"Why don't I tell you why I am here? I actually came to see you, Mr. Edwards."

"Please, I think we can all be on first-name terms here. Call me Tyler."

"Well, Tyler. I understand from a friend that you have been seeing a bit of my daughter, Madeleine. I have been extremely worried about her. It has taken me nearly two years to find her here, but that isn't the main reason I am here. God, this is difficult. I'm not sure how much you know."

"If you'd have asked me that yesterday morning, I would have said absolutely nothing. This morning, however, I'm guessing the three guys sitting before you, actually know more than you."

"Why don't you tell us what you know, Brian. Then perhaps we can fill in the gaps."

Brian smiled at Mason and nodded.

"Well, I was out at sea at the time. We had been sent away for what was meant to be a normal six-month tour. Unfortunately, that turned out to be nearly a year. When I came back home, I found my girlfriend and her son in the house, which wasn't surprising. The surprising part was finding them there with a young baby, and not Madds. Of course, I assumed the worst at the time. That my girlfriend had cheated on me and got pregnant. It was only after I calmed down that I found out that Rosie was my granddaughter, and that Maddie had abandoned her and left. Well, at least that is what I was told.

I have spent the past two years trying to find Madds, trying to work out where she was and why she left the house and her daughter behind. I got a lead last week while I was finishing up my tour, which is why I am here today. I didn't want to just turn up at her work, so thought it would be best if I came here first. I'm worried about Rosie. I think Thomas is up to something. He has already suggested that we get her adopted, that Michelle and he can't afford to keep the house running with a toddler. But I think there is more to it than that. Having overheard a couple of conversations Thomas had on the phone recently raised a few suspicions for me. I hate to say, I think Thomas is Rosie's Dad and possibly trying to sell his own daughter to the highest bidder."

He glanced around at all of us as he said it, hoping for a shocked reaction from his assumption. I guess from the look on our faces he realised the truth.

"It's true, isn't it? Thomas is Rosie's dad. I can see from the look on your faces that you aren't surprised by this."

I was a nervous wreck. I was meeting the father of the woman I loved for the first time. She didn't know he was here, and it looked like I had to be the one to tell him he was right. Thomas was Rosie's father and she was conceived because his arsehole of a 'stepson,' for want of a better word, raped his daughter. How the hell did I tell him that? I was saved from this when Mason started to speak again.

"Brian, I hate to say that you are right. Look, there is no easy way to tell you what happened. As Tyler said, until last night, none of us knew anything about Maddie's past. She finally opened up to us and Tyler yesterday. We were actually in a meeting about how we were going to get Rosie back. The thing is …"

Mason looked over to me, asking for permission to tell Brian. I couldn't let Mason be the one to do it. It had to be me. I would never forgive myself if I allowed the relationship he had with Maddie to be ruined because he had been the one to let her secret out.

"I think I should be the one to tell him, Mason."

Mason smiled and gave me a chin lift of confirmation.

"Brian, I have been in love with your daughter since she arrived here in Kings View. There was always something holding her back though. An invisible force stopped her from ever getting close to me. For a while, I thought it was just me, but as time went on, I had a sinking feeling that something happened to her in the past before she came here. My thoughts were confirmed one night when we fell asleep together on the sofa and I witnessed one of her nightmares. I knew then something had happened, something terrible. It wasn't until last night that I found out exactly what that was."

I took a deep breath.

"I think I should allow Maddie to tell you the full story of exactly what happened. It's not really my place to say. Safe to say it's not something I would like to happen to my daughter if I had one, or even to any woman I know."

If I thought Mason's reaction was bad enough, it was nothing compared to how Brian reacted. Even without telling him the full story, judging by what happened next he had already put two and two together. The chair he was sitting in, flew across the room as he got off of it with such force.

"I'll fucking kill him. How dare he do that to my only daughter. What the fuck did he think he was doing?"

Brandon, always the calm one, got up from his chair and carefully walked over to the now fuming and pacing Brian. Slowly he placed a hand on his shoulder, looking ready to move at any moment from a jerk reaction. Brian spun around, but Brandon just stood there.

"Brian, I know this is hard to hear. Hell, I was in the same state as you when I heard last night, and Maddie is only a friend to me. Well, I suppose that isn't strictly true. Kings is like one big family and as she works for Mason's fiancé, Jess, we all consider Maddie part of our family. Almost a little sister to us all. But the fact of the matter is, we can't go in all guns blazing, much as we would all like to. We need to make sure that Rosie is both safe and with Maddie permanently. We don't want to do anything that could jeopardise that."

Brian looked around the room at the three of us and just hung his head. I wasn't sure if it was in shame or sadness. Looking at him now, you could see the vulnerability that losing his daughter and possibly granddaughter could bring upon a strong man like him. Nodding his head, he picked up the chair and sat back down, taking a deep breath.

"I'm sorry. I shouldn't have let my emotions run away with me like that. It's funny. Like I'm sure you have, we are taught in the forces to bury our emotions, but when it is something close to home, it is very difficult to do."

"Don't worry, Brian. We understand better than most. One day, I hope we can sit down and we will tell you the stories of how we ended up with our women. But that isn't for now. Now we need to work on a plan to get Rosie back for good."

"Thank you. I'm pleased to know that Madds has found a place where she is loved and protected. I can see how much you all care for her. And Tyler, I guess I don't have to worry about you ever hurting my sweet girl?"

"Sir, if I ever hurt my sweetheart, I personally give you permission to shoot and bury me where I can never be found. I have loved her from afar for two years, and my feelings are never going to change. From what I have seen of Rosie, she is adorable, and I have already asked Madds if she will allow me to be part of her family. I have also said that I will respect Madd's wishes, and if she doesn't want me in her life then I will let her be. But I will never be too far away if she or Rosie needs help."

Brian smiled over at me and then extended his hand for a handshake. I took it with a firm grip.

"I guess I should welcome you to the family then."

"Let's not get ahead of ourselves, but thank you for the vote of confidence. So where would you like to go from here?"

"If possible, I would like to go and see Madds. I won't say anything about what we spoke about here. I'm hoping that she will open up to me."

"Let me get hold of Ashleigh and ask her to look after the shop for the afternoon. That way you and Maddie can go up to her flat and talk in private. I'm sure she would prefer that. I know Jess was there this morning, but she may want to go home at some point."

"Good plan, Brandon."

Brandon walked off to contact Ashleigh and arrange for her to come down. As they were still staying in town, I knew it wouldn't take long for her to get to the shop. Richard had already gone to get lunch and was going to say I was tied up in a discussion with a new client so as not to arouse suspicion. Brandon walked back into the room and confirmed that Ashleigh would text as soon as she arrived at the coffee shop.

"So, I guess while we are waiting, I will bring you up to date with what we were discussing before you came in this morning."

The four of us sat there and discussed how we were going to go about getting Rosie back. Currently, it was just a waiting game to hear back from the solicitors about the legal ramifications of what we were trying to do.

"The only worry I have is that Thomas is planning something. He has been living in my house in Plymouth for a while now. But I know he has links to Kent, and I am worried that he is going to take Rosie down there away from me."

"Do you know where in Kent? Richard and I can investigate and keep tabs on the area just in case he does make a run for it."

"I'm sure it was down near Canterbury. Chartham, I think. It's a small village just outside of the city. I don't know much more than that I'm afraid."

"Well, if you can get me as much detail as possible on Thomas, car reg, etc, we can start looking at cameras on the way down there. Just in case he does a runner."

"Give me your email address, and I will send it all over to you. I'll give you my mobile number as well so you can contact me if you need anything."

I wrote down my email address and passed it to Brian as he entered his mobile number into my phone, just as Brandon received a notification on his.

"Ashleigh is at the coffee shop. Jess is still there as well, so

Maddie isn't very suspicious at the moment. But I don't know how long that will last."

"Okay, I guess it's time to head down to see your daughter then."

"Lead the way."

Chapter Twenty-Two

Madeleine

⸻ ❧ ⸻

There wasn't much that could put me in a bad mood today. I was on cloud nine when I woke up this morning in Tyler's arms after a fantastic night. Even Mason making his sarcastic comments when he and Jess walked in this morning couldn't dampen my mood. Sitting down with Jess first thing this morning was good. Finally being able to talk about everything in my life had taken a weight from my shoulders I hadn't even realised was there. The customers that came in noticed it too, all commenting that I seemed so happy today and those that I knew well, like Mr. Duncan and Mr. Stewart, were both pleased that Tyler and myself were finally seeing each other.

I wasn't overly surprised when Ashleigh walked through the door near lunchtime and sat down with Jess. But when she walked up and asked if there was anything she could help with

I was both surprised and suspicious. Being January, our trade was quite slack with only residents of the town coming in, and as most of our normal customers had come in already, I wasn't expecting any kind of rush. I told her I was fine and just to sit down and chat with Jess. I was going to join them after Tyler had come to get the lunches anyway, so between us, we could run the shop without an issue.

Hearing the door go, I looked up to see Richard walk in. I must admit I was slightly disappointed to see him. I had hoped that Tyler would be collecting the lunches for the guys today.

"Hi, Richard. Are you here for the lunches?"

"Hi, Maddie. Yes. Tyler got caught up in a meeting with a new client, so he couldn't make it. He did say he would try to pop in when he was done. Sorry, you have to put up with me again."

"I didn't mean anything by it. Please don't think I'm disappointed ..."

"It's okay. I understand. No need to apologise. I know you would rather see your boyfriend than me."

"He told you?"

"Well, I think it might have been Mace that let slip, not Tyler."

"I should have known he wouldn't let that go when he left here, shouldn't I?"

"Well, he did go into a little bit of detail, yes."

I could feel myself starting to blush again as both Richard and Jess started to laugh.

"Maddie, you of all people should know what Mason is like. He wouldn't let that display go uncommented on. Especially if it meant he could get a rise from one of the guys."

"I know. It's just I'm not used to him embarrassing me; it's usually everyone else."

I smiled over at her, and turned back to Richard, passing him the box of lunches and drinks.

"I put some cake in there for you all as well, but don't tell Jayden, or he will get very jealous."

"Oh, you know I'm going to do exactly that when I go back to London, don't you?"

"Yes, I know. And I won't hear the last of it. Did you want anything else?"

"No, that's it. Mace said he would settle up at the end of the week as usual. I'll see you tomorrow, no doubt."

"Okay. Have a good day, won't you?"

"What, putting up with your extremely happy boyfriend? Yeah, thanks. See you later, ladies."

Before I could even answer his comment, he had walked out the door and was heading back to the office. I was left there looking at the door astounded at what he just said. I looked over at Jess and Ashleigh who looked about as shocked as I did. Richard wasn't one to talk much, especially as he really didn't spend much time down here and didn't know us that well. When we first met him he seemed rather shy, almost as if he was trying to hide something. After spending nearly two weeks down here with Tyler and the guys, it seemed he was finally coming out of his shell. I guess he just needed to get to know us better before his real personality came out.

I decided just to have a quick tidy-up out the back seeing as the lunchtime rush was now over. Walking out there I made sure everything was away and I was just picking up the tray of mugs to put back out front when I heard the door go again.

Walking back out I was just about to put the tray down on the counter when I stopped dead in my tracks. My hands immediately went to my face in shock, letting go of the tray and sending it crashing to the floor. Tyler stood in front of me. He wasn't the person that caused my shock though. Standing next to him was a man I hadn't seen except for in photos, for over three years. My Dad. The tears were already pouring down my face as I was sobbing uncontrollably.

"Hey, baby girl."

I could feel my legs starting to give out on me, the pain going through my body at seeing him again. Before I hit the floor, Tyler was at my side holding me tight as my body trembled in sobs. I couldn't understand why he was suddenly here, not comprehending what was actually happening to me. Tyler just held me as activity happened all around me. Ashleigh was there picking up glass mugs around me, but all I could do was feel Tyler's strong arms around me as I stared at the man standing in front of me. A worried smile on his face.

"It's okay, sweetheart. It's going to be okay. I'm here for you. I'm never going to leave you or let you go."

I buried my head in Tyler's neck, unable to look at the man in front of me. I was a huge disappointment to him. I knew that. I couldn't understand why he was here, or even how he had found me. It was only then I could feel the anger in me starting to rise. Tyler must have contacted him, that had to be the reason. He promised me he would help me and always be there for me, and he had immediately betrayed me by contacting my Dad. I went to push him away, the rage in me building. I wanted to hit him, to make him realise what he had done. Tyler sensed my change in mood, and if realising exactly what I thought he started to speak to me. Not letting me go, he just calmly spoke.

"Sweetheart, I didn't contact your Dad, if that's what you're thinking. He turned up at the office today after hiring his own PI to find you. Please don't think I had anything to do with this, sweetheart. I wouldn't have contacted him without asking you first."

I pulled my head out from his shoulder and looked into his eyes. I could see the pain in them, and immediately knew he was telling me the truth.

"Tyler is telling the truth, Madds. Don't blame him. I found you with the help of a private investigator. I thought it was best if I went to meet Tyler first, rather than just turning up here at your workplace. Plus, if I'm honest, I wanted his support, both for myself and you."

I looked over at my Dad and loosened my grip on Tyler. He realised immediately what I was going to do as he let me go so I could run into the arms of my Dad. I missed him so much. He was there for me all the time after my Mum died, and even in later years when he was away with the Navy. I often stayed with friends or family, and he would always check in with me as much as he could. I was engulfed in the biggest hug as I crashed against him. I couldn't really be angry with either of these men. I loved them both, more than anything in the world, except Rosie of course. The tears were pouring down both our faces now. We must have looked like a mess between us. I could sense Tyler walking up behind me as he placed his hand on my shoulder.

"Why don't we go upstairs to your flat. You can talk then without worrying about being disturbed."

"But the shop?"

Ashleigh spoke up. "Why do you think I'm here, Maddie? Sorry, I was in on it as well. Brandon asked me to come down and look after the shop. I guess because he knew you and your Dad would need time to talk. I can lock everything up and give the keys to Tyler or pop them up when I'm done. Jess will be here a while as well. I'm sure between us we can cope. If you need me to look after the place for a couple of days so you can spend time with your Dad, just let me know."

I didn't know what to say. Everyone had been so understanding and supportive of this. I could cry again, but held it together enough just to nod in agreement and went out to grab my bag and give the keys to Ashleigh. Walking out with Tyler and my Dad was surreal. I couldn't quite believe that he was here walking next to me. We walked up the stairs to my flat, all the time I was worried about what my Dad would think about where I was living. It was nice enough, but it was nothing like the place we shared together for my entire life.

"Don't worry about the flat, baby girl. I'm not expecting a penthouse suite. I know it must be hard keeping a place on the money you have been earning, in fact, I'm extremely proud that you have managed this long on your own."

His words gave me some comfort and a renewed sense of pride. I had done this all on my own. I had gotten myself through university and kept a place of my own and a job, with only a small amount of help from Jess and Mason. They had wanted to help me a lot more, but I would never accept it. I wanted to be independent like Jess had been before she met Mason, and although she was now engaged to a millionaire, her attitude towards life had never changed. In fact, Mason was just as humble as she was, even if he could afford just about everything he wanted. Walking into my flat, I immediately went into the kitchen to make some drinks.

"I'll get the coffee made, sweetheart. You sit down with your Dad and talk."

"You're not leaving, are you?"

"I'll stay as long as you want me to. But, I think you and your Dad need to have some of your conversations without me. It can't be easy for him to speak with me around. There are probably a lot of things he wants to say, but doesn't want me to hear."

"Tyler ... I love you."

"I love you too, sweetheart. Now go in there with your Dad before he starts to wonder what we are up to here."

I gave Tyler a kiss on the cheek and headed into the front room where my Dad was sitting, waiting for me to come in.

"Where do you want me to start?"

"Why don't you tell me what you want to, and we can go from there. I can then tell you why I am here."

I wasn't sure how much I should tell my Dad. Should I tell him everything? How Rosie was conceived? What Thomas did to me? My mind was going around in circles when Tyler walked in, placing the coffees down and sat next to me. Pulling me into his side he finally spoke.

"Madds, I know it was difficult to tell us what happened, but don't you think your Dad also deserves to know? No matter what, I am always going to be here by your side."

I smiled up at him as he placed a kiss on my head. He held me next to him as I recalled my whole story, warts and all to my Dad. I could see the anger in his eyes, especially when I told him what Thomas had done to me and how he and Michelle had treated me after Rosie was born. Throughout it all though, he never once shouted at me. Never once raised his voice towards me. He just sat there and listened, while Tyler gave me the support I needed by holding me and running his hand down my arm. When I finally finished, I looked up at my Dad and saw the tears in his eyes.

"I know I am a big disappointment to you, Dad. You wouldn't have wanted me to end up like this, and I know abandoning my own daughter is inexcusable. But I couldn't see any other way. They wouldn't let me take Rosie with me, and if I stayed, I wasn't sure what he would do to either me or her. I'm sorry."

As the tears started to fall, my Dad immediately got up from the chair and knelt in front of me, taking both my hands in his.

"Madds, baby girl. Do you really think that is what I feel about you? That you are a disappointment? I couldn't be prouder of the beautiful woman you have become. You have given me an adorable granddaughter, who idolises me, if I do say so myself."

I couldn't help but chuckle at that. I could see him giving her everything she ever wanted, and it was completely obvious how much she loved him from the photos he sent.

"More than that, you have kept your life together despite everything you have been through. You have a job, and while it might not be what you wanted to do, it is clear you enjoy it. And from what I have heard from Tyler here, the locals love you. Plus, you got yourself through university, and I am sure that Mason and his guys could use the knowledge you have every once in a while. But more than that, I see a woman in front of me, with a man that worships the ground you walk on. You know he would do anything for you, don't you?"

I looked at my Dad and then over to Tyler. I knew my Dad was right. Tyler would do anything I wanted, and that included walking away from me if that was my wish. I could never wish for that though. I knew that as soon as Rosie met Tyler, she would love him and that he would love her too. My Dad got up from the floor and sat back down in front of me. I had so many questions I wanted to ask him, so much about Rosie I wanted to know. But the only question that came into my mind was, why? Why now?

"I hope you don't mind me asking, Dad? Why are you here? Why now after all these years?"

"I guess it's time I come clean, to both of you. I have been looking for you since I came home and found Thomas and Michelle looking after a baby. For a while, I thought it was Michelle's, even after they told me the truth. I needed to know that you were okay, that you were still alive, but I could never get a break in finding you, no matter how much time or money

I spent.

As I said in my last message to you at New Year, my relationship with Michelle has become very strained. Part of that is because of you, not knowing where you were, along with the fact that I blamed Michelle for letting you leave. I guess now I know the truth. I was right to blame her, although perhaps I should have been blaming Thomas more. I've had a feeling for a while that something was off in the house. Michelle was going out all the time until the early hours of the morning, always saying she was just seeing friends. I suspect that isn't the case. I'm sure you probably know more about that than me.

But that wasn't the real reason I was determined to find you. Thomas has also been acting strangely recently. Not long after I found out about Rosie, he came to me and suggested that we should have her adopted. That as you had abandoned her you didn't want her, and they were struggling to keep her. Thomas couldn't get a job because he was the one looking after her all the time."

I could feel the hurt and pain building in me again. The fact that Thomas wasn't bothered about his own daughter killed me inside. If this had been the case, then why wouldn't he let me take her when I left the house. He wouldn't have been lumbered with her all this time. I felt Tyler squeeze me, sensing the distress I was feeling. I looked up at my Dad, who had stopped speaking for the same reason.

"Go on," I encouraged my Dad to continue.

"I overheard a conversation Thomas was having on the phone the other day, luckily not long before the PI I had hired told me where you were living and who you had been seen with. He was discussing with someone about birth certificates, and that if there was no father listed on the certificate the mother would have to be present for it to take place. I wish I had realised then what he was actually meaning, that he was Rosie's father. I started to think about why he would need this information and it was only when he mentioned a sum of money that he could get if he could get the deal done that I started to worry. I think he is trying to sell Rosie."

"He's what!"

"I was going to confront him but decided the best course of action was to find you first. He couldn't do anything without your presence, and he had been asking me recently if I was any closer to finding you. I didn't want to worry you with this, but after meeting Tyler, Mason, and Brandon today, I know they will do everything they can to help."

Chapter Twenty-Three

Tyler

I could both feel and see Maddie was starting to lose it. I understood now why Brian had come to see me first. He knew Maddie far better than me and knew what her reaction would be. When Brian had explained what he thought Thomas was up to, I thought she was going to smash the entire flat up. I held her tight feeling the rage and pain inside her as she trembled in my arms. I didn't know what else to do. I wanted to take the pain away from her, wanted to make everything in her world right. I just didn't know how I could do that right now. All I could do was hold her as the tears fell and give her as much love and support as I could.

"Sweetheart, I wish I could take all the pain away and click my fingers and make everything right, but I can't. All I can do is promise you that I will be next to you every step of the way. We will get Rosie back to you and I will be part of both of your lives.

I felt slightly embarrassed saying this in front of Brian, but when I looked over towards him, all I saw was a man who had a look of pride on his face. I would recognise the look anywhere, as it was the same look my father gave to me the day I graduated in the army. I knew then he truly had accepted me for his daughter, and he would back me all the way when it came to us. My only concern now was how to keep Maddie from doing anything stupid. I had a sneaking suspicion that she would immediately head off to find Thomas and try to get Rosie back on her own. I guess that was why Brian had asked me to come along with him, thinking I would have more influence over her than he did. Unfortunately, I wasn't so sure that was the case, and I just had to hope that between us we could convince her.

I felt her sobs start to subside as I held her and she moved to pull away from me. Looking up into my eyes she smiled at me.

"I love you too, Tyler. I should have come to you sooner. I should have realised that keeping it to myself all this time was only hurting me more, that I should have realised that all of my friends would never blame me for what I did. I know that now and I am truly sorry."

"I know, sweetheart. As I said, that's in the past now. We just have to look forward. But I must ask you one thing. Please don't do anything stupid. Please let me and the guys deal with this. I don't want you trying to find Thomas and going to get Rosie by yourself. I don't trust him not to hurt either you or Rosie. And if what your Dad is saying is true, and he is thinking about selling Rosie, he will need you to be there. He will do whatever he can to get what he wants. Please promise me this, please."

"I promise, Tyler. If I never see Thomas again it will be too soon. Now, I think you should get back to work. I don't want to upset Mace before he helps me get Rosie back. I will be fine here with my Dad."

"Mace is fine with me taking the afternoon off. Richard has plenty to do, and I can carry on again tomorrow. It really isn't a problem."

I sat there for a moment studying her face. My guess was she wanted to spend some time alone with Brian but didn't want to hurt my feelings. I looked over at Brian who gently nodded his head to tell me they would be fine.

"Maddie, if you want to spend some time with your Dad, please just say so. I won't be upset or offended. I should've realised that you just wanted to catch up with him and shouldn't have intruded. I can head off back to the office."

"Tyler, it's not like that, I just ..."

"Sweetheart, honestly it's fine. I understand. How about I come back around this evening. We can spend an evening in front of the TV, watching a movie together, if you would like?"

"I would like that a lot. Thank you for understanding, Tyler."

"It's not a problem. I'll get us a takeaway on my way home. Would you like to join us, Brian?"

"No, I will let you spend some time together this evening. I'm staying at the B&B in town so I can grab something there. I will pop by and see you all tomorrow before I leave. And thank you again, Tyler for looking after my Madds. I know she is in good hands with you."

I walked over to Brian and shook his hand. It took everything in me not to salute him, with his rank and all.

"I'll do everything in my power to protect your daughter, and granddaughter, with my life if I have to. I'm just happy that you found us, and you are welcome down here anytime, especially when we get a house together."

"Don't get ahead of yourself, Tyler."

"Okay, I won't, sweetheart."

"I'll just see Tyler out, Dad."

Maddie walked out of the front room with me and to the door. Opening it, I turned before walking out. Bending down I placed a kiss on Maddie's lips.

"Is that all I get?"

"Later. Get back to your Dad, you have a lot to catch up on. I will see you later."

Before I decided to do anything else, I stepped out of the flat and headed back up to the office. I needed to get answers quickly before Maddie decided to take matters into her own hands.

I'd been back in the office for about thirty minutes when Mason called Richard and me into the conference room. I could only think that they had heard from the solicitor, regarding Thomas taking Rosie away. As we walked into the room, Mason beckoned us to sit down with him and Brandon, who was already there waiting for us.

"Thanks for coming in, both of you. As you have probably guessed we have heard from the solicitors regarding Thomas taking Rosie, and from what you and Brian have both mentioned, Tyler, it seems we are going to have to act fast. Although in the eyes of the law, things don't often work as fast as we would like them to.

Having not dealt with children and this kind of thing before, I wanted to make sure that we had everything covered here. The last thing we want to do is put Rosie in harm's way or do anything that would mean Thomas got full custody of her. So, Christian has come back to me and confirmed a few things that you would do in a normal breakup situation where children are involved. He knows this isn't a normal situation, but wanted to make us aware of the normal process.

Firstly, you would be expected to go to mediation to talk things through. He agrees with me that we are already past this point, especially as Thomas has been extremely violent towards Maddie. One thing to ask Maddie is if she has any evidence of what he did to her, pictures, etc., as this will help if things go to court. I know it is going to be difficult to ask that, but we can always use Jess and Ashleigh if need be."

I sat there listening to Mason. Part of me hoped that she didn't have any pictures of what he did, mainly because I wasn't sure how I would react when seeing them. Plus, if I ever did meet Thomas, I may actually be serving a prison sentence for what I would do to him. Looking up, I saw Brandon studying my face.

"I think it would be best if the girls asked. I'm not sure we want Tyler seeing any of those photos from the look on his face now. In fact, I'm not sure any of us want to see them. You have to remember, Tyler, we all know that Maddie is your girlfriend, but we all love her like a little sister and would do anything for her. That includes beating up the arsehole that is doing this to her."

I smiled and gave him a chin lift. I knew they loved her, and that was something I was going to have to get used to. The same as Mason and Brandon had to when it came to their women. We all loved Jess and Ashleigh and loved to rub it in their faces occasionally. I guess I had that to come.

"Anyway, getting back to the point of the meeting," Mason said, glancing between us, "the next course of action would be to apply to the courts for a 'prohibited steps order'. We're only likely to get a prohibited steps order if we can show that Thomas is trying to take Rosie away, for a reason that's not in her best interest."

"I would suggest selling her or giving her up for adoption without consulting Maddie isn't in Rosie's best interest."

"Both Christian and I agree on that, so I have already put everything in motion to go to the courts. We just need to get proof that was what Thomas was planning."

At this Richard spoke, "Didn't you say that Brian said he heard him speaking to someone?"

"Yes, but what proof is that?"

"Tyler, you really aren't thinking straight here, are you? We can hack into his phone. All we need is his number and we can read all his messages and everything that is on there."

"I will pretend I'm not hearing this, Richard. That is totally illegal and we as a company do not employ those tactics. Fucking brilliant, but definitely illegal," Mason replied with a smile and a wink of the eye.

"Okay, I definitely will not message Brian now and ask him for Thomas' phone number," I replied, despite having already started to send the message when Richard first suggested it.

"Glad you haven't done that because it means that I won't start looking into it as soon as the number doesn't come through."

I could see Brandon looking at us, thinking we had totally lost the plot. I had to admit, we did sound completely bonkers, talking like this. But we all knew what we were doing wasn't exactly legal, but then again, both myself and Richard had already bent the rules slightly with what we had done so far. This was just one step closer to jail time if we got found out.

"There is one thing worrying me though," Brandon spoke up.

"What's that?"

"If what we think is true, that Thomas is going to sell Rosie, we may not have enough time to go through the courts and stop him. What do we do then?"

"That is the other reason I brought you both in here. What I am about to say stays within this room. You know I am a stickler at following the rules and the law, but in this situation, I have a feeling we might have to work outside of the law and take matters into our own hands. We need to find out where Rosie is. If she is still at Brian's house, then that makes things easier. We can just get Brian to take Rosie out for the day and we can bring her back here to Maddie. As she is Rosie's Mum, we can then do things by the book and go down the court route.

However, if he has taken her away, as we suspect he has or is going to, then once we find out exactly where he is we need to come up with a plan to get her back. That will be difficult though as I am sure he will call the police. If it comes to that we may have to involve Maddie in going to get her. Before you say anything, Tyler, that is the last thing I want as well, but four guys turning up to snatch a child back, isn't going to look good unless we have the Mum with us for an explanation."

Much as I hated to hear it, I knew Mason was right. If we just went in there to grab Rosie, the police would arrest us all, and then Thomas would probably take Rosie somewhere we would never find her again.

"There is another possible outcome, one that is worrying me more. What if Maddie gets hold of Thomas? When Brian told her what he thought Thomas was up to, she lost it. I'm worried she is going to contact Thomas and go and get Rosie by herself. I'm guessing that Thomas could be very persuasive and tell her everything she wants to hear, just to get her down there to be able to get what he wants, and I'm guessing that is whatever figure of money he has agreed to sell Rosie for."

"We will have to cross that bridge if we come to it. I just hope you can persuade Maddie that this is not a course of action she should take. Anyway, this is all irrelevant at the moment as one, we don't actually know if Thomas is trying to sell Rosie, and two we have no idea where he is. Until we can find either of them out, it's business as usual. I still need you to go up to London on Thursday and Friday to get Richard totally set up there. If we get any leads you can work together up there. but let me remind you, say nothing to the rest of the guys for the moment. If I think they need to know I will tell Jayden."

Just as we were about to head out of the conference room, my phone alerted me to a new message. Looking down I saw a telephone number from Brian, Thomas' number to be precise. I looked up and saw Mason looking at me with a slightly tilted head as if asking me a question without saying any words. I just nodded my head slightly in confirmation.

"You know what to do, just be careful."

I nodded again and walked back to my office. I knew I didn't have long, but Richard and myself would work all night on this if we had to just to get the information we needed.

Chapter Twenty-Four

Madeleine

Spending the afternoon with my Dad was amazing. Much as I wanted Tyler to be with me, I needed to spend time with my Dad alone. There were things we both had to say to each other and Tyler being there would have made things difficult. I know that he would have been angry at some of the things I said, mainly because he cared about me so much. For years I had lived with the thought that my Dad would have been disappointed with me. But after plenty of tears and talking, we finally knew each other's feelings.

"Promise me when you go back home that you won't do anything stupid, Dad. Don't make Thomas suspicious of anything. Tyler promised me the guys will help me to get Rosie back, and I know they will."

"It will be difficult for me to keep quiet, Madds, knowing what he did to you. But I promise I will try to keep my temper. There is one promise I can definitely keep. After this, everything between Michelle and I will be over. I am pretty sure she has been unfaithful to me the entire time I have been away at sea. In fact, I'm positive she has been working as a prostitute all the time we've been together. When I look back at how I met her, it's pretty obvious now. I was just too blinded by lust to realise it back then. I'm just so sorry for everything I put you through. When we first got together, Michelle seemed to love and want to look after you. I can see now that was all a lie. The only thing I want at the end of this is an answer as to whether she knew what Thomas had done, and whether she was part of his plan to sell Rosie."

I smiled at my Dad, after everything that had gone on. After all the thoughts I had about him, I realised that I was wrong. Throughout all of this, the only person he had been thinking of was me. I thought for a long time that he was only worried about Michelle and he would turn his back on me because of her. That couldn't be further from the truth.

"Dad, you couldn't have known what was going to happen. I'm not going to forgive you, because there is nothing to forgive you for. Nothing that happened to me was down to you. It is all on Thomas, and Michelle for the way she treated me. Nothing you saw while you were at the house would have led you to believe what was going to happen."

"Madds, it's kind of you to say that, but ..."

"No buts, Dad. What is important now is me getting Rosie back and living my life together with her, and Tyler if he still wants that."

"Okay, baby girl, I won't mention it anymore. I will say this. Tyler is an amazing guy. I like him a lot. It's obvious to me how much he loves you and would do anything for you. The rest of the guys he works with as well seem to care about you so much. I'm so glad that you have this kind of family around you. I came here to try and convince you to come home with me, but after meeting Tyler and the rest of the guys, I immediately knew that wasn't an option. I can see how much you love it here, and how much you are loved. I would never ask you to leave what you have built here. In fact, I'm even considering moving closer when I retire from the Navy next year."

That was all I wanted to hear. My Dad loved Tyler and was happy for me to stay here. Having him move close by would only make things even better.

"I know how lucky I am to have Tyler. Any other man would have run a mile putting up with my mood swings and the times I tried to push him away. If they stayed up until that point, they wouldn't still be here now finding out the truth. Knowing that you like Tyler and are happy for me to be with him makes me happy. But knowing you would move away from somewhere you have called home all your life, just to be closer to me, completely fills me with joy. Thank you. Thank you for always being there for me and for understanding."

My Dad gave me a hug. He didn't need to say any more. Just knowing he was here, that he still cared and loved me was all I needed. His hug said more than any words ever could. I hadn't realised how long we had been sitting there talking until I heard a knock at the door and looked over to the clock.

"That must be Tyler. I didn't realise how late it was."

I got up from the settee and walked to the front door to find Tyler waiting outside, complete with dinner.

"Hi, sweetheart," he greeted me with a kiss on the cheek as he walked into the flat. Walking towards the kitchen, my Dad greeted him in the hallway.

"Hi, Tyler. Sorry, we didn't realise what the time was. It seemed to run away with us as we were talking. I'm just going so you don't need to worry."

"It's no worry, Brian. You know I am more than happy for you to join us. I have plenty of food here for all of us. I don't want to tear you away from Madds."

"Thanks for the offer, Tyler. But I think you need some time to talk as well. I will pop in and see both of you before I leave tomorrow. I want to get back home so I can let you know the state of play. We can work out where we go from there."

Walking over to my Dad, I gave him a hug. I was so happy to have him back in my life, and all I needed now was my daughter back and life would be fantastic now I had Tyler.

"I'll see you in the morning, baby girl. Thank you again for looking after her, Tyler," he said, holding out his hand to Tyler, who immediately took it. "I'll let myself out."

I watched as my Dad walked out of the flat and Tyler went into the kitchen to get our dinner served. Walking into the kitchen, Tyler had everything laid out with two plates ready. We both took what we wanted and headed back into the front room to eat. I had a small table and chairs in the kitchen, but we both preferred the comfort of the front room to eat.

"So how did things go with your Dad? You both seem happy. Well, except for the fact I can tell you've been crying."

"There were quite a few tears shed, yes. But, apart from that things went well. I hadn't realised quite how much I missed him until he was here. I'm sorry I thought you contacted him. It just seemed suspicious that the day after I told you he turned up out of the blue."

"I must admit that thought had crossed my mind as well. But I want you to realise that I will not make any decisions without speaking to you first. Which brings me to my next topic of conversation."

"Oh yeah, and what topic is that, Tyler?"

"The one about finding a house. I have been thinking about it a lot since last night, and I wanted to start looking for something as soon as we can. I want everything to be in place as soon as we can for when Rosie comes home."

"Tyler, I love that you are thinking about this, but I'm not sure what I can afford at the moment. I make a little money working at the coffee shop but with Rosie coming and the rent, I'm not sure how much ..."

"Sweetheart, I wasn't asking for you to pay. I was going to sort it all out for us. I meant what I said that I wanted to be a family with you and Rosie. That includes buying a house for us all to live in. Even if you decide it's not going to work between us, I want to know that I have given you a nice home for you and Rosie. Before you start, that is non-negotiable. I have more than enough money to help you out, and it's not charity, it's my gift to you. If things do work out between us, which I hope they do, then it will be our family home."

"Tyler, I don't know what to say. This is just too much."

"I said it's non-negotiable. Just say thank you." His smile as he said that filled my heart with warmth. I loved Tyler's smile. Most of the time it filled his face with mischief, but at times like this, all I could see was love and warmth.

"I love you, Tyler. Thank you, and yes you can start looking for houses. I'm sure anything you find will be good."

"Great, because I have a couple of houses in mind already. They are just outside the town, but still within reasonable walking distance. I knew you wouldn't want to be too far away from town."

I just smiled at Tyler. I knew there was no point in arguing with him about this. Once he had made his mind up, there was no turning back. I just had to hope that he wasn't spending his entire life savings on this place. Much as I loved him and wanted to spend the rest of my life with him, there was always that doubt in my mind that something would go wrong. It always did for me. We sat eating in relative silence, just passing the time in conversation every now and then.

After my conversation with my Dad, I still had so much going through my mind. I really didn't know what to do about the situation with Thomas. Part of me wanted to leave it in the hands of the guys, but I still had to face him and what he did to me. I couldn't let that go. I had to be brave and start to stand on my own two feet when it came to things like him. I couldn't allow others to do it for me. I had managed to survive two years of university and working by myself, so why couldn't I face my tormentor myself? I must have been lost in my own thoughts for a while, because Tyler had moved my plate and was now sitting beside me holding my hand, trying to get my attention.

I sat and looked at him blankly for a second, not registering what he was saying. It wasn't until I saw the look of worry in his eyes that I finally snapped out of my daze.

"Sorry, Tyler, I must have just got lost in my thoughts there for a second."

"I was starting to get worried, sweetheart. I have been trying to talk to you for the last five minutes. What's wrong?"

"Nothing really. I was just thinking, that's all."

"No secrets, remember? And that includes thoughts. What were you thinking about?"

"Not exactly what, but who. Thomas."

Instantly I felt Tyler stiffen next to me. I know how much he hated him, despite never meeting the guy, but this was a conversation that we needed to have. I needed to have.

"Tyler, I know you and the guys all want to help me get Rosie back, and it is probably the best course of action. But I feel as if I need to face him. I need to fight my own battle against him. I was thinking that perhaps I could give him a call and talk to him."

"Absolutely no fucking way, Madds! There is no way I want you talking to that guy, let alone confront him. Sweetheart, he already nearly put you in hospital. Please don't do anything stupid. If you really must speak to him to get over what happened to you, then let me be there with you. I just don't trust him not to hurt you again, or Rosie, come to mention it. I promise you we will get Rosie back, and you will have your say, but not without me there. Promise me that please, Madds."

"Tyler, I just …"

"Please, sweetheart."

The look of worry on Tyler's face as he begged me not to confront Thomas was too much. I couldn't say no to him.

"Okay, I promise not to speak to him without you around."

"Thank you, sweetheart. I will feel a lot better knowing that. Now let's clear this all up and spend the rest of the evening relaxing together."

I smiled and nodded at him, but there was still that thought in my mind. I needed to do this for myself. I needed to prove to myself that I could face him and was no longer scared of him. I would just call him, that's all. I wasn't stupid enough to face him without Tyler or someone else around, but I could tell him over the phone how I felt and prove to him and myself that I was no longer scared of him. I could always drop the call if it did get too much. All I had to do was convince my Dad to give me his number and then I would call him. I just had to keep Tyler happy and agree to what he asked. There was no reason for him to know that I would call Thomas. For now, I was going to enjoy an evening with my gorgeous boyfriend without worrying about anything.

"I know it's early, but let's just watch TV in bed shall we? Then if either of us falls asleep, we don't have to worry."

"Tyler, that sounds fantastic. Do you want to join me in the shower?

"That should be an offer that I can't refuse, but are you sure?"

I held out my hand to him and smiled. I was ready, I just had to prove it to him.

"Come on, I'm sure between us we can find a happy medium."

Starting to walk towards the bathroom, Tyler scooped me up into his arms.

"I'm sure we can, and have a lot of fun finding it."

Chapter Twenty-Five
Madeleine

W aking up before my alarm, I found myself in the arms of the man I loved. I still didn't know what it was about him that seemed to calm me so much. For two nights now I had been in Tyler's arms and never had one nightmare. That was almost unheard of in my world. I had spent the last three years waking up at least once sweating and breathing heavily because of that night and the months that followed. If there was ever a reason I knew this man lying next to me was right for me, that was the reason. He kept me safe and calm.

Guilt started to wash over me, knowing what I wanted to do. I knew Tyler would be mad if he found out that I was going to speak to Thomas. But I had to do it to find out if what my Dad thought he had planned was true, and if it was, I had to find some way to stop him. I felt Tyler stir next to me, and smile as he opened his eyes and they met mine.

"Now there is a beautiful sight to wake up to. Good morning, sweetheart," he said, placing a soft kiss against my lips.

We still hadn't had sex yet. He wasn't sure if I was ready for that quite yet. But the more time we spent together, the more adventurous we were. I had finally managed to get Tyler to allow me to pleasure him. It had been something I had done with other boyfriends in the past. Not that I had many. As soon as I freaked out when it came to having sex, they would run a mile. It was why I had learned to give a good blow job, just to keep them keen. I wanted to sleep with them, but knew I needed time, but none of them were happy to stick around, especially if they experienced one of my nightmares. The only one who had was Tyler. This amazing guy was lying next to me. Last night had been fun, and knowing that I could make him feel good just made me love him more. I just needed Tyler to realise that I was ready to sleep with him, or at least try. I couldn't guarantee that I wouldn't freak out slightly. But I knew that Tyler would be there with me, and would help me get through this. I guess that's why I felt so guilty about what I was going to try and do. Tyler was so caring and in some way I felt I was betraying the trust he put into me.

"Are you okay, sweetheart? You seem miles away there.," he said, pulling me from my thoughts.

"Mmm, I'm good. Was just thinking about last night."

"I think it should be me saying that. Especially how you made me feel," he returned with a huge smirk on his face and placed a kiss on my head as he pulled me close to his body.

Tyler wasn't as well built as Mason, Jayden or Brandon, and I wouldn't say he was the typical drop-dead gorgeous ex-military man like them. But to me, he was perfect. He was unconventionally handsome with his steel-grey eyes and facial hair. I had always been a sucker for a beard and moustache, especially when they were on Tyler. I had tried the clean-shaven guys, but there was something about feeling a beard brush against my skin that caused goosebumps to radiate across my body. Just like now as Tyler placed gentle kisses behind my ear and down towards the spot where my neck met my shoulders. I loved the feeling and couldn't stop the moan that left my lips.

"Now that's what I want to hear in the morning. My beautiful sweetheart, moaning next to me. Let's see how many more moans I can get from you before we get up this morning."

Much as I wanted to stay in bed and enjoy it, I knew that I had to get up and ready for the day ahead, whatever that may bring. That included speaking to my Dad before he went home.

"Much as I would love to spend more time with you in bed this morning, I need to get ready for work. I'm sure we can spend more time in bed together this evening."

"You really know how to put a dampener on the morning, don't you sweetheart?"

Smiling at him, I gave Tyler a quick kiss and jumped out the bed before he could grab me and pull me back. I knew that if I spent another minute in bed I would be late to get everything ready for the morning. Quickly going into my bathroom, I started the shower to get ready for the day.

<hr />

The morning had gone well so far, once I had managed to get Tyler off to the office. There was something about him this morning. I couldn't be certain, but I was sure he suspected what I was planning on doing. He seemed worried about me and was reluctant to leave me alone. I wasn't sure if that was because he had finally got me to admit my feelings towards him, or if he thought I was going to run off and find Thomas.

Although I wanted to speak to him, running off to find him was the last thing on my mind.

Mr. Duncan had already been in for his usual coffee and pastries and all my normal morning customers had come and gone. I was just about to start getting all the lunches ready when I heard the bell above the shop door go. Walking back out of the front, I couldn't stop the smile that spread across my face to see it was my Dad.

"Hey, Dad. Sit down and I will get you a coffee."

"You really don't have to, baby girl."

"I know, but I want to spend at least some time with you before you head home. I know you have a long journey ahead of you, so I won't keep you too long."

"Okay, just a quick one then. I want to say goodbye to Tyler and the rest of the guys before I leave."

I made my Dad a coffee, before going out back and quickly finishing the lunches, so I could sit down and speak to my Dad. I knew it being a Wednesday, there wouldn't be that many people in the shop today. It would only be one of the guys picking up their lunches, along with Mr. Duncan and Mr. Stewart. Walking back out, I grabbed my now cold latte, a normal occurrence for anyone running a shop, and sat down with my Dad.

"So when are you heading back down to Plymouth then?"

"As soon as I have said my goodbyes to you and Tyler. It's nearly a four-hour drive, so I don't want to leave too late. Hence why I am here so early."

"Dad, I'm sorry that I haven't answered any of your messages. I just didn't know what to say."

"Madds, it's okay. I do understand. Now I know what really happened, I can understand why you didn't. I won't tell you what Michelle and Thomas said about you, because I never believed a word of it. But I could understand that you would probably think I was disappointed in you. But that was far from the truth, I have always loved you and couldn't be happier that I am a granddad. So, we won't say any more about it, okay."

Smiling at my Dad, I couldn't be happier that he had accepted Rosie, especially knowing how she came into the world. That just made what I was about to ask him even more difficult.

"Dad, there is one thing I would like to ask you."

"Anything, baby girl."

"Can I have Thomas's phone number? I would like to speak to him. I never had it when I was at home."

I could see the hesitation in his face.

"I'm not sure that is a good idea, Madds. I know Tyler wouldn't be happy with me giving it to you. I also don't think it will help the situation."

"I'm not going to cause any trouble, Dad. I just need to face my past to be able to continue my future with Tyler. I have things I need to say to Thomas, so that he realises he hasn't got the hold over me he thinks he has. I need to prove to him that I can live a life with another man, despite him thinking otherwise."

"I really don't know, Madds."

"Please, Dad."

I know I sounded like a pouty little girl, but I really needed to speak to him.

"Just promise me you won't do anything stupid."

"I won't. And don't say anything to Tyler. He worries about me enough as it is. I don't want him to worry about something he doesn't need to."

"I won't say anything, unless you do something stupid."

"I won't."

Dad just finished putting the number into my phone, when the shop door opened and Tyler and Richard walked in. Walking straight over to me, with a big smile on his face, he placed a kiss on my cheek.

"I missed you, sweetheart. Sorry, Brian, but your daughter is far better looking than you."

"No problem, Tyler. I totally agree."

I could feel the heat rise up my face and knew I must be blushing like mad. The way all three men in the shop started to laugh I guessed that was the case. I decided that I needed to get out of the situation and went out of the back to get all the lunches for the guys. It wasn't long before Tyler had walked out back to see me.

"I'm sorry. I didn't mean to embarrass you like that."

Turning in his arms that he had now placed around me, I smiled up at him.

"It's okay. I know you didn't mean to. I guess I will just have to get used to it. Especially as I have been winding up the rest of the guys as they found their girlfriends. Are you coming round again tonight?"

"Definitely. I did want to speak to you first. I have to go up to London with Richard tomorrow until Friday night, so I wanted to spend as much time as possible with you tonight."

"Let's make it special then," I said, placing my arms around his neck and lifting up to place my lips on his. It didn't take more than a few seconds for our kiss to get heated only to be interrupted by a small cough and laugh from the entrance to the kitchen.

"Sorry to interrupt, but if we don't get back to the office soon Mace will send out a search party."

Tyler placed his forehead on mine and laughed.

"I guess we best get the coffees made so I can head back. We can continue this tonight," placing a quick kiss on my cheek and picking up the lunches for the guys.

Walking out front I quickly got the coffees ready for Richard and Tyler to take with them. Passing them over, Richard thanked me with a smile.

"I'll see you later, sweetheart."

I smiled and just nodded my head.

"Wait a sec, Tyler. I'm going to come along and say goodbye to Mason and Brandon, before I leave," my Dad said, then turning to me, he pulled me into a hug.

"I'll see you again soon, and don't do anything stupid, will you?"

Luckily, he spoke quietly enough that no one but us could hear it. I just gave him a squeeze as reassurance, regardless that I was dying inside. I was going to go against both my Dad and boyfriend. But I had to do this, I had to face Thomas at some point, and that was going to be today.

I waited until the lunch rush had finished. Wednesday afternoon was always extremely quiet. Most of the time I was working on my coursework, but now that my degree was finished, I would either spend my time deep cleaning the shop, getting stuff ready for the rest of the week or just sit and read. Today though, I had other plans. Today I was finally going to stand up for myself. I was going to call Thomas. I knew that I wouldn't get a visit from Jess or Ashleigh as they had gone out for the day with Joan, Mason and Jayden's Mum. This afternoon it was just going to be me, so there was no stopping me. So, why was I staring down at his number on my phone? I knew why. It was because of the hold he still had over me. The memories of that night no longer held me back in my life, but they still affected me.

I couldn't let him do this to me anymore. I had to call. Finally clicking the button, I waited for the call to connect. Part of me hoped that it would go straight to voicemail, but the other part of me just wanted to get this over. The ringing tone in my ear continued, bringing a sinking feeling inside. He wasn't going to answer. If it went to voicemail, did I leave a message? Did I want him to know it was me calling without speaking to me? I was just about to hang up when I heard his voice. It was hesitant, but it was definitely him.

"Hello?"

"Thomas?"

"Yes, who is this?"

"It's Maddie ... Madeleine."

Chapter Twenty-Six

Thomas

———— ❧ ————

"It's Maddie ... Madeleine."

I heard her voice speaking at the end of the phone, but still couldn't quite get my head around the fact that she was talking to me. How the hell had she got my number? I had never given it to her, and even if I had, why after all this time was she calling me? I should be grateful, since it was costing me a fucking fortune to try and find her. The only thing I could think of was Brian had finally found her and she had got my number somehow. But I wasn't sure why Brian would agree to that. I was sure he had started to suspect something. The older Rosie was getting the more you could see certain characteristics of mine in her. Madeleine must have thought that I had hung up on her when she spoke.

"Thomas, are you still there?"

"Yes, I'm still here. Just a little surprised to hear your voice. I thought I made it clear last time we saw each other that I never wanted to see or hear from you again. Didn't you get enough last time? Or are you just missing being fucked by a real man? I told you I would ruin it for you with any other man you met. Did I succeed?"

Yes, I was being a real dick, but I couldn't care less. I never liked Madeleine. Just needed to get laid that one night. What I hadn't expected was to become a father at the same time. Although, at the moment, that was a real asset. I just had to convince her to name me as the father on the birth certificate and then I could sell the brat.

"Whatever, Thomas. I didn't call to go on a trip down memory lane. We need to talk."

Wow, my timid little mouse had finally got a backbone. This could be an issue. I needed to control and dominate her again like I did that night. I'd break her again, and I knew exactly how. I'd take her back to that evening, then tell her what I could do to poor little Rosie.

"And what, pray tell, do we need to talk about?"

I knew what was coming. It was the reason why I was packed and ready to leave with Rosie. I wanted to get out of here before Brian got back. His trip had given me the perfect opportunity to leave with Rosie. My Mum knew what I was trying to do. She got bored with Brian very quickly, and realised that he wasn't going to give her the life she wanted. That was why she was out all night shagging whatever bloke she could. That and because she wanted the income it gave her. She wanted out and so was onboard with my plan. Hell, she was more than onboard, she was practically begging me to get the deal done, even to the point she was willing to pose as Rosie's Mum just to do it. That wouldn't be necessary now. Not now that I had Madeleine on the phone.

"We need to talk about Rosie. I want her back. She is my daughter after all."

"Our daughter, Madeleine. Don't you forget that. I have just as much right to look after her as you do."

"That would be true if you would admit to everyone that she is your daughter."

"Besides the point, Madeleine. But that isn't why you are calling, is it? You never answered my question. You haven't found a guy to satisfy you as much as I did that night, have you? You've never felt the way you did when I was fucking you hard that evening."

I needed her to remember, needed her to feel the pain and fear that I had given her that evening. That fear was going to get me exactly what I needed. Her, with me, so I could sell Rosie to the buyers I had lined up.

"Fuck you, Thomas. Yes, I have found a guy who makes me feel a hundred times better than you did, and that's without having sex. Not that it is any of your fucking business. Now, I want Rosie back and I am going to do everything I can to get her back."

This was an interesting turn of events. She had found a guy. This could be both an advantage and a complication. But the fact she was willing to do anything to get Rosie back, could play directly into my plans. I just needed to convince her to meet with me down in Canterbury. Once I had her with me, then I could tell her the truth.

"Well, what if I said I didn't want to give Rosie up? That I had fallen in love with the little girl and had decided to raise her myself? I'm sorry, Madeleine, but it's not as easy as you thought. However, I do have one solution."

I stopped speaking, waiting to see what her reaction would be. Up until that point I thought she would be screaming down the phone at me. It had seemed that little Madds had grown up and grown some teeth. But I suspected under all the bravado, the timid, frightened little girl was still there. The longer the silence went on, the longer I knew that was the case. Finally, she spoke.

"What solution?"

Perfect, she was falling into the trap I had set.

"If you want to see Rosie again, then you need to come live with me. That's the deal. It's me and Rosie, or I will make it extremely difficult for you to ever see her again."

When I heard her gasp at the end of the phone, I knew I had her, the insecure Madeleine that I'd pleasured myself on all those years ago.

"Thomas, you don't want me or Rosie. You just want to hurt and manipulate me. I'm happy here, at least as happy as I can be without my daughter. I've built a good life for myself. I have friends here and a guy that loves me. You can't expect me to give all that up to live a lie with you. You know you'll get bored with me in a couple of weeks and where would I be then?"

I had to convince her somehow.

"People change, Madeleine. You of all people should know that. Doesn't Rosie deserve to have her Mum and Dad around her?"

It almost made me sick to say those words. I didn't want Madeleine. I didn't want Rosie either. But if it got me the fifty grand I was promised then I would sell my own mother.

"I need to think about this."

"Well don't think about it too long. I am taking Rosie on a trip to see some of my family. I will be in Canterbury tomorrow. You have twenty-four hours to make a decision and meet me there. If you decide you will meet me, send me a message to let me know you are on your way and I will arrange a meeting place. Twenty-four hours, Madeleine."

I hung the phone up before she could argue with me or give me an answer. I sat there for a moment running through the past twenty minutes in my head. Had I done enough to convince her? I was sure I had. She had to say she would come down. There was no way she would leave Rosie in my hands. She would message me and come down to Canterbury. Then I could get my name placed on the birth certificate and get rid of the brat. By the end of Monday, I would be fifty grand richer, and on my way to living the life I wanted abroad.

Shame I hadn't told my mother this. There was no way she was getting a penny of the money. She may have thought I was working with her, but she was nothing but a prostitute, and I wanted nothing more to do with her. I had a little surprise for her though. Well actually, Brian. I had plenty of photos with her and numerous men in the throes of passion. As soon as I was on my way out of the country they would be delivered to Brian. I would destroy both of them for everything they had done to me.

Looking at the time, I saw it was nearly two o'clock. Time to get moving as it was nearly a seven hour drive down to Canterbury. Grabbing our cases, I went and put them in the car. Heading back in, I went to get Rosie and found her sitting with my Mum.

"I thought you were going out."

"I was, but Brian has called to say he is on his way home. He should be here around four."

"I better make a move then. Oh, and by the way, I've just had a very interesting conversation. With Madeleine."

"When did she call you?"

"About twenty minutes ago. I'm guessing Brian has finally found her, and she managed to get my number from him. I've given her twenty-four hours to agree and get to Canterbury. I'm sure she will turn up. Once she does, we will be able to put the plan in action without a hitch."

I could see my Mum looking at me worried. I knew she wasn't sure whether this would work.

"Well if she doesn't, I'm still happy to pose as her to get the deal done. Just let me know what's going on. I can be there in a day. I need to get out of here Thomas. Brian suspects something, I know it."

He would more than suspect when I was finished. But for the moment I may still need her. Prostitute or not, she was still my mother, and could be useful.

"It will be fine, Mum. By Monday evening, I will have the money, either way, and we can be out of the country by Tuesday. I'll message you."

"Be sure you do."

"Come on, Rosie. Want to go on a trip?"

I picked Rosie up and put her in a light coat. Even I knew not to put a child in a big coat in the car. Picking up her winter all-in-one suit, I headed out of the door and put her in the car seat behind the passenger seat. As I drove off, I nearly shouted 'yes'. This was it. This was the point I could finally say I was going to get out of here and away from my mother.

There was no way Madeleine wouldn't come down to Canterbury, and when she contacted me I would make sure she didn't tell anyone where she was going. I didn't want her new boyfriend to turn up and make things difficult. Then I would have her to myself for the whole weekend. I hadn't been with anyone for a while, so was keen to get laid, and Madeleine was just the woman I wanted to do it with. Hearing her scream again was already playing on my mind, and I had a whole two days to do with her as I pleased before Monday.

By then she would be so scared and downtrodden that she would do anything I said. I would make sure of that. Then after I got rid of the brat and got my money, I would dump her back at the train station and head down to the Channel Tunnel. Then over to France and Europe would be my oyster. I hadn't decided where yet, but I was sure it wouldn't take long for me to decide.

Chapter Twenty-Seven

Tyler

E ven as I left the coffee shop with Richard and Brian, I was still worried about Maddie. I should be so happy that I finally had the woman that I loved, but she seemed a little distant, almost worried about something. I couldn't put my finger on exactly what it was, but I knew there was one way to find out. Walking up towards the office, I decided to ask Brian.

"Brian, did Madds seem okay when you spoke to her this morning? It might just be me, but she seemed lost in her thoughts, possibly worrying about something."

I glanced over at Brian as I spoke. There was no change in his demeanour, but I noticed his brows frown as I asked. He knew something, but I was sure he wasn't going to say anything.

"She's probably just worried about Thomas trying to sell Rosie.

I'm sure she will be fine. She didn't say anything to worry me when I spoke to her, anyway."

"You're probably right. I just worry about her. She was talking last night about contacting Thomas. I just don't want her to do anything stupid. Forget it, I'm just being an overprotective boyfriend I guess."

Again the frown of the eyebrows. He definitely knew something. I just had to hope that my talk with Maddie last night was enough. Walking into the office we were greeted by Mason and Brandon. Richard must have messaged ahead to let him know that Brian was coming with us.

"Brian, good to see you again. Are you heading back home?"

"You too, Mason. Yes, I'm going back to Plymouth now. I want to keep an eye on Thomas and see my gorgeous granddaughter as well. Hopefully nothing has happened while I have been away."

"Well, we have plenty of leads if he does, and I believe Richard and Tyler here have gained some very interesting info from his phone."

"I cannot thank you all enough for how you have looked after my daughter these past two years. Especially you, Tyler. I know I am leaving her in good hands here."

I didn't have to say a word when I looked over at Brian. His face said it all. I just gave him a curt nod to let him know my feelings towards what he had just said. Both of us being in the military made it easy to have a conversation with meaning and not say any words.

"Well, I guess I better be making a move. I just wanted to say goodbye and thank you to you all. Hopefully when this is all over I can come back down and meet you all."

"That would be great, Brian. I often have BBQs at my house

when everyone is down. Sometimes we have a couple of our friends from the met police as well. You would always be welcome."

"I look forward to it, Mason. Let me know if you need any more help and I will let you know if anything changes."

"Will do."

We all said our goodbyes and Brian left to head back home to Plymouth. I could see Brandon looking at me. He knew something was bothering me. Richard had noticed it too.

"Do we need to talk?"

"I think we do, Brandon. All of us."

"Okay, looks like a working lunch in the boardroom then," Mason replied, picking up our lunches and heading into the room. We all followed him and sat down to eat and work.

"So, what's the problem, Tyler?"

"Maddie is up to something, and I don't know what. I think she is going to do something stupid."

"Like what?"

"I think she is going to contact Thomas. She spoke to me about it last night. Said that she felt she had to face him, to get over her fears. I asked her not to, but this morning she seemed really distant. I'm sure she was worrying about something. When I asked Brian about it, although his demeanour didn't change, I saw him starting to frown. I think he may have given her Thomas' phone number."

"Shit, Tyler. You don't think she would call him, do you?"

"That's exactly what I think. If he has as great a hold over her as I think he has. He may convince her to meet up with him. God knows what he will do then."

"I guess we have to hope that he doesn't have that kind of hold then. Or, we just have to ramp up the investigation. What do we have so far, Richard?"

"Well, we have all the text conversations from his phone. The problem is, although they are pretty damning evidence, we can't use them. We would have to get the police to gain the information for us to be able to do that. I also have alerts set up for every road from Plymouth to let us know if his car drives down there."

"So, if he makes a move, we will know about it."

"Yes."

"Good. Do you think it is a good idea to head to London, tomorrow? Or do you want to stay down here and go next week?"

"Mace, we can't put the business on hold, just because something may happen. I'm only a couple of hours away should I need to get back. Richard needs to get set up in London. You know Jayden is already pissed he has spent this much time down here. He needs him up there to help him out."

"Well, if you are sure."

"I'm sure, Mace. Now I'm going to go and get some work done as I want to spend the night with Maddie before I'm away for two days."

I could hear the guys all laughing as I left the room. I knew they didn't mean anything by it. They knew exactly how I was feeling at the moment. I'm sure that would change over time, and being apart for a couple of days would keep us both sane. But for now, I didn't want to spend any time away from my sweetheart. Especially now that I had finally got her. Plus, I had a feeling from our earlier conversation that tonight was going to be special. If that was the case, then I wanted to make sure that this was a night Maddie wanted to remember, a night to remove all thoughts and memories of her only night with Thomas.

———————— ❦ ————————

It was just after five when I headed up to see Maddie. I wasn't sure if she would still be in the shop or had locked up for the day. Being January, I knew trade was quite sparse, so Maddie quite often locked up around four and headed home. Stepping up to the door I saw Maddie cleaning the counters, so headed inside.

"Hey, sweetheart. You're working late tonight."

"I had the book club ladies in. They've decided to come here once a month to enjoy the cakes that we have. Plus, it means they get to have lattes all afternoon instead of instant coffee. Also gives a nice profit for Jess once a month."

"Also gives you a chance to talk about all those filthy books you've started to read?" I said it more as a question than a reply.

"Since when have you been reading my books on my kindle, Tyler?"

"Ah, so you don't deny it then."

I saw the blush rise up on her cheeks and couldn't help but walk over to her and place my hand over it.

"You look so cute when you do that. Sorry I shouldn't tease you, should I? Come on, are you finished for the day?"

She just nodded her response.

"Let's get out of here then."

I picked up the keys from where they were hanging and locked the shop door, turning the open sign to closed, as I walked back out to the kitchen where Maddie had gone. I noticed a dish wrapped in foil on the countertop and looked over at Maddie with raised eyebrows as she turned to see me walk in.

"I made us a quiche. I thought I could warm it up in the oven and we could have it with some chips and salad for dinner tonight. I can't let you keep buying dinner for us. Especially if you are going to be buying a house. We need to save some money and I can cook."

I smiled at how thoughtful she was. She had no idea that me buying a house wouldn't put much of a dent in the money I had in my account. I was a computer geek for Christ's sake. I had made thousands on the crypto currency markets. Okay, I didn't have as much as Mason and Jayden, but me and the other guys in the firm had made quite a killing on the markets. I had to be good for something and the rest of the team were quite happy with what I had made them.

"We can survive, sweetheart. Even if I do buy dinner every night. But thank you for worrying about me and my financial situation. Believe me though, you don't have to."

We headed out of the shop, locking everything behind us and went upstairs to her flat. I couldn't wait to get her out of here. Despite knowing who owned it. She didn't realise that a short while after Mason had met Jess the flat was going to be put on the market. Mason had found out and bought it. He wanted to make sure that Maddie had a place to live, but he was using the same letting agent, so Maddie was none the wiser. Except for the fact that he had lowered the rent, much to the agent's surprise. It was a nice flat, and Maddie had done everything she could to make it a home. But I wanted more for her and little Rosie. I wanted her to have a proper home, with or without me. I knew Mason didn't mind. He would probably keep it empty when Maddie moved out and use it as a base if one of the guys came down from London. Plus, as the business was growing, we could end up having more guys working for us who may need a place to stay.

The only thing that mattered now though, was spending the evening with the wonderful lady at my side. Try as I might, I still couldn't believe how lucky I was to have her. I was going to make sure she knew that every day of her life.

"I'll get some chips going and then we can sit down and relax. There is a beer in the fridge if you want it, or some wine. Can you pour me a glass as well, please?"

I knew Maddie drank occasionally, but not normally when she had work the next day. Not unless there was something that was worrying her. I had a feeling I knew what that reason was this evening, and it was the one thing I didn't want her to worry about. Walking over, I placed my arms around her after she had finished at the oven. She turned in my arms and looked up at me with a smile that didn't quite meet her eyes.

"Sweetheart, I don't want you to drink because you are worried about what is going to happen tonight. I would rather just hold off until you are ready. I love you and us not having sex isn't going to change that."

I leaned down and gave her a soft kiss on the lips. I needed her to realise that sex for me was not the be all and end all of our relationship. Yes, I wanted it to happen, but not if it was going to cause Maddie such distress.

"I know you love me, and you don't care whether we have sex or not. But I do. I want to have that physical relationship with you. I guess I'm just feeling a little nervous."

"We will take it one step at a time, sweetheart, and then only if you are comfortable. But I will not do anything if you get drunk. I need you to be totally in control of yourself and the situation. Okay?"

"Okay?"

Placing another kiss on the lips, I pulled her into a hug.

"I'm going to grab a quick shower if that is okay. If you want to grab one after me, I can keep an eye on dinner."

"That would be great, thank you."

After we had both showered and enjoyed the meal Maddie had prepared we sat on the settee together. I held Maddie close to me as I brushed her arm with my hand. I could feel she was tense and worried about what was going to happen tonight. Or what she thought was going to happen. That was why we were just sitting here, with the TV on. I didn't want to rush into this. We had two beautiful nights together and I didn't want to lose that. I wanted this to happen naturally. I felt Maddie shift in my arms and looked down to see her eyes looking into mine. Slowly I leaned down and placed my lips on hers. Our kiss deepened and I could feel the want in her. I knew she thought she was ready for this, but I wasn't so sure. I had to take things slowly. I needed to make this as good for her as possible, help her to have something good to remember from having sex. Her hands snaked up my body and rested behind my head, pulling me closer as our kiss continued. Pulling away I spoke.

"Sweetheart, remember we don't have to do this. I don't want to do anything that could hurt you."

"I want this, Tyler. I wish you could have been my first, but that ship has sailed. But I want you to be the first man to make me feel good. Please take me to bed."

I still wasn't sure that she was ready. I loved her more than any woman I had ever been with, not that there had been many. But none of them had meant as much as the woman in my arms now. Switching off the TV, I carefully got up from the settee and held my hand out to Maddie. As she took it, I pulled her up from her seated position and led her into the bedroom. We had been here for the past two nights, and I had made her feel things she hadn't felt before. But tonight would be different. Tonight, would be the first time I made love to the woman I was going to spend the rest of my life with.

"I want you to tell me if I hurt you, or you need me to stop, sweetheart. If it doesn't happen tonight, then we can try again another time. I don't want this to be a traumatic experience for you. I want you to be able to enjoy it."

"I want this, Tyler. I want you. But I will say if I need you to stop, okay?"

I didn't answer her with words. Gently, I pulled the top she was wearing over her head bearing her beautiful breasts to the coldness of the room. Guiding my hands down her body, I pulled down the shorts she was wearing, until she stood in front of me in all her glorious nakedness. Being naked together was not an issue. We had already done that. It was just the next step that was the worry.

Smiling, Maddie got onto the bed as I took off the sweatpants I was wearing and got onto the bed next to her. I knew I couldn't just take her. I needed her to be relaxed and in the moment before that happened. Taking a nipple into my mouth, I gently caressed her other breast with my hand. Pinching and rolling her nipple between my fingers. Hearing Maddie moaning in pleasure was now by far one of my favourite things to listen to. I could feel my cock already getting hard from the noise. Gently I grazed the fingers of my free hand down her body and rested them just above her mound. I wanted to use my fingers first to bring her to a climax.

Slowly I circled her clit, eliciting a moan from her lips. Deciding to take it a step further I glided my finger down into her wetness. She was so wet for me, and I need her to realise that. Placing kisses up her jaw and between her shoulder and next, I leaned up and whispered into her ear.

"You're so wet, sweetheart. Is that all for me?"

"Yes, Tyler, please, I'm so close."

I knew I had to distract her slightly before I entered her with my finger. I needed to keep her talking.

"What do you need, sweetheart? What do you want me to do?"

"Anything, everything, Tyler. I want you inside me."

I could hear her breathing speeding up, I knew she was close to coming just with the gentle circling I was doing around her clit. Gently I pushed my finger inside her and stroked the spot that I knew would drive her wild. I could feel her trembling underneath me, her skin glowing with a sheen of sweat. She took a sharp intake of breath as my finger entered her and for a moment, I thought she was going to ask me to stop. But then I could feel her hips starting to move, riding my finger.

"More, Tyler. Please, I need more."

Carefully, I placed a second finger into her and only a few seconds later, I felt her clamping down on me and her face full of ecstasy as she came undone in my arms. I don't think I had ever seen anything more beautiful than that. But the best was yet to come.

Chapter Twenty-Eight

Madeleine

F eeling Tyler's second finger enter my core was all I needed to push me over the edge. This was by far the best orgasm I had ever had in my life. Feeling the waves throughout my body I couldn't help but say his name.
"Tyler, oh God, yes."

My body was pulsating in waves of pleasure, and it took a few moments before I registered that I needed to breathe. My skin felt so sensitive as Tyler placed gentle kisses up my body and then pulled me into his arms placing a soft kiss on the top of my head.

"You're so beautiful when you come, sweetheart."

I felt safe in Tyler's arms. I felt I could conquer anything and there was just one last thing I needed to do.

"Tyler."

"Yes, sweetheart."

"Please make love to me."

"Madds, I'm not sure …"

I wasn't going to allow him to continue. I needed this. I needed him to be with me on this. I loved him so much and knew I could do this. Turning slightly in his arms I looked into his steel blue eyes.

"Tyler, what we just did was amazing. You are the first man that I have allowed to do anything like that to me. I want to go to the next step with you. I love you, Tyler, and I want this with you."

I could see there was still some hesitation in his eyes. I needed him to realise how serious I was about this. Placing my lips on his, I started to kiss him, pouring as much as I could into it.

"Madds, please. I'm holding on by a thread here."

"I don't want you to hold back, Tyler. I want you. Please, Tyler."

Immediately he pulled away from me and I missed the warmth of his body next to mine. I was about to plead with him again when he reached down and pulled out the foil packet he had placed in his pocket. Laying back down next to me, he gently pushed me down onto my back.

"Madds, are you really sure about this, sweetheart?"

"I have never been more certain."

Lifting slightly, I took the packet from his hand and ripped it open. Taking his cock into my hand, I gently ran my fingers up and down. Seeing Tyler's reaction to my touch was a wonderful thing to see. I had waited nearly three years for this moment and could feel my nerves starting to kick in as I unravelled the condom over his hard length. I wasn't sure if I could do this, but I had to try. I knew Tyler would never hurt me, but the fear was still there. As if sensing my uncertainty, Tyler placed soft kisses in the crook of my neck.

"Remember, sweetheart, it's just me and you. If you need me to stop, just say. I want you to remember this night. Are you ready?"

I nodded my head, unable to say anything. Carefully he moved over me and rested in between my legs, pushing them slightly apart. I could feel my heart beating in my chest, partly from the fear of what Thomas had done to me, and partly in anticipation of what was to come. I felt Tyler gently run the head of his cock through my folds, coating it in my juices. Slowly he pressed into me, slowly and deliberately entering my body. I held my breath, waiting for the pain to come, the pain I remembered from my first time. But there was no pain, just a growing sensation of pleasure within me.

"I need you to breathe, sweetheart. Just breathe and feel everything I'm about to do to you."

I relaxed and allowed the breaths to come as Tyler slowly and completely filled me. It felt amazing and for a moment I wanted us to just stay in this moment forever. But I needed him to move. Needed him to make me feel alive like he had with his fingers and tongue. Tyler must have read my thoughts as he slowly pulled out from me and then back in. His strokes caused electricity to build within me. With every stroke, Tyler placed kisses over my body, whispering words of encouragement as I felt my orgasm start to build.

This was a moment unlike any I had ever had. I had been with guys before Tyler who had brought me some pleasure, but nothing compared to this. Nothing, to the man that I loved with all my heart making love to me. I knew Tyler was taking it slowly and being as gentle as he could. Part of me wanted him to just let go, but with the way he was making me feel I had no reason to complain.

I could feel my orgasm teetering on the edge, and Tyler must have as well as he increased his pace slightly.

"Come for me, sweetheart. Come undone for me."

It was all I needed to allow my orgasm to crash over me. I could feel myself pulsing on Tyler's cock as he chased his own orgasm, increasing his pace. He was breaking, now fucking me, but not as hard as I knew he probably could. I could tell the exact moment when Tyler came, the point when his erratic movements pushed him over as he moaned my name. I felt him twitch inside of me as he released.

Nearly collapsing on me, he managed to twist us both onto our sides without pulling out of me. He just held me close to him. It was only then that the enormity of what we had just done hit me and my emotions flooded to the surface as the tears started to fall. They weren't tears of pain, but tears of joy.

"Sweetheart, please don't cry. I'm sorry if I hurt you. I lost control. Please don't be upset."

"I'm not upset, Tyler. That was amazing, thank you. Thank you. Thank you."

I kept placing kisses on his lips as the tears were falling down my face.

"I need to take care of this. Stay right there."

Gently pulling out of me, Tyler went to the bathroom to take care of the condom. Then he was back by my side, pulling my body into his and covering us both.

"Thank you, sweetheart. Thank you for allowing me to have this moment with you. Believe me, it's one I will never forget. For now, though, you need your sleep."

Unable to argue with him, my body spent from our

lovemaking. I nestled into him and closed my eyes. Falling asleep in the arms of the man I loved.

Last night had been beyond my wildest dreams. Waking up in the arms of the man who loved me and took care of me was something I had wanted all my life. I never thought after what Thomas had done to me, I would ever have an experience like it. The problem was that it just made what I was going to do today even worse. I had contacted Ashleigh and asked her if she could mind the shop for the day. She had asked a few questions, but I just said that I had something I wanted to do for Tyler for the weekend and needed to get some bits together.

I knew Jess would be in the shop today as she would want all the gossip of what had happened between me and Tyler, along with wanting to find out how things went with my Dad. Waiting for Ashleigh to arrive, I picked up my phone and messaged Thomas.

"Heading to Canterbury today. Will be there around six tonight. Where do you want to meet? I have a place to stay for tonight but have to be out by 10:00 tomorrow morning."

I only had to wait a few minutes before I received his reply.

"Meet me in Dane John Gardens by the bandstand, tomorrow at 12:30. Make sure you don't tell anyone where you are going or you will never see me or Rosie again."

A feeling of dread came over me. I didn't want to spend the rest of my life with him, and something deep inside me told me that neither did Thomas. Everything screamed of a trap, but I had to go. I had to stop him from selling Rosie or even just giving her away. I knew I was risking my relationship with Tyler. There was a chance he would never forgive me. But I needed to get my daughter back and I wasn't sure that Tyler and the rest of the guys would be able to stop him in time. In my mind this was the only way.

When I heard the bell over the shop door ring, I looked up to see Ashleigh walk through the door.

"Hi, Maddie. How are you? I must say you look amazing. I take it things are good between you and Tyler?"

"Things are more than good. Last night was one of the best nights of my life. We finally slept together. I finally managed to put the past behind me and can now look forward."

"I'm so happy for you both, you especially. I understand how much this has taken over your life."

I knew she meant every word she said. I hated that I was lying again to everyone, but I had to think of my daughter.

"Are you okay to look after things here for a moment? I just need to get a few bits from upstairs and then I can come back down and we can have a chat."

"Not a problem. You know I will always help out when I can. Go on, get what you need to get done and then you can fill me in with all the juicy gossip."

Laughing I headed out the back to go and pack a bag for my trip. I hadn't had a chance to do it the day before due to the extra customers I'd had towards the end of the day. Grabbing a small suitcase, I filled it with enough clothes for a few days. I could always buy some more stuff if I needed it while I was down there. Before I left there was one last thing I had to do. I had to apologise to both Jess and Tyler. But I couldn't do it in person or by phone. Both of them would try and stop me, and this could be my only chance to get Rosie back. I couldn't afford to wait for the guys to find Thomas and risk the chance of him leaving with her.

Sitting at my table, I started to write.

My Dearest Jess,

I'm sorry to leave you like this, but I must. I love you all like my own family, but I cannot risk losing Rosie forever.

I have been given twenty-four hours to make this decision and it is one I have to make to have my daughter in my life. I know you will understand now that you have Callum in yours.

I hope that you can forgive me and that when this is over we can still be friends. If everything goes to plan, I will return with Rosie and I hope that my job will still be there for me. If it doesn't, then this is goodbye.

Please look after Tyler and give him the letter I have written. Try to convince him to continue his life without me should I not return, and tell him how much I love him.

Love you always,

Maddie

Hard as that was to write, I knew it would be nothing compared to what I needed to say to Tyler. How would he ever forgive me for what I was about to do? I had made promises to both him and my Dad, and here I was about to break every single one. Placing the letter to Jess in an envelope, I sealed it and began to write everything I needed to say to the only man besides my dad I loved in my life. The tears were pouring down my face as I wrote. I tried to tell him how much I loved him, but Rosie would always come first in my life. I was a hypocrite if the truth be known. How could I say that when at the first sign of trouble I left my daughter with the one man that had caused all of my pain and anguish.

Signing off the letter, I placed it in an envelope and addressed it to him. I needed to get back down to the shop to say my goodbyes to Ashleigh. I just had to pray that Jess wasn't already there and would try and convince me to stay. I only had thirty minutes now before my train left for London. Then I needed to get across London to get my train down to Canterbury. Grabbing my case I locked up my flat and headed down to the shop. Walking through the back, I was pleased to see that the shop was empty and only Ashleigh was there.

"Did you get everything done, Maddie?"

"Yes I did. ... Ashleigh, I need to do something and I don't want you to ask me any questions. Please don't say a word, just give this letter to Jess. It will explain everything. Also, I need you to give this to Tyler."

"Maddie, what are you doing?"

"Please, Ashleigh. Don't ask any questions. Just promise me you will do this one thing for me and give Jess and Tyler those letters."

"Maddie, we want to help you. We can help you. Please don't do anything stupid."

"I need to do this Ashleigh. If I don't, it will break me. Just promise me you will be there for Tyler and help him get over this. I love you all, but I have to go. I need to be on a train. I hope one day you will all forgive me."

I couldn't stand and argue any more. I needed to get to the train station, and I was about to break. Quickly I grabbed my case and headed out of the door. I knew it wouldn't be long before one of the guys would try and catch me up and stop me from leaving. I had to get on the train before they could get to me.

Walking up the road towards the station, I could feel my heart starting to break. I had made a life here from nothing. I made friends, no I had gained a family and I was walking away from it again. Just like I had to Rosie two years ago. I didn't deserve any of this. Didn't deserve my daughter or these people in my life. Perhaps I should just leave and start afresh and forget them all, but I couldn't. I had to at least try to get my daughter back.

Getting to the station with just a few minutes to spare, I waited for the train to arrive. All the time, worried that Mason or Brandon would arrive and try to talk me out of it. I was relieved when the train arrived and they weren't anywhere in sight. Finding a seat, I sat down and allowed the tears to fall. Pulling away from Kings View, I hoped that one day I could come back. But whether I would ever be forgiven was yet to be seen.

Chapter Twenty-Nine

Tyler

⸻ ❦ ⸻

Richard and I had arrived in London mid-morning and I was going to be staying with him in Jayden's old flat. We probably would have got here sooner, but I didn't want to leave Maddie behind. Last night was amazing. I couldn't have asked for a better night. In the grand scheme of things, it wasn't the best sex I had ever had, but that didn't matter. The fact it was with the woman that I wanted to spend the rest of my life with made it the best. After everything she had gone through, she had finally let me in and allowed me to get close enough to her to help her forget what Thomas had done to her. We hadn't heard anything from Brian, so we had to assume everything was fine down in Plymouth.

We had been working away for a couple of hours when I received a message on my phone. Looking down I was suddenly filled with a sinking feeling. Richard looked over and must have seen my concern.

"What's wrong, Tyler?"

"Suddenly I have this feeling that everything is going to fall down around me. I've just got a message from Brian."

Opening up my messages I started to read and immediately dropped my phone at what I saw.

"Tyler, what's happened? It can't be anything bad as we haven't received any alerts."

He picked the phone up and started to read out loud.

> *Tyler, call me as soon as you get this message, please. Thomas and Rosie have gone. Brian.*

"What the fuck! How? We have his car flagged to alert us if he moves anywhere out of Plymouth."

I just sat there, unable to comprehend everything that was happening. I had let Maddie down. I had promised we would keep Rosie safe and I had failed. She would never forgive me if we couldn't find her. My whole world was crashing around me and there wasn't a thing I could do about it. Richard must have dialled Brian's number because I could hear him talking.

"Hi, Brian ... No it's Richard. Tyler is a little shell-shocked at the moment, so I thought it best if I called ... Shit, that's why we haven't heard anything ... Okay, can you give me the reg number then and I'll see if I can find him ... What time do you think he left? ... Okay, I will keep you updated ... No, don't contact her, let us deal with this ... No, I'm sure he will be fine when I snap him out of his daze ... Okay, I will speak soon. Speak later."

I sat there staring into space. I hadn't realised that Richard had called Jayden into the office, or that he was now kneeling in front of me trying to snap me out of my funk. How could I have let this happen? How could I have not seen this coming? This was going to be the end of me and Maddie, I knew it. I couldn't even keep one promise, one that I had made only a couple of days ago.

"Tyler. Tyler, snap out of it man. I need you with me. We haven't lost her yet. We can find her. But I need your help. I can only do so much."

I sat there looking around me. My face was completely void of any emotion. I was numb. I looked at the worried faces of my colleagues next to me.

"Is someone going to tell me what the hell is going on?"

"Do you want me to explain, Tyler?"

I looked up at Richard, finally realising what was going on and just nodded my head. I wasn't sure if I could speak, let alone explain everything to my best friend.

"Okay, this isn't going to be good, but long story short. Maddie was raped around three years ago by the son of the woman her Dad was going out with. She got pregnant and had a little girl, Rosie. Thomas, Rosie's Dad, is planning to sell Rosie and has made off with her. We had a trace on his car set up, but it appears he has taken his Mum's car which is why we didn't receive an alert."

"Fuck. Is this what you were trying to say the other day about not knowing the entire story?"

Finally, I trusted myself to speak.

"Yes. I didn't want to get into it then because it was all a bit raw. I had only found out the night before."

"Well, what do you need us to do?"

"I've just started a trace on the car. It's going to take a little longer as we are playing catch-up instead of getting alerts while he is driving. We have a rough idea of where he may be heading, but it's a pretty big area," Richard replied. I couldn't thank him enough for taking the reins on this. I was the best at what I did, but that was only when I had my head on straight. Currently my mind was going around in circles and anything I tried to do would lead us nowhere.

"Do you need any help from Nathan and Kye? I can pull them off the jobs they are working on if you need them."

"Not at the moment. I just need to let this program run. I'm going to grab a coffee and give Mason a call to let him know what's going on."

"Thanks, Richard."

As soon as I heard Jayden thank Richard, I knew this was the time I was going to get the lecture. The one we had all given, Mason, Jayden and Brandon when they had lost their woman. But this was different. This was a three-year-old girl we had lost.

"Tyler, don't start to …"

"Jayden, I don't want the fucking lecture about everything is going to be okay. That it wasn't my fault and not to lose hope. I fucking failed her. I failed Maddie and I failed Rosie. I promised to keep them both safe from that bastard and what the fuck happens? He fucking takes her the day after I made that promise. So don't fucking lecture me."

The anger was building inside of me. I was angry that we had let Thomas slip through our net. I was angry that I had let the woman I loved down. But, most of all I was angry at myself for making that damned promise in the first place. Standing up quickly, the chair I was sitting on flew across the room. I was ready to hit something, someone.

"If you need to take it out on someone, take it out on me. But don't fucking give up. Don't ever give up. It's taken both you and Maddie years to admit your feelings for each other. You can't let her go, Tyler. Please."

Kye and Nathan must have heard the commotion and immediately came barging in the door. Seeing Jayden standing in front of me and my stance with tears on my face, they immediately knew something was wrong. Before they could say a word, Jayden spoke to them both.

"Just give us some space, guys. Everything is okay. I'll explain later. No need for you to worry."

I could see the look of concern on both their faces, most of all Nathan's. We had been friends since primary school, and although we had grown apart recently, we both knew we would do anything for each other. The fact that he couldn't help me now cut through me like a knife.

"I'm okay. Sorry if I startled you."

Nathan walked over to me slowly, hesitant to get too close in case I did lash out. Tentatively he placed his hand on my shoulder.

"If there is anything we can do, we are here for you, bro. Brothers in arms to the end, remember that."

"I know, and thank you, Nathan. I just need some time to get myself together. No one is hurt, so there is no need to worry much."

Nathan's gaze went from mine to Jayden. Jayden just gave him a curt nod and both he and Kye left the room. Walking over to where the chair had landed, I picked it up and put it back in front of my desk. I looked at Jayden standing there. I knew I owed him an apology. I shouldn't have spoken to him like that, no matter how I was feeling. Hell, not only was he one of my best friends, but he was also my boss. Any other company would have fired me on the spot for speaking like that.

"Jayden, look I'm ..."

"No need to say it, Tyler. You don't need to apologise to me. I know you're upset. I've been there. We all react differently. Mason and I lost it completely and shut down. Brandon wasn't really in any fit state to do anything after his beating. You just got angry. I understand, but what I said still holds true. Don't give up. Richard has already started the groundwork to find them. Once we know where they are then we can go from there. No need to let Maddie know yet. I can get Richard to contact her Dad and ask him not to let her know yet, not until we need to. But you need to be on the top of your game. You're the best at what you do for a reason, and we are going to need that skill to find them," he paused for a second to allow his words to sink in. "Are you good now?"

"Yeah, I'm good, but I do need to say I'm sorry. I should never have lost it with you. You and Nathan have been my friends for years. I know I never confided in you about Madds, but that was because I didn't know how to. The only reason Brandon knew was because we had a long conversation when he was in hospital. I guess what I am trying to say is that I love you like a brother and don't want us to lose that, no matter what."

"Don't worry about it. As I said, we all deal with things in different ways. You just lashed out, no big deal. Now, what do you need me to do?"

Just at that moment, Richard walked back into the office.

"I guessed it was safe to come back in now as the commotion seemed to have died down. Mason has been updated on the situation and is immediately getting on the Christian to update him and get things moving with the courts."

"Thanks, Richard. At least you're the calm one here at the moment. I'm not sure I would have been able to do what you have today."

"No problem. Are we working on this now, or do we have to continue with our other work as well?"

"Everything else can go on hold. I can contact the client and let him know we are dealing with a child abduction. I'm sure they will understand. They don't need to know it has something to do with a member of the team."

"Okay, I'll get onto them."

We spent the rest of the morning and into early afternoon trying to trace where Thomas had gone. We tracked him as far as Andover so far. He was obviously using the A303 heading nearly past Kings View in the process. We guessed that Brian's thoughts about him heading towards Canterbury in Kent was probably correct. We just needed to make sure. Brian had spoken to Mason and given him as much info as he could to hand over to Christian.

"How are things going?"

"We have got as far as Andover, so about halfway to Canterbury if that is where he is heading. We don't want to start looking straight there in case he didn't head that way. We could just be wasting time we don't have."

"That makes sense ..." Jayden was just about to continue when his phone rang. "Hi, Mace. What's happening?"

I saw his face almost run white as a sheet as he listened to what Mason was saying to him. I knew it had something to do with Maddie as soon as he looked over to me. His face was full of worry and concern.

"Yeah, I'm still here, Mason ... Yes he is here with me ... I'm not sure if that is such a good idea."

"Pass me the fucking phone," I grabbed the phone from Jayden. I needed to know what was going on. I had a sinking feeling again that everything was starting to fall apart in my life.

"Mason, what the fuck is going on? What's happened to Maddie?"

"How do you know something has happened to Maddie?"

"Mason, don't fuck with me now. I can tell something has happened by the way Jayden is looking at me. Just tell me."

Mason went dead silent. This was bad. I knew it. For one I hadn't got reprimanded for the way I had just spoken to the boss and owner. Two, he really didn't know how to break the news he obviously had.

"Tyler ... Jess went to the shop today and ... Ashleigh gave her a letter from Maddie. She's gone. She didn't say where, and she didn't specifically say she was going to meet Thomas, but she did say she had twenty-four hours to make a decision that kept Rosie in her life. There's a letter for you as well ... Tyler ... Tyler, are you still there?"

I couldn't take much more. I couldn't listen to what Mason was saying to me. It was all too much. Not only had I let them down, but now Maddie was doing everything she had promised she wouldn't. She was putting herself, and Rosie for that matter, in danger. She couldn't even trust me to help. For the second time that day the chair I had been sitting on flew across the room, this time narrowly missing Nathan who had walked into the room. I stormed out of my office and headed out the front door, shocking Jackie, our receptionist, in the process, and headed out the front door.

I didn't get very far when a hand grabbed me by the arm. I swung round to punch whoever had grabbed me, my military instincts immediately taking over and found Kye standing there holding me.

"That's not going to get her back is it?"

"You fucking knew. You knew and didn't say anything. You bastard."

I went to punch him again. The anger radiating through me. Not so much at him, but at the whole situation. He just held both my arms and somehow turned me to pin them behind my back and restrain me. How the hell he managed it I will never know.

"Before you start taking everything out on me, no, I didn't know. But it's obvious it has something to do with Maddie the way you are acting. With everything that is going on I just assumed she had taken matters into her own hands and gone to find Rosie and Thomas. And before you say anything, yes, Jayden did fill us in. We needed to know, especially when it has something to do with one of us. I know I haven't been around long, but I still see you all as family. I've done some shit things in my time, kidnapping Sienna being one of them, but you guys have taken me in and looked past my prior actions. I'm here for you, just as much as every one of those guys in there and back at Kings View. Now if you still want to take your anger out on me, go for it. Believe me though, I won't be as easy a pushover as your best friends in there. I'll fight back."

I knew he was right. It wasn't any of their fault, what was happening. Just one big fucked up situation that we had to deal with. That I had to deal with. The adrenaline of my anger rapidly dissipated and the pain and hurt started to sink in. I felt Kye's grip loosen as he let go of both of my arms.

"You good?" I could feel his hand resting on my arm, just in case I flew again, but he never moved. I nodded my response.

"Come on then, let's get back in there and plan out how we are going to get your girl and new daughter back."

We walked back into the office block and I gave an apologetic smile to Jackie as I walked past. Walking back into my office, I saw Jayden just hanging up the phone with Mason. All eyes went to me as I walked through the door.

"I'm sorry, guys. I shouldn't have blown up like that."

"No harm done. Although from the sounds of things, you owe both Jackie and Mason an apology. So, what's the plan?"

"Head back down to Kings View and read the letter I guess. I'll grab my stuff and head down there tonight."

To my surprise it was Richard who spoke next.

"Tyler, it's nearly five o'clock. There is no way you are going down there tonight. From the timeframe that Mason has given us, Maddie won't have got to Canterbury yet, if that is even where she is going. We need to know exactly where Thomas has taken Rosie before we go off all guns blazing. We should have an answer by the morning. Then, and only then, I will drive us down to Kings View. You are not driving anywhere. You're liable to get yourself killed. This isn't fucking negotiable."

We all stood there staring at Richard. I don't think any of us had ever heard him talk like this before, and definitely hadn't heard him swear. He left no room for argument. Even if he had, I don't think Jayden would have let me go by myself anyway.

"I couldn't have put it better myself, Richard. We'll make a military guy out of you yet."

I stood and looked at the guys around me. I couldn't ask for a better bunch of colleagues or friends if I wished for them. They were all there for me, and for that I would be eternally grateful.

Chapter Thirty

Madeleine

I arrived in Canterbury around six o'clock last night. I had countless missed calls and messages from just about every member of Kings Brothers, Jess, and Ashleigh. I had only replied once to Ashleigh to let her know I was fine and not to worry, that I knew exactly what I was doing. The problem was, I didn't. What the hell was I going to do to get Rosie back? I knew I couldn't fight Thomas. That had turned out bad every time I had tried before. I was frightened of him. No matter how I had turned my life around, how I had managed to put what he did to me to the back of my mind, I was still scared of him and what he could do to me and Rosie. I really hadn't thought this through. I reacted immediately to his ultimatum. I didn't think of the consequences of what I was about to do. I could lose everything, not only my daughter but the man that I loved. Or I could get my daughter back, but still be without Tyler. I wasn't sure he would ever forgive me for what I was about to do.

My meeting with Thomas wasn't until 12:30. I wasn't sure what I was going to say, or what I was going to do. I didn't have any plan in my head. My only thought was getting here and saving Rosie. I couldn't face breakfast. I hadn't eaten since yesterday morning. The thought of food just turned my stomach. I was far too worried about what today may hold in store for me. I packed up my stuff and got ready for the day ahead. I had to be out of the hotel room by 10:00, so I would have a couple of hours before I had to meet up with Thomas and Rosie. Just enough time to do a little bit of sightseeing around Canterbury. Not that I really wanted to. All I wanted to do now was to see my little girl.

As I sat there waiting for my time to leave, I wondered if she would remember me. I know my Dad had mentioned me all the time to her and made sure to show her pictures of me in the hope she wouldn't forget. But she was so young. Would she remember who I was, and would she still love me? Would she have bonded so much with Thomas that she couldn't bear to be parted from him? It made me sick to think that he would have built a relationship with her. He had point blank refused to accept her as his daughter, saying he wanted nothing to do with either her or me. So, why was he doing this now? Why was he even suggesting we should be a family? Was he telling the truth, or was it just another lie, to get me to come down here to meet him? I couldn't take that chance though. I had to come here to make sure Rosie was okay.

Then there was Tyler. Had I ruined everything we had between us? Would he ever forgive me for not telling him what I was going to do? I knew if I had, then he would have stopped me from coming down. Then again, if I had told him, he could have come down here and got Rosie back. But would Thomas have planned for that situation? Would he have thought that I might bring someone with me and snatch Rosie while he was distracted? It was too late to think about the what ifs now. I was here and I had made my decision. I just had to hope that everything would turn out for the best and then try to regain the relationship I had with Tyler. If he wouldn't, then that would be on me, and I would have to live with that. But at least if I had Rosie in my life, I could carry on living. Without her, my life was empty.

Looking at the time, I realised it was nearly ten and I needed to be out of the hotel room. Grabbing all my stuff, I went and checked out of the hotel. Just over two hours to waste now before I would finally see my daughter again. Unfortunately, with that came the tormentor himself. I would finally have to face Thomas after two years away. I just hoped I was strong enough to fight for what was right, for what I deserved, for Rosie.

I'd been walking around Canterbury for just over two hours. I'd done all of the touristy things, visited the Cathedral, walked around the shops. But my heart wasn't in it. All I wanted was Rosie back in my arms. I had missed her so much these past two years. There wasn't a day that I hadn't thought about her. I'd been wondering what she was doing, what her first word was? I had missed it all. Missed her starting to talk. Missed her first steps. I really didn't deserve to be her Mum, but I was. I was her Mum and all of that was going to change today. No matter what, I was going to become the Mum that my own mother was to me. She loved me unconditionally while she was alive.

She was always there for me. I just wish she had still been with us. She would have known exactly what to do. But then again, if she had still been with us, perhaps I wouldn't have been in this mess. There would have been no reason for Dad to start seeing Michelle. No reason for Thomas to be living with us. And no Thomas would have meant no Rosie. As much as I hated him, hated what he did to me, I couldn't help but think without him I wouldn't have a beautiful daughter. I guess fate deals us some funny cards at times, because no matter what, I couldn't see my life without Rosie in it.

Walking past the bus station, I could see the entrance to the gardens in front of me. I had no idea what was waiting for me there. Should I just call Tyler now and tell him where I was? Even if I did, what could he do? He was nearly three hours away. No, the time for that had long gone. I just needed to face my fears and walk in. At least I would get to see Rosie again. I just hoped it wasn't for the last time. If my Dad was correct and Thomas wanted to sell her, how would I stop him? I just had to hope that I could convince him that her place was with me. If it was just about money, then I should have spoken to Mason and Jess. I'm sure they would have lent me the money to pay Thomas off. Then again, would that have stopped him, or would he just have come back for more when he had spent it?

All these questions whirling around in my head were irrelevant now. I was here and there was no going back, not without the prospect of losing my only daughter. Walking through the entrance I saw the bandstand up ahead, a lone figure standing by it. At first I couldn't make out if it was Thomas or not, then when the figure turned around it hit me like a ton of bricks. I froze on the spot. All those emotions from two years ago hit me. The way he had stood there taunting me, punching and kicking me came flooding back. Then the realisation struck that he was alone. Rosie wasn't with him. Had he already gotten rid of her? Maternal instincts kicked in and I started to run towards him, anger building inside of me.

"Where's Rosie?" Were the first words that left my mouth as I came up beside him.

"Well, you certainly seemed pleased to see me, my darling Madeleine. I must say I am surprised you are that eager to see me again. Was it that good for you that you couldn't wait for a repeat?"

"Thomas, you're a bastard and I never wanted to see you again. But I didn't have a choice, did I? Now you haven't answered my question. Where's Rosie? You said to meet you here, so where is she?"

The fear was growing in me the longer I stood here. Could he have been that cruel to make me come all the way down here just to tell me he had sold Rosie? I never thought he would be that brutal, but the longer this went on the more I started to wonder.

"My, you have grown a feisty attitude in the past two years, haven't you Madeleine? To answer your question, Rosie is with my cousin being well looked after. Once I get you settled in our place I will go and get her. Then you can be reunited with our daughter."

How dare he say that. How dare he call Rosie our daughter. The anger in me was building. That the man in front of me had the audacity to say that after everything that had happened.

"My daughter. You wanted nothing to do with her, remember Thomas? You wanted both of us out of your life, then decided she was too important to you to let go. You can't have it both ways. You either want to be a father to her or you don't."

"Madeleine, Madeleine, please calm down. I told you over the phone that I do want her to be in my life. Both of you. I want us to be a family together."

I had to believe he was telling me the truth, much as I hated to admit it. If he wasn't, then I may never see her again.

"Okay, so where are we going?"

"My car is parked over in the car park. I will take us to our new home, then I can go and get Rosie."

"Let's go then."

Going to carry my case, I was surprised when Thomas actually picked it up. I never saw him as the gentlemanly type. He was full of surprises. Perhaps he had changed. But even if he had, would I want to spend the rest of my life with this man? I followed him to his car, but realised that it wasn't his. I had always liked his car. Even if I couldn't stand the guy, his car was awesome. Instead he had Michelle's car. I had to wonder if he had done that on purpose.

He placed my case in the boot, and we got in the car together. I noticed Rosie's car seat in the back. He might be a jerk, but at least he tried to keep her safe when he was driving. I suppose I had to give him some credit for that. We headed off out of the city.

"So where are we going?"

"Just to a house I have rented in Chartham Hatch. It's just outside of the city, only a short drive. My cousin lives in the village. I wanted her to meet Rosie."

"Have you finally admitted to someone that she is yours?"

"No, and you are the only person apart from me that will ever know. Oh, and Rosie of course, once she grows up."

Something in his voice was setting off alarm bells again. The drive to the house was as short as Thomas had said. Within ten minutes we were parked outside a small bungalow in the middle of the village. Getting out of the car, Thomas grabbed my bags and we headed inside the bungalow. As I walked in I started to look around. It was very homely. I was impressed that Thomas could live like this. I'm sure it had to have been a furnished rental property, because Thomas couldn't have done this. He wouldn't have the gumption to have this much furniture in a home. You walked directly into the front room, which had a three piece suite, TV, coffee table and a large open fire, which reminded me very much of the one in Mason and Jess' cottage back in Kings View. I could see the door open to the kitchen, which although old, was still clean and tidy with a dining table and four chairs. Thomas must have taken my bag into a room because he was no longer in the front room with me. Loudly I spoke to him.

"This is nice. I'm surprised you found somewhere like this."

Hearing footsteps behind me, I looked around to see Thomas standing there with a smirk on his face.

"It is, I managed to get it on a short-term rent. One week at a time. I don't plan on staying here that long."

"But … I … thought," my mind was going a mile a minute as I spoke. He wasn't going to stay here long. Did that mean?

"Did you really think I wanted to be a family, Madeleine? Did you really think I had changed that much, that I wanted to spend the rest of my life with you and the brat? Dear, dear, dear. You are far too gullible. I only got you here so you could name me as Rosie's father. It's the last thing I need to be able to put my plan into effect. I can't sell Rosie if I am not named as the father. Therefore, as soon as I can get an appointment on Monday morning at the registrar's office, you will name me as Rosie's father and I will sell her."

Realisation started to hit. It was all a lie. I had made a massive mistake by coming down here. I needed to run, but where would I run too? I still had my phone so I could call for a cab, or the police, or Tyler, anyone. I made a bolt for the door, but only got a few feet before I felt two strong arms around me, lifting me up from the floor. I struggled as much as I could and tried to kick him as he held onto me tight. But it was no use. There was no way I was going to escape his grasp. He carried me into one of the bedrooms and threw me down on the bed. Without hesitating, he walked out of the room and locked the door behind him.

"I'm sorry, Madeleine, but this is for your own good. I can't have you running off to your boyfriend now, can I? And before you look, I have your phone, so you won't be able to contact anyone."

I quickly went to my bag and found my phone missing.

"Now be a good girl and be quiet. I have to go and get Rosie. Then you can cook me something. I haven't eaten anything except McDonalds for the past two days."

With that, I heard him walking away from the door. A few moments later I heard the front door slam shut. I sank to the bed, tears pouring from my eyes. What had I done? I never should have believed him and left Kings View. But it was too late now. There was nothing I could do about it. I was going to lose Rosie, and I was going to lose Tyler, and it was all my fault.

Chapter Thirty-One

Tyler

I t was only 7:30 in the morning when we pulled up outside the offices in Kings View. We had left early because neither Richard nor I could sleep. We had been up most of the night trying to establish exactly where Thomas was. We had got as far as Maidstone when we left at 5:30. It did appear that he was heading to Canterbury, but where? Richard wouldn't let me drive this morning. He joked that he wanted to make it here alive. I had to admit that he was probably right, there was also the chance that we wouldn't have ended up here, and I would have driven straight down to Canterbury. Although we had discussed it throughout the night, it wasn't the best idea I'd had. We didn't know for sure he was there. He could have been leading us on a wild goose chase to throw us off the trail.

Parking up, I noticed that Mason's car was already here. I wasn't sure if that was because he had brought Jess into work, or if he was working himself. As I got out of the car, I got my answer. Mason and Brandon walked around the corner. They must have dropped the girls off at the shop this morning and grabbed breakfast, because they were holding coffees and a bag of pastries in their hands.

"Well, this is a fine mess we find ourselves in, isn't it?"

"I'm not really in the mood for jokes, Mace."

I saw the glint of humour in his eyes immediately disappear. As if the realisation and memories of Jess disappearing came flooding back to him. Brandon also stood there with a solemn look on his face.

"I'm sorry, Tyler. I should have known better than to make light of the situation. How are you holding up?"

"Well, apart from only getting a couple of hours of sleep last night, I'm good. Neither of us slept much. Let's get inside and I can get you up to date with what we have found out so far."

Walking into the office, we all headed for the conference room to go through everything and get a plan together. We all sat down, and I grabbed my coffee from the holder. I knew it was mine as it was the only one with a name on. Jess always made the best gingerbread lattes, and she must have known that I needed one this morning. Taking a sip, I let out the breath of anticipation that I always had with my first coffee of the morning.

"Jess thought you would need that. She said she would bring some more down a little later on."

"I'll thank her when I see her. I just want to th ..."

"No need to thank us, Tyler. You have been there to help us out the past few years. This is our way of saying thank you. We will get Maddie and Rosie back unharmed. As long as Thomas hasn't managed to get an appointment today, we have the whole weekend. Once we can establish where exactly he is, I can get Callum to contact the local registrar's office. Perhaps he can buy us more time, maybe get them to say they don't have any appointments until the middle of next week. That could give us a few extra days to track him down and get a plan together."

I was about to thank him again, but stopped short when I looked up at him. I know none of these guys here expected me to thank them. They would do anything to see us all happy and settled down. They also all loved Maddie like a little sister, so wanted to protect her. But that was my job, or at least it was until last night.

"I guess I should give you this first, Tyler. None of us have opened it."

Mason passed me the letter Maddie had left for me. I looked down at it for a while, afraid of what it said inside.

"Do you want to be alone for a moment?"

I looked up at Brandon who asked the question.

"After the way I reacted yesterday, probably best if you stayed."

Opening the envelope, I unfolded the letter and began to read.

> *My dearest Tyler,*
>
> *I can only say to you that I'm sorry. I never meant things to turn out this way. I hope that one day you will be able to forgive me. I really wanted to tell you what I was doing, but I wasn't given a choice.*
>
> *Thomas gave me twenty-four hours to meet with him, or he was taking Rosie away from me for good. He says he has changed, that he wants the three of us to be a family. I'm not sure I believe him, but what choice did I have? He said he would know if I told someone and had already made plans to take Rosie should that happen.*

I love you, Tyler. I have never loved another man before you, and I don't think I ever will again. But Rosie is my daughter. I left her once and I can't do that again. If there is a remote chance that Thomas has changed, at least Rosie will grow up knowing both of her parents. But I will never love him. I will never share a bed with him again in my life.

If I can convince him to let me bring Rosie back, then I will. I just hope that I haven't ruined any chance of being with you forever. I guess I may never know.

I will contact you when I can to let you know I am safe. If you don't hear from me in a few days, then something has gone wrong. Only then should you come to find me. Please not before. I cannot risk losing Rosie.

Just remember I love you and that I'm sorry. Thank you for our nights together. I will never forget them.

Your Sweetheart, Madds

I sat there reading the letter over and over again. Why hadn't she come to me? We could have put a plan in place where she could have met Thomas, but we would have been close by to help. I didn't know what to say or do. I just sat there. It was Richard who finally spoke.

"Tyler, we're here for you. But we need to know what the letter said."

I passed him the letter for him to read. He read it out loud to Mason and Brandon. I felt the tears start to well in my eyes. She had gone. She had really gone. Worst of all, she made the decision to leave. I know she was convinced by Thomas, but still, she had been the one to leave. The room was filled with stunned silence. No one knew exactly what to say. Again it was Richard that spoke first.

"Tyler, Maddie did this because Thomas has manipulated her. You have read all the messages he sent. He doesn't want her or

Rosie. We need to find them and get them back. Don't give up."

"But what if she is happy with him, Richard?"

"She won't be because he doesn't want her."

Just as he spoke, he received a message on his laptop.

"Well, I guess this message answers our question, Tyler. Thomas has just sent a message to his Mum. *Bitch has arrived but can't get an appointment at the registrar until Wednesday, so I have to put up with both of them until then. Stay where you are unless it gets bad. I will keep in touch. Don't worry, by Wednesday evening we will be on our way.*"

Immediately after he stopped speaking another message came through.

"And it appears that he was in Canterbury this morning and was last seen heading out on the A28 towards Ashford. Which would take him right through Chartham. Brian was right. I will start to trace houses that have been let in the area to Thomas Smith. Could be a long shot, but we might find something. Hopefully there aren't many in the area."

"I'll get onto Callum as well. With our combined resources we may be able to find him quicker. At least we don't have to try and put in a delay to the registrar, and we also know that we have until Wednesday to find them."

I was still sitting there, staring at the letter that was now on the desk in front of me. What did it mean? Was this her goodbye letter to me, the same as Brandon got from Ashleigh? Was that the end for us? I know Brandon got Ashleigh back, but I wasn't so sure that would happen between me and Maddie.

The room had gone quiet again and I looked up to find everyone except Richard had left the room.

"Tyler, I'm not going to give you a lecture on how you feel. All

I'm going to say is it's obvious Maddie has been spun a web of lies. She is so worried that she is going to lose Rosie for good that she is making irrational decisions. Well, we can see they are irrational, but to her they are the only decisions she feels she can make. Let's find her and let her tell us what she wants. If she tells us all to fuck off, that she is happy where she is, then so be it. We can deal with that if and when the time comes. But I know that the only man she wants to be with is you. She wants you to be part of Rosie's life and to be a family together.

What you must decide is, do you want to let her go? You've spent the past two years trying to get her to go out with you. You never gave up until she eventually told you the truth three days ago. Are you willing to let those two years go to waste, or are you going to go and get your woman and her daughter back?"

There was only one answer I could give Richard. But my answer didn't matter if Madeleine didn't want me.

"I think you know my answer to that without even asking. But what does my answer matter if she doesn't want me?"

"Then you fucking fight for her, Tyler. I may not have known you long, but I know that you love Maddie and would do anything for her. Don't let that go because you think she doesn't want you. We may as well give up on all this now if that's what you're going to do."

All the anger that I had been feeling suddenly morphed into a feeling of dread and fear. The pain and tears that I had been holding back, couldn't stay concealed for much longer. With only Richard in the office, I could let the hurt and worry free. Allowing the tears to start to fall, I sat there silently sobbing. I had to let my emotions out in any form before I exploded. Richard didn't say a word, just came and sat next to me, allowing me the release without any judgement. Eventually he spoke.

"Let it all out, Tyler. You're no use to anyone unless you're thinking straight. With all that pent up emotion you have in you, something is going to snap. Better to let it out now than in front of Maddie and Rosie when they need you. And before you argue with me, they do need you. Maddie might not realise it at the moment because her judgement is impaired by lies, but she will realise, and it will break her if you aren't there for her. So, with that in mind, I'm going to ask you again. This time I want a definite answer. Do you want to fight for her?"

Without a single hesitation I answered him.

"Yes."

"Then let's work out what we are going to do to get her back."

We spent most of the morning running traces and ringing local letting agents trying to establish where Thomas was. Mason had called Callum and he was doing the same. Brian had been updated on exactly what was happening, and it was all Mason could do to stop him from getting in his car and heading down to Canterbury to find them himself. Mason had just about managed to convince him to stay there, to try and make things look as normal as possible. Instead he needed to look around and see if he could find an address book with an address for Michelle and Thomas' relatives down in Canterbury.

The office was a hive of activity, but we didn't appear to be getting anywhere closer to finding her. I needed to be close to her. At least if I was in Canterbury, then I would feel like I was actually doing something instead of just sitting here in front of a laptop watching traces run through.

"I can't sit here much longer, guys. I need to be down in Canterbury looking for her. I'm not getting anywhere just sitting here."

"We still don't know for definite that they are anywhere near Canterbury. The new trace I set up hasn't pinged to say they have moved, but they may have done before we set it up. It could take a couple of days before it picks them up."

"That could be true, Richard. But they could also be staying at a house near Canterbury and not moving until Wednesday. If you guys want to stay here, then fine. But I'm going to head off down to Canterbury after lunch. I need to do this. I need to feel close to her. I'm losing my mind just sitting here."

Brandon and Richard looked at me, and then turned to look at Mason who was just sitting there looking at me. Neither of them would agree to my plan without Mason's say so. He was the boss after all. But I didn't care what he said or thought. I was going to Canterbury this afternoon, come what may. They were either with me, or I would do this on my own. For a long while, no one said a word. Everyone was just waiting to hear what Mason said.

"Okay. If that is what you want, Tyler. I will speak to Jess and Ashleigh and let them know we will be away for a while. I will have to get Jess's car so she can get home this evening. Brandon it might be worth Ashleigh staying at my place until we get back. I think we would both be happier if they were together. We can get Nathan or Kye to come down and stay with them if you want?"

"I'm sure they will be okay on their own. Anyone that wanted to hurt them has been locked up. But I let you make that call."

"Well, it looks like we're going on a road trip then. We best take two cars with us. With two extra passengers for the way back, one won't be enough. But you aren't driving, Tyler. No arguments on that one. You can either go with Richard or me, but you will not be in charge of a vehicle in your current mindset. There is no argument to be had here. It's either my way, or no way."

I looked up at him and nodded in agreement.

"Right, well as that is settled. Let's get everything we need together and go get your girls back."

Chapter Thirty-Two

Madeleine

························ ✦ ·······················

I wasn't sure how long it had been since Thomas left to go and get Rosie. It must have been a while since I had fallen asleep, and it was now dark outside. I couldn't work out how I had managed to sleep with everything that was going on, but I must have been exhausted from crying for so long. I should never have come here. I should have known that Thomas was lying to me. He had never been truthful in all the time I had known him, so why would he suddenly change now? I sat up on the bed resting my back on the headboard. I should have gone to Tyler. He would have found a way for me to meet Thomas and get Rosie back. But "should have" wouldn't get me out of the situation I was currently in. I just had to hope that Tyler hadn't given up on me and was trying to find us. If not Tyler, then at least Mason and Brandon.

Sitting there, I noticed that the house wasn't silent. I could hear a muffled noise through the door. A child's cry. Rosie was here and she was upset. I wanted to shout out to Thomas, but I needed to keep quiet. If I upset him in any way, I wasn't sure exactly what he would do to me. I heard footsteps heading towards the door, and Rosie's cries started to get louder the closer the footsteps got. The next thing I knew, the door to my room unlocked and an angry Thomas burst through the door with Rosie in his arms. I was overwhelmed with emotion seeing him there with our daughter in his arms. It had been two long years since I had last seen or held her. All those missed evenings of tucking her into bed and reading her a bedtime story, I had missed them. I was close to tears of joy seeing her again. But my mood soon changed as soon as Thomas spoke.

"Deal with your brat of a daughter. I'm not putting up with her cries much longer. Keep her fucking quiet, or I will, and I'm not sure if you want to know how I will do it!"

Anger built in me. How dare he talk about my daughter, our daughter in that way. I was going to answer him back, but realised that would only cause me pain. I had to be sensible here and stay safe for Rosie. The longer I could stay safe, the longer she would be safe, and that would also give the guys more time to find me. Knowing it was now night-time, and a Friday, I knew I had at least the weekend before he could get to the registrar's office. I just needed to play the game. Slowly getting up off the bed, I walked over to Thomas and took Rosie into my arms. She was the most important person in my life right now, and I needed to comfort her. I tried to reassure her with my words, hoping that somehow my voice would both comfort her and jog her memory of who I was.

"Come on Poppet, no more tears baby. Mummy's here now. Come on, let's have a cuddle on the bed."

Rosie was still crying in my arms and struggling to get loose as though she didn't know who I was, or that she didn't want to be with me. I could feel myself start to panic. Had she already forgotten me? What had Thomas and Michelle told her about me? Deciding just to persevere I got up onto the bed, and held her in my arms, never once acknowledging or speaking to Thomas. It clearly didn't bother him as he just walked out of the room and shut the door behind him again. Finally, I felt at home. Rosie was safe in my arms. I had missed her so much. Dad had sent me plenty of pictures over the years, but it wasn't the same as actually having her with me, in my arms like she was now. I just hoped that she would realise who I was and still want to be with me.

I could hear Rosie's cries slow down as she calmed in my arms and started to snuggle into me. I started to feel some relief as she appeared to realise exactly who I was. She started to wiggle about and as I looked down at her I found her staring up at me. She had a puzzled look on her face as if she was trying to work out exactly who I was. All of a sudden a big smile came on her face as she flung her arms around me.

"Mummy, it is you."

"Yes, it is, Poppet. Did you miss me?"

"Gandad, said you be back. Where is Gandad?"

"We will see Grandad soon, pops. Hopefully you will get to have lots of new friends too. Has Thomas been looking after you?"

"Don't like him. He is mean. Don't like nanny either."

I hated that she had started calling Michelle Nanny. Hopefully once this was all over, we would never see either of them again. I sat there just holding her. I loved this little girl so much. I still regretted leaving her behind, leaving her with him for two years. But at the time it was the only thing I could do. I didn't have anyone to help me.

"Mummy."

"Yes, poppet."

"Do you love me? Gandad says you do, but Nanny says you don't."

If I ever got hold of that woman, I would kill her. How dare she tell my own daughter that I didn't love her. Perhaps she should have been saying that about her own son seeing as he didn't even want to acknowledge she was his.

"Of course, I love you, Rosie. I'm sorry I had to go away. I wanted to take you with me, but I wasn't allowed."

"Why?"

Shit, we had already got to that stage. The constant why question.

"Because they wouldn't let me take you with me to the school I went to," much easier than explaining what a university was I thought. "But I have finished school now, so you can come home with me and meet all my friends."

"Will Gandad be there?"

"Not to start with, but he will be after a while."

"How about Nanny and Thomas?"

"No, it will just be me and you, Poppet. Well, maybe Tyler as well."

"Who is Tyer?"

"It's Tyler, and he is my friend. Now, come on, it's getting late. We can talk more tomorrow. Right now, I think it's time for you to go to sleep. No more questions and no more tears. Just snuggles with my favourite little girl."

"Mummy ... I love you."

"I love you too, Poppet," I replied as she let out a big yawn and snuggled into me to go to sleep.

I lay there with her in my arms wondering how she would take to everyone in Kings View. Would she like them? I knew they would all love her. Well, I knew all except for maybe one person. Tyler had said that he thought she was adorable and wanted her in his life, but was that just to make me happy? Did he really still want us to be a family together? I hoped so. I so wanted Rosie to sit there and call him Dad. He would be a fantastic Dad to her, I knew that. But, that was only if it was what he wanted. I heard the soft breaths from Rosie next to me as she slept soundly. All was quiet again, that was until I heard the footsteps.

It wasn't until the door opened that I realised Thomas hadn't locked me in the room.

"Is she asleep?"

"Yes, she can stay here with me if you like. I can look after her."

"We need to talk. You can either leave her here or put her in her room. That bed has bars on it so she doesn't fall out. She does like to move around a bit."

Carefully I picked Rosie up and carried her into the other bedroom. I didn't want her falling out of my bed and hurting herself. As I placed her down on the bed she stirred slightly.

"It's okay, Poppet. Mummy just needs to talk to Thomas. If you wake up you can come and find me in my room, or I can come and sleep in here. Night, night."

"Night, Mummy."

I walked out of the room and carefully closed the door behind me. Walking into the front room, I found Thomas sitting there with a drink in his hand. Some things never changed. I just hoped he had stayed sober whenever he was looking after Rosie.

"What do you want to talk about?"

"Sit down and we'll talk."

I sat down on the settee opposite him. There was no way I was going to get close.

"As I said earlier, I don't want you and I don't want Rosie. Before you say anything, I'm not letting you have her either. When I said she was far too valuable when I chucked you out, I meant it. Do you know how much people who cannot have kids will pay for a child? Even one of Rosie's age. Well, I do. Fifty grand. That's how much I can get for the brat. If I could have sold her when she was a baby I would have got a lot more, but that ship has sailed. I have no intention of becoming a family with you, or anyone for that fact. And I am certainly not allowing you to leave here with Rosie. Something good has got to come out of this fucked up situation, and the only thing that is going to be is me getting enough money to fuck off out of this country and away from you, that brat, and my whore of a mother."

"I feel sorry for Brian. All these years he has been in love with a prostitute. That's all she was ever good for, opening her legs and getting fucked for money. Why do you think I ended up the way I did? She never really wanted me. I was just a result of one of her drunken fucks. Neither of us saw my Dad again. In fact, I'm not sure my Mum even knows who my father is."

I sat there shocked at Thomas's admission to me. I guessed what Michelle had been doing, but to find out that she never wanted Thomas made a lot of sense to me with the way he acted and how he treated his Mum and other people around him.

"Thomas, if it is money, you want then I can get it for you. I can get you fifty grand, and I still get to keep Rosie. No one needs to know she is your daughter. I won't tell anyone."

"You can get fifty grand. Yeah right. You can barely look after yourself, let alone get that kind of money."

"I can, Thomas. I have a friend that could lend it to me. Please don't sell Rosie. Please."

I saw something in his expression. A sudden change in his demeanour. But as soon as I saw it, it was gone, and the Thomas I knew and hated was back.

"You expect me to believe that? That you have a friend that can lay their hands on that kind of money. Forget it. I have already made the arrangements, and believe me, the people I am dealing with won't be too happy if I back out of the deal.

But I won't let you think I am heartless. You have a choice how the rest of our time together goes. Much as I want to fuck the life out of you, I won't. But that is if, and only if, you behave yourself, look after me and Rosie for the next few days, and agree to everything I ask you to do. That means you will come to the registrar's office with me and name me as Rosie's Dad. You will not cause a scene when we go to sell her. If you agree to this, then you can have free reign of the house and I will not touch you. However, if you try to escape with Rosie, or you cause any problems in any way," he paused for a second as I looked into his eyes and a cruel smirk came on his face.

"If you cause any problems, then I will lock you in the room and will use you in any way I see fit, whenever I want. And I have a very vivid imagination and strong sexual appetite. What do you say?"

I knew I didn't have a choice. He would make good on his threat. I knew I still had until Monday at least. Two days for the guys to come and find me and Rosie. I could be nice for two days.

"I guess I don't have a choice."

"Oh, you have a choice, Maddie. Far be it from me to dictate to you."

"I will do whatever you ask. Just let me spend the next couple of days with Rosie, please. Let me at least get to say goodbye properly."

"I can agree to that. I don't want to have to deal with her until Wednesday afternoon on my own anyway."

"Wednesday?"

"Yes, we have an appointment on Wednesday morning with the registrar. Unfortunately, that was the first appointment I could get, especially as we should have done this in Plymouth. I have another meeting set up for Wednesday afternoon. Then you can have your phone back and get home to wherever it is you live. I must say, I was hoping you would choose the hard option. I could have done with a good fuck. Oh well, I guess I will have to wait a few days. Unless?"

I looked up at him. Did he really think I would agree to sleep with him after everything he had done?

"No, I guess not."

"I'm going to go and cook something to eat. Are you hungry?"

"No, I ate earlier."

"Okay. Well, I guess I will say goodnight then. I will eat in my bedroom, so you don't have to deal with my presence. If Rosie wakes up I will deal with her, so you can sleep."

I walked into the kitchen. I wasn't really hungry, but I just needed to get away from him. At least I knew I had until Wednesday. That gave the guys more time to find me. I had to hope they were looking for me.

Chapter Thirty-Three
Thomas

·······━━━◆✦◆ ❦ ✦◆✦◆·······

I sat in the quiet room, a large scotch in my hand. I knew Madeleine would agree to my demands. She really didn't have that much of a choice. Part of me wanted her to fight. I wanted that one more time with her. She may have been a virgin when I took her, and might not have been ready for what I did, and had no experience. But fuck, I can still remember how tight she was and how good I felt ramming into her. My friends would say I'm sick for having these thoughts, and I guess I was, but I never liked the easy sex. I never liked the women who just laid down and opened their legs for me. Women like my mother.

No, I preferred it rough, when they put up a fight. It was probably the number one reason why I was still single. No woman would put up with being treated like that in the bedroom. It didn't matter how much I looked after them and cared for them outside of the room, one night with me and they would run a mile. I definitely preferred virgins, and I'd had a few. They didn't know what to expect from sex. I had my limits though. I would never go with a girl. They had to be way over legal age. I wasn't sick, not in that way. I had a few friends who liked to sleep with barely legal girls, but that wasn't for me.

I wonder if Madeleine had slept with another guy since me? She said that she had been with another guy, and he had made her feel very good, but they hadn't had sex. I wondered how true that was. I'd said I would ruin it for every bloke that came along, but I wondered if that was true? Was I that much of an arsehole? Why was I even thinking about her? It was just one fuck. Was I jealous of what she had? She had parents who loved her. I know her Mum wasn't around anymore, but Brian loved her with all his heart. If he had to make a choice between her and my Mum, I knew without a doubt he would always choose Madeleine. Was that why I did it? Was I jealous of what Madeleine had so I wanted to take something away from her? Did I want to take her daughter away from her because of how my Mum had treated me? Did I want her to feel the way my mother made me feel?

Sitting here I realised that I was either really fucked up in the head or drunk. I was going to go with the latter because the former was too painful to consider. I just had to get through the next few days and then that would be it. I would be free of them all forever. I wasn't stupid enough to think that fifty grand would change my life forever, but it would get me out of this country and then perhaps I could get my shit together. Maybe I'd find myself a woman I loved and start a family. I must be fucking drunk if I'm having these thoughts. I placed the glass back on the table, looking at the bottle of scotch I had bought earlier in the day. Almost empty. I needed to stop drinking. It was not the answer to everything in my life.

Grabbing my phone, I looked through the messages I had received this evening. Plenty from my Mum telling me how Brian had absolutely lost it when he got back and found me gone. He gave her a week to get out of the house and not come back. He told her if she knew what was best for her, she would tell him exactly where I was so he could come and get Rosie. She promised that she hadn't told him, but I wasn't so sure. It was the reason why the only people who knew where I was currently living were me, Madeleine, and the letting agent I'd used for this place. Even my own cousin didn't know how close by I was.

Then there was a message from my contact, confirming the arrangements of the meeting on Wednesday when we would give Rosie to her new family. I sent a quick message off to him to let him know I would be there at the designated time with all the paperwork he needed and Rosie. I wasn't going to ask how he had managed to arrange it all. After all, what I was doing was illegal. Selling a child to the highest bidder amounted to human trafficking, for want of a better description. But he had managed it and I wasn't going to question how. It was another reason why I was leaving that evening. I didn't want to be around when Maddie went to the police. I knew she would, but I wouldn't be anywhere near for them to find me. I would be slowly making my way across Europe. I didn't know where I would settle, but I had plenty of time to find out.

My phone started to ring and I looked down to see it was my mother. Part of me just wanted to turn it off. I couldn't be bothered to speak to her. But I knew if I didn't she wouldn't leave me alone. So reluctantly, I answered.

"Yes, Mum. What did you want?"

"I need to get out of here. I can't stay here much longer with Brian. He is driving me insane. Please let me come down and stay with you."

"I've already told you. You can't be anywhere near here at the moment. You know as soon as you leave, Brian will follow you here. Then we risk losing everything."

That was only partly true. Yes, I did think that Brian would follow her and could take Rosie and Madeleine away. But the real reason I didn't want her down here was because it would then be difficult to leave the country without her knowing. If she was still over in Plymouth, I could get out of the country and then call her to drop the bombshell.

"If it's that bad, why don't you go and stay with one of your regulars?"

"What do you mean, stay with one of my regulars?"

"Mum, don't try to fucking fool me. I know you're on the game. You have been my entire fucking life. Just go and stay with one of them."

"How dare you even suggest that. I'm not on the game. Just because my male friends like to look after me, you're saying I'm a prostitute."

"That's exactly what I am saying."

"Even if I was, all those guys have families of their own, so they aren't going to want me around. They wouldn't even acknowledge me in the street."

She was saying this, but then saying she wasn't a prostitute. I hated her. Hated the sight of her. Listening to her lies over and over again, I just didn't want to hear it anymore.

"Whatever, Mum. You are not coming down here. I have got Madeleine to agree to everything. If you turn up then the chances are she will change her mind and cause complications. Everything is set up for Wednesday afternoon, as I said. It's only a few more days. If I can put up with her and the brat for that time, you can put up with Brian or stay in a hotel."

"I can just come down to Canterbury. I don't have to stay with you. I just need to get away."

"I'm not in Canterbury. I had to get an appointment at another town."

"But, Thomas ..."

"No, Mum. Just stick to the plan we made. If we start making changes, there is more chance of things going wrong. It's just five days. I'm sure you can live with that."

"Thomas."

"Look, I have to go. I will call you once everything is done and we can meet up to get away. I'll see you on Wednesday."

Before she could say anymore, I hung up the call. I couldn't stand to hear any more of her fucking whining. I needed to keep my distance from her, the further the better. I just hoped that she didn't decide to drive down here and show up at her nephew's place. I knew it was getting late and Rosie would be up at the crack of dawn. I hoped things would be easier with Madeleine here. It did seem Rosie was happy to be around her.

That meant that I could go to sleep in my current state and not have to worry about getting up with her in the morning. Yeah, I could put up with this for a few days. Getting up from the settee, I headed off into my bedroom. I stopped outside Madeleine's room. For a moment I thought about walking in there and repeating what I had done three years ago. But I would for once be a man of my word. As long as she did exactly as I said, I would leave her alone. Once I got what I wanted, maybe I would change my mind. I would just head to my room and dream of that night together.

Chapter Thirty-Four

Tyler

.... ⋙⋘ ....

We had been in Canterbury now for nearly twenty-four hours and were still no closer to pinpointing exactly where Thomas and Maddie were staying. I was infuriated at how long it was taking. We should have been able to find him easily, but every lead we thought we had come up short. According to all of the letting agents we had spoken to so far they had not rented out any short-term lets in the past week. We weren't sure if any of them just didn't want to give us the information or if they were telling us the truth.

His car hadn't been seen since Friday morning when it left Canterbury towards Ashford. We were starting to wonder whether he was actually still in the area or if he had gone further afield. The only thing that had us thinking he was still in the area was the car he was using had not entered Ashford where we would have found it on one of the cameras that they had there.

I was starting to get worried. I hoped that he wasn't doing anything to Maddie while she was staying with him. It had taken her so long to be able to get close to me. If Thomas had tried or done anything to her, then the chances were that we would be back to square one again. Maybe she would never let me or another man get close to her ever again.

Callum had been trying just as hard to help, but even he couldn't find any information. Brian had contacted me and offered to come down and help. I said that it was probably best if he stayed away. If he really needed to get away from Michelle, then he should head back down to Kings View. Mason had offered for him to stay at his house, although I think that was partly so there was someone there to look after Jess, Ashleigh, and baby Callum. He had said that he would wait to hear from us and would head down as soon as he knew Maddie and Rosie were safe, but if there was anything he could do to help he would. He was trying to get as much information as he could from Michelle but so far, she had denied knowing anything. Unfortunately, I had a feeling that was the truth. I suspected that Thomas didn't want anything to do with his mother.

To me it was obvious that everything he had told Maddie was a lie. He wanted nothing to do with either her or Rosie. I just couldn't believe that he had managed to manipulate Maddie to make her believe his lies. I know she loved Rosie, but she had already agreed to let us deal with things for her.

I was going out of my mind just sitting here in the hotel room. We were staying at the Howfield Manor Country Hotel in Chartham Hatch. We wanted to be as close to where we thought Thomas was staying to be able to get there quickly if we needed to. The problem was we could be sitting right next to him and wouldn't be any closer to finding him. Brandon and Mason had gone out a couple of hours ago to check out the area and to follow up on a couple of the letting agents that hadn't gotten back to me. So, Richard and I were just sitting here, going through various leads on the computer.

"We have got to be missing something, Tyler. We have tried everything and we are still no closer to finding Maddie. What the fuck are we doing wrong?"

I could tell Richard was as worried as I was. He hadn't known Maddie long, but like everyone who ever met her, you couldn't help but feel as if she was your best friend. She was always so welcoming to anyone she met, including Kye. She knew exactly what part he had played in Sienna's kidnapping, but like the rest of us, we all looked past that and brought him into the folds of our close circle.

"I know. I just wish that Maddie would contact me. I know she said she didn't want me to contact her, but I think I should at least try."

"Fuck, that's it, Tyler. That's the one thing we haven't done, run a trace on her phone again. Hopefully she may have switched it back on. God that should have been the first thing we did once we got down here. Why didn't we think of that already?"

"Probably because the pair of us haven't slept for two days and clearly aren't thinking straight. I'm sure Mason and Brandon have already tried, but it's worth another go. I'll send her a message and we can see if we get a reply. Either way we should be able to trace it."

"I'll start the trace now. Can you put her number in?"

I entered her number into the trace program, along with Thomas's. It would probably be best to check both. I sent off a message asking her to please contact me, and we both sat there and waited to see whether we got either a message back or got a trace on the phones.

It only took about ten minutes for my phone to notify me that I had received a message. Looking down I was filled with hope when I saw it was from Maddie's phone. That hope was completely dashed when I opened it up and read the message out loud.

> *Tyler, fuck off and leave me alone. I don't want anything more to do with you. I'm happy here with Thomas and Rosie. We are going to stay together and be a family. Don't contact me again. Madeleine.*

"Tyler, don't get upset. It's obvious that Thomas has Maddie's phone. Look how she has signed it, Madeleine. She never calls herself that, she doesn't like it. All the other messages she has sent you have all said Madds or Maddie. He has fallen into the trap. Don't get disheartened. This is good because the trace will happen a lot quicker now he has used the phone. You know that, Tyler."

I did know that. But it still didn't stop the pain and hurt that I was currently feeling. Maddie was with the one man that had caused her both pain and happiness with Rosie. Richard got up from his chair and walked over to me. In the past two weeks Richard and I had grown closer than even me and Nathan. There was a part of me that regretted that. I didn't have my best friend with me, but Nathan had distanced himself from both myself and Jayden recently. Neither of us knew why, but at the moment, I was just glad to have someone to help me through everything I was going through. He placed a hand on my shoulder.

"We will find them both. I promise you that, and no matter what I will be there for you. You've become a real friend to me, one I'm not sure I really deserve. You have accepted me for who I am, even knowing my preferences. There are a lot of guys out there that would run a mile, afraid that I would come on to them. But you haven't, and I can't thank you enough for that. You know, if things don't work out between you and Maddie ..."

I knew exactly where he was going with this conversation, I

just didn't know how serious he was.

"Richard, I'm flattered you could think of me in that way. But you would hate to see me naked."

The pair of us just looked at each other and burst out laughing. We both needed the release, despite seeming misplaced. We had been working on minimal hours of sleep and had hardly eaten the past few days. How we were even functioning was a miracle. Probably one of the reasons why we hadn't even thought about one of the simplest things we could do to find Maddie. As we both continued to laugh at our shared joke, Richard's laptop notified us that it had found something and Richard immediately went over to see.

"You're not going to fucking believe this. They are less than a mile away from us!"

"What?"

We had been joined again by Mason and Brandon and had now pinpointed the exact house where Thomas had Maddie and Rosie. It was all they could do to stop me from running up there to go and get him. We were now trying to trace where Thomas was renting the house from. We had a plan in place, but to put it in motion we had to get the letting agent on board. I was pacing the hotel room trying to calm myself down. Much to the annoyance of Mason and Brandon, Richard just seemed to be engrossed in what was happening on his laptop.

"Will you fucking stand still for a moment, Tyler? We know where she is, and we have a camera set up at the only road out of where he is staying. If he makes a move, we will know about it and can follow him. Brandon and I have already been up to the bungalow and all seems quiet. Just calm the fuck down."

"That's easy for you to say, Mason. Just remember how you

fucking felt when Chris had Jess, or how Brandon felt when Nikolaos had Ashleigh. Just remember that and then say that again."

I knew I was out of order speaking to the pair of them like this. They had both been through hell when their woman had been taken, but that should also make them realise what I was currently going through. I was completely lost without her.

"That was out of order, Tyler, and you know it. But I'm sorry for losing it with you. Look, we are all on edge as much as you. Jess hasn't stopped messaging me trying to find out what's going on. Told me if I didn't bring her best friend back that I might as well not bother coming home myself. None of us have slept properly and we are all living on our nerves. I guess we all need to let off some steam, but that doesn't mean we should be taking it out on each other."

Looking at the guys around me, I knew there wasn't anyone else I wanted to help me. Sure, I loved Jayden and Nathan, even Kye to some degree. But there was something about having friends help that weren't close friends. In the same way I had been there for Brandon instead of Mason. Jayden had turned to Justin instead of me or Nathan. Mason was the only one who needed his best friend. I guess that says a lot about him, or it says more about us.

"I'm sorry. I was out of order. I guess it's because we are so close, yet so far away from getting them back. I just worry about what he could be doing to her."

"I'm sure she is fine, Tyler. I don't think he would do anything to jeopardise getting what he needs. He might threaten her, but I don't think he'd follow through this time. None of the messages suggest that anyway."

I still couldn't be sure. All I wanted to do was pulverise the guy. Mason had contacted Callum, and they were also working on finding out who had rented the bungalow. We were hoping to speak to the letting agent or the owner to arrange a house inspection. They could use the excuse that it hadn't been done before they had taken over the residency. Mason and Brandon were going to do the inspection and then take it from there. But before any of that could happen, we needed to find out who it was. All we could do was sit here and wait for the info to come to us.

We were just all sitting here, waiting. Time passes so slowly when you're waiting. The old saying a watched pot never boils, well it definitely held more understanding for me now as we sat there in silence. Nearly all of us jumped when Mason's phone broke the silence.

"Mason King ... Hi, Callum. Let me put you on speaker phone so I don't have to explain a second time to Tyler. There you go."

"Hi, guys. So I have the letting agent that is renting out the bungalow to Thomas. I have spoken to them and let them know you will be contacting them and to help in any way you can. I've also taken the liberty to contact Kent Constabulary so they are aware of the situation should you need them, or they are called."

"Thanks, Callum. I really appreciate it."

"No problem, Tyler. It seems to be a full-time job lately, helping out with your women. Just try to remind the rest of the guys that I am a Detective Inspector with the Met police and not your personal law enforcement," letting out a laugh, none of us could stop ourselves laughing along. We all knew Callum and the rest of his team well. Mason and Brandon most of all as they had been stationed together in the SAS. "Anyway, enough of that. What's the plan?"

"We thought about going for a house inspection. Brandon and I could head in there and pretend to do an inspection. Say one couldn't be done before they took over. Then overpower Thomas and get Maddie and Rosie."

"Nice plan, as long as he isn't tooled up."

"Callum, this is a guy that rapes young women. Sorry to say that, but it's the truth. He isn't going to be any match for us. He was frightened of Maddie's Dad. Although he is in the forces, he's a kitten compared to me and Brandon. Although I would never say that to his face."

Mason smiled over at me as he said that. He was right. None of us would dare say that to his face. I had a feeling that there was more to Brian than the man we met three days ago, and I'm sure whatever he was hiding from us, was not something any of us would like to see.

"Sounds like a good plan. I'll make a detective out of you yet Mason King."

"In your dreams, Callum. I like the independence of running my own business too much to join the police. I was ordered about enough in the forces, thank you. I'll call if we need any assistance, but I think we have this one covered."

"No problem, Mason. And Tyler, we expect another wedding invitation. The guys have them stacking up at the moment. This will be the fourth. I'll send the details over to your phone, Mason. Good luck."

We were all still laughing as Mason said his goodbyes to Callum. He had taken the phone off speaker mode and walked out of the room. I suppose because there were things he needed to say without any of us hearing. He was gone a lot longer than we all expected and when he walked back into the room we all turned as the room went silent, waiting to hear what he had to say.

"We have an appointment tomorrow morning at 10:00. The letting agent is going to phone him today and let him know. Any problems and they will get back to me. Just one more night, Tyler. Tomorrow, Maddie and Rosie will be back with us."

"But will they?"

"We've come this far, Tyler. Don't give up yet. We will deal with anything as and when it comes up. For now, just have faith in the guys sitting in this room with you."

Nodding my head, I left it there. I had the utmost faith in every single member of my team. What I wasn't sure about is whether I still had a life with Maddie at the end of this. I had one more night to get through before I found out. All I could do now was hope and pray that we came out of this unscathed and as a family together.

Chapter Thirty-Five

Thomas

⸻ ❧ ⸻

I was amazed that I had woken up this morning without a hangover. The amount of scotch I had put away last night I should have felt like shit, but I had woken remarkably well. Madeleine had kept her distance and had kept Rosie amused all day. So that just meant I could finally relax and forget about everything.

Much to my surprise, Madeleine had cooked us a lovely roast for lunch. I had to admit that it was always nice at home when she was there. We always had something good to eat, even if she hated both me and my Mum, she never let us starve. We even managed to have a civil conversation over the table, and in different circumstances I could almost find myself enjoying her company. But I couldn't allow myself that kind of closeness. She was here for one reason and one reason alone. So, I could get the fifty grand that came from selling Rosie.

Nothing could stamper my good mood, until my phone rang that was.

"Thomas Smith."

"Hello, Mr. Smith. It's Greg here from Canterbury City Lettings. Sorry to bother you on a Sunday afternoon but we have noticed in our paperwork that we didn't do a house inspection before you moved into the bungalow you are renting."

"Well, I'm only here until Friday, so can't you do it when I leave."

"I'm very sorry, Mr. Thomas, but part of our agreement with the owner is we have to do an inspection before every changeover. I wondered whether it would be okay for us to come round tomorrow morning at ten?"

"Do I really have a choice?"

"Well, I hoped that you would understand. If the time isn't convenient then we can arrange another time."

"No, I guess that will be fine. I will be here with my girlfriend and our daughter. Will that be a problem?"

"That will be fine, Mr. Smith. Thank you for being so understanding. It will be a Mr. Mason King and a Mr. Brandon James who will be coming around. It should only take about thirty minutes. We won't inconvenience you too much. Thank you."

"Okay, well we will see them then."

I hung up the phone. I would have to talk to Madeleine. Make sure she knew exactly how to act around them. This could cause trouble, but I was sure that I would be able to get her to act correctly, if she wanted to stay untouched by me anyway. I would leave that discussion until tomorrow morning though. No need to dampen her day as much as mine. Plus I was hoping for some form of meal for the evening. I just hoped they didn't suspect anything when they turned up, or trouble could ensue.

I was still reeling over the telephone call I had yesterday afternoon. Why would they suddenly want to do a house inspection? I had only rented the property for one week. It was more like an Airbnb than renting. So why did they want to check the house? I know they said it was because they hadn't done one before I moved in, but still. I just had to keep my cool. They would only be here for thirty minutes tops. It wouldn't take that long to go around the place, hell it was only one level so probably would only take them around fifteen minutes. I just had to make sure that Maddie kept Rosie occupied and played the part of my doting girlfriend. I heard her moving about in the bedroom, so I waited for her to come into the kitchen. I knew she had to have her coffee every morning, so she would head straight here. I wasn't wrong and she walked in.

"Oh sorry, I didn't realise you were up. I'll come back when you're done."

"No, please, we need to talk. Take a seat."

I could see the hesitation in her eyes, full of concern and worry. Any other time I would be happy that I had put that fear in her, but this morning I was more worried for myself. Worried about what this meeting would do to our dynamic. Would she scream for help as soon as the agents walked through the door? I hoped not because I was told two agents were arriving at ten. If she said anything to them then I could have the police here in no time. I had to make sure that Madeleine would do exactly as she was told. Looking up, I saw she had finally got a mug of coffee and was now sitting at the table with me.

"What do we need to talk about?"

"We have visitors coming today. The letting agents that I rented this place from didn't have a chance to inspect the property before I moved in. So, they are sending out two guys to do an inspection today. I just wanted to remind you what is at stake if you do anything stupid. As far as they are concerned, we are a happy family just on a week's break and this was all we could find. I just need you to keep Rosie occupied and your mouth shut, okay?"

"I won't say or do anything, Thomas. I will just stay out of the way in the front room and read to Rosie. I will let you deal with everything."

"Just see you do that. Well, I guess we better make sure the house is presentable.

We spent the next hour making sure that the house was tidy and presentable. All of Rosie's toys were kept in one place in the corner. It didn't take us that long as we hadn't made that much of a mess. Even I wasn't that much of an untidy bachelor. I didn't like to live in a mess. I wasn't a neat freak, but I kept most places neat and tidy, just some clothes that needed to be put away and the washing up from breakfast to be done.

The place was clean by 9:30 so I made another pot of coffee and waited in the kitchen while Madeleine dealt with Rosie who was now wide awake and demanding attention.

"I'm just going to sit down with Rosie and read to her. I will keep out of your way while the letting agents are here. I'll smile sweetly and act like your doting girlfriend."

"I would appreciate that, thank you."

I watched as she walked into the front room and sat down with Rosie and started to read to her. Even I had to admit that it was nice to see them together. Part of me actually felt sorry for taking them away from each other. But then the materialistic part of myself reminded me that the girl was worth fifty grand.

I sat at the table in the kitchen waiting for our visitors to arrive.

It was just after ten when the doorbell rang. Getting up I walked over to the door and was greeted by two guys in suits. To be fair, they looked more like policemen than they did letting agents. My guard was immediately raised until one of them spoke.

"Mr. Thomas?"

"Yes."

"Good morning, my name is Mason King, and this is Brandon James from Canterbury City Lettings. I believe you are expecting us."

"Yes, please come in."

I showed our guests into the house.

"Where would you like to start? You will have to forgive us, my girlfriend is just keeping our daughter amused in the front room. Perhaps you would like to start there to keep the distraction down to a minimum for her."

"That would probably be best."

I showed them into the front room and spoke to Madeleine."

"Madeleine, this is Mr. King and Mr. James from the letting agency."

"Very pleased to meet you both."

I instantly saw a look of shock as she glanced up and spoke to the two men standing in front of her. She recognised them. I was sure of it. Her expression quickly turned neutral in a matter of seconds, but I had already seen it. There was something going on. I just needed to find out what.

"And you. Sorry to bother you, we will be out of the way soon."

Chapter Thirty-Six

Madeleine

I couldn't believe that Mason and Brandon had just walked into the house. I was sitting there almost shaking when I realised who it was. I hadn't heard them introduce themselves to Thomas, so it came as a little bit of a shock when Thomas introduced them as Mr. King and Mr. James. At first, I didn't put two and two together, until I looked up to acknowledge them there. I could see Thomas looking directly at me as Brandon signalled me to stay calm. I tried to not give anything away with the way I spoke or my facial expression, but I was sure that Thomas had realised something was wrong.

I went back to reading the story to Rosie, thinking that this might put Thomas at ease. However, it was obvious that Thomas was now on edge. Glancing back as he walked out of the door with Mason and Brandon, I just smiled at him and continued to read. Knowing they were here meant that Tyler was close. Did I make a break out of the front door or did I stay exactly where I was? I was in two minds. I was about to make my move, get out of the house and head for safety. But I couldn't be sure of exactly where Thomas was. Was he in a room with Mason and Brandon, where he would not see me leave, or was he outside looking to make sure I didn't go anywhere? I got my answer when I saw Thomas standing just outside the door to the front room. He obviously didn't trust me to stay where I was. I didn't look over at him, I daren't. I just continued to read. But I knew he was there. If I was going to get out of this house with Rosie, then it would be down to whatever plan Mason had come up with. They must have had one to turn up under the pretence of being with the letting agent.

My only concern was that they would leave me here with Thomas. I'm not sure I could handle what would come as soon as they walked out the door. Thomas must have realised by now that I knew these guys, because he was not going to let me out of his sight, no matter how causally I acted.

I could hear them walking around the bungalow. Pretending to be making notes on the condition of the place. All the while Thomas was glancing from me to the back of the bungalow. I tried to stay calm and continue to read to Rosie.

"Mr. Smith, could I just borrow you for a second? I just want to check something with you."

I looked up at Thomas as I heard Brandon calling out to him.

"Don't even think about moving, Madeleine. I can get to you a lot quicker than you can get out of this house."

"I wasn't planning on going anywhere. Where would I go even if I did get out of the house? It's not like we are close to any form of public transport now is it, Thomas?"

"Good, make sure you don't."

I could feel my heart rate increasing as he walked back to where Brandon and Mason were looking. A few moments later, I heard footsteps walking back down the hallway. Expecting to see Thomas come back into view, I was shocked when I saw Mason walk into the room and over to me. In an almost whisper he spoke to me.

"I don't think we have long. But we are here to get you out of here. Tyler and Richard are waiting outside. You will be leaving with us and not Thomas today. You and Rosie ..."

Before he could say anything else, Thomas was running into the front room. A look of pure anger on his face.

"What the fuck do you think you are doing? You don't work for the letting agents, do you? Who the fuck are you and what do you want with Madeleine?"

I could see Brandon walking up behind Thomas who flew around and faced him, pulling out a flip knife in the process. Not wanting any confrontation, Brandon immediately put his hands up in a form of surrender. I knew that either one of them could take Thomas down, but I also knew they would try to talk him down first. Neither of them liked any form of confrontation. I had realised that from all the time we spent together in the coffee shop when Jess had been kidnapped by Chris.

"Thomas, just put the knife down a second so we can talk," Brandon said looking directly at him, his hands still raised in surrender.

"Not until I've got some answers. Get in there with your buddy."

Thomas motioned Brandon to step into the front room next to Mason and then turned to me.

"Okay, which one of these two are you shagging? I assume that's why they are here, to come and get you. I must say your taste in men has improved after the dicks you were going out with after me."

"Thomas, I'm not shagging either of them. I don't know who they are. I thought ..."

"Don't give me that crap. I heard Mr. King here. I heard him say you and Rosie would be leaving with them and not me. Well, it's not happening. No one is taking either of them. They are mine to use and own."

"Thomas, let's just calm down here. No, we aren't from the letting agents, although they did set this meeting up for us. Yes, we are here for Maddie and Rosie. What you are planning to do is illegal, and it's not happening. Even if you had made it to the Registrar's office on Wednesday, they wouldn't have given you a new birth certificate. The only thing that would have been happening was you being arrested by the police for trying to sell a child. The police know everything. There is no way you are going to get out of this with what you want."

"You haven't got any proof."

"Oh, we have plenty of proof. We have all of the text messages that you have been sending your associate. And as we currently speak the police are on their way to arrest Mr. Roger Golding. That is the gentleman you have been dealing with, isn't it?"

I saw the look of worry and anger go across Thomas' face. I could see this wasn't going to end well. Someone was going to get hurt, and I didn't want that to be one of my friends. If it was going to be anyone, it would be me. I slowly stood, still with Rosie in my arms. I could see Mason looking at me with worried eyes, pleading with me not to do anything stupid. I wasn't going to get close to Thomas, I just wanted to be on the same level as him. Not that I was anywhere near as tall as him, but I just wanted to look him as close as I could in the eye. I knew he wasn't all bad, just dealt a shitty life by Michelle. Quietly, and as calmly as I could given the current situation, I spoke.

"Thomas, is it really worth it, all of this? Is it worth getting hurt or even killed, spending time in jail for trying to sell a child? Yes, I do know Mason and Brandon, but I didn't plan this. I had nothing to do with this. They are private investigators. I work for Mason's fiancé, Jess. It was obvious as soon as I walked away from where I live, they were going to try and find me. That's what friends do. They love me, and I know deep down somewhere in you, you love Rosie too. I have seen how you are with her. She's your daughter, Thomas. How can you think about selling her just to get fifty grand? I know you hate me, and you don't regret anything you did to me. I can live with that and have learnt to deal with it. But what about Rosie? For her sake don't do anything stupid. You could still be part of her life if you give yourself up now."

"I don't want to hear another thing from you, bitch," Thomas said as he swung round to me holding the knife towards me. I could see Brandon and Mason ready to pounce on him if he made another move. I just looked over, trying to stay as calm as possible and shook my head. He wouldn't attack me and Rosie, I could sense he was already starting to doubt his plan. I held out my hand.

"Give me the knife, Thomas. It's not worth it. It's over. Please. Think of yourself and Rosie. We can get you help, get you away from Michelle. If it's money you need, then I will do everything I can to help you out. I have some savings. It's not much, but I can get a loan, anything. Just please don't take Rosie away from me. I can't live without her."

I saw him hesitate slightly, and for a brief moment I thought he was going to give me the knife.

"You think your little speech is going to change my mind, Madeleine? I never wanted you or the brat. You were just a means to get laid in my drunken state, it was a bonus to find out you were a fucking virgin. But I never wanted you or a fucking child. The only good thing to come out of this is the fifty grand I'm going to get on Wednesday afternoon. Now hand Rosie over."

There was nothing I could say or do to make him change his mind. I could only see rage and anger in his eyes now. He was never going to give this up without a fight. I just had to hope that we all came out of this unharmed. I felt the tears as they started to fall from my eyes. The fear finally took over my body. But I had to try and stay strong for Rosie, for myself. I couldn't let him see that he was affecting me in this way. In his mind he would have won if he did. Mason started to speak again.

"Look, Thomas. Nothing good is going to come of this. The police could be here in a matter of minutes if we call them. They know we are here and what is going on. If you give yourself up now, then you will be given a much lighter sentence than if you carry on this charade. Don't be stupid, Thomas. We're ex SAS soldiers, we can take you down in a matter of seconds if you force us to. But we want to stop this amicably. Just give me the knife."

Mason was trying to reason with him, but I knew Thomas would not give up without a fight. He never had.

"I have already told you once. You are not taking what is rightfully mine. Rosie is my daughter, and I can do whatever I damn well please with her. If that means I sell her to the highest bidder, then that is what I am going to do. And you two PIs aren't going to do a damn thing about it. Madeleine, come here."

"I'm not going anywhere with you, Thomas. Neither is Rosie. She is my daughter too and I refuse to let you sell her. She belongs with me and always has. It was just your greed and selfishness that kept me away from her for so long. The lies you and Michelle told my Dad nearly broke him. Rosie and I are going to be a family again, and there is nothing you can do about it.

"We'll see about that."

In a matter of seconds Thomas was lunging toward me with the knife. My automatic reaction was to turn my back to him to protect Rosie. I was waiting to feel the pain of Thomas running into me and plunging the knife in. But that pain never came. I turned to see him fighting with Mason and Brandon. The pair of them had blocked Thomas' path to me and were now trying to dodge his knife attack.

I could see Thomas slashing the knife towards Mason and Brandon and was terrified they were both going to be hurt. I had to stop this now. It couldn't carry on. Thomas was acting like a madman who couldn't see that this was a battle he was never going to win. The sound of the three of them fighting carried throughout the room. There was a smash of glass as Thomas threw a vase that was on the coffee table towards Brandon's head. Brandon just ducked in time as it flew past him and smashed against the wall. I couldn't take it much more.

"THOMAS, NO!"

I was screaming at him to stop, everything was happening so fast. When I saw the blood on the ground I screamed. I wasn't sure whose blood it was, but I hoped that it wasn't Mason or Brandon's. Rosie was crying in my arms, and I could barely stand with the fear that was going through me. I wasn't sure how long I stood there before the door burst open. Looking up I saw him. Tyler. The man that I loved. I ran around Mason and Brandon who had finally got Thomas pinned on the ground, arms held behind his back as he struggled to break free. I didn't stop until I flung myself into Tyler's arms.

Chapter Thirty-Seven

Tyler

⸺⸺⸺ ✦ ⸺⸺⸺

I t was just before ten o'clock and we were about to head up to where Thomas was holding Maddie and Rosie. I was under strict instructions by Mason that I was to stay outside with Richard. Every part of my body was on edge. I wanted to be the one to go in there with him. I knew he was right though, as soon as I walked through the door and saw Maddie standing there, I would want to grab her into my arms. Not really the right entrance for someone who is meant to be doing a house inspection. The plan Mason had come up with was a good one, the right one. I just had to sit and wait it out. Any sign of trouble and we could phone the police and be there in a matter of seconds.

I just wished I was still in the army. I know I didn't see much front line action like Jayden and Nathan, but I knew how to use a gun, and I would feel a lot more comfortable right now if I had one. I just had to hope that Thomas didn't. This situation could go from bad to deadly in a matter of seconds if he did. We had seen too many guns in the past year to have to deal with more. We were just lucky that both Kye and Ashleigh had come out of both situations alive, not unscathed, but at least alive.

We had agreed with the hotel Manager that they would keep our rooms for us for the day and night, which of course, had nothing to do with the huge payment that Mason had given them for doing so. All in all, if the situation had been different, our stay would have been an extremely pleasant one. Mason walked out of his room to meet us in the lobby.

"Are we all ready for this?

"As ready as I'll ever be," I replied with a hint of fear in my voice.

"It will be okay, Tyler. You just need to let us do what we are good at. I know we are all trained for this kind of thing, but Brandon and myself have always worked well together in situations like this. Just trust us to keep Maddie and Rosie safe. We will call for help if we need it. I just need you to stay calm and not come barrelling in at the first sign of trouble, okay?"

I nodded my head in agreement with him. I wasn't going to make any promises. Not yet anyway. The woman I love was in that bungalow, along with her daughter who I had already claimed as my own, even if I was the only one who knew that. But as soon as this was over, I was going to make sure everyone knew, and I was going to make it happen. Amelia seemed happy to have Jayden and Sienna as parents after they adopted her, so why couldn't I do the same with Rosie?

"Let's get this show on the road, shall we?"

We all headed out of the hotel lobby and headed out to our cars. Mason and Brandon were going to head up first and we would follow about five minutes later to give them a chance to get inside. They had already scoped out the area and chosen a place for us to park where we could see the bungalow in plain sight, but it wouldn't be suspicious to anyone inside or walking past. There weren't any other homes nearby, so we didn't have to worry about nosey neighbours getting involved or calling the police. It also helped that they were aware of everything that was happening, another reason why Mason was in charge, he thought of everything.

I saw them drive up the road and immediately felt a mixture of emotions. Excitement, worry, anticipation, dread. The latter being the one I most feared. What would I do if this all went tits up? What would become of me if I lost the only woman I had ever or would ever love. It wasn't a thought I wanted to contemplate, but it was the only thing going around in my head. As if sensing my internal turmoil, Richard placed his hand on my shoulder. I don't know what I would have done without him these past few weeks. He had always been there for me, always knew exactly what to say or do when I went to that dark place in my mind. If he was my partner, or lover, you would say he had been my rock. But that is exactly what he had been. I just hoped he found someone who loved him as much as I did Maddie. He deserved to have someone in his life to be there for him. He would always have my friendship, but sometimes that wasn't enough, and Richard was the kind of guy that should have someone in his life to love and care for him. Immediately I felt hopeful, not just for me and Maddie, but for everyone we cared for and loved. I knew we could get through this. We had each other after all.

"It's time to make a move, Tyler," Richard said, pulling me from my thoughts. I smiled at him and did the only thing I needed to do at that moment. I pulled him into a hug. I loved him like a brother, and right then I just needed to make him realise that. Pulling away, I saw a slight look of shock on his face.

"Thank you, Richard. Thank you for everything, for being

there for me. For knowing exactly what to say when I needed to hear it."

"Tyler, you don't have to say ..."

"I do. I need to say this to you while I still can. Before we get wrapped up in the emotions of the day. You may have come into our lives because of Sienna, may not have been with us during our time in the army. But I still see you as one of my best friends, a brother, and I just wanted you to know. I love you, man."

"God, you can be a sappy shit at times can't you. But I love you too. No chance of ..."

"No there fucking isn't, now let's go get my girl."

We both knew we were joking with each other. There would never be any romantic feelings between us. Just brotherly love. But the friendship we had grown over the past few weeks allowed us that kind of intimacy, even if it was joking. I couldn't ask for a better man to call my friend, especially now, when by one simple statement he had set me at ease. He allowed me to clear my head so I could face what was about to come. We walked to the car and got in to head up to the bungalow.

It was only a five-minute drive, if that, and we parked exactly where Mason had indicated we should. We could see his truck parked outside and there was no sign of either of them. Good, they must already be inside. All we had to do now was wait. I was back on edge again. I wanted to be in there, wanted to know exactly what was going on. Sitting outside and just waiting, well, I was starting to realise exactly what Mason and Brandon had been through with Jess and Sienna. I had a new respect for both of them.

"Look, I know it's easy for me to say this sitting here, especially as I am only a friend of Maddie's. But the two guys in there are two of the best. I have known a lot of ex military guys and none of them are a patch on Brandon and Mason. They are always calm, no matter what is going on around them. You just have to trust them, the same as you would any of your friends. They would do anything for you and Maddie. I promise you that she will be fine."

"I wish you could make and keep that promise, Richard. Yes, I trust those guys with all our lives, Maddie and Rosie included. But there is one factor, or one person we can't account for, and that's Thomas. What if he has a gun? We all know how to use one properly, but does he? Anything can happen with someone who isn't properly trained. I have seen plenty of so-called gun users accidentally discharging their weapon. If Maddie or Rosie are anywhere near ..."

"Don't even think about it, Tyler. We just need to stay calm, and you need to be there when she comes out. You need to be her strength. I saw what William did to Sienna, and I'm not talking about the abuse. She needed someone to be her rock, and that turned out to be Jayden. You need to be that for Maddie and little Rosie. You need to keep a clear head and be ready to hold her, to make her feel safe and at home."

"I know, but I can't help it. I guess one day you will find out. Well, I hope you don't, but the way things are going, all four of us that have found our partners have had to deal with some kind of crisis to get there. I guess the odds are stacked against you here."

I hoped that this would be the end of it. I hoped that Nathan, Kye, and Richard all found the loves of their life without any issues. I think all of us had been through enough to last us a lifetime, and that was without five of us entering war zones as we had. It was only then I realised exactly what Richard was doing, what he did best, distracting me. He would have been fantastic in the army. I could see him having all of us in stitches on every mission, just to keep us grounded. In fact, he was exactly the same as Mark. That was probably why Jayden got on so well with Richard, and had pressed for him to work for us. It was his way of remembering Mark.

"I hope one day I can find someone, Tyler. But I don't hold out much hope."

The silence fell between us again. I guess we had both said as much as we could say to keep each other's minds off what was going on in the bungalow. I knew Richard was just as worried as I was. We all were. The unknown of what was going to happen in that bungalow today, weighed heavy on all our minds. We all had to hope that Mason and Brandon were as good as we all knew they were. But it would all be down to how unstable Thomas was, and from what I had seen and heard, he was a very unstable character. Not quite as unstable as Chris who had taken Jess, but still enough to make us all worry.

With the windows of our truck open, we would hear if there were any problems inside the place. But all there was, was silence. Well as silent as the countryside could be. I had always been a city boy, the same as Jayden and Richard. But there was a lot to be said about the life in the country that Mason and Brandon had now chosen. The serene quietness was soothing to the mind and body. It was something I had learned to appreciate the more time I spent in Kings View. I'm not sure I could live as far out of the town as they did. I still needed the closeness of other people to feel at home, but the more relaxed pace of life was definitely something I could get used to. I would have to, if we could ever get Maddie and Rosie out of that place and away from Thomas.

I was immediately brought back into the present with that thought. What was taking them so long? They had been in there for nearly forty minutes now. It shouldn't take that long for them to overpower one guy. The worry was building inside of me. Something must have gone wrong. What if one of them got hurt? We hadn't heard any gunshots, so there was some relief in that. But that wasn't to say that no one in there was hurt.

I could see Richard starting to fidget next to me. His restlessness and worry, mimicking my own. We were both eager to get in there and deal with whatever situation we found. We may be computer geeks, but we still wanted to be part of the action. It was only then that I heard the most distressing sound of all. One that made my entire being shiver. That coldness that goes through you as if someone has just walked over your grave as they say. A scream. We both heard her as clear as day. Maddie was screaming at Thomas to stop. Before he could grab me, I was out of the truck with Richard shouting behind me.

"Tyler, we don't know what is happening in there. You might be walking into a trap."

I could hear him running behind me, trying to catch me up to stop me. But no one was going to stop me from getting in there, to my woman and girl. I had already noted the front door when we arrived. It was an old wooden door. It wouldn't take much for me to break it down. I ran up to it and placed two kicks onto it. The door flew open and I almost ran inside to the pleas of Richard behind me.

"Tyler, don't go in there please. Tyler!"

I wasn't listening. I had long since blocked him from my mind. My only thought now was to get into that bungalow and see Maddie. She and Rosie were my only priority, and fuck everything else. I stopped in the doorway and my eyes immediately met those of Maddie, my woman. The tears were pouring down her face as she held a crying Rosie close to her. She was safe. Nothing had happened to them. It was only when she started running towards me that I looked around to see Brandon holding Thomas on the floor and placing zip ties around his wrists to control him. Then I saw the blood and was immediately concerned for Maddie.

She crashed into my arms and it was all I could do to not fall onto the floor with the force she reached me with. Carefully I held her. I wanted to squeeze her so tightly, but I had to remember little Rosie was in her arms.

"Are you hurt?"

"Tyler, I love you."

"I love you too, sweetheart, but I need to know if you or Rosie are hurt. The blood. Is any of it yours?"

"I'm fine. Just hold me Tyler. Let me feel that you're real."

I stood there as the relief suddenly hit me, and the tears I had been holding back started to fall. It was over. I had my girls in my arms, and I was never letting them go again.

Chapter Thirty-Eight

Tyler

I t was finally over. I had my girls in my arms where I needed them to be. The tears were pouring down both our faces, but there was just one thing I needed to do. I placed my lips against hers. Running my tongue across her lip I could taste the saltiness of both our tears on them. She gratefully parted her lips and deepened the kiss. We both needed this. Both needed the grounding that came from being connected in this way. I pulled away from the kiss to look into her tear filled eyes. "I was so worried, sweetheart. I'm not going to argue with you about what you did. All I know is you are safe. Both of you, and that is all I care about. Just say you will never leave me again."

"I have everything I need right here, Tyler. You and Rosie, there is no other place I would rather be. Except at home."

We both smiled at each other. It was only then that Thomas

decided to cause a scene.

"Let me fucking go, you bastards! You're not taking Rosie away from me. She's mine to sell and I will fucking do it when I get these fucking ties off my wrists. Let me go NOW!"

With one swift punch, Mason knocked him out.

"That's better. I can't stand hearing that kind of language in front of a lady and a child. Maddie, are you okay?"

"I'm fine, but what about you and Brandon? You've both been cut."

"Nothing we can't handle. We've been in worse states than this, haven't we Brandon?"

I watched Brandon get up from the floor and saw the cuts to his arms, the same as Mason. Luckily they hadn't got any cuts to the face. I think Jess and Ashleigh would have killed them and me if they had.

"Yeah, I'm good. Takes more than this idiot to put us down."

Richard casually walked into the room, phone in his hand.

"Took you long enough to get in here, and you did a piss poor job of keeping him out."

"Hey, Mason. I kept him out for forty-five minutes. All bets were off when Maddie screamed. If I'd been outside I could have stopped him. But nooooo, you said to stay in the car. I didn't have a chance. Anyway, the police are on their way along with an ambulance. I have let everyone know Maddie and Rosie are safe and Brian is about thirty minutes away from your place. Jayden, Nathan, and Kye are also heading down."

"Wow, you have been busy."

"Group chat, one message. Get with the times, Brandon. Anyone would think you were a dinosaur."

The whole room erupted into laughter, as we heard the sirens arriving in the distance.

"I guess I should introduce you to Rosie, now that everything has calmed down. Rosie, these are the friends I was telling you about. We can meet them all later when we get home. Say hello to them all, Poppet."

"Heyo, evyone."

There was a chorus of *hello, Rosie*, from all of us in the room and the smile on her face was adorable. She looked up at me while I was still holding Maddie and gave me an amazing smile.

"Tyer?"

"Yes, that's me. I'm Tyler, and I am very pleased to meet you, Rosie."

She moved her hands where she had been holding onto Maddie and held them up to me. I looked over at Maddie who just smiled and shrugged her shoulders. I was shocked that she wanted me to hold her. I let go of Maddie and took Rosie in my arms, she flung hers around my neck, gave me a big squeeze, and kissed me on the cheek. I could have burst into tears of joy right there and then. This little girl who I had never met but loved already, was showing me all the love she could in her own way. In that one moment, it appeared that she had completely accepted me.

"I think she likes you, Tyler," Maddie said.

"Do you like me, Rosie?"

"I love Tyer. Mummy can Tyer stay wiv us? Don't want to go back to Nanny."

"I don't know, Poppet. Tyler might not want to stay with us. You'll have to ask him."

"Tyer, pweese stay wiv me and Mummy."

"How can I resist, when you ask so nicely? Yes, I will stay with you and Mummy. We can talk about it more when we get home. There are lots of people that want to say hello, and I think Grandad might be there too."

"Yay, gandad!"

It was right at that moment when the police and paramedics parked outside. I hadn't realised that while we were talking, Mason and Brandon had gone outside to meet them, and Richard had stayed where he could see if Thomas came round, but still gave us some privacy. He stuck his head around the corner.

"Tyler, the police and ambulance are here. They will want to speak to Maddie and make sure they are both okay. You might want to bring them outside now. The sooner we get this over with, the sooner we can get home. I'm sure little Rosie is tired."

"Not tired."

"Okay, Rosie. Sorry, you are not tired. But you must be hungry."

"Macs?"

"Don't tell Mummy, but I'm sure we can convince Mason to stop at McDonald's on the way back."

"Fank you, Tyer. You are the best."

"I know, Pops. Can I call you Pops, Rosie?"

"Yes, Tyer. Can I call you Daddy?"

I couldn't believe what this little girl in my arms had just asked me. I looked over at Maddie and saw the tears in her eyes. I knew they were happy tears as she had the biggest smile on her face.

"Let's talk about that later, Pops. First let's get some food and home as quickly as we can, shall we?"

"Okay, Daddy."

I wasn't going to correct her. I was loving it if I was truthful.

"Come, let's get you both checked out and then we can head off home."

I placed my arm around Maddie and led her back out of the bungalow to the waiting ambulance and police. After being checked out by the medics and giving her statement to the police, it was time for us to all head back home. I had left the girls in the front room talking to the police. I didn't want to hear what Maddie went through, not yet. We would talk later tonight once everything had calmed down and we got Rosie settled. I'd already decided that I would stay on the couch until we could get a new house sorted for us. I would let Maddie and Rosie share her bed. It was the least I could do for them. I walked over to where the guys were waiting.

"How are you both doing? Looking at it, the blood looked worse than the actual wounds were."

"Yeah, just surface wounds really. Could have been a lot worse, if we didn't know what we were doing, and Thomas knew what he was. The paramedics said we would live, but they didn't recommend it."

"Very funny, Mason. The girls are just finishing up with the police and then we should be able to leave."

"How is Rosie? I have to admit she is adorable. Especially asking to call you Daddy."

"You heard that then, Richard? Yeah, she seems perfectly okay. I think she was just a little upset because Maddie was upset, but she wants me to stay with them, so I think all is good there."

"And, another one bites the dust. Only three of you left now, eh Richard?"

"Don't get your hopes up there, Brandon. It will take a special kind of person to end up with Richard, won't it bro?"

"You know it, Tyler."

I smiled at Richard. Our own private little joke. I could see the perplexed look on the faces of Brandon and Mason. They would find out soon enough, but it wasn't my place to say anything, but I would stand next to Richard when he did finally feel the need to tell them, for moral support. Although I knew he wouldn't really need it.

"Can we stop off and get McDonalds for Rosie on the way home? I promised I would convince you to stop. If we do it before we get too far, then I think she will probably be asleep within thirty minutes. I believe there is a car seat in Thomas's car we can use that for the moment."

"No problem. Is Maddie okay with it?"

"I kind of promised Rosie without asking. I was so caught up with her asking to call me Daddy, I forgot to ask. I'm sure she will be fine this one time. I won't make a habit of it. Not without Maddie's knowledge anyway. Come on, I have to be the one to spoil her more than Brian."

We all stood there laughing as Maddie and Rosie walked out with the detective behind her. Thomas had already been taken away after coming conscious not long after the police had arrived. They ignored his pleas that we had gone in there and beaten him up, but that might have had something to do with all the cuts on Mason and Brandon.

"You are all free to leave now. But we may need you to come back down for some questions, so please don't leave the country."

"Don't worry, sir, we all know the rules. One of my army buddies is a detective in the Met. We will make sure we are available for any questions you may have."

"Thank you, Mr. King. Have a safe journey home."

With that, he headed off with the rest of the police. Maddie walked over to me with Rosie and put her arm around my waist. I kissed her on the top of her head.

"Are you ready to head home?"

"More than ready. Let's go."

***

It was a little after three o'clock when we all got back to Mason's house at Kings view. The front of the house was full of vehicles. When they said everyone was going to be here they weren't wrong. If I wasn't mistaken, Jayden and Mason's parents were here too. I helped Maddie out of the car and gently got Rosie out of her seat. As I had guessed, within ten minutes of us leaving McDonalds, she was fast asleep and was still asleep now. I didn't want to wake her. Today had been very hectic and probably quite traumatic for her. I knew she shouldn't sleep too much, but I was guessing as soon as she heard Brian's voice, she would wake up quite quickly. She adored her grandad after all.

We walked into the house and the place was buzzing. I thought for a moment that Mason was going to lose it, but a swift hug and kiss from Jess as he walked in soon calmed him slightly. Although I think he would have much preferred to do something far better than deal with a house full of guests.

"The guys are out back having a beer, and before you start complaining, it's low alcohol, and Jayden brought them with him. Your drinks cabinet is still intact. Now get out of the way. I need to see my bestie."

Jess came barrelling over and grabbed Maddie into a hug. Mason walked over to me.

"Do you want to put Rosie down in one of the bedrooms?"

"No, I'll just sit outside with her. She will probably wake up as soon as she hears Brian's voice. I don't want her waking up and not knowing where she is. She has been through enough these past few days. I'll leave Maddie with the girls and come outside with you."

I gave Maddie a quick kiss and left her to chat with Jess, Ashleigh, Sienna and Joan, and headed out the back with a still sleeping Rosie in my arms. Walking outside I could see the guys all gathered on the deck. Jayden immediately got out of his chair to allow me to sit down with her. Before I could even get there, Brian had walked over to me.

"Thank you, Tyler. Thank you for bringing my girls home. I don't know what I would have done if I had lost both of them."

"You don't have to thank me, Brian. I wouldn't have been able to do much if I hadn't brought them home myself. Let me sit down and grab a drink. Mace, have you got any bourbon? I think I need something a little stronger than beer."

"I'll grab you a glass."

I walked over to the chair vacated by Jayden and sat down, nestling Rosie into my side. The guys all gathered around.

"Looks like she has taken a shine to you, Tyler. How much have you bribed her?"

"Very funny, Nathan. For your information she has already decided that I have to stay with her and Maddie, and that she is going to call me Daddy, and that was before I promised her Maccy D's on the way home."

The laughter from the guys caused Rosie to jump and she started to wake up next to me.

"Where am I, Daddy?"

"We are at Uncle Mason's," I decided to follow the same explanation to her as all of the kids in the group. All these men in front of me were going to be Rosie's uncles. It might be confusing when she gets a bit older, but for now, I wanted her to be part of the family. "These are all my friends. When you are a bit more awake you can meet them all, but why don't you just say hello for the moment. Then you can see your surprise."

"Supwise?"

"Yes, but you have to say hello to everyone first."

"Heyo, evyone. Now where is my supwise?"

The whole team burst out laughing. Typical child, surprise first, everything else later.

"Well, if you look behind me, you might see someone you wanted to see."

She carefully lifted up and looked behind me. Her entire face lit up as she stood up on my legs, lifted her arms and shouted. "Gandad!" It took everything in me to hold her and stop her falling from the chair as she wiggled and fought me to get to Brian. Looking around I saw Brian walking over.

"There is my little princess. Come to grandad."

Brian took Rosie out of my lap and gave her a big hug that only a grandad could. I hoped that he moved closer to us in the future. I loved seeing them together and wanted to know that they could see each other whenever they wanted.

"Gandad, Daddy said he will live with me and Mummy."

I saw Brian look over at me and raise his eyebrows. The only thing I could do was shrug an answer. How could I tell her not to call me Daddy, when she sounded so adorable when she said it?

"Daddy, princess?"

"Yes, Tyer is my new Daddy. I decided."

"Okay, princess. But Tyler might not want to be your Daddy quite yet. He has only just met you. But we can all talk about that another time. Come and say hello to all of Mummy's other friends. I want you to meet little Amelia too."

I watched them walk back into the house and turned to look at a stunned group of men in front of me. I knew I was the last person they expected to settle down with a ready-made family, but it was all I wanted. I wanted to be Rosie's Dad, and I wanted Maddie as my wife. All I had to do now was convince Maddie that she wanted that too.

"I think that little girl in there has completely fallen for you, Tyler, and I couldn't be happier. I'll give you the details of our solicitor so you can look into adopting her if you would like? I know you have to speak it over with Maddie, but that little girl in there seems to have already made up her mind."

"I know, Jayden. I've asked her to call me Tyler, but as you say, she's made her mind up. I just hope Maddie is happy with that. I don't want to do anything to push her into a relationship, but Rosie seems to be doing just that."

"Well, we can deal with that when the time comes. We can stand here and chat for a while, then I think we need to head back inside. Those four women in there, combined with my mother, are a recipe for disaster."

"I'll drink to that."

Chapter Thirty-Nine

Madeleine

—————— ⊱✦⊰ ——————

I wasn't sure what to expect when I walked into Mason's house. I had been so worried all the drive home about how I was going to face Jess and Ashleigh. I had walked out on Jess and left Ashleigh to pick up the pieces. Would either of them ever forgive me? Getting out of the car, I just stood there looking at the front door as Tyler got Rosie out from her seat. I wanted to go straight home, afraid to face the mess I had left behind on Thursday. Mason walked in and Tyler followed behind him. I knew I had to face the music at some point, so I headed up into the house, walked inside and stood tensely behind Tyler.

I saw Jess talking to Mason and Tyler in front of me, and I put my gaze down to the floor. I couldn't bear to look at her. I had let her down, and in my mind I lost the friendship that we had built these past few years. I only looked up when I heard her say one thing.

"Now get out of the way. I need to see my bestie."

She came striding over to me and flung her arms around me. I had never been happier to see someone since I saw Tyler standing in the doorway of the bungalow a few hours ago. I couldn't help but let all the worry out as soon as she held me. Everything had built up since I had made that phone call, and then probably one of the biggest mistakes in my life was when I went to meet Thomas, leaving everyone I loved behind. Except Rosie of course.

"I'm sorry, Jess. I'm so, so sorry," the tears were pouring down my face. Jess just stood there hugging me and I could feel the quiet sobs as she held me close.

"I was so worried about you, Maddie. Why didn't you come to us? We would have helped you. Why did you have to go and face him yourself?"

I pulled out of her embrace. I knew I should have gone to them, but hindsight is a wonderful thing.

"I'm sorry, Jess. I know I should have come for help. But Thomas was threatening to sell Rosie, with or without me. He convinced me that if we got together we could be a family. I guess I thought I could buy myself some time. At least I would have Rosie with me. I know I was stupid. I just couldn't see any other way."

"Stop apologising. I don't care as long as you and little Rosie are safe. Come on, I reckon you could use a drink, and Sienna has brought some lovely bottles of wine down, even if she can't drink them."

Tyler had told me that Sienna was pregnant. We were all happy to hear that everything was going well with the pregnancy after what happened to them before. It was heart-breaking to lose a child. I was lucky that I had my Rosie back, but to never know what your child would look like, was something I couldn't imagine. I knew that Sienna must have been a strong woman to go through all of that and come out the other side. We walked into the living room and I found Ashleigh, Sienna and Joan there, along with baby Callum and Amelia.

"Auntie Maddie, you're home. I missed you at the shop today with my nanny."

She came running up to me and gave me a big hug. You couldn't help but love this little girl. I can understand why Sienna and Jayden wanted to adopt her. After everything she had been through she was still the most loveable girl there could be.

"I'm sorry I wasn't there earlier, Aims. I'm back now and I have my little girl with me as well. Her name's Rosie. I hope you can be friends."

"I would like that, Auntie Maddie. I'm going to go and find Daddy and Uncle Mason."

With that, she ran out of the room and I was left with three women looking at me.

"Before anyone says anything, I'm sorry. I know what I did was stupid, but I truly wasn't thinking straight. I know I put you in a terrible position, Ashleigh, and I cannot tell you how sorry I am."

"Don't say any more, Maddie. You and Rosie are home and are safe. Let's just think about that. I don't know what you must have been going through, so I have no reason to judge. All I know now is you can live your life again with Rosie. Talking of Rosie, where is she?"

"Probably still asleep in Tyler's arms. She has become very attached to him already. She's decided that he is going to be her Dad. She is even calling him Daddy. Tyler asked her to just call him Tyler, but she just keeps saying Daddy. I don't think either of us has the heart to say no. I just hope ..."

"I don't think you have any worries there, Maddie. Tyler was out of his mind when he read the letter. I don't think you will get rid of him that easily. I think he is more worried that you won't want him."

"He really thinks that?"

"I think the pair of you just need to sit down and have a long chat. Not today, give it a few days and then sit down together and talk. You have both been through a lot. I think you both just need to relax for a while. I can mind the shop with Joan, and I'm sure Mason won't mind Tyler having a few days off. Richard can stay down here if need be. But let's forget all of that now. Tell us what happened."

I spent the next thirty minutes going through everything that happened. I was glad to talk to someone. I needed to let it all out, and doing that with Tyler was probably not a good thing. Jess and Ashleigh had been there for me when I first decided to tell them the truth and it helped when I needed to tell Tyler. I just hoped that this would do the same.

"So, he never hurt or touched you throughout it all?"

"No. In fact at one point we were having quite a normal conversation. Part of me can't hate him, knowing what his mother is like. She was probably behind it all. He doesn't even know who his father is. In fact, Michelle probably doesn't know either."

"You mean ..."

"Yes, she was on the game. Even while she has been living with my Dad as his girlfriend. I'm not sure how I am going to tell him."

"You don't need to. I already know, Madds. I guessed as much a long time ago. But you have just confirmed it."

I looked up at my Dad, who was holding Rosie in his arms. Luckily, she wouldn't understand any of the conversation we were having. But it was one I didn't really want to have with her in the room.

"I think we will discuss this another time. Poppet, I would like you to meet all of my friends. This is Jess who lives here with Mason and Callum. She owns the coffee shop I work in. This is Ashleigh, and over there is Joan, who is Mason and Jayden's Mum. And this is Sienna."

"That's Amam's Mummy. She lives with Uncle Jayden."

"That's right, Poppet."

"Hello, evyone. Do you live here, Mummy?"

"No, Poppet, I live above Jess's shop."

"It's Auntie Jess, Mummy. Amam told me that evyone is auntie and uncle, except Nanny Joan and Nanny Lizbet. Are they my nannies too?"

"Well, Rosie. I don't …"

"If you want to call me Nanny Joan the same as Amelia, you can, Rosie. But I'm not really your nanny darling. But you have your Grandad and wait until you meet Tyler's Mum and Dad. They are going to love you."

I could feel the tears starting to form in my eyes again. I was so lucky to have such loving friends around me. No, not friends, they were an extended family. And the fact that Rosie had accepted them as her new family, and they had accepted her, I couldn't hold it back any longer.

"Mummy don't cry. We have Daddy now, and Gandad and lots of new friends. Please be happy."

"I am happy, Poppet. Mummy is just being silly."

She gave me the biggest hug ever, and I knew then what I was doing was right. I still wasn't sure how things would work at the shop, but we would find a way together.

"Mummy, can I go play with Amam and Monty, please?"

"Yes, go on and have some fun."

I placed Rosie down and looked up at my Dad. He smiled and just put his arms around me, protecting me in the only way a Dad can.

"Let's go for a walk."

I turned to speak to all my friends and didn't even need to ask before Joan spoke.

"You need some time with your Dad. Go. We will still be here when you get back. I haven't had a chance to catch up with everyone in ages. One of us will let Tyler know if he comes looking, but I think he needs a while to decompress with his friends as well."

"Thank you."

We walked out the front of the house and out to the pergola. It always seemed to be the place everyone went when they needed to talk. We sat down together and just took in the countryside around us.

"Dad, I ..."

"No, baby girl. Don't say anything. Please just listen. I know we have had this conversation already, but I need to say it again. I am so sorry that I left you with Thomas and Michelle. I can't imagine what you have been through. But it's over. Completely over. I chucked Michelle out of the house this morning before I changed the locks on the house and headed down here. She is out of my life completely. I guess I never really loved her, and that makes what happened to you even worse."

I went to speak, but he just held his hand up to stop me.

"I've been thinking a lot this morning on the way down here, and have had a long chat with Edward before you arrived. I'm retiring from the Navy in a few months, so I won't be going on any more tours, and there is nothing to keep me in Plymouth now. I'm thinking of moving down this way. Perhaps somewhere in Winchester. I wouldn't be too far away from you and little Rosie, but far enough to give you your own space. Edward and Joan have offered me a room in their place if I don't find something straight away, but I want to start looking soon. What do you think?"

I flung my arms around him. I couldn't think of anything I liked better than having my Dad so close to me. Well there was only one thing I would like better, and even with all the things Ashleigh and Jess had said, I still wasn't sure if Tyler would want me after everything I had done these past few days.

"What's wrong, Madd's? I thought you would be happy."

"I am, it's just ... what if I have ruined any chance of a relationship with Tyler. He trusted me to tell him everything, and I just left him and went to do everything myself. I put myself and Rosie in danger. What if he can't forgive me?"

"I'm sure you've already had this conversation with your friends. I'm also sure they have told you the exact same thing I am going to say to you now. He loves you. He is just as worried that you don't want him around anymore. He's petrified that you are going to take Rosie away from him. You know Jayden has already given him the details of a solicitor so he can put everything in place to adopt Rosie. He adores her, and from the sounds of things, Rosie has already decided she wants Tyler as her Dad."

"I know. That came as a bit of a shock to both of us. But would you be happy if I settled down with Tyler? Do you think he is the right man for me?"

"Baby girl, I don't know of another man that loves you as much as I do, except Tyler. I already gave him my permission to marry you the first day I met him. He worships the ground you walk on, you and Rosie. There aren't many men out there that would take on another man's child as their own. When I saw him walk into the garden, Rosie snuggled into him, fast asleep. I knew you had made the right choice. But it has to be right for both of you, and I think you both need to talk things through."

"Ashleigh said that to me as well."

"Well then your friends are very wise ladies, and you should listen to us all. Don't make a hasty decision either way. Relationships need to be built on trust and communication. You may think you have lost Tyler's trust, but if you explain everything to him, exactly what you were feeling and going through, he will understand."

He pulled me into another hug, as the tears fell again. I was on a real emotional rollercoaster today. Tears of joy and sadness were coming in waves. I knew everyone was right. Tyler and I needed to sit down and talk things through. But I first needed to know if there was a chance for us, whether we talked or not. I felt my Dad look up and he pulled away from me slightly.

"I know the question on your lips, Madds. You want to know if there is even a chance for you both to be together. Well now is the time to ask."

I looked around and saw Tyler standing a few feet away from us, not wanting to disturb our private moment together, but also needing to be with me.

"I'll leave you two alone."

Dad gave me a kiss on the head as he got up from his seat and walked over towards Tyler. As he got up to him, he said something that I couldn't hear. Tyler just nodded his head, never taking his eyes off of me. I saw my Dad look at Tyler, turned to look at me, and chuckled to himself as he walked back towards the house. Time seemed to stand still as Tyler stood there and looked at me. Neither of us wanted to move, frightened of what was going to happen between us. We had both said how much we loved each other earlier in the day. But when the adrenaline had worn off, did we both still mean what we said? I knew that I did, but did Tyler? Was Tyler standing there having the same internal conversation himself? I don't know how long it was before Tyler slowly started to walk over to me.

"Can I sit down?"

"Of course." I hesitated for a moment before both of us started to speak at the same time.

"Sweetheart." "Tyler."

We both laughed at each other, and Tyler took my hand in his.

"You go first, sweetheart."

"I think I've done enough damage for one day. You should go first, Tyler."

"If you're sure," I just nodded my head for him to continue. "I know we probably have a lot to talk about, and today isn't that day for that. But I want you to know, everything I said to you earlier, I meant every word of it. I want to stay with you and Rosie, I still want us to be a family together. I love Rosie calling me Daddy, and one day I hope that I can adopt her and make her legally mine. Plus I want us to have children of our own. I know that's a lot to take in, but I needed you to know that. If you don't, then that's fine too. I will always be there for you and Rosie, no matter what happens between us." He paused, waiting for me to say something, but I couldn't. I was too shocked by what he had just said to me. The silence between us was too much for Tyler to bear. "Please, say something, Maddie. Please ..."

I didn't say a word, just crashed my lips against his. There were no more words needed to be said. We still both felt the same way about each other. So why say it? I needed to show him how I felt. I loved him more than any other man I had met. I wanted him in Rosie and my lives. We kissed until both of us were gasping for air. Tyler placed his forehead on mine.

"I guess we need to start looking for a place then, one where we could be a family together. That's if you still want me in yours and Rosie's lives?"

"It's all I have ever wanted, Tyler."

With that, he pulled me into his arms and held me close.

Chapter Forty

Madeleine

I had been home with Rosie for a week now. We had got into a comfortable routine, and I was getting used to having my girl around me again. I had been back at work for a couple of days and things were getting back to normal, well, as normal as they could be with a nearly three-year-old in the mix. Rosie would spend the day with me at the shop. Most of the time, either Ashleigh or Jess would come in. Sometimes they would go up to the park for a walk with Monty if Mason had brought him into work. Or they would sit at their favourite table colouring together. I would join them when things were quiet. I was starting to really love my life.

Tyler was the other surprise. He had not left my flat since we had returned from Canterbury. Rosie was still adamant about calling him Daddy, and neither of us wanted to argue with her. She had made her decision and so had I. I was going to spend the rest of my life with him. I loved him so much and I didn't ever want to leave or lose him again. We had sat down and talked the past few days. I explained everything. Why I had left without speaking to him. How sorry I was and that I realised that I had been stupid to think I could sort things without him. He'd forgiven me the moment I was back in his arms at the bungalow, and he understood exactly why I had gone down to Canterbury. Many tears had been shed on both parts. But it brought us closer together.

The only thing that had been difficult was us spending time together alone. Despite Rosie going to bed early, it was difficult for us to be close. Always worrying that she was going to wake up, and only having one bedroom in the flat also made things difficult. Tyler chose to sleep either on the settee or the floor of the front room every night, just so he could be close to us. But it wasn't close enough for me. We had gone to look at a house the other evening that was just outside the main town. It was a beautiful cottage overlooking the Hampshire countryside. It was everything I could want in a place of our own. It had four bedrooms, one with its own ensuite, and the main family bathroom which was as big as my own front room. For a cottage it was pretty big, but that was because the previous owners had built an extension on the side, but had still managed to keep it in style with the old cottage.

All of us loved it, especially Rosie who decided that we should buy it and then get a puppy, so Monty had a friend of his own when he came over. I couldn't argue about the house. The puppy, maybe. But having seen how Tyler looked at Rosie when she suggested getting a dog, her big blue eyes looking up at him, I would be surprised if she didn't get her own way. Tyler would cave as he always did. Don't get me wrong, he didn't spoil her, but she usually got what she wanted with him. If he didn't give in, then my Dad usually did. We had put an offer in on the house and were just waiting to hear. We knew it might be a couple of days as the owners were away on holiday, but they were due back today and I had been on tender hooks all morning.

My Dad had also started looking for a house in Winchester already. In a short space of time, he had become good friends with Edward and Joan, and they were helping him to find a place to buy in town. He had seen a few places and was just waiting to see if the offer he had placed was going to be accepted too. I was slightly worried about how much Tyler was spending on our house. He assured me that the money wasn't an issue, that we wouldn't have a mortgage over our heads, but that wasn't the point that worried me the most. If things didn't work out between us, where would Rosie and I be then? Tyler said not to worry because we would always have the roof over our heads no matter what. We could live there as long as we wanted. But there was always that nagging doubt in my mind.

The morning at the coffee shop had been a pretty normal one. Rosie had always been an early riser so her being up at 5:30 wasn't usually a problem. If she wasn't awake before I left in the morning, then Tyler would stay at the flat until she woke up and brought her down before he went to work. However, this morning she had been up with the larks and had come down with us, after Tyler had spent the morning reading and writing with her. He loved to teach her things. She was already more proficient with a computer than I was. I believed she just wanted to be like Tyler. But she had enough time to decide what she wanted to do with her life.

My regular customers loved her. Mr. and Mrs. Duncan often brought her treats from the shop, treating her like their own granddaughter as they didn't get to see their own grandchildren very often. Ashleigh had been in most of the morning and was spending time with Rosie. She was brilliant with kids and would make a fantastic mother one day. I knew it would happen for them soon. They deserved to be parents more than anyone, and I just hoped that they could have a child of their own. But if not, there was going to be one very lucky child that they adopted.

I was currently starting to get the lunches ready for everyone when I heard my phone ringing. Seeing it was from Tyler, I answered it as quickly as I could.

"Hi, sweetheart. Are you sitting down?"

"Do I need to?"

"You might want to, I have some news."

I sat down on the chair closest to me, a feeling of dread running through me.

"I'm sitting down now. What's up? Has something happened to Dad, or someone we know?"

I looked up and saw Ashleigh glancing over at me, a worried look on her face.

"They've accepted our offer on the cottage. We exchange contracts in a couple of weeks. It's ours, sweetheart. We have our own home."

I squealed in delight at what he'd told me. I saw Ashleigh's worry immediately disappear when she saw me smiling.

"Is it really true? You're not trying to make me feel better?"

"No, sweetheart. It's true. Look I have to go, I just wanted to call you and let you know. I'll see you this evening."

I hung up the phone and turned to Ashleigh.

"I take it you got the house then?"

"Yes, we did. I can't wait to have a house of our own."

"I'm so happy for you both. Would you like Brandon and me to look after Rosie this evening? Give you and Tyler some time together on your own? I can bring her with me in the morning."

"I can't ask you to do that for us."

"Well, I do have an ulterior motive. We are going to look at some puppies this evening, and I know that Brandon won't be able to say no to Rosie."

"That's cruel, especially as she wants one herself. It would be just like Brandon to get two and we end up with one."

"I wouldn't put it past him. So, Rosie, would you like to help choose a new puppy for Uncle Brandon and me? You can have a sleepover at our house."

"Yayy, can I stay with Auntie Ash? Pwese, Mummy?"

"If you would like to, Poppet. Are you sure Brandon will be okay with it, Ashleigh?"

"Well, if he isn't, he will be sleeping on the settee tonight."

I was currently sitting in the arms of the man I loved after sharing a lovely meal with him. This was where I wanted to be, and I couldn't wait for us to be able to do this in our own home.

"What are you thinking about so hard, sweetheart?"

"I was just thinking how much I can't wait to be able to do this in our own home."

"Oh yeah, is that all you want to do in our own home? Snuggle on the settee?"

"Well, I can think of a few other things."

"Like what?"

Although we hadn't slept together properly since the night before I left for Canterbury, we had fooled around a lot, and I was far more confident being with Tyler than I had been. I know he was egging me on, trying to get me to bite on the conversation. And who was I to disappoint him? I slowly pulled myself up from my position on the settee and straddled him, making sure to rub down on him. I could feel he was already hard just from us sitting here together. A slight smirk came over his face as I looked down into his eyes.

"I could definitely get used to this, sweetheart."

"You better, because I have a lot of years of wasting my life to make up for."

Leaning down, I started to kiss him, although it was only a couple of seconds before Tyler started to take the lead. He slid his hands into my hair and positioned my head exactly where he wanted it to be able to access the crook of my neck. He knew that was one of my weak spots that would immediately make me agree to anything he said.

"I think we need an early night, don't you?"

I barely whispered the word yes before Tyler was lifting me up with him as he carried me into the bedroom. Placing me down on the bed, he continued to place kisses all along my neck as he undid the buttons on the blouse I had conveniently put on this evening. It wasn't until he undid the buttons that he realised I wasn't wearing a bra. I heard his breath hitch as he realised and smiled as he looked up at me.

"Someone ... was ... planning ... this." He placed kisses down my neck and shoulders between each word he spoke. I was about to answer him when he took one of my nipples in his mouth causing me to moan in pleasure.

"Mmmm, I think we are both wearing far too many clothes. Strip."

Tyler wasn't this demanding last time we were in the bedroom, but it was a side of him I liked. He showed me exactly how much he wanted me. I knew I didn't have the perfect body. I'd had a child, of course my body wasn't perfect. But that didn't matter to Tyler. He loved me and my body exactly the way it was. In a matter of minutes, we were both back on the bed, naked. Less than three weeks ago this would have caused so much anxiety in me. Now all I felt was anticipation, the kind that comes from knowing how good the man who is holding you in his arms can make you feel.

Feeling Tyler's fingers trace down my body caused goosebumps across my skin. The anticipation was building inside of me. Expecting him to enter my core like he had last time, I held my breath. What I didn't expect was Tyler to suddenly shift down the bed and between my legs. I didn't get a moment to think about what was going to happen next when I felt the electricity going through my core as he circled my clit with his tongue.

"God, Sweetheart, you taste so good. You don't know how long I have been wanting to do this again."

I couldn't say any words as he continued to pleasure me with his tongue. I had thought his fingers were good, but his tongue? Fuck, he was amazing with that. I could feel the pleasure building inside of me as he plunged his tongue deep inside me. I wasn't sure how he even managed it, but it was only a matter of minutes before I was moaning and screaming his name like a chant, over and over again. Tyler slowed his movement gently to bring me down from my euphoric state. It wasn't until my breaths became regular that he stopped and moved back up to my side on the bed. Placing his lips on mine, he kissed me. I was shocked at first when I could taste myself on his lips, but it was strangely arousing and I could feel myself starting to get wet again.

"You are so beautiful when you come, sweetheart. I could watch you every minute of every day, seeing you come undone from my touch."

"Tyler, I need you."

"And you can have me, sweetheart. Whenever you want me."

I wasn't going to let him say another word. I was going to take control of my sexual desires. For once I was going to call the shots. I had let so many guys before me tell me what I should and shouldn't do, but for once I was going to do what I wanted to do. I knew Tyler wasn't the same as the guys I had dated before, but what we had between us was going to be different. I wanted to show him what I wanted to do. With newfound strength, I pushed Tyler down on his back and straddled him, placing myself directly over his cock. The groan he let out only kindled the need in me. I leaned down and continued the kiss he had started only moments before, slowly rubbing against his cock, sliding it through my wetness.

"Sweetheart, you're killing me here. Please don't leave me hanging here. There are condoms in the drawer next to you, I need to be in you now."

I needed him too, but I needed to feel him. I didn't want any barrier between us. Tyler was it for me and I wanted him to realise that. I knew I was safe, I had been on the pill since Rosie was born. But I knew if it happened again then Tyler would be there for me. I looked down at Tyler, a smile forming on my face as I reached down and placed the tip of his cock at my entrance. I could see the look of concern on his face.

"Madds, you haven't put a ..."

I didn't let him finish before I pushed down, until he was fully in me. The difference from the last time we'd had sex was immediate to feel. Feeling his warm, thick cock filling me almost had me coming.

"Fuck, Madds. You feel so fucking good, sweetheart. But I need you to move, honey. I'm hanging on the edge here."

Slowly I lifted up and then glided back down, my confidence building with each stroke. Given that this was only the third time I'd had sex with a guy, I didn't know if I was doing it right, but I did know that this felt fucking amazing. Tyler started to mirror my thrusts and was soon setting the pace as I went along for the ride. If I'd realised how good it could feel to be with a guy, I would have given myself over to Tyler a long while ago. I could feel the beginnings of my orgasm starting to build inside me, or was it the end of the one Tyler had already given me? I couldn't tell which.

"Madds, sweetheart, I need you to come for me, baby."

I felt Tyler's finger press down on my clit, sending me over the edge as Tyler groaned as he released into me. I know he wanted to pull out, but I wasn't going to allow him. I wanted to feel him, all of him inside me as he came. I collapsed on top of him as he engulfed me in his arms and pulled me into his chest.

"You really shouldn't have done that, sweetheart. What if ..."

"Tyler, I'm on the pill. I needed to feel you, needed to show you that you are it for me. If by some chance I get pregnant, then I do. You wanted us to have a family together. If it happens sooner, then it happens."

"Could I love you any more than I do right now?"

"I'm sure you could show me how much you love me right now."

I placed chaste kisses all over his face, as he chuckled below me.

"Much as I would love that, we have to get up early tomorrow morning so you can open up the shop. Then, if you remember, we are going to meet my family."

"Shit, I had forgotten about that. What if they don't ..."

"They will love you as much as I do, Madds. You and Rosie. Now, let's take a shower together and get some sleep. Soon we will have a place of our own, and when we do, you will be regretting this newfound sexual vixen you seem to want to be."

Chapter Forty-One

Tyler

W aking up with Maddie in my arms was by far the best thing to happen in my life in a long time. It was only four in the morning, and we hadn't gotten much sleep, but I was wide awake. This was what I wanted for the rest of my life, to have the woman I loved in my arms forever. I wanted to be a family with her and little Rosie. I loved that girl as if she was my own, and it was obvious to everyone that she had decided no matter what, I was going to be her Dad.

We were weeks away from having our own house together, and it couldn't come a moment too soon. There was so much we needed to do and get. I wanted to give my little girl everything she wanted in her room. If she wanted Disney princesses, she could have them. Marvel superheroes, I didn't care what, I was going to give her whatever she wanted. I knew I would have a fight on my hands with Maddie, that she would say I was spoiling her rotten, but I didn't care. She was mine now, they both were, and neither of them would go without anything their hearts desired.

There was only one hurdle we had to overcome now, and that was meeting my family. I had called my parents and explained everything to them. Maddie knew this, and I think that is what worried her about meeting them. She thought they would judge her on what she had done. My Mum was horrified at what she had gone through and understood completely why she had taken the actions that she did. Even though I had explained this to Maddie, she was still worried about it. I was more worried about how they would react to Rosie calling me Daddy. Would they accept her and love her as I did?

I knew all the answers to these questions. They were all yes, and they would accept Maddie, and Rosie and love them as much as I did. But with Maddie worrying, it made me worry. I wanted everything in her life to be happy and simple. She had been through so much in her life and I wanted to make it all better. We had taken two of the problems out of the equation, Michelle and Thomas. But for how long? Thomas was currently in prison awaiting trial for trying to sell Rosie and for kidnapping. He could be looking at a sentence of anything up to fourteen years. We weren't expecting anything close to that, and in fact, we didn't care. He had no idea where we were living and by the time he did get out, Brian would have moved out of Plymouth and into Winchester. Michelle was more of a worry though. We had no idea where she was or what she was planning. Was she still in contact with Thomas, and if she was, what was her plan? Much as that was a worry, there was nothing we could do about it until she showed her cards. I just had to continue to build a life with Maddie and Rosie and protect them if and when the time came.

I must have dozed off again, with Maddie in my arms, because when I woke I saw that it was nearly 6:00, and being a Sunday, time to get ready for the day. Ashleigh wouldn't be at the coffee shop until around 10:00, I suspected, seeing as Rosie would probably sleep in. She loved spending time with both Ashleigh and Jess. Jess more so as she got to help with Callum and Monty. She was going to make an amazing big sister when the time came, already helping with Callum despite him being only a year or so younger than her. And as for Monty, well, I didn't think it would be too long before she convinced me to have a puppy. If Brandon hadn't already bought her one.

Feeling Maddie wake next to me, I pulled her into a hug and kissed her on the head. I was already getting used to the stolen moments between us. Being in bed together was a luxury I was looking forward to regularly when we all had our own rooms.

"Morning, sweetheart. Time for us both to get up, I'm afraid.

"Can we just stay in bed all day?"

"Much as I would love that, you have the shop to open, and we are due at my parents later today."

I heard the sigh of worry leave her lips as she tensed in my arms.

"We've already had this discussion. It will be fine. My Mum and Dad are going to love you and Rosie, and you get a sister in the mix too. I promise it will be okay. Just trust me."

I knew she trusted me to tell her the truth. She would be fine, I had already warned my parents that Maddie was it for me. And if they didn't like it., well, it was me, Maddie, and Rosie as part of their family, or none of us. I didn't like to give them that kind of ultimatum, but there was no way I was giving this wonderful woman and girl up for anyone, family or not.

"I guess I better get into the shower then."

"Now, that sounds like the best idea of the morning so far."

We were on our way to my parents. As I suspected, Ashleigh arrived at the shop just before 10:00 with an extremely excited Rosie and Brandon. Although, at the moment he wasn't exactly my favourite person. He had gone to see some spaniel puppies yesterday with both Ashleigh and Rosie. He used the excuse that Rosie had to help pick out a Sprocker puppy to live with them in their new house that was now nearly ready to move in. They had chosen a puppy for themselves, a boy that with Rosie's help they had named Oscar. That wasn't the problem. The problem was that Rosie had fallen in love with one of his sisters, so Poppy was now going to be a member of our family.

Much as I hated to admit it, I loved the idea of having a dog around the house. Monty was such a character and was always so affectionate. It was something that I had wanted to do when we were more settled, but it would appear that Brandon had other ideas about that.

"I can't believe Brandon went and bought us a puppy. I don't even know how to look after a puppy."

"Well, he said it was a housewarming gift, but from what I can gather it's more like a house-destroying gift. But it will be good for Rosie, and from what Ashleigh said, all hell would have broken loose if she didn't get her way. And Brandon was always the peacemaker of the group. I'm sure Poppy will fit in with us."

"When can we get Poppy, Daddy? Uncle Brandon said she is too small to leave her Mummy."

"That's right, Pops. She has to stay with her Mummy for a while. Once we move into our new house, we can go and get Poppy, or you can go with Uncle Brandon when he goes to get Oscar."

"Yayy, I like Uncle Brandon and Auntie Ash. They are fun."

"Why did you name her Poppy?"

"Because you call me Pops and Mummy calls me Poppet, so I wanted to call her Poppy, so she was the same as me."

I had to laugh at her thought process, although from the pictures Brandon had shown me, Poppy was a good name for her. Although I was sure there would be some confusion in the household after a while, what with Poppet, Pops and Poppy all being spoken at the same time.

We pulled up outside my parents' house just before 13:00. I could see the worry building on Maddie's face as I turned off the engine. Taking her hand in mine, I wanted to show her that no matter what, I was there for her.

"I can't say this to you enough, sweetheart. It will be fine. They will love both of you."

"I'm sorry, Tyler. I just can't help but think of what they think of me. Leaving a child behind at only a year old. What if they can't forgive me for that?"

"We all did, Madds. We understood what you were going through, and they do too. They know everything and are still eager to meet the woman who has captured my heart. They will love Rosie as well, as if she was my own daughter. As far as I am concerned, she is my daughter, and I love her as if she was my own. Let's go and meet them, shall we?"

I saw a slight smile and a nod form. I knew she was worried, but I also knew as soon as she met them she would be fine. I helped Rosie out of the car and walked round to Maddie's side. Rosie went rushing up to the door and eagerly knocked on it, wanting to be the first to say hello. The enthusiasm of the little girl I had only known for just over a week was amazing. She had allowed all of my friends into her heart and I couldn't wait for her to let my parents and sister in too.

My Dad opened the door and was immediately engulfed in a

hug from Rosie.

"Gandad Michael."

"Umph, you must be Rosie. Hello, princess. It's good to finally meet you."

I saw my Dad smile over at me as he picked Rosie up in his arms and started to walk over to an extremely nervous Maddie.

"And you must be Maddie. It's a pleasure to meet you my dear. My son told me how lovely you were, but forgot to mention how beautiful."

Hugging my woman, he gave her a quick peck on the cheek. You wanted to know where my smoothness came from, there it was right there. I learned from the best, especially when I looked over and saw the blush on my Maddie's cheeks.

"Dad, stop the sweet-talking. You're embarrassing Madds."

"As if, son. How are you?"

"I'm good, Dad. Let's get inside and meet Mum and Kelsey."

I guided Maddie into my family home. I knew from the reception she had received from my Dad that everything would be fine. Maddie just had to believe it now.

"Look who I found at the front door."

I saw Rosie squirming to get out of my Dad's arms. Realising she wanted to get down and over to my Mum, my Dad placed her down on the floor and she immediately ran over to my Mum and greeted her in the same way she had my Dad, with a massive hug.

"Nanny Jenfer."

"Hello, Rosie, my darling. It is so nice to see you. Tyler never told us you were a princess."

"Daddy, why didn't you tell Nanny Jenfer I was a princess?"

I saw both my parents' eyes rise when they heard Rosie call me Daddy. It was a big shock to everyone who heard it, especially me, and I had told them exactly what to expect. The look of surprise on their faces was still clear to see.

"I wanted them to see for themselves, Pops. We all know you are a princess, but everyone has to see that with their own eyes.."

"Okay, Daddy. I understand. Is Auntie Kesey here?"

As if she had a second sense, Kelsey walked right through the door as Rosie spoke. Although she hadn't met any of my family, I had shown her lots of pictures of our lives together. I wanted her to feel part of my family before she met them. Brian had already accepted me, and I just wanted Rosie to accept mine too.

"So this is where my little niece has got to."

"Auntie Kesey, Daddy has shown me pictures of you. You are very pwetty, just like he said."

"He said that, did he? Well you are very pretty too. A real-life princess."

I looked over at my sister and smiled. We may argue and fight, but she was still my sister, and she had grown into a beautiful woman.

"I will introduce myself, Maddie. I'm Kelsey and I'm this one's sister. I must admit I have no idea what you see in him, but to each their own."

"Kelsey."

"He knows I'm joking, Mum."

"It's lovely to meet all of you. You are all so kind, thank you. I'm sorry, I'm just very nervous to meet you all."

"There is no need for you to be nervous. If you have gained

my son's heart, then you will have gained ours. He has never brought a woman back to meet us in his entire life. That must mean you are special. And bringing us this little one, we definitely know you are."

I knew then I had made the right choice to bring them both here. They were now truly part of my family.

"Well, with that said, you two can go off and do whatever you men do to bond, I need to spend some time with my new daughter-in-law and get to know her better."

With that, my father and I were ushered out of the kitchen. My sister decided that she was going to get to know her new niece, so we both decided to go out on the back deck and have a beer.

"Say what you have to say, Dad. You know everything. Tell me I'm a fool to fall for her, that she is no good for me."

"Yes, we do know what happened to her. What that young lady in there has had to live with these past two years! She lied to you and all your friends. But, there was one thing you forgot to tell us. That little girl in there, Rosie, she tells us more in a few words than you ever have. She hasn't even met us, just heard what you have told her and the pictures you have shown her. Yet she came running into all of our arms and accepted us as her grandparents. As her family. That tells me more than anything you could about Maddie. That tells me that despite the fact she left her daughter for two years, she loved her. That she taught her how to love. It's obvious to me that the little girl in there has decided who she wants to be part of her life and be her family. I'm not going to argue or disappoint her, are you?"

"How could I? I love her as much if not more than I do her mother. If I never have a child of my own, I still have her. I don't care who her biological father is. As far as I'm concerned, she is mine, and no one is ever going to say differently or take her away from me again."

"Then that is all that matters. And for the record, I love Maddie. She hasn't said much, but it took a lot of courage to walk in here and face us. She must have worried that we would judge her, knowing what she had done, but she still did it. Do you want to know why?"

"Why?"

"Because she is madly in love with you. That much I can see. If you fuck this up, son, I will kill you."

I looked at his face for a second, worried about his last statement. It was only then that he allowed the smile to form on his face. I knew he meant what he said, maybe not that he would kill me, but I knew if I did muck this up with Maddie, he would never forgive me. He was getting the one thing he had always wanted, a grandchild. I hoped it wouldn't be the only one, but if it was, I knew that he would love and spoil her for the rest of her life.

"Thank you, Dad. That means a lot to me. And if I do muck this up, there will be a long line of people ready to hurt me before you."

"That's good to hear."

Chapter Forty-Two
Madeleine

I was now standing alone in the kitchen with Jennifer after she had ordered Tyler and Michael to leave. Kelsey had decided to spend some time with Rosie. This was it. This was the moment when I was going to find out what they really thought about me. This was the time when I was going to be told that their son was too good for the likes of me, and I should leave before Rosie became too attached. I could feel my anxiety start to rise as I stood there in silence waiting for the conversation to start.

Jennifer checked the meat that was in the oven and then turned to me.

"Why don't you sit down, Maddie? I assume you prefer to be called Maddie and not Madeleine?"

"Maddie is fine. Do you prefer Jennifer, Jen or Jenny?"

"Jen or Jenny is fine. I don't mind either. Only my mother used to call me Jennifer, and from the sounds of things, little Rosie. Why don't we have a coffee, and you can fill me in with all the information about yourself that Tyler forgot to tell me."

She made us both a coffee and as she placed it down in front of me, I asked her the one question I didn't want to ask, despite knowing that Tyler had told them everything.

"What do you want to know? I'm guessing Tyler told you everything about my past, about what I did."

I guess she could hear the fear in my voice as I spoke, because she immediately put her hand over mine and smiled.

"Tyler told us everything that happened to you, Maddie. Before you say any more, I am not going to judge what you did. How can I? I have never been in a situation where I have had to make that kind of decision. I can't imagine what you must have gone through after what he did to you. Then, to raise a child under his shadow all the time! You are an extremely strong woman, Maddie, and you have raised an amazing daughter. It's obvious to me how much she is loved by the way she accepts everyone she meets as part of her family. The fact she wants our son as her Dad, is beyond me. But she is too young to see the error of her ways. She will when she gets older."

I suddenly met Jen's eyes at what she had just said. I could see the glint in them, the kind that only a mother could have when she was talking about her own child. She just started to laugh.

"I'm sorry, I shouldn't joke like that with everything you have been through. I know you are worried about what we would think. But if our son loves you, then that is all that matters to me. I know he has done some bad things in the past, nothing that he wasn't ordered to do in the army, of course. But still, they are things no man should have to do. No one is perfect, and all I care about is that he finds someone that loves him. So, my only question to you is, do you love him?"

It wasn't a question in my mind that I had any doubt over. I didn't even need to think about my answer.

"Yes. I love Tyler with all my heart. I always have. I just went about showing it the wrong way. I'm truly sorry for everything I have put Tyler through. Rosie and I don't deserve his love, but he still chose to give it to us. I would rather die than hurt him again."

"That's all I needed to know. The rest of it doesn't matter to me. I just want to see my son happy. I hope one day he will have a child, or children of his own. But, if that doesn't happen, having little Rosie in my life, calling me Nanny, will be something I will always be grateful for. And for the record, you really do not need to go to that extreme for me. Being a family is never easy, it is something you must work at. You will argue and get on each other's nerves. Lord, I don't know how many times I've wanted to murder Michael. But I love him and my family, and that includes you and Rosie. I know you don't have your Mum around anymore, and I can never replace her, but to me you are another daughter in my life. If you ever need to talk, I'm here for you."

Tears were pouring down both our faces now. I had been accepted into Tyler's family. It was more than I could have ever expected four weeks ago. I had let so much time pass me by worrying about what everyone would think of me if I told them the truth. It was only now I realised how stupid I'd been. I felt Jen's arms come around me in a hug. I felt at home, loved and I only wished I'd done this sooner.

"Don't think about what you should have done. It's in the past. Let's just look forward to what we have to come."

"Thank you, thank you for accepting me and Rosie into your lives."

It was then that our moment of peace was shattered by Rosie running into the kitchen.

"Mummy, where is Daddy's phone? I want to show Auntie Kesey, Poppy."

"I think Daddy has it out with Grandad Michael."

"Thank you, Mummy."

She was out the door before anyone could say anything else.

"Poppy?"

"It's a long story. Probably best if we explain it over lunch to everyone. Although I am sure Kelsey already knows the whole story. Now, what can I help with?"

"Absolutely nothing, just sit there and chat with me. Everything is in the oven, so we just need to open a bottle of wine and drink."

"Sounds like my kind of lunch."

Lunch had been amazing with Tyler's family. All my worries had come to nothing. They didn't care about what had happened in my past, only about the future. As long as I loved Tyler and wanted to spend the rest of my life with him, like he did with me, that was all that mattered to them. Rosie absolutely adored her new grandparents, and now she had an auntie all of her own, one that didn't belong to anyone else. That would be until Tyler and I had a child of our own. There was now no doubt in my mind, that was what I wanted. I wanted a family of our own together. I knew that Tyler would always love Rosie as if she was his own child. I also knew he was already looking to adopt her, but he wanted his own son or daughter, and that was something that I was going to make sure would happen.

We were all sitting in the front room, with Rosie snuggled in Michael's arms almost falling asleep. In fact, it wouldn't be too long before she was sound asleep. We had spoken about everything except for one person, Kelsey. I know that Tyler worried about her a lot, especially her relationship with his best friend, Nathan. They had grown up together and Tyler said it was obvious to him that Kelsey once had a crush on Nathan. I'd heard him warn Nathan off a few times, but something told me that there was more to their relationship than they would admit.

I wanted to talk to Kelsey about it. I was almost her age, just a couple of years younger than her. I wanted her to see me as a sister that she could talk to about anything. I was going to say something when she asked if any of us wanted a coffee.

"Does anyone want tea or coffee?"

"Sounds like an amazing idea. I'll give you a hand."

"Maddie, you don't have to help. You're a guest here."

"It's not a problem, Jen. It gives me a chance to get all the gossip on Tyler that only a little sister will tell me."

I smiled over at Tyler, who immediately looked worried.

"Don't worry, I'm sure she will only tell me the good stuff."

I got up from the settee and followed Kelsey out into the kitchen.

"So, what do you want to know about my brother then?"

"I don't. I want to speak to you, about you. I only know what Tyler has told me. So, I want you to tell me the truth, not what Tyler thinks."

"There isn't much to tell really. I'm twenty-five, single, just moved out of my parents' house and a just qualified accountant. What's more to know?"

"Single, really? There is no one special in your life?"

"Look if Tyler wants to know about …"

"Tyler hasn't sent me in here to find out if you are seeing

Nathan, if that was what you were going to say. But you are seeing him, aren't you?"

I saw a look of shock and worry cross her face. Oh yes, she was seeing him alright. If I was to hazard a guess, she was totally in love with him. I knew Jess suspected that he had someone in his life, and Jayden had made passing comments every now and then. But standing here looking at her, I didn't need to put two and two together to come up with four.

"Maddie."

"I won't say a word to anyone. I know how difficult it is, not having anyone to talk to. I want to be a friend, a little sister that you can turn to when you need to talk. Look, you don't have to say anything to me now, and as I said, I won't say a word to anyone. And I mean anyone, including Nathan. Just know if you need someone to talk to, I'm here for you and I hope I can talk to you as well."

Seeing the smile of relief on her face filled me with warmth. I knew she may not speak to me anytime soon, but she would come to me at some point. When she was ready. The next words that came out of her mouth however knocked me for six.

"I love him, Maddie. I've completely fallen for Nathan. I know he loves me too, but he's scared of what my brother will do. He is trying to push me away. I've had a crush on him my whole teenage life. My friends were always so jealous of me having a good-looking brother and his best friend around my house all the time. I guess that's why I had so many friends, just because of them. It meant I spent all my time at home alone with them. I didn't want to share him. In my mind, he was always mine."

"As I grew up, my feelings for him only grew stronger, but he would always keep his distance. Except once when I was sixteen, I asked him to be my first kiss. I didn't want it to be awkward when I kissed a boy, and I felt comfortable with

Nathan. The problem was from that moment on, I didn't want to be with anyone else. I tried desperately to find a guy I liked, but they just weren't Nathan. It was only about six months ago that I happened to see him in a club I go to. He was on his own for a change. I guess Tyler was down with you in Kings View. We got talking and I stayed the night at his place. Nothing happened, nothing has happened past us kissing."

"I know my brother wouldn't agree. Says that he treats women badly, but I know for a fact that he hasn't been with another woman for six months."

"Do you know that for certain?"

"Yes, because most of the time he has been with me. It helps that my new job is in London, so I tend to stay up there during the week and only come home some weekends. The only reason I am here today was because you were coming here. I'm driving back to see him at my place this evening. He has changed, Maddie. I just need Tyler to see that. I want to take things to the next level. I just need to convince Nathan."

"What do your Mum and Dad think of him?"

"Dad sees him as another son, and Mum has always assumed that we would get together. She would be happy if we did. It's just Tyler. What the hell do I do, Maddie?"

"Well, first, don't worry about Tyler. We will deal with him when the time comes. I will support you and stand with you all the way. But make sure Nathan is the one you really want. I'm not going to lie that it will affect your relationship with Tyler. But if it is really what you want, then he will get over it."

"It is. I want to live the rest of my life with him. I've never met a man I love more."

"Well, in that case, I say go for it. I'm always here if you need me, any time day or night. No matter what happens, we will get through this."

I could see the tears starting to appear in her eyes. I quickly walked over to her and pulled her into a hug.

"Don't worry, Kelsey. You will be fine, and I'm sure with some help, you will get the guy. Just don't take two years to do it like I did. And I promise that I will not tell anyone."

"Thank you, sis."

"You're welcome, sis."

I was so pleased to have this new friendship with Kelsey. No matter what, I wouldn't say anything to Tyler about her relationship with Nathan. But I was going to find a way to make him see how good together they would be.

"I guess we better take this coffee back to them before Tyler sends a search party to find us. I think he is worried about what you are going to tell me."

"Come on then, I don't want him to ban me from seeing my new bestie."

Laughing we carried the mugs into the living room. I could see Rosie was now fast asleep in Michael's arms.

"Would you like me to take her from you? She can be a bit of a lump after a while."

"No way. You're not getting my new granddaughter away from me that easily. You will be lucky if you get to take her home tonight."

That was the last thing I needed for all my worry and anxiety to leave my body, the fact that Michael didn't want Rosie to leave him. I knew that Rosie was going to have a fantastic family around her, one that loved and cherished her. I looked over at Tyler and smiled. All I needed now was for Tyler to agree to marry me and my life would finally be complete.

Epilogue

Tyler

⋯⋯⋯⋯⋯⋯✦⋯⋯ ❦ ⋯⋯✦⋯⋯⋯⋯⋯⋯

Today was the day we finally picked up the keys to our own home. Rosie was excited as anything, because that also meant that Poppy could finally come home with us. We were planning on picking her up tomorrow once we had settled in. All the furniture that I had ordered was being delivered this afternoon, and the guys were coming round to help us move everything in and get it arranged in the house.

Rosie had declared that she wanted to be a big girl like her Auntie Kelsey, so she was going to have flowers all over her bedroom. Part of me was pleased about that, but part of me wanted her to be a little girl for a while longer. She was three next month, and should be thinking about having Disney princesses all over her bedroom. I guess being around grown ups for most of her life made her a lot older than she actually was. We agreed that over the weekend we were going to go down to B&Q and pick out some wallpaper. Although I already knew what she would choose. It would be yellow. That seemed to be her favourite colour of the moment. All her clothes had to be yellow, or at least have some yellow in them.

Rosie was currently at the coffee shop with Maddie, Ashleigh, and Jess. They were running it together today, while the guys and I were getting everything ready at the house. I was somewhat pleased about that, because it meant I could head down to Winchester to pick up the keys, and the one other thing I needed for the evening. I'd designed a ring for Maddie, my engagement ring to her. I had already spoken to Brian about it, and asked him for his permission, which he had given me without question. All I needed now was for Maddie to say yes.

Dad was coming over later to help with the move and to bring the dinner that Mum was preparing for us. It wasn't anything fancy, but it was something that I could just put in the oven to warm up, served with crusty bread and a good bottle of wine. She would probably put in something for dessert as well because she knew I had a major sweet tooth. They knew how special the night was going to be, so they had also offered to take Rosie for the weekend, but as I'd promised to take her to pick up Poppy tomorrow morning, I didn't want to let her down. So I would make sure she had something to eat, put her to bed, and then I would be able to put my plan into action.

I was currently driving into Winchester to get the keys to our first house together. I said our first, but honestly, I couldn't see us living anywhere else in our lives. As far as I was concerned, we would grow old together in this house. Parking in the town centre, I first headed over to the estate agent to pick up the keys to the house. Walking in, I was immediately greeted by Duncan who had been the agent that sold us the house.

"Mr. Edwards, so good to see you again."

"Please, I'm sure you can call me Tyler by now, Duncan. The number of times we have spoken over the past few weeks, we are almost friends."

"Well, I must say you have kept me on my toes, Tyler. You will be pleased to know that the confirmation has been sent through for the funds transfer, so I can hand the keys over to you right now."

"Thank you for all your help, Duncan. I know I can be a little demanding, but you have dealt with everything amazingly. I will be recommending you to all my friends and colleagues. In fact, I believe a Mr. Brian Lewis has already been in to see you about a couple of houses here in Winchester."

"Yes. I believe he is going to look at them tomorrow with me. Is he a friend?"

"My soon to be father-in-law, I hope. If everything goes well this evening, anyway."

"Well, I will wish you well and hand you these keys. I hope we can do business again, but I suspect you will not want to move out of Sunflower Cottage, because it is beautiful."

"It is, and no, I don't plan on moving. Thank you again for all your help."

"You're welcome. Just let us all know how tonight goes and please send us some pictures when you are settled. We love seeing how things look once our clients move in."

"Will do. I hate to run, but I have one more stop at the jewellers before I go back. See you soon."

"And you, Tyler. All the best."

I headed down the high street to the jeweller's where I had commissioned Maddie's ring. We were lucky in Winchester to have lots of little artisan shops that would deal with custom requests. I had chosen a white gold band with a ruby to match the colour of Maddie's hair which I loved. It was then surrounded by diamonds in the shape of a heart. I only hoped that we had guessed her ring size correctly. Ashleigh had taken her shopping the other week and suggested they try on rings. The shop assistant was helpful enough to get her ring size for us. Walking into the shop, I was greeted by the owner, who was also the man creating the ring for me.

"Ah, Mr. Edwards. So good to see you again. I take it you are here to pick up the ring?"

"Yes, I am hoping it is ready."

"It is, and it is a masterpiece if I do say so myself. I took the liberty of placing it in a red box as well. I thought it would continue the theme."

He passed me over the box and I opened it. It was beautiful, and exactly how I had imagined it in my head.

"It's perfect. I really do not know what else to say I'm speechless. Thank you so much."

"I hope your good lady feels the same way."

"So do I, believe me. I think this is more nerve wracking than moving into our new house today. Talking of which, I better head off, the furniture will be arriving soon. Do I owe you anything?"

"No, you are all paid up. Good Luck."

"Thank you."

Sending a quick text to the guys saying I was heading back with the keys and to meet me at the cottage, I made the short journey back to Kings View. I arrived at the cottage to find everyone there and the furniture van just turning up.

"Took your time, didn't you? I thought you were just going to get the keys."

"I had to make another stop, for your information, Nathan."

"Did you get it?"

"Yes, Brandon, and it's perfect."

I took the box out of my pocket and passed it to Brandon for him to see.

"Definitely Maddie. Well done, Tyler."

"Is that what I think it is?"

"Yep, I'm going to ask her tonight. After we have put Rosie to bed. I have a dinner planned, which Mum has cooked for me, and I just have to heat it up. Then, I will ask her."

"That's brilliant news, but I have a better idea. Give me a minute," Mason said as he wandered off on his phone.

"Let's get all of this furniture in the house, then you can all enjoy your weekend."

We started helping the delivery guys move all the furniture in the house. I decided we would put it in the right rooms and arrange it as best we could. Then Maddie and I could decide exactly where we wanted everything to go permanently. I knew Maddie would want a say in how we arranged everything, so as long as it was in the right room and we could sleep tonight, that was all I was worried about.

Mason walked into the house and over to me.

"It's all arranged. Rosie is having a sleepover at ours tonight, as we have Jayden, Sienna and Amelia there. The kids can all sleep together and you can pick her up tomorrow in time to get Poppy."

"I can't ask you to do that, Mace."

"You didn't. I arranged it. Call it payback for what you did for me and Jess."

"Thanks, Mace."

"Don't mention it. Now let's get this all moved in."

It was a little after four in the afternoon when we had everything moved into the house and arranged so we could at least sleep and eat for a couple of days. I had booked a few days off the following week to get us fully settled in and to decorate at least Rosie's room. My Dad had been down and brought dinner with him. As I suspected, Mum had also put in some of her chocolate fudge cake with cream for dessert. She knew how to look after her son well. So it just left me and the rest of the guys to go rescue our women from the coffee shop and the kids. We all walked into the shop to find no customers, but all the kids sat at one of the tables drawing pictures.

"Daddy," came the chorus from all three children as our women sat there and looked up at us.

"Now there is a pleasant sight. Four of the most gorgeous guys, walking into our little shop. Have we all died and gone to heaven?"

"I hope I'm the only one you are looking at, babe."

"Of course, Mason my darling. Why would I want any other man when I have you?"

"God, they have gotten worse over the years. How do you all put up with it down here?"

"The same way everyone probably puts up with you in London, Jayden. Don't worry, I've heard your side of some of your conversations with Sienna. Believe me, guys, they are a lot worse than that, and I don't mean sickeningly sweet."

I saw Sienna start to blush at my comment, causing Mason and Brandon to start snickering beside me.

"Okay, I think that is enough from you. Did you want a coffee, or are you heading straight off?"

"No, we are going to head off, Maddie. Oh, and Rosie is coming for a sleepover with Amelia and Callum this evening. Give you a chance to get settled before all hell breaks loose with Poppy arriving tomorrow."

"You don't have to do that, Mason, really."

"It's all arranged, and you can close up as soon as we are gone. Ashleigh has a spare set of keys so she will be opening up for the next few days. Just get settled into the house and we will see you again on Monday. No arguments."

I smiled at the two ladies in front of me. They were absolute angels. They had obviously spoken about what I was planning tonight and had given me two whole days with Maddie to spend time together.

"Come on, kids. Let's get home to Monty. We can take him for a walk together. We have some clothes at our house, Rosie, so no need for you to head home."

We all said goodbye to everyone and promised that we would have everyone round in a couple of weeks to christen the new house. Although I was definitely going to christen a few rooms before then, just in a completely different way. We locked up the shop once we had finished off clearing up and headed up to our new home. It was about a fifteen-minute walk from the shop, but it was a lovely day, so we just enjoyed the walk together. As I got to the front door of the cottage, I unlocked the door and before Maddie could even step in, I swooped her up in my arms and carried her across the threshold, bridal style.

"Tyler, put me down, you silly sod, we haven't got married. You don't need to carry me over the threshold."

"I want to do this right, sweetheart. It's our first night in our new home together. So, I am going to carry you in. I have dinner in the oven, chocolate fudge cake for dessert, and a bottle of wine cooling in the fridge. All I want you to do is relax and enjoy the evening."

"Could I love you any more?"

"You can ask that question again at the end of the evening, after I have spoiled you rotten. Now why don't you go and relax in a nice hot bath, while I check on dinner?"

"Sounds like bliss."

I watched as she walked into our bedroom. The great thing about our master bathroom was that not only did it have a built-in shower big enough for two, but it also had an amazing slipper bath in the middle of the floor. If you kept the door open, you could look out through the bedroom and onto the beautiful Hampshire countryside. It was one of the best features of the cottage, especially as our bedroom was in the new annex with a lovely balcony, much to the envy of Mason, who was currently trying to plan the same for his house.

Maddie had suitably relaxed in her bath for a while, and came down just in time for me to serve up the fantastic dinner that Mum had prepared for me.

"I must say I am suitably impressed by all this."

"I'm not going to lie. Mum did it for us. I can cook, but nothing like this. She thought we might like a decent meal at the end of the day, and I knew she wouldn't let me down with the chocolate fudge cake."

"I guessed your Mum would have something to do with it, especially when your Dad stopped by the shop to see Rosie before he left. I said they should pop down next weekend for dinner. I can get everything prepared and you can just put it in the oven ready for when I get home. I can invite Kelsey too, but I suspect she will leave it for a while. I know she is busy at work."

"I'm glad you have gotten close to Kelsey. I really worry about her. Especially her infatuation with Nath."

"She's a big girl, Tyler. You have to let her make her own mistakes. We will all be there to pick up the pieces if things go wrong. And is Nathan really that bad? Have you seen him playing the field lately?"

"A leopard never changes his spots, sweetheart."

"Jayden did."

"Be that as it may, Nath isn't good enough for Kelsey. I will make sure he never dates her."

"I'm not going to argue with you tonight. All I will say is Kelsey is an adult and as such can make her own decisions. Let her be."

Maddie was right, we shouldn't be arguing tonight, especially with what I had planned. Perhaps I was too protective of Kelsey. But she was my younger sister and that is what big brothers do. The problem was, I knew Nathan would protect her as well if not better than me. I guess I just had to let her live her life and hope my warnings were heeded by Nathan.

We sat down and ate the wonderful dinner that Mum had prepared along with a glass of wine. When the time came for dessert, I had to take the liberty of feeding Maddie a few bites. She of course returned the favour. So, we were now snuggled on the settee together in our front room and clearing everything away, watching the fire burning in front of us. We didn't bother putting anything on the TV, just decided we wanted to relax here in each other's arms enjoying the peace while we had it. I had made sure that the ring was in the pocket away from Maddie, I didn't want her realising what I was about to do before I gained the courage to take the plunge. I was just about to move when Maddie spoke.

"Tyler, shall we go out on the balcony of our bedroom and watch the sunset? We still have a little while. We can lay on one of the loungers together with a blanket and just enjoy the sunset together, without Rosie about."

Why hadn't I thought of that? It would be the perfect setting to propose.

"Sounds perfect, sweetheart."

We got up from the settee and headed to our bedroom. I grabbed a blanket and passed it to Maddie.

"Why don't you go out and get yourself comfortable? I will just check that everything is locked up."

"Don't take too long. You don't want to miss the sunset."

I placed a kiss on her cheek and watched her walk out onto the balcony. I didn't need to check any of the locks. I had done that when Maddie was relaxing in the bath. I just needed her to get comfy and gain the courage to walk out and ask the one question I had been waiting to ask for the past two years. Giving her a couple of minutes, I walked out to find her relaxed on the lounger, looking across the downs at the setting sun. I still had a while before the sun finally started to set on the horizon. Walking over to her, I took the ring box out of my pocket and kneeled down beside her, taking her hand into mine. I could feel myself shaking as I started to speak.

"Maddie, sweetheart. I have loved you from afar for over two years now, always wanting to be the man to help heal whatever it was that kept us apart. Our love hasn't had an easy path, but it has made us stronger. Not only do I have a beautiful woman to call mine, but I have an amazing daughter in Rosie. I cannot see myself with anyone but you and Rosie in my life. Madeleine Lewis, would you please make me the happiest man alive and agree to become my wife? Marry me, sweetheart."

As proposals went, it wasn't the best. But it was heartfelt and I meant every single word of it. I saw the tears starting to appear in her eyes as she smiled up at me. All I needed now was her answer. I needed to know that she wanted us to be a family.

"I thought you would never ask. Yes, Tyler Edwards, yes, I want to be with you for the rest of my life and become Mrs. Edwards. Yes, I will marry you."

She had hardly let the words leave her mouth before her lips came crashing down onto mine. We kissed for a little while until I broke away, conscious that we were meant to be watching the sunset together. Gently, I joined her on the lounger and passed her the box with the ring that she still hadn't seen.

"We still have a few minutes if you want to open it."

When she opened the box and looked at the ring I had designed she let out a gasp.

"It's perfect, Tyler."

Pulling it out of the box, I placed it on her finger and placed a kiss on it. Turning to face her, I placed a kiss on her lips.

"I thought so too when I designed it. But it isn't as perfect as you."

I pulled her into my side as we lay there together watching the sun set across the downs. This moment couldn't be any more perfect. I had the woman I loved in my arms, my fiancé, a beautiful daughter who I was already in the process of adopting as my own, and we were in our own home, watching the sunset in front of us. It really didn't get any better than this. As if mirroring my thoughts, Maddie spoke.

"Tonight couldn't be any more perfect. I love you, Tyler. Thank you for never giving up on me."

"I could never give up on you, Maddie. You were always mine, and you and Rosie always will be. I love you too, sweetheart."

As we said those words to each other, the sun went down to end the day. We lay there in each other's arms knowing that tomorrow it would rise again and a new chapter in our life would start.

About the Author

Clarice Jayne is a new Author who published her first book Jessica's King in May 2021.

Living in Kent, The Garden of England, with her husband, daughter and dog, she started writing as a hobby when someone suggested she should publish a book. Jessica's King was the outcome.

Clarice writes mystery and suspense romances based in the south of England. All of her books include mystery, a little danger, passion, family, and a happily ever-after.

When she is not writing, Clarice works full time in the healthcare industry, drinks copious amounts of coffee and enjoys spending time with her family.

Next from Clarice Jayne

Kelsey's King

Nathan Mitchell has been friends with Tyler Edwards since they were kids. They have grown up together, went through school and the army together, along with Jayden he considers them both as brothers. But Nathan has a secret he has been keeping from Tyler for a while, he is in love with his sister Kelsey. He has tried to keep his distance, but every time he tries, he falls harder for her.

Kelsey loves her brother and knows her relationship with Nathan will cause all kinds of issues. But she can't let Nathan go, she doesn't want to let him go. With secret rendezvous, and stolen moments, Kelsey wants to come clean to Tyler. But fate takes things in another direction.

When a past job comes back to haunt Tyler, he fears for his girlfriend Madeleine and their daughter Rosie. The problem is, it was never going to be them that the mystery man would go after. It was always going to be Kelsey.

Unfortunately, the King Brothers team realised this too late to stop him. Can Nathan and the team save the woman he loves? And will Tyler ever forgive him when the truth comes out about his relationship with Kelsey?

Kelsey's King is a stand-alone mystery, suspense romance with a happily ever after, and is the fifth book in the King Brothers Investigation series.

Also from Clarice Jayne

Kings Brothers Investigation Series

❧

Jessica's King

Sienna's King

Ashleigh's King

Madeleine's King

Kelsey's King – Coming Autumn 2022

Printed by Amazon Italia Logistica S.r.l.
Torrazza Piemonte (TO), Italy

39857613R00208